P9-BZJ-270

Also by Terry Spear

NIGHT OF THE
Billionaire
WOLF

TERRY
SPEAR

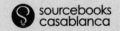

sourcebooks
casablanca

Published by Sourcebooks Casablanca, an imprint of Sourcebooks
P.O. Box 4410, Naperville, Illinois 60567-4410
(630) 961-3900
sourcebooks.com

Printed and bound in the United States of America
OPM 10 9 8 7 6 5 4 3 2 1

Thanks to Bonnie Harrington Hauser for helping my friend Kelley Granzow send soldier boxes filled with books for troops overseas for Christmas! And thanks, Bonnie, for enjoying the series and then collecting all of the books for your mother, Phyllis Harrington, to read as well. I'm glad you're both enjoying them!

CHAPTER 1

"ACCORDING TO MY WEATHER APP, THE DELUGE OF rain starts again in two hours," Lexi Summerfield warned her personal assistant, Kate Hanover, while looking at the app on her cell phone. They only had three days to locate the message, or it would no longer be relevant. The text she had received made it clear she had only one shot at this, and then it could be too late. They had to locate the message before the men who were hired to kill her father got wind of it.

As a gray wolf, Lexi hated that she couldn't be close to her father like she'd always been. Not now that he was in the Witness Protection Program with a different identity, location, and job. None of which she knew. In fact, she didn't want to know about any of it, or she could put his life in jeopardy, should the reason he was in witness protection— Joe Tremaine—send more of his thugs to try to learn from her where her father was. She didn't know what her father had to tell her, but it was important enough he'd contacted her surreptitiously, putting both their lives at risk.

As she and Kate packed their backpacks for the hike, tension and stress filled Lexi with dread that she might not be able to find the message in time. She paused to take another drink of water, her mouth dry and her darn hands sweaty. She was fighting the urge to clench her teeth.

It wasn't just that she missed her dad and wanted to keep him safe. A year ago, she'd lost her mother when a ferry crashed into a bridge in Brazil, sending her mother's car and another plunging into the water, and none of the bodies had ever been found. Her mom had helped Lexi with her business, encouraging her all the way. She was the reason Lexi had stuck with it during the highs and lows of starting her cosmetics company.

So many things reminded Lexi of her mother, whose hobby was growing flowers from seeds and cross-pollinating them to create new varieties. She'd even named one, a purple daylily, Lexi Love because purple flowers were Lexi's favorite. The fragrance of her mother's roses, gardenia, jasmine, and honeysuckle scenting the air was one of Lexi's fondest memories, and when she had a chance, she was re-creating her mother's garden in her own yard as a memorial. Her mother had been a pediatrician and loved taking care of sick kids and making them feel better, which was why she'd been in Brazil—taking care of Mexican wolf shifter kids in a pack for two months before she died. Lexi missed her, and so did her patients.

Lexi packed away her camera, determined to take pictures as good as her mother's and to use all the tips her mother had taught her—how to make the lights and shadows and colors pop. How to compose the pictures for the most appealing result. Photography had been another of her mother's hobbies, and she had taken the pictures of Lexi's cosmetics to use for her website and product promotions. Lexi could hire someone else to do them now, but she felt connected to her mother when she took the photos herself, now that she was gone.

She regretted every day her mother wasn't here. Just as Lexi missed seeing her dad whenever he wasn't busy working in his family practice clinic doctoring patients. She wondered what her father was even working at, now that he couldn't work as a doctor. She hoped he was doing well and that he was happy. But she suspected he missed her and her mom as much as she missed them both.

"Do you have your noisemaker in case we run into any black bears?" Lexi asked Kate, getting her mind back on the business at hand.

"The horn is in my backpack. Relaxing and communing with nature as wolves is just what you need, even if this is a high-priority mission." Kate brought out their protein bars and filled her own travel mug with water. "You have a full schedule of appearances next week, and the tea and dinner engagement with the Denalis. You really have to take a break every once in a while."

Not that this was a real break. Well, sure, Lexi was enjoying Redwood National Park as a wolf, trying to relax when she wasn't looking for the message. As far as she knew, she was the only one of her kind who had made over a billion dollars in the cosmetic industry. Work would always be waiting for her, and sometimes a body just needed to have some fun for a change. Not that her work was all work. She enjoyed what she did, but always being on a schedule could be exhausting.

She still had to locate the message her dad had sent her, buried like treasure in the redwoods. He'd Facebook-messaged her with a cryptic note that only she'd know how to decipher—Wolf at Red Fish Falls—and included a simple, hand-drawn map that indicated where he'd buried the message. They'd vacationed here some years ago, she and her family, and her father had fondly referred to the area where they'd seen several fish in the creek below one of the waterfalls as Red Fish Falls.

Kate slipped her 9mm into her holster and pulled her lightweight backpack over her shoulders. "Ready to go?"

"Yep." Even though Lexi didn't feel she really needed a bodyguard all the time, she felt having Kate serve as *both* her personal assistant and her bodyguard worked well. She hadn't thought she could get used to living with someone she didn't know, but she was thoroughly enjoying Kate's company, as if she'd found a sister.

With a double black belt in a couple of different martial arts forms, all her combat arms training, and a degree in marketing, not to mention being a she-wolf, Kate was perfect for the job. Several male wolves had applied for the position, but Lexi felt it was easier not having to fend off a potential suitor's advances, if one became attached to the idea that he might mate her and enjoy her wealth too. The money could be a real draw for roguish types.

"It's fun being with you because your presence is so sought after," Kate said, her short black hair in a bob, her blue eyes sparkling. "Sure, all the attention is on you, but it's exciting to bask in your limelight. I know you like your solitude, so I'm glad you enjoy my company when we're on our own."

"You're great at coming up with fun activities. I always feel comfortable around you, not needing to have a public face for show all the time."

"Not at first though," Kate said, smiling. "We had to have ice cream cones dripping all over us in the heat last summer, and we laughed so hard that we lost the rest on the sandy beach. That was my second day on the job, and our relationship was totally transformed."

Lexi smiled. "I had never considered eating ice cream on the beach. Now I know why. The heat and ocean breeze were too much for the soft, top-heavy swirl of ice cream to manage. We couldn't lick it fast enough."

"Yeah. I don't think I've ever been that much of a sticky mess before at the ocean, even when I was a kid. That was definitely an icebreaker."

"I agree." Lexi sighed. She had never been popular around males or females, mostly because she'd been shy. Some attributed her "aloofness" to being a snob because she was the daughter of physicians, but it wasn't like that. She just wasn't all that outgoing, and when she finished her public appearances to promote her business, she loved retreating to the solitude of her ocean-view estate.

The tabloids often mentioned that Lexi was one of the most sought-after, eligible bachelorettes, and that didn't help either. Numerous human males had tried to meet her and told her she was beautiful, intelligent, sweet, desirable, and anything else they could come up with to try to convince her they were really interested in her and not her wealth. If they only knew she had a real growly side to her personality and no human mate would do!

After several disastrous dates with wolves who had an agenda, she'd made a new rule for herself: Three dates was all she'd allow herself with a wolf. If he didn't have what it took to be in a relationship with her for longer than that, she was calling it quits. Kate thought it might take longer than that, but Lexi was afraid if she dated a guy more than three times and wasn't serious about mating him, it wouldn't be fair to him.

She looked over the hand-drawn map of where they were supposed to search for the message again. Waterfall. North of the cabins. Rocks.

No matter what, she couldn't have reporters learning her dad was very much alive. As far as everyone knew, he was dead. Her mom had died before her father witnessed

the district attorney's murder in San Antonio and testified against the drug lord. He hadn't had any choice. Joe
Tremaine had seen her father witness the murder. If the
drug lord had been a wolf, her father could have just killed
him himself, if he'd had the chance. As it was, her father had
to be taken into the Witness Protection Program and then
officially declared dead. Lexi wasn't supposed to ever have
any contact with him. She loved him for having asked her
first whether he should testify against Joe Tremaine.

Despite having to cut ties with her father, Lexi knew
it was the only thing he could do. He was a marked man
anyway. She knew in her heart that he had to put the drug
lord behind bars and pretend he was dead while Tremaine
was locked away. Hopefully, her father would remain alive.

The U.S. Marshals would kick her father out of the
Witness Protection Program if they learned he'd met with
her though. Her father's mention of Wolf at Red Fish Falls
had to mean he wanted to meet her as a wolf, if she could
locate the message he'd buried out here for her to find and
learn where the meeting would take place.

"We need to do some more martial arts training," Kate
told her, bringing Lexi's attention back to her friend.

Kate had taught Lexi some of her black-belt jujitsu
moves, which Lexi hadn't expected when she hired Kate.
But she loved it.

"I thought we were on a break," Lexi cheerfully reminded
her. Except for trying to find her father's message.

"Right, but think of how much fun it would be to get a
workout at the cabin. Fresh air—"

"Rain's coming."

"Well, we can practice inside the cabin then. We can
move some furniture out of the way."

"Okay, sure."

Dressed in jean shorts, hiking boots, and T-shirts, and both wearing lightweight backpacks carrying their water, bug spray, protein bars, satellite phones, cameras, ponchos, a couple of garden trowels, and first aid kits, they headed down the trail from the cabin. Lexi also had a Glock tucked into her backpack, figuring she really wouldn't need to use it. But she was aware Joe Tremaine's men could still be searching for her father if they weren't convinced he had died in the car crash. And they could be watching her, too, to see if she and her father met up with each other.

While Lexi and Kate hiked along the rugged stretch of northern California's coastline, they talked about different marketing options for Lexi's Clair de Lune Cosmetics, the French name meaning "light of the moon." Their voices would help scare off any bears that might be in the area. Lexi loved taking pictures of the redwoods in all their glory, battling the winds and the salty sea air as she and Kate hiked toward the location where they believed the message was buried. She was soaking up the scents of the redwoods, and the squirrels and rabbits that lived here.

"You know you have your pet rehoming party coming up. When are you going to bring home your own little cutie pie?" Kate asked. "I know you lost your Misty some years ago, but don't you think it's time to give another needy pet a home?"

"My problem is I want to take all of them home: fluffy and shorthaired, large and small, any breed, any mix. If I can't give them all a home, I feel it's not fair to the others. They look at me with their sad eyes and just beg me to love them. All of them. Not only that, but the last two parties I sponsored, the dogs I fell in love with went to families who will give them tons of loving and attention. Maybe the next pet party." Lexi glanced at Kate. "Don't tell me *you* want a dog."

"Me? No, I'd just take care of him or her when you didn't have time. I mean, just call it an additional duty."

Lexi smiled at her. "You *do* want a dog."

"I love dogs. I haven't had one since I was a kid, but in my line of work, I can't possibly have one of my own."

"Okay, now you can."

"But what about you?"

"We'll need two, you know. So they can play with each other. The problem is that not all dogs like us if we haven't raised them from puppies, so we need to find two that are not afraid of our wolf scent and who are okay when we shift. I'd hate to have to rehome my own rehomed pet."

"Agreed." Kate was smiling.

"You know you could have asked me."

"I just kept thinking you'd get one, and with this party coming up, I thought I'd mention it."

"They'll have venders at the party, so we can pick up whatever we need for the dogs right there. Plus, a percentage of the proceeds goes to the Fur Babies Rescue Center."

"Oh, that's good," Kate said.

They'd walked for about an hour at a good brisk pace in the heavily damp air, except when they'd paused to take pictures of the towering redwoods and more birds—Steller's jays, a golden-crowned kinglet, and a pileated woodpecker. The ancient and majestic trees gathered moisture from the dense coastal fog, making Lexi feel as though she was in a magical fairy garden. The redwoods were so tall and wide that they seemed part of a mythical, primeval landscape.

"I hear the waterfall nearby." Kate slipped a little on the

muddier part of a trail. "He said it was near the waterfall, right?"

"According to this map, yes. Unless it's a different waterfall." Lexi sure hoped not.

They finally reached the falls, the rush of water flowing over the cliff and running into the stream below.

They both looked at the simply sketched map.

"Maybe we just have to move rocks over there," Kate said. "Instead of digging for it. This looks like the drawing of rocks on the map."

"Over there? By the big one?" Lexi pointed at the area that looked similar.

"Yeah."

They headed for the larger rock, and at the base, they began moving the rounded river rocks away from the big one, but after several minutes, they reached soil.

"Do we dig now?" Kate asked.

"Yeah, let's try that." Lexi pulled out her trowel, and Kate did the same with hers.

Both of them began to dig, but after several minutes, they hadn't found anything. They filled the hole back up, then moved the rocks back to where they'd been and started working at another spot. Two more times they moved rocks, dug in the dirt, then replaced the disturbed materials. Lexi paused to take a picture of the waterfall.

"I'm wondering if it's located at a different waterfall." Disappointed, Lexi had really believed she would find the message at the first place she looked. She shouldn't have been so optimistic. "It's hard to tell from this simple map. There aren't any features that would indicate this place over any others."

"Except his map indicated that the site was northwest of

the cabins, and this is the first set of waterfalls located in that direction," Kate said.

Lexi hadn't told Kate what the secret message was about or who it was from. She'd let it slip that the person who had buried it was a he, so she'd left it at that. She'd hoped she'd smell her father's scent when she looked for the message, but she didn't smell any sign of him anywhere. She'd only received the text message from him this morning, and then she and Kate had needed to pack and travel here in a rush to begin to look for it.

They'd seen several waterfalls, and all the creeks had fish swimming in them, so that didn't help in narrowing things down to a particular waterfall. Her family had been to several on their vacation here, and her father had said the same thing about all of them.

Lexi had informed Kate that she couldn't tell her any more about the message or its sender or she'd have to kill her. Kate had laughed, but the truth was that Lexi worried about someone else killing Kate *and* her, if they knew Lexi's father was still alive. Since Kate wouldn't let Lexi search for the message on her own, Lexi had taken her into her confidence—at least as far as searching for the message.

"How long do we have to find it?" Kate asked.

"Three days. After that, the location of the message will be irrelevant."

"So we keep searching. You know, I was thinking more about our marketing. We always do kind of a high-fashion setup for the promo videos. I was thinking we could do some out here. More for the outdoorsy girl—like us— with an outdoor-woodsy theme, a getting-back-to-nature concept. The idea would be that no matter whether you're in the city or roughing it in the woods, your makeup will last and protect you from the elements and enhance your natural beauty."

"Now see, that's why I hired you! You're perfect for this job. We could do some of that now while we're staying at the cabin."

"That's what I was thinking. I figure we could slip in some promo, and we'd both have fun doing it in between trying to locate the message." Kate glanced at the rocks they'd replaced. "We'll find it."

Lexi hoped. She pulled out the park map. "There's another set of falls over here. Still northwest of the cabins, just a little farther north." Her phone rang, and she struggled to free it from a zippered pocket on her backpack. She recognized the phone number on her caller ID and scoffed. "It's hopeful suitor number three." She answered the call and said in her most professional business voice, "Lexi Summerfield, how may I help you?" The breeze blowing the branches and birds singing in the background would be a sure giveaway that she wasn't at home and on the job.

"It's Randy Wolfman. I want to take you out for dinner on Monday night at six."

"Randy, you're a nice guy, but you and I don't really have what it takes to be a couple. I'm sorry, but it was nice that we had a couple of dates anyway." Three, but who was counting? Once she'd decided on her new rule, she'd become determined to stick to her plan: give the guy three chances to change her mind and then move on. She truly was a romantic at heart, and she worried that Mr. Right Wolf—who really was the one for her and not seeing her just because she was sitting on a load of money—would show up, and here she'd be dating Mr. Wrong Wolf. She was afraid she'd lose her only chance at having the wolf of her dreams.

"Aww, come on, Lexi. We'll have a great time," Randy said.

She thought he liked going out with her because they each paid for their own meals, since she didn't want the wolf to feel he had paid his way into her life. "Sorry, it wouldn't work out between us. I hope you find the right wolf for you."

"But—"

She ended the call and blocked his phone number.

Kate was smiling at her. "He would never take no for an answer."

"You're right. And I have a hard time rejecting people. I just need to start telling them I'm not interested."

"Are you afraid you might dismiss the wrong guy?"

"No. If one of them was the right wolf, I'd smell his interest and our pheromones would go through the roof when we got close. I danced with all five wolves who have asked me out on separate occasions, and not one of them did that for me. Sure, they wanted to have sex, that much was obvious from their full-blown erections, although that would mean mating for life. But our pheromones were a fizzle, no interest at all."

"Which begs the question: Can we find more than one wolf who can do that for us?" Kate asked quite seriously.

"I think so. I don't believe only one wolf in the whole wide world would be the one for each of us. We might never find that wolf. I'm sure it has something to do with genetic predisposition, what physical qualities a potential mate has that suit our physical needs in order to create the best offspring. That's all on the pheromonal side of us. Then there's the human equation, the needs and wants and desires. The social and emotional compatibility. It's complicated. But I can tell you right now that these guys were more interested in money than me. They were trying way too hard to prove they really were into me, and it wasn't working."

"You're easy to like."

"Friendship is fine. Mating for life is a whole other story." Lexi had never checked into their backgrounds, something she would definitely have done if one of the wolves had really moved her.

"I agree with you there."

The rain-saturated breeze switched, and Lexi smelled the scent of a male wolf and a black bear that had passed through there recently.

"The wolf has to be a *lupus garou* like us," Kate said, "since no one has reported any sightings of wolves in the area. Maybe the wolf was the one who left the message?"

"I don't believe so." Lexi didn't think her father would ask another wolf to get involved in this. The fewer people who knew about it, the better. "And there's a female black bear, by the smell of her, roaming the area. Keep your eyes peeled and continue to make noise. We need to head on back before the rain starts anyway. We can check the other location later. It will take us about an hour to reach the cabin."

Kate laughed. "How often does the weatherman get it right?"

Lexi saw a fairy ring of mushrooms and took another picture. "Yeah, I know. But you know me. I always try to give him the benefit of the doubt."

Light rain began to fall, and then the drops grew bigger. Lexi hurried to put away her camera, and both laughing, they pulled out their ponchos. They were already soaked by the time they got the ponchos on. Still, they'd be protected somewhat from the continuing rainfall.

A couple of young bear cubs cried out somewhere in the distance, and Lexi's adrenaline surged. "Do you hear that?"

"Yeah, they're close by. It sounds like danger to me."

"They're crying for their mother. They have to be in trouble. I'll see if the park rangers can rescue them." Lexi hurried to get her phone out and called the ranger service. "Hi, my friend and I were hiking, and we heard the distress calls of a couple of bear cubs."

"We've got our hands full with a family of hikers who have lost their way, including one who's badly injured. And a search party is looking for another missing hiker. We can look into the cubs' situation after we've taken care of the hikers in distress."

"Thanks." Lexi ended the call.

"You didn't tell them where the bear cubs are."

"The park rangers are too busy with human distress calls. You're my bodyguard. You can protect me." Lexi left the designated trail, which she wouldn't normally do as a human because she didn't want to trample the vegetation. The bear cubs' cries guiding her, she raced through the forest as best she could, trying not to stumble over tree branches and fall into the ferns filling the understory.

Kate trailed close behind her. "This is a dangerous idea. Where there are cubs, there's a mother bear nearby. The female bear we smelled, I betcha."

"Unless something has happened to her. And then we need to rescue them."

"What do you propose we do? Take them home with you?"

Lexi was sure Kate wasn't being serious. Wolves raising bear cubs at her oceanside home? No way.

"Once we rescue them, I'll call the park rangers to pick

up the cubs and take care of them if the mother doesn't come for them. The rangers can find a home for them. As young as the cubs' cries sounded, they wouldn't be able to make it on their own."

Lexi and Kate continued to move quickly through the underbrush in the direction of the cliffs. Lexi's skin prickled with unease, her stomach twisting in knots. From the sound of the cubs' cries, they were way down below the cliffs, and the only way to reach them quickly would be climbing down there. That terrified her. Worse, her fearful scent would clue Kate in.

No way had Lexi wanted anyone to know what had happened to make her fear cliffs. She prided herself on keeping her secret. But even now, she suffered a flashback: gasping as a wolf as the soil and rocks at the edge of the cliff gave way, free-falling toward the rocky ground, praying some of the tree branches would help to break her fall. They did, scraping and bruising her, but she still landed badly on the rocks below and broke her left hind leg. Just from the memory, she felt a shock of phantom pain shoot up her left leg. That would be the last time she'd fight with a boyfriend and take off on her own without telling anyone where she'd be.

It had been a stupid thing to do, something she had seen others do in videos on *I Shouldn't Be Alive*—in other words, going alone, not telling anyone where she'd be, not having a satellite phone in remote areas, and not having water with her—though as a wolf, that was understandable. She'd sworn she'd never do anything that dumb herself. Worse, she'd been in her wolf form and couldn't climb to safety with a broken leg, so she'd had to shift into her human *naked* form before help arrived.

She and Kate finally reached a steep cliff and Lexi hesitated, not wanting to get near the edge that, according to forest ranger reports on the area, were known to crumble. Chills raced down her bare arms and legs. She had to force herself to move toward the cliff's edge. Slowly, so she wouldn't end up falling and breaking a leg like she'd done before.

"Are you okay?" Kate asked.

"Yeah, sure. The cliff face is unstable. I'm just being careful." But it was a lot more than that.

"Okay, yeah, you're smart to do that. I guess I can't talk you out of taking this dangerous route and looking for a safer way to get down there instead."

"I don't want to risk delaying the rescue." Lexi finally reached the edge. She observed the rocky cliff, looking for the best way to climb down, terrified she would fall. The mewling cries were coming from the base of the cliff near a couple of trees.

"This is not what I had in mind when I signed up to… Holy shit," Kate said, peering over the edge of the cliff.

Lexi looked down at the swollen creek rushing along the banks of the cliff. "The creek's risen because of all the rain. The cubs are crying in a den down below. They could drown. We have to save them." Lexi started down the cliff, grabbing whatever she could—rocks, tree roots, vines—to keep from falling to her death or breaking a leg or more. She grabbed what looked like a stable rock, but as soon as she tried to hold it and move her right foot to another rock, the one in her left hand pulled free. She fell and cried out, grabbing for anything that could stop her fall. She grasped a tree root and hung on for dear life, her breath coming out in harried puffs.

"Oh God, hang on, Lexi. I *really* didn't sign up for this." Kate waited to descend so she didn't cause an avalanche of rocks and dirt to collapse on Lexi.

"You don't have to do it."

"Are you kidding? Then you'd be able to take all the glory!"

Lexi smiled, then frowned. If the mother bear attacked them, there wouldn't be much glory in that.

CHAPTER 2

RYDER GALLAGHER—WHO FORMERLY WENT BY HIS first name, Ted—had changed it due to issues he was having with a man of the same name that credit card companies were after. And, of course, all Ryder's friends were having trouble with the transition. He was taking another hike, killing time before his friend Mike Stallings arrived at the cabin campgrounds. Ryder thought he heard women's voices every once in a while and took a trail headed in their direction. He wasn't the kind of guy who liked solitude. Though this was better than just sitting in the cabin waiting for Mike to turn up. Not that Ryder planned to hike with the ladies.

One of the women squealed and then both laughed. He smiled. He didn't want to intrude too much. He wasn't interested in befriending a couple of human women, but he was drawn to check them out.

Their good humor lightened his mood, which had been somewhat dampened by the sudden change in plans. Mike had needed to stop and see his parents on his way to the cabin. They were gray wolves, so family was important, but Mike's parents' anniversary had slipped his mind. Ryder and Mike didn't want to lose their cabin rental reservation for the rest of the week, so Ryder had shown up alone until Mike could join him. Their jobs as bodyguards were stressful, and they needed all the vacation time they could get.

Ryder reached the place on the trail where he thought

he'd run into the two women, but there was no sign of them, and he didn't smell their scents in the area. He heard their voices again, farther away. What trail had they taken? He had been sure this one would intersect with theirs.

Then from a different direction, he heard bear cubs crying out in distress. The women forgotten, Ryder immediately went into rescue mode. He ran through the ferns in the direction he thought the cubs were, but knew he'd find them faster if he ran as a wolf. Already well off the trail, he pulled off his backpack and began to strip out of his shorts, socks, hiking boots, boxer briefs, and T-shirt. He shoved his clothes into his backpack, then hid it in the ferns.

Off and running, he headed for the cliff where he'd heard the bears crying, wishing Mike was here to help him. At least he was glad he had detoured to the other trail in an attempt to run into the ladies, which had made it possible for him to hear the bears' cries much more distinctly and reach them faster. Now he just had to get to them before it was too late.

Her heart hammering, Lexi was still trying to make her way down the cliff, her fingers clinging precariously to the loose rocks, dirt, and mud, the water rising steadily down below, the poncho hampering her efforts. If she hadn't been so concerned about reaching the cubs as quickly as possible, she would have thought to shove her poncho in her backpack. "Remove your poncho before you climb down. Mine's getting in the way while I try to find footholds."

The earth crumbled more, and she knew she was going to be cut and scraped up, just like Kate would be. Hopefully, that would be the worst of it. If she could only extract the bear cubs without getting into a confrontation with the mother bear!

The rain was still coming down, making it worse. Her hands were wet and so were the rocks she was trying to hold on to, which meant everything was slippery. Suddenly, the rocks supporting her gave way. Her heart beating hard, Lexi cried out as she tumbled down the last ten feet. She landed in the rising water with a splash.

"Lexi! Ohmigod!"

"I'm okay. I'm at the base of the cliff. I'm okay." Short of breath, her heart beating way too fast, Lexi scrambled to her feet.

"Are you sure?"

Lexi knew Kate would do anything to help rescue the cubs too.

"Yeah, just don't fall like I did." As if Lexi could have prevented it. "Just scraped and bruised, sore muscles, but no broken bones."

"Okay. God, you scared me." Kate removed her poncho and shoved it into her bag, then pulled her backpack back over her shoulders and began her climb down.

The water was swirling around Lexi's shins and she was edgy, waiting to catch Kate if she fell. "You would have done this on your own if I hadn't made the decision to aid them and gone down first."

Rocks skittered down the cliff below. Lexi's stomach clenched, her body tense, ready to spring into action if Kate lost her hold on the rocks. Lexi wasn't sure if it was harder watching Kate trying to make her way down safely or doing it herself.

The rock Kate was holding on to came loose and she cursed, sliding down a few feet, grabbing for something to stop her fall. Lexi's heart caught in her throat, and she lunged forward in rescue mode, arms outstretched.

Kate finally caught a tree root and held on for dear life as she found rocks jutting out where she could plant the toes of her boots. Panting, she said, "Yeah, I would have. We're going to be a mess when we return to the cabin."

"We'll heal quickly from our scrapes and bruises." As *lupus garous*, they healed twice as fast as humans. Of course, Lexi wasn't taking into account tangling with a black bear sow if they were faced with her next. "Are you okay?"

"Yeah, just catching my breath."

Lexi heard the bear cubs again, crying for their momma. She worried about the mother. She glanced across the creek, and sure enough, the momma bear was watching her from the other side of the bank, half-hidden in the trees. She was glad to see the momma bear was alive. Lexi just hoped the bear didn't attack her and Kate when they tried to rescue the cubs.

"We don't have to worry about the momma bear abandoning them or that she's been killed."

Kate glanced in the direction of the creek. "Great. Good news. Oh, she…uh, looks so big."

"Yeah, she is." Waiting for Kate to start her descent again, Lexi peered through a tangle of tree roots beneath a dead tree. "Okay, I found the den."

"And the mother is now pacing across the creek, watching us," Kate warned, still paused halfway down the cliff. She had moved over a few feet from where Lexi had come down, the cliff crumbling just as much, but she seemed to be frozen in place.

"Don't rush the descent, watch your footing. As soon as you're down here, I'll go in after the cubs." Lexi waited for

Kate to move again. "When you get down, you can be the lookout and tell me if the mother bear heads this way."

"And protect you, right?" Kate said.

Lexi gave her a half smile. "It's your job. Or…one of your jobs."

"I think I need a pay raise."

"You might be right." If Lexi was going to make Kate help her with stuff like this, she definitely had earned a pay raise.

Kate finally got the courage to begin again and started climbing down. Good, she was finally making some progress. "Sorry it's taking me so long. You made it look a lot easier than this."

"No worries. Take your time, really. The cliff is crumbling so much that it makes the descent much more treacherous."

One of Kate's feet slipped first, and then the other, suspending all her weight from the two rocks she was holding on to, which gave way under her weight. She cried out and fell, Lexi trying to catch her. She did, but she couldn't keep her footing under Kate's weight, and they both fell into the water at the base. Kate was sitting on Lexi's lap, scrambling to get off her, each of them asking, "Are you all right?"

"Yes, I am," Lexi said, figuring she'd have a couple of new bruises on her butt.

"I am too," Kate said. "You cushioned my fall nicely. Thanks."

"You're welcome. I just hadn't planned to fall too."

Lexi and Kate helped each other up. Then Lexi steadied her breathing, yanked off her poncho, and dropped it on the ground while Kate fished her poncho out of her backpack and slipped it on.

Lexi peered into the den and saw four beady little eyes

peering at her from deep inside their large home, the water already filling their burrow. She ducked into the den on her hands and knees. Now she wished she'd worn jeans and not jeans shorts. "There are two of them, about twelve weeks old."

"Okay, bring one out to me, and I can carry him across the creek, and you can… *Holy crap*."

"What?" Lexi's heart was already drumming hard. She was afraid the mother bear was crossing the creek and charging Kate.

"A male wolf just…um…arrived to…um…help."

Lexi frowned. Now *that* she hadn't expected. The wolf had to be a *lupus garou*, and they didn't need his help, unless he wanted to run interference with the mother bear.

Sure enough, the light from outside the den suddenly dimmed and she turned to see a very hot, muscular, *very* naked man crouched at the entrance, rainwater streaming down his tanned skin, his dark reddish-brown hair dripping wet. "If you'll hand me one of the cubs, I'll take him out and you can grab the other." A couple days' beard growth gave him an even more rugged appearance, his eyes appearing dark-brown in the low light of the damp, earthy den. And he smelled like a wolf—all male, his adrenaline surging, testosterone spiking.

Even though Lexi figured she and Kate had this well in hand themselves, an upset momma bear could be totally unpredictable. Any help from a fellow wolf would be welcome.

Lexi took ahold of one of the cubs by the scruff of his neck—like his momma would do, except the bear would use her teeth—and passed him to the male stranger.

"Ryder Gallagher," he offered, then carried the cub into the rain so Lexi could grab the other cub and leave the den.

Ryder. She imagined riding the cowboy in the throes of passion—and why that visual came to mind when she had a dangerous rescue mission, she hadn't a clue.

The cubs' fur was soft, and they both were still crying, which worried her. The momma bear roared. And that concerned Lexi even more.

Don't charge. Don't charge. As soon as Lexi backed out of the den, Ryder reached down with his free hand and helped her up, which was a good thing because she was having trouble getting to her feet under the weight of the bear cub. She tucked the bear cub close to her body, trying to keep him warm.

"I'm Lexi," she said, intentionally not giving the wolf her last name, though he probably wouldn't know who she was anyway. It was no doubt just paranoia on her part.

"I'm Kate," her assistant said, smiling at the hunk when she was *supposed* to be watching the mother bear.

Ryder was already searching for a safe place to set the cubs down so the mother could come for them. "The creek's rising. We'll have to get across it and leave them on the side where the mother is, a safe distance from her. If we don't hurry, we could get caught in the floodwaters ourselves."

Lexi already knew that, but she agreed they needed to move quickly if they were going to get the cubs safely to their mom and not be swept away by the rising water themselves. But she was afraid of getting too close to the mother bear roaring again to her babies.

"I've got my gun," Kate said.

Both Lexi and Ryder looked shocked.

"To shoot up in the air. Jeez, not to shoot the poor, frantic mother. Just to keep her away from us."

"Okay, good thinking." Lexi thought the mother might not be deterred if she wanted to protect her cubs badly enough.

Ryder started making his way across the creek and Lexi followed him, keeping the cub as dry as she could, but the water was deeper and the current stronger the deeper she got, and the rocks on the bed of the creek were mossy, making them slippery.

Lexi concentrated on her footing while observing the heartthrob wolf specimen in front of her. Muscular legs swallowed up by the water, a gluteus maximus that rated a solid ten, now also covered by water, a sturdy back, broad shoulders, muscular arms—all dripping with rainwater as the rain pelted them even harder now.

Other than enjoying the show in front of her, Lexi was ready to return to the cabin and dry out. Though she realized she hadn't grabbed her poncho. She hadn't seen it when she exited the den. Then again, a naked male wolf and the sow and the bear cubs had garnered most of her attention.

Kate was trying to make it across the current, too, attempting to place herself between the mother and Lexi. She didn't want Kate to take the risk, but Kate did have her gun and noisemaker out to help scare the mother bear enough to keep her from attacking—hopefully.

Kate slipped on the rocks and bumped into Lexi. Lexi nearly fell, but Ryder's hand shot out to catch her arm and help steady her.

"Thanks," Lexi said. He really came in handy, and despite not wanting to feel that way, she really liked having his strong hand on her arm for the moment.

"Sorry," Kate told her.

"It's not your fault. It's really slippery," Lexi said, and then she lost her footing again, tumbling into the water.

CHAPTER 3

SO FAR, SO GOOD. THE MOTHER BEAR HADN'T MADE A move toward them, and Ryder hoped the bear realized they were only bringing her cubs to her. Lexi's light-brown hair and clothes were drenched, everything clinging to her curves, her green eyes unusually big, her dark lashes long and luscious, her lips glistening with raindrops, sexy and kissable. And why he would be thinking about that in the middle of this mess was only because he was a wolf, he figured.

Then Lexi slipped on more mossy stones next to him and fell before he could grab ahold of her arm a second time. His heart nearly giving out, he and Kate grabbed for her in the same instant. His bear cub tucked against his body, he wished he was wearing a heavy-duty, lined raincoat to keep the cub warmer, and not his hairless man suit.

They finally got Lexi to her feet, and she was even wetter than before. So was the cub, and that added weight to her handful. He prayed she'd make it the rest of the way, but he continued to hold on to her arm to keep her on her feet the best he could.

"The cub is throwing you off-balance," he said, wanting to assist her without losing his footing too.

He gripped Lexi's arm, hoping he didn't bruise her, and they continued to make their way across the creek with the bears in their grasp. She slipped a couple more times, and Kate went down once but hurried to get to her feet as best she could, saying, "I'm okay."

Which was good because Ryder couldn't help but one damsel in distress at a time.

They finally reached the shore, all of them stumbling a little on the wet, mossy rocks. Ryder let go of Lexi once she had her footing and moved farther up the bank away from the water. "Okay, we can release them here." He set his charge on the ground.

Lexi released her cub next to his sibling, telling them, "Go to Momma."

The bear cubs bounded toward the mother bear, looking eager to be with their momma. Ryder and the women backed away from the bears as quickly as they could on the uneven terrain, keeping the mother bear in their sights. He just hoped none of them stumbled as they moved away from the potential threat.

When the cubs reached their mother, she checked them over. Once she reassured herself they were fine, the three bears hurried off into the woods, vanishing from sight.

Sounding relieved, Lexi said to Ryder, "Thanks for helping with the bear cubs. Come on, Kate. Let's get back to our cabin."

"I'll go with you to make sure you get there all right." Ryder was determined to see them safely home.

Frowning, Lexi opened her mouth to say something, but Ryder spoke again in case she was going to tell him they didn't need his help. Maybe they didn't, but if they didn't know another way back, at least he did.

"You saw how the cliff sediment and rocks gave way, even for me as a wolf. As humans, we can't make it back that way. Probably not as wolves either. Not only that, but the water's rapidly rising. If you're staying at one of the Redwood Cabins, I am, too, and I know another way back."

"All right, lead the way," Lexi said with almost a challenge in her voice.

Kate was smiling at her, though she was glancing back in the direction the bears had gone. Ryder was also concerned the mother bear might return to deal with them for man-handling her cubs, but she didn't seem to want to.

"Good, I'll lead you back then." Ryder shifted into his wolf and started to walk along the bank of the flooded creek. It had rained since Ryder had been here, putting a damper on the trip. Not that it bothered him while running as a wolf, but hiking in the rain as a human wasn't much fun.

When he'd heard the bear cubs crying in distress, he'd figured he was going to get himself killed if he had to fight a sow to save her cubs. Even so, he would have done anything to rescue them. What he *hadn't* expected was to find two pretty she-wolves attempting to save the cubs. Much to his surprise, he'd recognized their voices as the two women he'd heard conversing with each other in the woods on the other trail. If he'd known they were wolves all along, he would have been racing to meet them.

If the situation hadn't been so dangerous, he would have laughed at the expression Lexi wore when she turned to see him at the entrance of the den peering in—a mixture of shock, incredulity, and annoyance. Maybe a little bit of intrigue. He could tell she believed he was intruding on her and her friend's mission to save the cubs, but he hadn't been about to leave them to their fate, should the mother bear cause them trouble. He was glad Kate had been serving as a lookout too.

Now he hoped things were looking up and he wouldn't have to spend his vacation alone until his buddy arrived in a couple of days, if the ladies wouldn't mind visiting with him for a bit. He glanced back at the women following him, both looking over their shoulders for danger.

The she-wolves were both pretty women, but Lexi especially appealed because of her take-charge attitude, how she was willing to brave the danger to save helpless creatures by entering the bears' den, and that said a lot in his book. Not that Kate wasn't there to help too. He hadn't smelled any male wolves' scents on either of them, so he suspected they were here on their own, vacationing like him.

When he wasn't needed as a bodyguard, he loved cooking, just like his partner, Mike, did. And that made him think of preparing a tasty dinner for the ladies, if they were up for some male companionship. Things could definitely be looking up.

Lexi realized the male wolf scent she and Kate had smelled earlier on their hike belonged to Ryder. She watched as he led them through the forest where no path existed, with no indication they were headed for civilization. She hoped he knew where he was taking them. He was a beautiful gray wolf with a black-tipped tail, black guard hairs on the saddle on his back, and blond on his stomach, paws, and face. His bushy tail was held high as he made his way back to the cabins, alpha posturing all the way.

Kate smiled at Lexi again, like she was interested in the wolf. Lexi wished she could shift so her outer wolf coat would repel the rainwater like it was doing for him. She felt like she and Kate were starring in a wet T-shirt/shorts' contest, their clothes plastered to their bodies. But shifting would mean leaving all their things in the middle of the forest.

"Hold up." Kate pulled off her pack, tucked her gun and horn away, and pulled out Lexi's poncho.

"Thanks, I thought I'd left it behind." Lexi slipped it over her head.

"No way. We don't want to litter the redwood forest." Kate extracted her poncho and slipped it over her head.

They were both so wet, Lexi didn't think wearing the ponchos would make a whole lot of difference.

After about an hour of hiking, Lexi felt the telltale start of a blister on the back of her heel, and she paused in front of Kate. "I've got a blister from the wet socks and boots." Even though their hiking boots were water-resistant, they weren't fully waterproof. If she'd had time, she would have taken off her boots and socks. Then again, once they'd reached the base of the cliff, they had been standing in ankle-deep water. That was another advantage of wearing a wolf coat. No blisters.

Lexi sat down on a log and pulled her pack off, then fished out her first aid kit. Kate held out her poncho to cover Lexi while she removed her socks and boots and then applied liquid bandage to the blisters and any red, chafed area that could form new blisters.

Ryder sat down nearby, watching to ensure the bear didn't follow them but also glancing around at the area, probably concerned someone might see him as a wolf. If someone did, Lexi would quickly call him her dog. No wolf liked to be referred to that way, but in a pinch, it would have to do. Though dogs were only allowed on leash in the campgrounds, on park roads, and in developed areas, not on the trails or in the forest. She could see getting a fine for having an unleashed "dog" in the park where it didn't belong.

Lexi put on dry socks, but she wasn't sure that would

help with wet boots. Then she slipped her wet boots on and Kate changed places with her. Lexi shielded her with her poncho and watched as Kate applied first aid to her blisters.

"We're a pair," Lexi said.

"Yeah, my boots are good for shallow creek crossings and rain, but not for being submersed in water." Kate packed her bag and Lexi did the same; then they took off again.

It took them nearly an hour to reach a real trail that led them to a footbridge. Relieved to see it, Lexi had wondered if they would have ever found a way to cross the creek and reach the top of the cliff. She had to admit she was glad they'd run into Ryder. He'd been a real help.

They hurried across the creaky bridge to the other side of the creek and then ascended stone stairs set into the earth until they reached the top of the cliffs. This was a much better way to get down to the other side of the creek, but she hadn't felt they'd had any choice when they needed to rescue the bear cubs in a hurry. They walked another hour along the trail, finally reaching their log cabins hidden from view from each other in the forest.

Kate was raising her brows at Lexi, motioning with her head to the wolf before he turned to see her antics. Lexi knew Kate thought she should invite him for supper because he'd helped them with the bear cubs and had made sure they found their way back to the cabins safe and sound.

Lexi felt inviting him to have dinner was against her better judgment, but he had helped them, and she'd graciously offer. Maybe she'd get lucky and he'd turn her down, or nothing more would come of it. "Hey, thanks for helping us with the bear cubs and ensuring we made it back to the cabins safely. Would you like to have steaks with us at our cabin tonight?"

The wolf's eyes smiled at her and he nodded, wagging his tail vigorously. So much for him declining the invitation.

Kate was smiling, looking thrilled to have some male companionship.

Lexi wanted to roll her eyes. "Okay, come at six. We're in cabin number four."

He woofed and raced off.

"You did your good deed for the day," Kate said as they walked into their two-bedroom cabin. She closed and locked the door. After pulling off her backpack, she set it on the floor by the door.

"Rescuing the bear cubs, yes." Lexi set her backpack next to Kate's.

Kate smiled. "I mean inviting Ryder over to eat with us. He did get us home safe and sound. Going back the way we came could have been deadly. Besides, he took us on a nice little jaunt that gave us even more exercise. So...are you going to invite him to run as a wolf tonight with us?"

"I'm sure he has better things to do than to spend all his time with us."

"I bet if we offered, he'd wag his tail even harder. What if we run into another bear? It wouldn't hurt to have him tag along with us. If he's alone, which he appears to be, he probably wouldn't mind the company."

"Unless he's a lone wolf."

"He would have said no to dinner then."

Of course Kate was right. "Do you want to shower first?" Lexi always asked, but Kate always let her go first.

"No, go ahead, though I'm going to strip out of these wet clothes and throw on a robe in the meantime." Kate disappeared into her bedroom.

"Thanks." Lexi took off her boots at the door, then grabbed

some fresh clothes from her bedroom and went into the bathroom to take a nice, hot shower. She couldn't wait to get out of her cold, wet clothes. After she showered, she doctored up all her scrapes and cuts, then put on a pair of capris, a halter top, and sandals. She grabbed her wet clothes to hang out on the covered deck to drip-dry but saw Kate sitting at her laptop at the kitchen table.

"Bathroom's free." Lexi set her clothes outside, then went back inside and grabbed her camera and bottle of water out of her backpack. "You don't have to keep up with the business twenty-four seven. You're supposed to be taking a break too." She set her camera down on the table and then took a drink of water from her container.

"I'm just looking for anything I might find on our sexy mystery wolf."

Lexi was about to take another swig of her water when she paused. She was surprised Kate would be so interested in learning more about the guy, though Lexi shouldn't be. He was a ruggedly handsome male wolf, and his assistance couldn't have been better timed. Not to mention he had good rescue instincts.

"You know, you can go out with him if you'd like. I keep telling you this is your vacation too." Lexi appreciated that Kate was such a workaholic, but she didn't expect her to work all the time.

"Are you kidding? After the bear situation? No way. You need my protection."

Lexi laughed. "At the cabin? I'd be fine. The two of you could have some fun."

"He's interested in *you*." Kate's clear-blue eyes filled with mirth. "First, because you make all the decisions. I can tell he likes an alpha. Yet, he appreciated that when you needed a little help to cross the creek, you accepted his assistance. And also because you were the one brave enough to go into the den to rescue the bear cubs."

"Only one of us needed to do that, and you were safeguarding me in case the sow charged us. She was a much greater threat, and you were brave to stand guard." Lexi was trying not to show any interest in what Kate might have learned about the wolf, but wolves were curious by nature. She was glad she and Kate had hit it off so well. They were more like good friends, except that she paid Kate a big salary for her business acumen. As to guarding Lexi? Today was the first time in a long time Lexi might have needed her services in that regard. Though Kate, in her human form— who wouldn't have wanted to try to kill the mother bear— wouldn't have stood a chance against the raging animal.

Kate got up from the table without telling Lexi what she'd learned about the wolf. Lexi wasn't going to ask her about him, not wanting Kate to see she was dying to know more.

Kate motioned to her laptop. "I was just catching up on work emails."

Didn't she just say she was researching the wolf? And why did that intrigue Lexi more than answering business issues? "Are we having any more problems with Spring Cosmetics?" Lexi was irritated with Silky Spring, the owner of the small, upstart competitor that, for whatever reason, was targeting Lexi's cosmetics company with negative customer reviews. Why was Spring Cosmetics going after only Lexi's business?

"I keep telling you that you should hire a private investigator to dig up dirt on the new company."

Lexi figured Spring Cosmetics might fail on its own

without her help. Companies were launched all the time, and they shut down just as fast.

"There are no more reviews saying that her cosmetics are better than yours," Kate said.

"Hmm. Maybe they're laying off for now." Lexi towel-dried her hair.

"You've made a gold mine on your cosmetics. She wants what you have but doesn't want to do all the work, like paying for the marketing, researching, and spending all the countless hours. She just wants money like you have now. Like many politicians, she figures she'll just throw dirt at your products and hope your customers will turn to her company and buy hers instead."

"But why attack *my* cosmetic lines only? You said yourself you checked on other cosmetic sales sites, and they aren't having the same review problem we are."

"Which is why I still think you need to get a PI to look into her. *Thoroughly.* Find out who she is. And use it against her."

"I will, if I need to." All they knew was the woman was a pretty redhead named Silky Spring, and she had a mean streak where Lexi was concerned.

"I'm off to shower." Kate retired to the bathroom, and after a few minutes, she turned on the water.

Lexi swore she would never do anything like this, but it was killing her not to know more about Ryder Gallagher. She sat down at Kate's laptop and did a search for him. A number of men by that name popped up on websites, Facebook, Twitter, and Instagram, but none of them matched the wolf she had invited to dinner. A ghost. There was nothing about him online anywhere. No wonder Kate hadn't told her anything about him. He didn't exist.

How could anybody in this day and age not have some kind of digital footprint? Unless he wasn't who he said he was. Because of her situation with her father, that worried her.

CHAPTER 4

RELIEVED THE BEAR CUBS WERE SAFE WITH THEIR mother again and feeling good that he'd met the she-wolves, Ryder reached his clothes in the woods, shifted, dressed, and headed back to his cabin. Thinking he saw someone off in the distant woods on the trail, he figured it was just another hiker. Nothing to worry about. As a bodyguard for billionaire Aidan Denali and his mate, Holly, Ryder was always wary of his surroundings when he wasn't guarding the good doctors. Some of his caution was also due to being a wolf.

When he reached his cabin, he stripped off his clothes inside, showered, and dressed. He knew by Lexi's hesitation that she hadn't wanted him to come over. He should have declined the offer, but dinner with the she-wolves could be fun. He felt sorry for having had to take them such a round-about way to their cabin.

He could have offered to carry one of the women, but then the other would have been without a knight. And he really didn't want to get caught walking naked all that distance.

Dressed in jeans, a T-shirt, and boots, he got on his cell and called his partner. "Hey, Mike, you really missed out on all the excitement here." He told him everything that had happened.

"Two beautiful she-wolves, unattached, and all to yourself? And they got to see you in rescue mode? How did you get so lucky?"

Ryder laughed. Maybe it was because Mike wasn't here to steal the show.

Wanting to keep her anonymity, Lexi didn't even know what they could talk about with Ryder. She didn't want to mention what she did for a living. But then she figured even if she mentioned she sold cosmetics, he wouldn't assume she had over a billion dollars to her name, just that she might sell them at a cosmetics counter in a department store, or something like that.

"I take it you don't want Ryder to know your last name or who you really are." Kate set the table for three.

"No."

"Or to mention what I do? If he knows I'm your personal assistant and bodyguard, he'll probably assume you don't just sell Mary Kay cosmetics. You know, you've started that line of men's skin-care products. He'd be the perfect model." Kate smiled.

Lexi winked. "Without his clothes."

Kate laughed. "I knew you thought he was hot."

"I'm sure he's a macho wolf who might not be interested in men's skin-care products."

"I'm sure you're right. So what do I say I do?" Kate paused to look at the table setting.

Kate was right. If she mentioned marketing or any other part of her job, it would most likely be a giveaway.

"Okay, I sell cosmetics too," Kate said. "I mean, I do, through all my marketing plans for you."

"That's it. Perfect." Still, Lexi was afraid if they saw much more of Ryder, the truth would come out. Not that she'd necessarily have trouble with him like she'd had with the other male wolves who had already known about her wealth and had sought her out. But she was tired of opening herself up to that kind of harassment. Especially since she hadn't told the four wolves she had recently seen that there wouldn't be any more dates.

—␣∿␣—

When Ryder went over to the ladies' cabin for dinner, he brought a bottle of merlot as his contribution to the meal, hoping they'd like it. He was wearing jeans, a blue shirt that was a little dressier than a T-shirt, and hiking boots, not wanting them to think he was a man on a date, but still wanting to make a favorable impression. He hadn't felt this anxious about sharing a meal with a couple of she-wolves since he was a teen. He didn't know what had come over him, but his hands tingled with apprehension when he arrived at the cabin.

Lexi opened the door and ushered him in. "Oh, the wine looks good. Thanks for bringing it."

"You're welcome. I wanted to contribute something to the meal." He still couldn't get over the feeling that he was on a date with a she-wolf, and he couldn't *believe* he was feeling this way. "Do you come here often?" He poured the wine and the ladies served up the steaks, mashed potatoes, gravy, and a spinach salad. "Dinner smells good."

"Thanks. A few times. What about you?" Lexi took a seat at the head of the table. She still appeared to be in charge.

"I've been here too many times to count. Mostly with others I've worked with."

Kate took a seat at the center of the table. He was tempted to sit at the other end, alpha posturing, but he preferred being closer to both ladies, so he sat opposite Kate at the center of the table.

"Thanks for inviting me over. The food looks great." But he really didn't care about the food as much as having the company. He wasn't a lone-wolf kind of guy. He thought he would be fine running as a wolf and just enjoying the wilderness until Mike arrived, but he realized he much preferred running and visiting with someone, rather than being on his own.

"You're welcome. Do you often come to the park alone?" Lexi cut up a couple of pieces of her steak.

"No. But my partner couldn't make it. He had to see his parents." Ryder poured some blue cheese dressing on his salad.

"What do you do for a living?" Kate took a bite of her steak.

"I'm a bodyguard for Drs. Aidan and Holly Denali. Do you know them?"

"Oh." Lexi eyes widened, and she sounded really surprised.

Kate looked just as surprised.

Why? Because he knew the famous doctor duo? At least the doctors were famous among the wolf populations.

"They found the cure for our enhanced longevity." This time Lexi's voice sounded impressed. "They tested our blood."

"Right. I've helped organize some of their research"— which Ryder was proud of—"but my basic job is serving as their bodyguard. Along with my partner, Mike Stallings. Attempts have been made on Aidan's life, so his brother, Rafe, hired us to watch over him."

"Because Aidan didn't believe he needed a bodyguard," Lexi said.

"Yeah. Between the work he was doing and his wealth, he

needed us. Of course, now we're safeguarding his mate too. And when they have little ones, them too."

"But you're here," Lexi said.

"Uh, yeah. He has a couple of guard details that he uses, so we can swap off and see our families. What about you? What do you do?"

"Cosmetic sales," both women said at the same time.

"You're not sisters, are you? You don't look all that similar." And their voices were different, but they seemed to be thinking in sync like siblings would.

"No, we're just good friends," Lexi said.

Kate smiled at her, and Ryder sensed something more was up. A secret they weren't willing to share with him. Not that he blamed them. They didn't know him from Adam.

"I was planning to run tonight through the woods as a wolf. Would you like to join me?" Ryder thought Kate looked like she wanted to jump at the chance, her eyes bright, her lips lifted, but then she glanced at Lexi.

Lexi was definitely the alpha in charge, but she was hesitant. Which wasn't really an alpha behavior. Either she did or she didn't want to go running with him, and she should have just let him know one way or the other. He could practically see her thinking over the reasons why she shouldn't go running with him and considering why it would be okay to do so. He couldn't figure out why she seemed to worry about having him around. He wondered if she had run into trouble with another male wolf that had made her wary of bachelor males. He wouldn't be surprised.

"The food is perfection. But I'm enjoying the company too," Ryder said.

Lexi stiffened a little.

Yep, he was invading her space, as if telling her he planned to spend all his time in their company as long as they were all here. Which wasn't happening. Now, he wished he hadn't mentioned running with them as wolves tonight, as nice as it would be.

Kate glanced at Lexi, and he swore she was silently pleading with her to agree. He knew the women had suffered blisters from the earlier hike, but the blisters had been on the back of their heels. The wounds wouldn't bother them while they ran as wolves.

Lexi let out her breath as if she'd lost the battle with her friend and nodded. "We'll meet you around nine out on our back deck. By the way, why were you running in the woods as a wolf during the day?"

Her tone of voice implied he shouldn't have been, and normally he wouldn't have been. "I was searching for the bear cubs' den. I'd heard them cry out earlier while I was on a hike, but I couldn't locate them. They'd sounded like they were in distress. I stopped and shifted to cover more ground as a wolf. I wasn't following any of the main trails." He wasn't foolhardy.

"Okay, I wondered." Lexi sipped some of her wine. "What are the doctors up to these days?"

"They're still monitoring wolves to ensure the cure for the aging process is permanent, and they're doing other kinds of research, but I'm not at liberty to say."

"Oh, I know," Kate said, "if others learn of it, they're liable to steal the research." She immediately looked at Lexi, as if she'd made a slip about something.

Lexi's cheeks grew pinker and she quickly said, "Sure. I can imagine that's a real problem for them."

Kate relaxed marginally. It made Ryder wonder what the two women were up to. Then he realized they'd never given him their last names so he couldn't even do a search on them.

"Are you from around here?" Ryder couldn't help how curious he was about the women.

"Yes," Kate said, while Lexi said, "No," at the same exact time.

"I'm from this area originally," Kate clarified.

"I'm not," Lexi said, not saying where she was from. "What about you?"

"Sacramento, originally," Ryder said. "California wolf stock, bred and raised."

The ladies both smiled at that.

"Me too," Kate said.

Lexi didn't say anything.

"No problem. Californians are friendly sorts, and we don't hold it against you if you're from somewhere else," Ryder said, trying to ease the tension. He should have concentrated on enjoying Kate's company, but he was known to go the most difficult route that presented itself. He wanted Lexi to know he was safe to be around. That she had nothing to worry about where he was concerned. He truly saw himself as one of the good guys.

At least for an instant, he'd made Lexi smile.

Ryder reminded himself he had to be wary of meeting wolves he didn't know though, with regard to his own employment. Rafe had often mentioned the staff should do a background check on anyone they came in contact with for an extended period of time and who might have a dark interest in the doctors' research. Not that Lexi seemed interested in spending more time with Ryder, but Kate, now, she was a different story.

He didn't believe the women had already known he was

staying at the cabins or that he had any ties to the doctors. He thought he was being paranoid because Aidan's brother was. Then again, Aidan had issues with wolves trying to steal his research, so there was some basis for it.

They finished dinner, and he thanked the ladies and told them he looked forward to seeing them again on the wolf run. He thought it would be fun if he prepared a meal for them tomorrow because he loved to cook, but then again, he should probably just do the run tonight and let the ladies contact him if they wanted to spend more time with him. He was sure Lexi wouldn't want to.

"I'm glad you enjoyed the meal," Lexi said, as he helped to clear the dishes away. "We'll see you in a little bit."

Kate was all smiles as she began to clean the dishes.

Lexi walked Ryder to the door. "Thanks for everything."

"Thanks for the dinner. And really, you helped me find the bear cubs too."

She smiled. He liked it when she smiled. He was a pushover for making a she-wolf's day—or night—a little brighter, particularly when she held some unfathomable fascination for him.

Then he left and was glad she'd agreed to go running with him. He still wanted to know more about the two women though.

———

"I'm so sorry," Kate told Lexi as she finished cleaning the dishes.

Lexi laughed. "Don't worry about it. He's wondering what we're all about. Keep him guessing. It's all good."

"What if he wants to get together with us again?" Kate put the clean dishes away in the cabinet.

"We'll play it by ear."

"Really? I thought you'd say no way."

Lexi smiled. "He's too curious for his own good. But I doubt he's into intellectual property theft so we don't have to worry about him stealing our research."

"Because he's a hot wolf," Kate said.

Lexi shook her head. "That would be a good way for one of our competitors to try to get into our business. But if he works for the Denali doctors, he wouldn't be trying to steal our research. He's doing just what he said he's doing." Still, she got on her phone and called Aidan Denali. "Hey, this is Lexi. We'll be seeing you at your brother's place to have a tea party with the ladies and dinner with all of you next week. My personal assistant, Kate, and I are staying at the Redwood Cabins, and we ran into a man who says he's your bodyguard."

"Uh, Ted, I mean Ryder Gallagher. He decided to go by his middle name a few weeks ago. Yeah. He was supposed to go with Mike Stallings to the cabin. But Mike couldn't make it right away. Is everything okay?"

"Uh, yeah, he helped us rescue some bear cubs."

Aidan laughed. "Mike will be disappointed he didn't get to take part in that."

"Well, I was just checking to make sure he truly works for you."

"He does, and he's great at his job and a good friend."

"Okay, thanks, Aidan. We'll be seeing you next week."

"Looking forward to it."

They ended the call after that. "Ryder works for Aidan and Holly," Lexi said.

Kate snorted and got on her laptop to answer emails. "I could have told you that."

Lexi smiled at her. "It's good to be sure about it."

"I agree. And if you hadn't done it, I would have suggested it because I couldn't find anything on the social network sites for him, which had me worried."

"Me too."

Kate glanced at her and smiled. "You did some research on him when I was in the shower. Interesting."

"Yeah, I was curious about him. I still am. Why not be on any social network sites?"

"Maybe he's afraid someone would befriend him and try to reach Aidan that way."

"You could be right." Lexi hated when her imagination took hold and she saw danger when there wasn't any.

At the appointed hour, Lexi and Kate were standing on the back deck as wolves, waiting for Ryder. He arrived right on time, his tail and head held high. He looked grateful to see they were ready to go with him. The three of them took off through the woods, having a grand time. Lexi figured she wouldn't be able to keep who she was secret from him when she went to the ladies' tea and dinner at Rafe Denali's home, but by then it wouldn't matter. She wouldn't be spending more time like this with him. Kate was welcome to see him if she was interested.

Lexi loved being successful, but it truly wreaked havoc with finding a mate who wanted to be with her and *only* her and not because she was so wealthy. Maybe someday she would get lucky.

In the meantime, she needed to figure out where her father's message might have been hidden. She knew he had to hide it well, so no one else would find it. But did that have to include her?

CHAPTER 5

RYDER COULDN'T HELP BUT BE WATCHFUL AS HE AND the she-wolves ran through the woods. The rain was no longer falling, although the sky was still overcast with only a hint of the full moon shining through. Wind blew through the redwoods, the whooshing sound soothing to Ryder's ear. He glanced in the direction of his she-wolf companions. Lexi had a blonder wolf face and body than Kate, and her legs were a little longer. Both were pretty wolves, and they bumped into each other every once in a while in a playful fun way that made him smile.

A couple of black-tailed deer bounded in front of them and darted out of the wolves' path, startling the wolves, the smell of panic surrounding the deer. Ryder and the she-wolves were keeping off the trails, running through the ferns and dense huckleberry shrubs, feeling the wind in their fur. Even though they were well equipped to handle the rain while in their wolf coats, he was glad it was no longer raining.

He was enjoying the run with the two she-wolves when he saw movement in the trees and turned to look. A black-haired, bearded man wearing camouflage pants and shirt, camo boots, and a hat was shooting pictures or video of them from a distance. Ryder's heartbeat accelerated, and in warning, he barked at the women to run out of the photographer's view.

He hesitated, allowing the women time to run off ahead

of him so he could watch their backs. To his astonishment, Lexi turned and raced toward the man as if she was in killer attack form. *What the hell?*

She was bound to put all wolves into hot water when they had worked so hard to show they weren't monstrous predators.

Kate chased after Lexi as if she was part of her hungry-for-prey wolf pack.

Ryder normally always had a plan. This time? He didn't know whether to rescue the man, fight off the she-wolves, or take off to show the guy that Ryder wasn't part of any of the wild wolf rampage.

Hell. He couldn't let the she-wolves hurt the photographer. He chased after them, trying to shorten the distance between them. He wished he could head them off before they reached the man with the camera, who had immediately grabbed his camera bag and made a mad dash through the woods. There was no way the man could outrun the wolves.

Though the *lupus garous* tried to stay out of the news, some hiker taking photographs shouldn't be that big a deal. Sure, they'd probably end up on some social media sites— didn't just about everything?—and sure, some of their kind would know it was Ryder and question how he got caught at it. But this would be way worse.

Lexi caught up with the man, jumping at his back and forcing him facedown in the ferns. He cried out. "Don't eat me! Don't eat me!"

Lexi was growling furiously, the camera in her mouth, trying to yank it from his hands like she was playing tug-of-war.

Ryder had almost reached them when Lexi managed to

yank the camera from the man's grasp. Kate grabbed his camera bag, and the two she-wolves raced off in the direction they'd come.

Ryder stared at the man, who was practically hyperventilating. But the she-wolves hadn't bitten him. They'd just taken his camera and camera bag. Ryder smelled the man's overriding scent—fear—and recognized the guy as Don Morgan, an independent photographer with a nose for news who wrote for the tabloids. A paparazzo. As far as Ryder knew, Don might be a celebrity chaser, but he wasn't a bad guy.

Ryder told himself that Lexi—and Kate—might have a very good reason for attacking the man. Who knew what past experience could shape a person? Still, he couldn't believe they'd reacted the way they did, putting wolves at risk. Don would undoubtedly report the attack to the park rangers, and they'd be out looking for a crazed pack of wolves that didn't like having their pictures taken. If they believed him. More likely, they'd think it was a pack of wild dogs.

As wolves, they ran fast, covering a lot of ground. Ryder had been here so often, he thought he knew where they were headed: to an isolated waterfall, though he easily followed their scent.

He was right. They finally reached the waterfall cascading through all the greenery. Kate set the bag down on the ground, and Lexi did the same with the camera. The adrenaline was still rushing through his bloodstream, and he could hear the women's hearts beating hard.

They were still panting, but they all stopped to sip from the cold water. An owl hooted, the water splashed down the mossy rocks of the waterfall, and crickets chirped in the darkness.

Standing next to the stream, Lexi shifted, her creamy skin and curves glistening in the moonlight, her rosy nipples erect in the cool air. Then she picked up the camera and began looking at the pictures Don had taken.

Kate was still in her wolf form, the bag she'd taken sitting nearby.

Then Kate shifted and began rummaging through the camera bag. It was full of lenses, scandisks, and battery chargers. The camera had to have a night-vision lens so Don could capture night shots. Kate shifted back into her wolf form.

Ryder looked over the camera, but Lexi hadn't damaged it. He wondered if she just planned to remove the memory cards so Don wouldn't have any pictures of them.

"We can't have photographs taken of us here." Lexi shifted into her wolf, grabbed the camera, and headed back to her cabin.

"Right, we shouldn't, but it happened, and we don't attack humans for it." Ryder shifted, then picked up the camera bag for Kate.

She woofed at him in appreciation, and they chased after Lexi.

When they finally reached the back deck of Lexi's place, he set the camera bag down.

Lexi set the camera on the deck, shifted, opened the door, and grabbed the camera bag and camera. "Thanks for the lovely wolf run," she said, by way of dismissal.

Kate headed inside the cabin.

He wasn't going to be dismissed. He shifted. "Don't you think that was rather a rash way of dealing with him for taking pictures of us?"

"If I thought so, I wouldn't have done it. Good night,

Ryder." Then Lexi walked inside and shut the door. The lock clicked.

Hell. He was still staring at the door, not believing what had happened. He wondered how Mike would have handled the situation.

"Do you even *know* who the photographer is?" Ryder asked at the door, not knowing if either Lexi or Kate had returned to their bedrooms and could hear him.

Lexi opened the door dressed in a pink, lace-trimmed, floral pajama shorts set. She looked sweet and innocent, the vision before him at odds with the sight of the she-wolf who had made the mad dash to tackle Don and steal his camera. "Don Morgan, paparazzo. Good night, Ryder."

That she knew him surprised Ryder. He couldn't imagine Don had hassled her for any reason, which made him again wonder exactly who she was. Ryder quickly offered, "Breakfast in the morning on me? Something special?" He had to hear the whole story. He smiled amiably at her. "I'm not just a bodyguard. I cook."

Lexi opened her mouth to say something, but clamped it shut. Then she smiled a little, appearing amused.

Wearing pj's featuring sunflowers, Kate poked her head out the door. "I'm game."

Lexi let out her breath. "You can join him, if you want."

"*Not* without you."

Ryder waited for Lexi to agree. Man, if he wanted to date Kate, she seemed perfectly agreeable. So why was he so hung up on the woman who wasn't interested in him?

"Eight… No, make it nine," Lexi said.

He thought that would make for a late breakfast, but maybe the ladies were sleeping in a bit on their vacation. "Is there anything you'd like in particular, or anything you don't care to eat? Anything gourmet that appeals?" Ryder asked.

"Strawberry crepes filled with light vanilla cream," Lexi said.

Ryder smiled at her, assuming she figured he couldn't prepare such a meal. True, he'd have to run to the grocery store to pick up the ingredients, but he could do it. "And you, Kate?"

"That sounds yummy."

He was thinking of something more filling. "Anything else?"

"That's it, but if it's not substantial enough for you, feel free to fix something else for yourself," Lexi said.

Yeah, he was thinking he'd add some ham and hash browns on the side. "See you then." He shifted and took off for his cabin, eager to head for the grocery store and pick up the ingredients he would need for the crepes. He hoped Lexi understood he had every intention of questioning her actions further, but he suspected she must have had a run-in with Don Morgan over something and this had been personal.

When he reached his cabin, he shifted, entered the place, and then locked the door. He called Mike. "Hey, you know those two she-wolves I met?"

"More exciting news? I should have gone with you."

"I'll say." Ryder explained what had happened while he got dressed. "What would you have done in my place?"

"Hell. Rogue wolves?" Mike asked.

"I suspect it's something else. The first thing that came to mind is that Lexi has been hurt by a photographer before when she was in her wolf form. But if it isn't that—"

"Don't tell me. Don's gone after her because she's someone important. What did you say her last name was?"

"She didn't give it to me. Neither did her friend Kate."

"A celebrity?"

"Maybe. I don't get out to the movies much. Singer? I don't know."

"Hell, well, get a picture of her and maybe I'll know who she is."

Ryder laughed. "I can see her taking my phone away from me and deleting all *my* photos."

"I have *got* to meet this woman. I'll be there in two days. Let me know if anything else goes on with her, will you?"

"Yeah, will do. Maybe she'll tell me something tomorrow." At least Ryder sure hoped so.

"Call me when you learn what's up."

"I will." If she'd had a run-in with Don before as a human, Ryder could see that, but as a wolf? He still couldn't figure that out.

"I can't believe he is out here." Kate was making them blender margaritas.

"Don Morgan?" Lexi let out her breath. "I swear he's like a hound dog when it comes to knowing where I am. I'm sure he wouldn't be here for any other reason. If I didn't want to be responsible for him and his wife and two kids, I'd turn him."

Kate smiled and handed her a drink. "What if Don returns with another camera? Maybe he's got a couple of spares in his vehicle or wherever he's staying?"

"I know. I thought the same thing. He can't see us digging for that message. That's why I had to take his camera. I hoped it would scare him off and he'd return home and give up trying to take pictures of me out here. How did he even learn we were out here?" Lexi took a good swallow of her margarita. "Perfection."

"Thanks. You don't think he knows about our wolf secret, do you?"

"No. I think he just stumbled across what he thought would make a good story: wolves that aren't supposed to be in the redwoods."

"What are you going to do with all this camera equipment?" Kate loaded the pictures from the camera to her laptop.

"I'd give it to the rangers at the ranger station, saying we found it, but that might corroborate his story that wolves ran off with it and then we found it abandoned. I'd rather no one finds any of it."

"Plus, we are taking the memory cards, and he would probably assume whoever turned the equipment in stole them. The wolves wouldn't remove them. I wondered how he could take pictures of us in the dark, but this is a video camera with night vision."

Lexi joined her to look at the photographs. "He took several shots of us before Ryder saw him and warned us."

"Before that, he took all kinds of shots of celebrities. He'll hate to lose all this, unless he backed it up already."

"He wouldn't have any of the pictures he took of us as wolves tonight. Are there any of us that show us hiking earlier?" Lexi asked.

"Yeah a couple of us hiking. You were right. He was out here looking for you," Kate said. "This is a picture of one of the ranger stations."

Lexi peered at the photos some more. "Looks like he didn't take any photos of us at the bear den when Ryder shifted as a wolf and joined us."

"No. He would have had to have been where we were at the time and then climbed down the cliff. He couldn't have managed it without us being aware of it. Though if he'd gotten shots of us crossing the creek with a naked man carrying a bear cub, he would have had a sensational hit once he sold the story to a magazine," Kate said.

"Good thing he didn't. He doesn't have any of our cabin either."

Kate said, "Maybe he doesn't know where we're staying yet. Okay, so when we have breakfast with Ryder tomorrow, you know he is going to ask you how you know Don and why you terrorized him by chasing him down and stealing his camera."

"Yeah, he will. Don sure has a powerful grip. I didn't think I would manage to yank his camera free from his grasp unless I bit him. Which"—Lexi smiled at Kate as she raised her brows—"I wouldn't have done. And thanks for grabbing Don's camera bag. He won't be coming around here for a while. Not until he gets another camera. Hopefully he'll be gone until we locate the message."

"What are you going to say to Ryder tomorrow? You shocked the wolf to pieces when you took Don down. Ryder was looking him over for bite marks, making sure you hadn't killed the man, but of course him hovering over Don must have terrified him even more. I'm sure Ryder thought we were both crazy."

"I'll play it by ear." It looked like Lexi would have to tell Ryder who she was. Don was a royal pain in the ass. She was certain he wouldn't give up his quest to get pictures of her while she stayed here.

He just couldn't catch her looking for the message from her father.

CHAPTER 6

BEFORE DAWN THE NEXT MORNING, LEXI AND KATE took off through the woods, determined to locate the message at the other waterfall, hoping this wouldn't be a bust like the other two times. Lexi planned to get back in plenty of time for breakfast. She just hoped they didn't run into Don out here.

"I'm glad you told Ryder we'd have breakfast at nine because we still haven't reached the other waterfall and we need time to dig," Kate said. Lexi was really pushing to get there as quickly as she could, Kate following close behind.

The whole time they were headed for the waterfall, they were watching for signs of Don. They didn't see him, and they hoped he wasn't still hanging around the redwoods.

Lexi sighed. "And hike back. Right. I should have gotten Ryder's phone number in case we were delayed. I can imagine him worrying about us and then tracking us here."

"Let's hope not. Is he listed in a directory? Do you want me to call Aidan and get Ryder's cell number?" Kate skipped over a rock.

"Yeah, sure." Lexi would rather Kate ask for it, making it sound more…businesslike.

"Hey, Aidan, this is Kate. Do you have Ryder's cell number handy? We're supposed to have breakfast with him and we're on a hike, so if we're late returning, we need to let him know." Kate smiled. "Okay, putting it in my contacts. Thanks! Bye."

They finally reached the next waterfall, and it was as beautiful as the first. Ferns embraced the rocks on either side of the falls, the water crystal clear, the sound of the rushing stream relaxing and refreshing. Despite wanting to start moving rocks, Lexi pulled out her camera to take some pictures. She was getting to be just like her mom.

Kate began moving rocks. Then Lexi tucked her camera away and started to help. When they reached the soil, they dug, didn't find anything, and moved everything back. And moved on to a new place. They did the same routine three more times.

"Is there another waterfall in this vicinity?" Kate asked.

"Let me look at the map, but it's getting too late to trek to a new location and start digging again."

"We could continue this later, after breakfast," Kate said.

Lexi stopped to look at the map and discovered a location above the falls where a second set of falls were located and pointed to it. "Yeah, that's a great idea."

"What if Ryder wants to come along?"

"He's out of luck. I can't get anyone else involved in this. *You* shouldn't be involved."

Kate sighed. "All right."

"Okay, let's head back. I thought we'd have more time at this, but this was a lot farther from our cabin than the other location." They packed up their gear and headed back. They didn't see any indication that Don was anywhere around, though they'd been smelling for his scent and watching and listening. Lexi hadn't smelled any sign of her father up here either.

They'd also been watching for bears, but they didn't see any. They finally reached the cabin, washed up, and changed clothes. "Are you ready to go?" Lexi asked.

Kate smiled. "Yeah. I couldn't believe you asked him for strawberry crepes."

"That's because he said he made gourmet food."

"And you wanted him to prove it."

"Naturally. And for the grief I know he's going to give me over stealing the paparazzo's camera and equipment."

"True. But you're a she-wolf, and Ryder is damned interested in you."

"He wants to interrogate me, and he's trying to offer a fancy carrot to get me to talk." Lexi opened the front door.

"Well, I for one am glad you ordered the strawberry crepes. If he does them right, this will be a real treat."

Except that when Lexi told him who she was, the dynamics between them would no doubt change, and not in a good way.

⁓⁓⁓

Eager to see if Lexi and Kate liked the meal he had prepared, and just as eager to learn more about them, Ryder opened the door to Lexi's knock and smiled. "Come in. The meal is ready."

Lexi and Kate smiled when they saw they crepes filled with cream cheese and whipped cream, with strawberries and more whipped cream on top.

"I have sliced ham and hash browns, too, if you'd like something more to eat with your crepes." Ryder started putting the ham and potatoes in two separate dishes so the ladies could help themselves.

"Sure. Glad you made extra, and it looks just as delicious," Lexi said.

Pleased they would like some of the other food he had fixed, Ryder made everyone cups of coffee. They sat at the table and began eating.

Lexi shook her head. "I can't believe you're not a gourmet chef working for a five-star restaurant." She took a bite of the crunchy hash browns, potatoes freshly cut, and practically purred.

"Yeah, this is so good. The Denalis are sure lucky to have you." Kate slipped another slice of ham onto her plate.

"Aidan was so busy with his research that Mike and I had to fix meals for ourselves—and for him. We started creating gourmet meals when we didn't have guard duty to do. We enjoy a little friendly competition."

"Well, this is great," Lexi said, motioning to all of the meal.

"I'm glad you like it." He wanted to ask about last night, but he was trying to enjoy breakfast with them and not start with the questions right away.

Thankfully, Lexi let him off the hook. "Just for your information, I've had run-ins with Don Morgan before."

Frowning, Ryder again wondered if Lexi was someone famous. She had to be for Don to be interested in making up a story about her for the tabloids. "Over?"

"He thrives on celebrity news."

"Celebrity." Ryder didn't know what to think.

Lexi smiled. "You didn't know you were in the company of a celebrity, did you?"

"Uh, no." He didn't believe she was a movie star. Wouldn't *that* be something if she was! Still, life would be a lot less complicated if she was just a regular she-wolf, not someone who was famous.

"Are you going to be guarding the Denalis at the tea party and dinner next week?" Lexi asked Ryder.

Looking relieved that Lexi was going to tell Ryder who she was, Kate let out her breath.

Ryder raised a brow, surprised to hear Lexi knew about it. "Uh, yes, I am." Then he snapped his fingers, the light dawning. "Lexi Summerfield and Kate Hanover, your personal assistant. Cosmetics. Hell, when you first mentioned you sold cosmetics, I thought you were Mary Kay ladies. You have the successful Clair de Lune Cosmetics company."

Lexi smiled.

"I'm a personal assistant *and* bodyguard," Kate corrected him. "I can do more than one job at a time."

"Like me and cooking."

"You certainly can do that well," Lexi said.

"What kind of a story did Don do that prompted you to relieve him of his camera and gear?" Ryder asked.

"He's trouble for me, all right? Yes, he has concocted annoying stories about me, telling the tabloids that I have this lover or that lover, whatever will sell news. Every time he sees me with a wolf on a date, he speculates—in print—if this is Mr. Right. But that's not the problem."

"Hell, I'll make sure he stays clear of you." Ryder was damn determined to make it so.

Lexi smiled. She appeared ready to take him up on it. Unless she was just amused that he'd offer.

Ryder served them more coffee. "I'm serious. That's what I do for a living. While you're here, I'm on the job."

"You can't question me about what I'm doing." Lexi took a sip of her coffee and set the mug on the table.

Surprised at Lexi's comment, Ryder didn't say anything for a moment. "Okay." He didn't think she'd be doing anything illegal, but why was she being so secretive about something? Unless it had to do with her cosmetics research, as it often was with Aidan and Holly's research. But in the redwoods?

"After lunch, we're taking a long hike to the upper falls,

northwest of the cabins. You make sure we're not on Don's radar. He might have to pick up more camera equipment, so it might take him a little time to return. On the other hand, he could be located nearby and have more stashed there. No matter what, I can't chance that he'll be following us." Lexi sounded dead serious. "I can't have him reporting on what I'm doing. Our lives depend on it."

Ryder couldn't believe the women would be in trouble. Here he'd thought he was going to have to lecture Lexi on terrorizing a human. Now he didn't know what to think. Of course he was dying to know what it was all about, but he promised to let it go for now. All he cared about was protecting Lexi's secret, whatever it was, from one nosy reporter.

"Oh, and on the pictures he took, he shot several of us as wolves before you warned us. He also had a couple of Kate and me hiking before we climbed the cliff after the bear cubs," Lexi said.

"But none of us carrying the cubs across the creek?" Alarmed, Ryder had never expected paparazzi to be snapping shots of anyone in the redwoods.

"No. He must have lost us at some point when we were hiking on the trail. To have taken pictures of us near the cliff, he would have had to leave the trail. And to get pictures of us with the bears, he would have had to climb down there like we did. One of us would have seen him. Besides, who, but us, would dare get close to a mother bear like that? There were no pictures of us returning to the cabins with a wolf either," Lexi said.

"Good." Ryder let out his breath, not believing he'd ever say this. "It was good that you took his camera then."

"I'm so glad you think so." Lexi smiled at him. "So, do you have a Facebook page? Twitter? Instagram?"

Wearing a hint of a smile, Kate glanced at her.

Amused that she'd ask, Ryder finished his breakfast and sat back against his chair. "You looked for my profile, didn't you?"

"Yeah, we had to make sure you were one of the good guys, but you're a ghost." Lexi finished off her last crepe.

"Being on social networks doesn't prove you're one of the good guys. There are lots of scam artists out there. I just don't feel the need to be on any of the social network sites. And I did worry that someone might try to befriend me on a site to get to Aidan and his research. Now for you, I can understand the importance of being out there."

"Okay, true," Lexi said.

He hoped the reason she had looked wasn't just because she wanted to see if he was one of the good guys, but to learn more about his interests, when he knew he shouldn't be thinking along those lines. Not when her income was way above his pay grade. How could he take her out to places when she could afford to go anywhere on her own?

Then Lexi got a call and glanced at the caller ID. "Hello, this is Lexi Summerfield." She rolled her eyes at Kate. "Um, Freddie."

"I'll help you clean up the dishes." Kate jumped up to clear the empty plates from the table.

Ryder began helping her, but he was super interested in what Lexi had to say to the man. From the looks she shared with Kate, the guy was bothering her.

"It's not going to work out between us. I'm sorry. I allow myself only three dates with a wolf, and after that, I move on. If we're not right for each other, we're not right for each other. You know the old saying about getting blood out of a turnip."

Ryder caught himself before he chuckled. What if he was the one who had dated her three times and *his* head was on the chopping block?

"No, I'm sorry. We don't have the kind of interest in each other that would warrant any more time together. I've got to go now. I shouldn't have answered the phone. I'm on a date now." Lexi glanced at Ryder.

"This doesn't count," Ryder quickly said, surprised she was calling this a date. He certainly had something more impressive in mind. If all she allowed were three dates? He'd definitely wasted this one already.

Kate patted his arm consolingly. He bet *Kate* didn't have a three-date limit.

"Good luck with finding the right she-wolf," Lexi said, then she paused, smiled, and ended the call. She did something on her phone before she placed it on the table.

"Lexi just blocked his calls. One more male wolf bites the dust." Kate placed the cleaned plates in the cabinet. "You have Ryder worried, you know, Lexi. He thinks he ruined a perfectly good date with you, and he's only got two more to prove he's the right wolf for you."

"Nonsense. He's had two dates with me already. Remember the hike we took?"

He just chuckled. He wasn't going to win this conversation, and if she really wanted to date him, he would have to come up with something special for the last one. He wondered how many wolves she'd dated.

"Besides, the dates that are unplanned can be the most fun," Lexi continued. "Before we go on the hike, we have to return for our backpacks and change our clothes."

He finished picking up the serving dishes off the table. "I'll grab my backpack and then follow you over to your cabin, if that works for you. I can keep a lookout for Don if he's sneaking around the place."

"That will be fine," Lexi said. "When we return, you can make us a gourmet lunch."

Not expecting Lexi to invite herself and Kate over for lunch, he chuckled. She gave him a brilliant smile. He wasn't sure what he'd gotten himself into. Here he was supposed to be on vacation, and now he was doing the same kind of work he did for the Denalis. Except this was different. Lexi was intriguing, secretive, and mysterious. With the Denalis, he knew what to expect most of the time. With Lexi? Never.

"Oh, yeah," Kate said. "That would be great."

"We'll leave the menu up to you this time. Surprise us," Lexi said.

Good thing, or he'd have to run to the grocery store again.

With her wealth, Lexi could have hired anyone to take care of whatever she was doing. Which made the situation even more baffling. He suspected Kate must know what was going on.

He couldn't help but see Lexi in a different light. Instead of being a cute she-wolf who saved bear cubs and sold cosmetics, she was someone prominent. He realized that was probably why she hadn't revealed who she was earlier— afraid he might be interested in her money. He could understand that.

Then Ryder and the ladies left his cabin, and he walked them to their place. Instead of going inside with them when they did, he circled the perimeter, checking for any signs Don was around, scoping out the place. Ryder didn't smell him anywhere in the vicinity, which he took as a good sign.

The ladies both left the cabin after that, carrying their backpacks, ready to hike.

"Would he know where you're going?" Ryder asked. If Don did, he could be lying in wait up ahead.

"No. Then again, he shouldn't have known about us being here in the first place," Lexi said. "We're very careful to book under pseudonyms and not mention that we're going away for any length of time."

"That's the same with the Denalis," Ryder said.

"It pays to be careful. I'm not like a movie-star celebrity. But in some circles, people know me."

Normally, Ryder would have advised the ladies to go as quietly as they could while hiking through the redwoods, but with the possible threat of startling a black bear, he kept quiet, while they talked about creating a woodland marketing video.

Ryder did consider that if the word got out, Don might not be the only one who learned Lexi was staying here with her personal assistant.

After an hour and a half of hiking and a lot of climbing, they finally reached the upper falls. When they arrived, he checked the place over to ensure Don wasn't around. "No one is here now."

"Okay. You can watch for anyone who might come up that path." Lexi waited for him to move off before she did whatever she'd come here to do.

Ryder moved away from the women to the edge of the steep incline where they'd made their climb up moss-covered, timber-braced stairs and kept an eye out for any movement below. What he hadn't expected was to hear the sound of rocks being moved and stacked near where they had rested. Then two trowels dug into the earth.

He turned to watch the women. They were both digging away with garden tools. They were on a treasure hunt? But this was federal property. He shook his head and continued to observe the path below.

Rocks were moved again, but then Kate cried out.

Ryder whipped around, afraid something bad had happened to one of the women on his watch.

Kate was shaking her hand out and then favoring it.

"Is everything all right?" He didn't move from his spot since he was still supposed to be watching for any sign of people.

"Uh, yeah. I just dropped a rock on my fingers, dummy me. No broken bones. Just bruised, I'm sure," Kate said.

Lexi motioned to the two of them. "Can you two switch places? You can help me with this, and Kate can be the lookout. Just don't ask what this is all about."

"If you're in some kind of trouble, Rafe has an army of ex-military wolves he served with who will drop everything to come to your aid." Ryder switched places with Kate. He was serious about that. Rafe would call in the troops in a heartbeat if he knew Lexi was having difficulties with anyone.

Lexi shook her head. "No one else can know what this is about."

"Okay." But he didn't like it. He was used to using muscle to take care of a situation, and if someone was causing problems for her, he wanted to help her in any way he could. "What do you want me to do?"

"Move rocks over there. Then we dig."

"For buried treasure?"

She gave him a look to be serious. He *was* serious.

"We're looking for a message. That's all Kate knows. That's all you need to know."

"All right." It wasn't, but once they found the message, maybe he'd learn what this was all about.

They moved the rocks, then when they reached soil, Lexi began to dig.

"I smelled an old scent of a male wolf," he said, helping her to dig.

Lexi didn't respond.

"Did he leave the message?" Ryder suspected so.

"No questions."

"Okay, no more questions about that, but how do you know something is buried here as opposed to somewhere else?" He asked because they weren't getting anywhere with this, and he wondered if she didn't remember where the message was buried.

She pulled off her backpack, dug around in it, brought out a hand-drawn map, and pointed at a spot on it. "Right there where the circle is. That's where it's supposed to be."

"That's the waterfall by the creek where we rescued the bear cubs."

She stared at the map. He turned it around for her. "You're looking at it upside down."

"No." Frowning, she peered at it.

"Yeah. Here's a faded compass symbol. If you hold it up to the filtered sunlight, you can see it a little better. That's the creek that passes by where the cubs' den was."

"But the 'N' for north is here." She pointed to a large N in one corner of the map.

"It's a red herring. It shows the faded Rose of the Winds on the map. That's the compass rose." Ryder again pointed at the faded compass symbol.

"Oh, right. My dad had talked to me about that as a kid. I'd forgotten. A compass rose was also called a wind rose or Rose of the Winds."

"The bear and her cubs won't return there."

"Yeah, but what if the location is flooded?"

"It hasn't rained since yesterday afternoon. Come on. We can use the footbridge this time, instead of trying to break our necks climbing down the cliff."

Lexi turned the map this way and that. "Okay." She folded up the map and tucked it in the pocket of her backpack. "You'd better be right."

"I am." He smiled at her. At least he hoped he was right.

"You'd better be right," Kate echoed Lexi's sentiment.

"Do you want me to get your backpack?" he asked Kate. It shouldn't be that much of a problem for her, except if she needed to grab it with her injured hand, but he had to ask.

"No. Thanks for asking though. I'm good."

"Everyone needs to keep a lookout for you-know-who," Lexi warned.

"Eyes peeled," Kate assured her.

They climbed down the steps, Kate leading the way, Lexi in between, and Ryder bringing up the rear. He was watching for any signs of Don, but he couldn't help but think of Lexi at the same time, wondering what kind of a date he could ask her out on to really impress her. What could he give the woman who must have everything?

When they reached the bottom of the steps, they continued the long hike down the hill toward the cabins, and then in the direction of the footbridge. The whole time, they were keeping a lookout for any sign of Don. Ryder didn't think the guy would give up that easily. But maybe he did have to return to the city to get more camera equipment. Ryder had thought of just suggesting the ladies leave here and go someplace Don wouldn't know about, but if they were here because of some message, he guessed that wasn't a viable option. And he guessed that's what was so important to keep secret from the paparazzo.

He just hoped they'd find the message where he thought it would be. If it was where they had just been, but in a slightly different spot, he could imagine how annoyed she'd be with him. Forget third dates.

CHAPTER 7

LEXI, KATE, AND RYDER FINALLY REACHED THE footbridge and hurried across it. But when they hiked to the area where Ryder thought the message should be, Lexi saw everything was underwater. "Just great." Why hadn't her dad left the message at the last location where they'd been? If he'd left it way above at the upper falls, the message wouldn't be underwater.

"It should be just past the cubs' den, if the map is accurate," Ryder assured her.

"Underwater," she said.

"We can do this," Kate said. "We'll find it."

Lexi loved that Kate was always the optimist. Lexi was usually one too. That made the two of them dangerous at times.

"The weather app said we're not going to have any rain for three days," Ryder assured her. "The water levels will be going down. If you don't have to do this right away, we can wait a bit. But if not, let me try to find it for you."

"You are a real Boy Scout," Lexi said, meaning it in a good way. "But we do have to find it soon."

He gave her a little smirk. "Okay. I'm just trying to do my good deed for today."

"You seem to be doing a lot of good deeds. Do you often do this on your vacation?" Lexi asked.

"I got lucky this time."

Lexi smiled. She was in the middle of the thigh-high water,

trying to search with Ryder while Kate watched out for anyone who might come upon them.

"It's no use." As much as Lexi hated to tell Ryder he was right because she didn't want to quit, she realized this was futile. Every time she moved rocks under the water, the silt would be stirred up and cloud the clear water. After a half hour, she was done.

"I'm sorry, Lexi," Ryder said.

"It's not your fault. I'm sure...I'm sure this wasn't something anyone had planned for. We'll find it."

"So what are you fixing us for lunch?" Kate asked, upbeat as ever.

Both Lexi and Ryder chuckled.

"He probably doesn't have all the ingredients he would need to make us another gourmet meal. But I'm sure whatever he makes for us will be outstanding." Or he wouldn't have offered. Lexi knew he was trying to make a winning impression on them. It was nice having a chef here to cook their meals, though she was thinking they'd grill spareribs for him tonight. When had this chance encounter turned into spending all her time with him?

When the paparazzi became a problem.

"I'll fix something I hope you both enjoy," Ryder said.

"I'm looking forward to it. We'll head back to the cabin then. Kate and I are going to do some promotional videos for the company," Lexi said.

"All right. When you're done, you can come over for lunch. If you need me to, I'll hang around where you'll be shooting the video and make sure Don, or any other paparazzo, doesn't show up and cause problems for you."

"Thanks. That would be most appreciated." Lexi was glad he had offered. She hadn't wanted to ask him to do

anything for her unless he volunteered, so she was glad he
wanted to help out more.

———

Before they set up for the video promo, Ryder did some
checking into Lexi's background. Her mother, Adelaide
Summerfield, had died in a ferryboat-bridge crash, the ferry-
boat hitting a pillar and taking a six-hundred-fifty-foot span
of the bridge down, causing two cars to fall into the water
at the mouth of the Amazon River basin. Lexi's mother, a
pediatrician, had been driving a rental car across the bridge
when the accident occurred. Rescuers had never found her
body. He imagined Lexi hated not having closure. He certainly would have felt that way. He'd also learned her father
was a family physician, Kurt Summerfield, and had witnessed Joe Tremaine—kingpin crime boss, drug trafficker,
and arms dealer—kill a district attorney in cold blood in
San Antonio, Texas. Then Dr. Kurt Summerfield had died
in a fiery car crash.

Ryder really felt bad for Lexi for the losses she'd suffered.
Family meant everything to wolves, and she'd lost both her
parents this past year in separate accidents.

He headed back out to help the ladies with their video.
Even though he had planned to guard them, he wanted to
watch the filming of their outdoor promotional video too.

First, though, he helped them build a nice little campfire
in the firepit by their cabin to set the outdoor scene, while
Kate set up the camera on the tripod to take the video that
would showcase the woods in the background, the fire in
the foreground, and Lexi sitting on a log where she would
be showing off her products. Lexi was busy setting up all the
cosmetics she would use in the video.

With the sound of the fire crackling, birds singing, and a breeze blowing through the trees in the background, Lexi began talking about her products while Kate filmed her.

Ryder was keeping a lookout, but he kept glancing back at Lexi to see her smiling, showing various cosmetic lines, and explaining how they were good for the outdoors—sunscreen and moisturizer, all dermatologist-approved.

He could see why she was so successful with her business. It wasn't that she just worked diligently or might have a really great product; she was also a super-saleswoman. Hell, he wasn't even in the market for what she was selling, but she had sold him on it.

He noticed two couples headed their way, wearing shorts, T-shirts, hiking boots, and backpacks. Though they looked like they were just vacationers, not reporters, he didn't want them messing up Lexi's video. Like a bouncer at a club, he walked toward them to head them off.

"That's Lexi Summerfield," the blond told him, her voice lowered so as not to mess up Lexi's video. "We thought we recognized her voice from the videos she makes. We watch all of them. We're just dying to meet her. Can we? We buy all her products."

"Wait until after she's finished making her video, and I'll ask her." Ryder felt like he'd joined Lexi's staff for good, and he actually liked the notion.

"Oh, thank you, thank you," the other woman said, her hands clutched together hopefully.

Both of the women were smiling and watching Lexi, and he hoped it would be all right with her to meet her fan club. He couldn't very well shoo them away when they weren't taking photos of her or causing any disruption of her work.

"I can't believe she's here making the video," the first

woman said as if Lexi were a famous movie star or singer. "It's like having front-row seats."

Ryder was used to seeing fan interest in Rafe, because he was much more of a public figure as a real estate mogul and hosted a lot of charity functions; not so much with Aidan because he isolated himself to continue his medical research.

For now, Ryder felt swept up in the enthusiasm for what Lexi represented, and he was proud of her.

When Lexi finished making her video, Ryder joined her. "You have a couple of customers from your fan club over there who want to meet you."

Lexi smiled at Ryder, then at the ladies. "Thanks, Ryder." She waved the women over. "Hi, I'm Lexi Summerfield."

The women hurried to meet with her, their boyfriends hanging back while Ryder went over to speak with them.

"When they heard Lexi speaking and then saw she was doing a video, that's all our girlfriends could talk about," the one guy said, smiling, his arms folded across his chest. "I didn't know she was a celebrity."

"Yeah, we were going on a hike. We didn't expect this," the other guy said.

"She's just up here on vacation like you appear to be."

"For a couple more days. This will be the highlight of the trip for our girlfriends," the first man said.

Kate carried the camera and tripod into the cabin, then returned with a couple of bags with Lexi's company's logo on them: a woman and a wolf, and a bright full moon.

Ryder smiled. Lexi had perfected her marketing down to a T.

The women each gave her hugs, taking pictures with their cell phones to commemorate the event, then gave Lexi another hug and thanked her. With their little complimentary gift bags in hand, they hurried to join their boyfriends.

Lexi had made their day.

Once the hikers were gone, Ryder asked Lexi, "Are you ready for lunch? I'll run over there and begin setting everything up."

"Yeah, that would be great," Lexi said. "Thanks for being our guard."

"No problem. No one other than the vacationers were here to check things out, and they were well behaved."

She laughed. "They're not always. Maybe having you here helped. So what are you fixing us for lunch?"

"Flour tortilla wraps—your choice of meat: ham, turkey, beef, or chicken, and toppings. I'll get it all ready, and everyone can make theirs the way they like it. Sorry it's not more gourmet."

"Oh, that sounds good. I'll have to try that sometime when I'm having a party."

"Yeah, it's great for parties." Ryder waited until Lexi was safely inside her cabin, and then he headed over to his place.

As soon as he began setting out the food, he got a call from Mike.

"Did you learn what was going on?"

"The women are Lexi Summerfield and her personal assistant, Kate."

"Lexi, the billionaire she-wolf? Hot damn! So I take it she's had problems with Don Morgan."

"Correct." Because Lexi had taken Ryder into her confidence, he didn't want to share with Mike that they were hunting for a buried message, unless she said it was okay.

"Okay, well, I'll be there tomorrow afternoon, just in case you need some extra help."

Ryder put the call on speakerphone and continued to set out the meat and toppings. "Good, you can help make the gourmet meals."

Mike laughed. "I knew you'd try to win them over with your cooking."

"You would, too, if you were here."

Mike paused. "Is there anything you want to tell me? Is there anything serious between you and one of the ladies?"

"Nah. Just being a good Boy Scout."

Mike laughed at that.

Ryder smiled. "Well, Lexi did say I was dating her, but I'm afraid this is our last date."

"Oh?"

"Yeah, she only dates a wolf three times and then he's outta her life."

"Then I'm coming at the right time."

Ryder laughed, but he hoped Mike wasn't serious. Ryder wasn't giving up this early in the game.

"How does dinner with Ryder sound to you?" Lexi asked Kate after they cleaned up and got ready to go over to Ryder's cabin for lunch.

Kate smiled. "Nothing's going on between the two of you, right?"

"He's assisting us in looking for the message and helping keep Don and others like him away. So no, there's nothing going on between the two of us. You would know. You're always with us."

"Easily remedied."

"No way. I'm not dating him."

Kate laughed. "You already told him he's used up two of

his dates. You know, there's that billionaire friend of Rafe and Aidan who is always trying to meet up with you at one of their shindigs. Derek Spencer. Only you're not there when he is, and he's not there when you are, except that one time. He's sexy and wolfish."

"I'm not interested."

"Just think, if the two of you got together, you'd double your billionaire status. He wouldn't be after you just for your money, like the other wolves at your door."

"There's more to a courtship between wolves than just money."

"Exactly. And you've only met him the one time. He has a hot body, keeps in shape, and you know you have to think of how that would affect your offspring. He's intelligent, kind, protective, and he's not the kind of guy who's just territorial."

"How do you know so much about him?" Lexi asked, surprised to hear Kate knew him. She hadn't been with Lexi at the time she'd met Derek.

"I interviewed for a position as his personal assistant before you were hiring. He preferred having a male personal assistant, afraid of what you were afraid of, only reversed. He was worried I'd be worming my way into his life and looking to get his money. He was really upfront with me about it." Kate shrugged. "Then I had the opportunity to interview for the job with you, and that was it. Perfect for both of us."

"I so agree. Come on. Our chef awaits." Lexi and Kate headed over to Ryder's cabin.

"Hey," Ryder said in greeting when he opened the door. "Mike's going to be here tomorrow, helping us."

"You didn't tell him about the message I'm looking for, did you?" Lexi asked.

"No, but he'll help us watch out for Don or anyone else who might show up here trying to do a news story on you."

Lexi let her breath out. "No one else was supposed to know about the message."

"*I* don't even know about it," Ryder said. "Mike is a good guy. He doesn't need to know anything about it, just that he's helping guard against trouble. I mentioned to Mike that Don was taking pictures of us, giving you grief."

"This other situation is really dangerous."

Ryder frowned at her. "Which makes me believe we should get Rafe involved."

"No, no one else, Ryder. No one. *You* shouldn't even know about it," Lexi repeated.

"Okay, Mike can stay here while we search for the message."

Lexi was ready to cancel lunch, but she knew Ryder thought he was being helpful in offering another body to assist them with guard duty. Instead, she switched topics. "Do you have any siblings?"

"Me?" Ryder seemed so surprised she'd change the subject. He finally finished making his turkey wrap and sat down with them to eat. "No. Not me. What about you and Kate?"

"Not me either." Lexi took a bit of her chicken wrap.

Kate didn't have any siblings either.

"What do you like to do when you're not working or searching for messages?" Ryder asked.

"I love to swim," Lexi said. "And boat and water-ski."

"Me too," Kate said. "I love to sail."

"Sailing, paddling, water-skiing. I love to do that too," Ryder said. "By the way, this doesn't really count as my third date, does it?"

Lexi and Kate laughed. If she'd really been counting their get-togethers, he'd already have surpassed the other guys in dates. It was time to concentrate on why they were here, and she was afraid Ryder would feel compelled to tell his friend what they were doing so he could help out. She didn't want to put anybody's life in jeopardy. It was bad enough Kate wouldn't let her do this on her own.

They talked about vacationing at other spots, and Ryder mentioned the trouble Aidan had had when he was looking for the cure for the wolves' longevity issues.

"I'm so glad he and Holly found each other and resolved the situation with her pack," Lexi said, finishing her sandwich. "I know a lot of wolves were afraid that our extended lives might be cut down to less than a human's lifetime, so it was good that they found a cure."

"I agree. It was great being there with them when it happened," Ryder said.

When they were done eating, they thanked Ryder for a nice lunch, but then made their excuses. "Kate and I are going to work on some more promo ideas."

"Good luck with that," Ryder said.

"Thanks." It looked like it was killing Ryder to not be able to spend more time with them, but as far as Lexi was concerned, she and Kate were looking for the message and watching out for trouble on their own.

"See you later," Lexi said, but she didn't really mean it.

"Great meal." Kate sounded a little guilty for eating and running. Kate would know Lexi was upset about Ryder telling Mike about anything. She followed her out the door. When they were drawing near Lexi's cabin, Kate said, "He only meant well."

"I meant what I said. No one else can become involved.

I understand where he's coming from though. It's the only reason I stayed for lunch."

"I understand. No dinner with him tonight then? You're just cutting him off like that?" Kate snapped her fingers to emphasize her point.

"Yeah, just like that. This is serious business. But don't let me ruin your plans. You can have dinner with him, Kate," Lexi said, meaning it. She would really like it if Kate enjoyed some male companionship. She didn't have to watch Lexi every minute of every day.

"No, I don't want to have dinner with him alone. I mean, I would, but he's not interested in me."

Lexi gave Kate a sideways glance as she opened the cabin door.

"Just don't tell me you don't want *me* to help you," Kate said as they entered the cabin and locked the door.

"I need you."

"Remember, he's the one who helped us with the map. We would have looked forever and never found it."

"We might still not find it there. He could be wrong," Lexi warned her.

"True. Are you sure you don't want to invite him over for dinner after he made us both lunch and breakfast today?" Kate asked.

Lexi gave her a look that said she wasn't changing her mind.

Kate shrugged. "Oh, all right. He's fun company, though, and until his friend arrives, he's all alone."

"Quit trying to convince me to change my mind. I'm not going to."

Kate shook her head. "I still think he'd be a big help tomorrow, even if we don't have a meal with him tonight."

"Let's go over some more promotional ideas you had for the summer collection." Lexi had to get Kate off the topic of Ryder before she agreed to anything more to do with him that she was sure to regret.

CHAPTER 8

RYDER WAS PLAYING A VIDEO GAME ON HIS LAPTOP, trying to keep his mind off Lexi, knowing she was pissed off that he'd mentioned anything to Mike about her trouble with Don Morgan, when someone knocked at the door, startling him. He was hopeful that Lexi, or maybe Kate, had returned to say everything was okay between them. When he peeked through the peephole, instead of seeing the women, he saw two men in dark-gray business suits standing in front of the door. One of the men had a crooked, bulbous nose that appeared to have been broken. The other guy had beady, blue eyes, a couple of nicks on his face where he'd recently shaved, and a scar that looked like someone had sliced his ruddy cheek with a knife.

Ryder opened the door. "Can I help you?"

"You can help Lexi Summerfield." The man was clean-cut, reminding Ryder of the FBI or CIA. He didn't like the implications of that already.

"Oh?" Ryder wondered what the hell was going on with Lexi, and his first thought was about the message she was trying to locate.

"When our dad died in a car crash, she had a mental breakdown. Tragic accident. She might not have told you, but she believes he's trying to get in contact with her. We don't want to have to recommit her, if it's not necessary, but we don't want you or anyone else feeding into her delusions."

"Who are you people?"

"Clifford and Joe Summerfield, her half brothers. Naturally, we were broken up about our dad's death too, but we have to move on. Lexi just hasn't been able to."

"Really. How do you know I've been visiting with her?"

"We saw her and her personal assistant just leave your cabin."

So they only knew of the one time they'd been together? At least Ryder hoped that was the case.

"Do you have some ID?"

"Just heed my words, Mr. Gallagher. You don't want to risk your career or anything else, should you pursue this." The guy shook his head. "Just letting you know."

Hell, he knew Ryder's name already? What else did he know about him? "Thank you. I'll take your words under consideration." Hell, the guys weren't wolves, so they'd lied about being her family. And she said she didn't have any siblings.

"See that you do."

Ryder shut the door in their faces, ran his hand through his hair, and pulled out his phone. He called Lexi, hoping these guys weren't monitoring their call, but he suspected they might have the technology to do so. "Lexi?"

"We're busy working on some promo," Lexi said.

"I just had a couple of visitors. Dark-gray suits. Scowly faces. They claimed they are your half brothers, looked like they were with the government—FBI or CIA—but I couldn't be sure of it and they wouldn't produce any ID. They said you had a mental breakdown when your dad died in the car crash."

"They were just at your cabin?" Lexi asked, sounding panicked.

"Yeah, they just left."

"Okay, thanks." She hung up on him.

"Wait!" *Hell.*

For a minute, Ryder wasn't sure what to do. Then he wondered if Lexi assumed the men were listening in on their conversation. What was she mixed up in?

He suspected she was looking for a message from her father. That he wasn't dead. Ryder knew she wasn't crazy. He wanted to call her back, but he suspected she wouldn't answer the phone a second time. He wanted to go over to her place, but he was afraid these men were monitoring both their cabins now.

Because of the work he did for Aidan and Holly, he always had monitoring devices packed in his bag in case anyone tried to learn anything about the research his bosses were doing. He pulled out his detector but didn't find any listening bugs anywhere inside his cabin. That was good, but he would have to check for listening devices anytime he returned to the cabin now.

He hadn't smelled their scents in the cabin before, either, though there were other scents in the cabin—human scents. But nothing new since he'd been here. They must have just arrived and seen the women leaving his place.

He left the cabin and started to circle around his place, looking for any indication the men were in the area. It didn't take him long to find that they had rented a cabin nearby.

He searched the area around Lexi's cabin and found a camera in a tree recording the activity at her place. They must have just set it up, or they would have seen them as wolves earlier.

He went around the back way to the cabin but didn't find any cameras in that direction. He knocked on the back door.

Kate answered the door and frowned at him. "What are you doing here?"

He entered the cabin and shut the door. Lexi frowned at him and folded her arms.

"Lexi, the man warned me not to have anything more to do with you. He said my career could suffer."

"He could be right."

"Well, the two of them are staying at a cabin near me. And they've got video security out front, watching your place. They'll know I'm here. They knew we were together for lunch, but I think they just found you. What the hell is this all about?" Ryder was ready to call in reinforcements, but he wanted to know what Lexi had to say about all this first. They couldn't take on the whole government, if that was who was after her.

"My father is in the Witness Protection Program. The men you saw may not be with the government. Even you said they didn't show you their ID." Lexi fixed them glasses of water.

"No, they didn't."

Kate's jaw dropped. "Ohmigod, Lexi, you should have told me. I wouldn't have said a word about it to anyone."

"Most likely, they are some of the guys who work for the man my dad testified against."

Which made Ryder want to take care of them personally. "What do we do about the message?"

"We leave it alone for now. If they get ahold of it and figure out where my father is, he's a dead man. Once you called, I burned the map. Dad and I will have to try again later. He's sure to know if I don't see him when I'm supposed to that the situation isn't safe."

"What do you intend to do? Go home?" Ryder hated that

they'd come here on a vacation, then this happened. Then again, maybe this was the real reason they came here, not for a vacation at all.

"No. I'm on vacation. We'll do some promo while we're here. We hadn't planned to, but we have more fun when we're working on something. And you can be our model for our men's skin-care products line," Lexi said.

Ryder's jaw dropped.

The women both smiled.

"No more digging in the dirt for a message that no longer matters. We have to do *something* with you," Lexi said.

Ryder smiled. "That's not exactly what I had in mind. Taking these guys down, finding your message, but modeling skin-care products?"

"Very natural. Not much of anything to it at all. We'll do a video."

"Don't tell me you have the products with you."

"We do. It must have been providence that you came here to help us."

Hell, he couldn't believe he'd gotten himself into modeling facial creams or whatever it was they had in store for him. He'd thought it would just be fun to be with two wolf ladies while he was on his own.

"If they want a show, we can put one on for them," Lexi said.

"Oh, great," he said.

"It's a great cover story. You're our part-time model. And we'll fix dinner," Lexi said.

"You've got a deal." Not that he wanted to be on a video that could be seen around the world—he could just imagine what Mike would say if he ever learned of it—but he was all for having dinner with the women. He suspected he was again in Lexi's good graces. "You sure you don't want me to get some muscle to take care of these guys?"

"No. It's too dangerous."

"All right."

Kate peered out the window. "Oh, no, Don's here, wearing a couple of cameras and heading for our cabin."

"Good," Lexi said, joining her at the window. "Now that these other men are here, we can use him."

"Oh?" Kate asked.

"I'm going to make him a proposition he won't be able to refuse." Lexi headed for the door.

"What's that?" Ryder hoped she knew what she was doing.

"An exclusive interview, if he'll harass the men in the other cabin."

"Couldn't that be risky for him, considering the other guys aren't the good guys? Assuming they aren't?" Ryder asked.

"We'll be there to watch his back. I'm sure these guys wouldn't want to get rid of all of us at once, not when they're more interested in me telling them where my father is."

"What about telling Mike what's going on when he gets here? He needs to know about it," Ryder said.

"If these guys take off, that might be the end of it for now. It's really best if we don't tell anyone else about it."

"He wouldn't mention it to anyone else, and the only reason to bring it up with him is that he's going to be here."

Lexi let out her breath. "Oh, all right, but I'm not usually this much of a pushover."

Ryder smiled. "I didn't think you were."

—⁓—

"Okay, wish me luck." Lexi opened the door to the cabin as she got ready to ask Don if he'd refocus his attention on Tremaine's men.

"Ask him to be a male model," Ryder said. "He might love it."

"That's an excellent idea, but it's not getting you off the hook." Lexi smiled at Ryder, then walked outside to join Don, who was setting up a camera on a tripod to take a picture of her cabin.

Don began snapping shots of her, as if he feared she'd duck back inside the cabin and he'd better make this worthwhile.

Her entourage of bodyguards came with her, and he glanced at each of them. "A couple of women uploaded some pictures that showed them meeting with you here while you were doing a promotional video. I figured you wouldn't mind me doing a little write-up then."

"It depends entirely on what you write about me. But I do have a proposition for you," Lexi said, smiling.

"Really?" Don's dark-brown eyes widened with speculation.

"Yeah. Two things. We're doing a promo video on male skincare products, and I don't want you filming or taking pictures while we're doing it," Lexi told Don. "But, if you'd like, you can be my other male model."

"Other male model?" Don glanced at Ryder again. "I thought for sure he was a bodyguard."

"He is. *And* he's my male model. Now, after we do the video shoot, I want you to harass, I mean, do a piece on the men in cabin—" Lexi glanced at Ryder.

"Cabin 5," he said.

"The two men staying there were harassing me, and they threatened Ryder."

Don looked in the direction of the other cabin that they couldn't see for the woods. "Has this anything to do with your dad's death?"

Even though Don made his money off celebrities, he was a good investigative reporter, when he wasn't taking photos of celebs.

"Maybe. They wouldn't identify themselves," Lexi said.

Glancing at Ryder again, Don looked like he was also dying to get a story on him, the male model.

"We'll include you in the video, free skin-care demonstration," she said.

"How much does it pay?" Don asked, sounding surprised.

"I'm just doing this for my modeling portfolio." Ryder folded his arms, looking growly, more like a bodyguard.

"Hell, you're being taken for a ride, pal. Do you know how much Lexi Summerfield's worth?" Don asked. "Plenty."

"Don, you don't have to be in the video, but you do have the outdoor, rugged look that would work for the line." Lexi was surprised Don hadn't laughed at the suggestion. "After doing the video, if you want, and the piece on the guys in Cabin 5, we can do an interview. No questions about my father though."

"All right. It's a deal. Except I'm not working as your male model for nothing. I don't have a model portfolio I need to set up."

"You never know when you might find a whole new role in life. Hollywood might even be calling."

Don laughed. "Right. Okay, let's do this."

This would be even more fun than the video Lexi did earlier for the women-in-the-woods cosmetics line. Who would have thought Lexi could have a couple of ruggedly handsome male models just show up for the video in the redwoods?

But she did worry about the men posing as her relations, and she hoped it didn't come down to having to kill them. Though to keep her father safe, she would do anything.

CHAPTER 9

TRYING NOT TO FEEL SELF-CONSCIOUS ABOUT BEING IN a skin-care product video, Ryder said to Don, "Why don't you go first."

"Nah. I want to see how a professional model does it before I have my turn."

Ryder sat down on one of the benches around the campfire, trying to keep a straight face. Of course he didn't have a clue how to act, and this was just too funny. Lexi was applying a facial cleanser and smiling and laughing while Kate was shooting the video. Even Don was grinning, and Kate was getting a big kick out of it.

Ryder couldn't believe how sexy Lexi's touch felt while she caressed his skin with a gentle stroke, brushing exfoliating lotion onto his skin with featherlight contact. It was about as intimate as could be. And he wanted to give her a kiss. Not to mention she was arousing him in ways he was trying to hide, hoping the camera was only focused on his face and not a lower part of his anatomy.

"That's how you would use the cleanser," Lexi said to the camera. "Once a week, use the exfoliator to refresh the skin. Doesn't he look great?" Then she used a toner, serum, and moisturizer.

Ryder sure hoped no one in his circles saw the video. But he did get a kick out of this.

Then it was Don's turn. Ryder was glad Don was on the hot seat, so to speak, for the rest of the video. He could just imagine what the bad guys in the suits were saying as they viewed the security video, observing Lexi using skincare products on two male "models."

Don looked relaxed when Lexi was applying moisturizer to his face, yet he appeared much more serious than Ryder had been while she was working on him.

When she finally ended the video, she said, "That was great. You did a super job, both of you. Kate will pay you, Don."

"Do I get a free supply of the skin-care products?" Don asked.

Lexi laughed. "Yes, I have free samples, if you'd like to have some."

"I'll get them." Kate went inside the cabin and returned with a gift bag, except instead of it being gold, it was silver— for the guys, Ryder figured.

Don was delighted, which surprised Ryder. He thought Don was kidding.

"Should we make plans about how to deal with the other guys?" Ryder said quietly to Lexi and Don while Kate carried the camera equipment into the cabin.

"Let's go to the back deck, since you said they don't have a security device monitoring us in that direction," Lexi said.

When they moved back there, Kate served them water and tea.

"All right, so how do you want to go about this?" Lexi asked. "You're the expert."

"Thanks." Don seemed to be pleased she would think so and not see him as trouble now. "I'm always after a story, you know. I wouldn't mind getting Ryder's too. I'm sure I could do an interesting angle on him being a male model."

Lexi smiled at Ryder.

Ryder wanted to laugh, but he kept the secret. Ryder wondered how Don was going to take care of the bad guys.

"I'll go to their door and ask about doing a story on them. Hopefully, they won't shoot me," Don said. "Then again, danger is my middle name."

They all laughed.

"I'll go with you," Ryder said.

"Two male models doing a story," Don said, chuckling.

"I'm a bodyguard. I just do this as a side hobby," Ryder said.

"Hell, all right."

"We'll go with you too," Lexi said.

"No. You stay with Kate at the cabin. You don't need to deal with these men." Ryder hadn't meant to sound so in charge, but he didn't want Lexi to have to come face-to-face with them.

"Okay, go take care of them then," Lexi said.

Ryder was expecting her to disagree with him. He was glad when she didn't.

"Come on, let's do this." Ryder suspected the photojournalist would be up for this. Don lived for the thrill of adventure and danger.

"Are you armed?" Lexi asked.

"Yeah. I'm a bodyguard."

His eyes widening, Don looked over at Ryder. "Hell, that's a good thing. Okay, let's go."

Ryder and Don walked toward the men's cabin, and when they reached it, Don knocked on the door. No one answered it right away. Then the man who had spoken to Ryder before opened the door with a jerk. "What do you want?"

"I'm Don Morgan, a photojournalist for the *Washington Post*, here to do a feature on you."

The guy gave him a really dark smile and glanced at Ryder. "And him?"

"My bodyguard. It's amazing how dangerous this work can be."

"A male model posing as a bodyguard or the other way around? I'm not sure how tough you can be, from what I saw of the two of you getting made up so nice and pretty."

"Looks can be deceiving," Ryder said, his voice dark with threat. He wasn't about to pretend he was Mr. Nice Guy.

The man shrugged. "I'm not sure why you would want to interview us. There's no story here."

"Sure there is," Don said. "You've been harassing Lexi Summerfield, and I'm the only one who's allowed to do that."

"Is that so?" The man turned his attention to Ryder. "Was Lexi surprised to hear from us?"

"Not at all. She wondered what had taken you so long," Ryder said.

The man snorted, then turned on Don. "Get that damned camera out of my face. We're not doing any damned interview. Get out of here. And, you, I told you that you should listen to me when I said not to get involved in this."

"I'm involved. I'm her bodyguard and model."

"That could be real inconvenient...for *you*."

"We're just on vacation here, so why don't you pack up your security videos and head on out of here," Ryder said.

The man gave him a dark smile. "We're just on vacation here too."

"Is that right? Then you won't mind if I remove the security camera you have doing surveillance on Lexi's cabin."

"Touch it and—" the other man said from inside the cabin, but the one they were talking to motioned for the other man to stop speaking.

"You're right. We're only worried about Lexi getting herself into trouble. Looks like with all her little helpers, she'll be just fine." He motioned to the other man. "Go ahead and get it."

The other man left the cabin and walked in the direction of Lexi's cabin. Ryder didn't believe for a moment they would leave well enough alone. And he suspected they'd set up the camera in another location.

"Now get that damned camera out of my face and get the hell out of here." The guy shut the door in their faces.

"Did you get anything for a story?" Ryder asked as they headed back to Lexi's cabin.

"Yeah, man. I provide the pictures, tell them the background, and they write up the story. This time, it's my story to tell," Don said.

"As long as it doesn't hurt Lexi."

Don smiled at him. "You've got a thing for her, don't you?"

"Don't you dare print that." Ryder could just imagine how irate Lexi would be over it.

"Yeah, see? I have a nose for news. When I do the interview, I promise it will only be to help her business."

"Unlike last time?" Ryder had no idea what Don had written up before concerning her, but he knew Don was into sensationalistic crap, so it wouldn't have been something that aided her business. Ryder didn't trust Don would do right by her this time either.

"Hell, I didn't know she was so accessible."

"Meaning?"

"I could have just asked her if she was getting serious about the other guys she was seeing."

"Well, she's *not* that accessible. You just got lucky this

time since you needed each other. Let her live her life in private. I'm sure you have plenty of other celebs you can hound concerning their love lives."

"What about you?"

"What do you mean, what about me?"

"You and Lexi."

Ryder just shook his head. "You don't want to go there."

"But you'll make sure I have a wedding invitation, right?"

"You don't ever let go when you've got a story you want to pursue, do you?"

"Nah, it's part of the territory. But I'd love to do a story on you."

"What? As a bodyguard?"

"No. A male model. Hell, I might be in on the ground floor of discovering a real sensation."

Ryder laughed. "Be serious."

"I am. Hell, I might be the one to make you famous."

"In a tabloid?"

"You never know."

When they reached Lexi's cabin, she opened the door. "We saw the guy removing the camera. Good job."

"But they're not leaving, I'm afraid," Ryder said.

"I'll keep an eye on them," Don said.

"So you're not leaving either?" Lexi asked. "You have your skin-care samples and I'll do the interview, so you have no reason to stay."

Don smiled at her. "I have to keep after these guys until you leave. You know I never listen when someone tells me they don't want to talk to me. Look at you. You're finally granting me my first interview."

"Okay, I'm ready." Lexi moved onto the back deck.

Ryder suspected she didn't want Don to take pictures

of the inside of their cabin. Ryder didn't blame her. She needed to keep her privacy as much as she could.

He and Kate moved to the deck with her and waited while they talked.

"What's your real relationship with Ryder?" Don asked her.

Lexi's lips parted, and she appeared to be taken aback by the question.

Don chuckled. "I don't have to make up anything about it."

"Nothing is going on between us," Lexi said. "And don't you *dare* publish anything that says there is." She gave Ryder a harsh look that told him he'd better not be feeding into Don's fantasy.

Ryder smiled. Don did, too, and Ryder figured that's just what he planned to do. There was no making concessions with someone like that.

When Don finished the interview, Ryder halfway expected Lexi to invite him for dinner, too, but she didn't. He could understand her reluctance to get too friendly with Don. Who knew what he would actually say to the magazine he was going to sell the story to. They wouldn't want to have to guard what they said over dinner. Ryder was relieved Don was leaving.

But he had to talk to Don about a mission he needed to go on tonight. He didn't want Lexi or Kate to know about it though. Ryder was certain the thugs in suits would be watching her place. They might even set up a security camera behind Lexi's cabin. In a way, Ryder wished the ladies would leave. On the other hand, for selfish reasons, he didn't want Lexi to go. Not that he had any chance with her, but he enjoyed her company. Plus, by his count, he was up to at least four dates with her. Wasn't that a good sign? He'd passed the three-dates-and-you're-out limit?

"Are you staying at the cabins or somewhere else?" Ryder asked Don, wanting to know how close by he was staying.

"In town at a hotel. All of the cabins were already booked."

Good. "But you're parked here somewhere, right?"

"Uh. Yeah. It's too far to walk."

"I'll walk you to your car."

Lexi smiled, looking appreciative that Ryder would make sure Don left the resort. Not that the guy would stay away permanently. Don could come back later.

"Sure. That way I don't get lost." Dan sounded facetious.

"See you in a few," Ryder told Lexi.

"All right."

Ryder walked outside with Don and said, "You must have a night-vision lens to be able to shoot pictures at night."

"I do. The damnedest thing happened to me last night. I was just playing around with my new lens to see how well it did when I saw four wolves. I began shooting them, thinking it had to be a rarity and it would make for a good story. I've never heard of them being in the park before."

"Oh?" Ryder was amused the number of wolves Don had seen had gone from three to four.

"Yeah, hell, the four wolves attacked me. Maybe five. I was in a panic to get away, believe you me."

Ryder made a point to look Don's arms and legs over. "They bit you?"

"Well, no. I told you it was bizarre. They stole my camera and equipment. They tore the camera right out of my hands."

"You don't say." Ryder smiled at him as if to say it sounded like a tall tale to him.

"Hey, I'm not making this stuff up. I told the park rangers, but they said they haven't had any sightings of wolves in the park. And they said if there were that many wolves, someone else would have reported seeing them. I told them they have that many now. Then they learned who I was, and my credibility was shot to hell. They figured I made it up to sell the story to a magazine. They assumed everything I said was just a hoax."

"It wasn't?"

"No! I had pictures of them even. The wolves took off with my camera and equipment!"

Ryder shoved his hands in his pockets. "Wolves don't attack people, and they don't steal stuff like that. Food maybe, if you had any on you. If they're starving. They would avoid people. But stealing cameras and camera equipment? No."

"These wolves looked like they were getting plenty of meals. They were well fed. I had to drive miles to reach a reputable camera shop to replace my camera equipment. I swear it's all true." Don glanced at Ryder. "So why are you walking me out to my car? Are you afraid I won't really leave?"

"I need you to make sure those guys don't leave their cabin tonight," Ryder said, not answering Don's question.

"What are you planning to do?"

"Something for Lexi. I'm sure, after those men removed the video camera that was set up to watch Lexi's cabin, they moved it to a new location and they're still observing her place."

"What's in it for me?"

Ryder shook his head. "Don't you ever do anything nice for anyone just on principle?"

"You get all the glory, and I get all the grief. You're the trained bodyguard. Why don't *you* keep those guys at the cabin, and I'll do whatever it was you were going to do."

"It won't work, and I can't say why."

"You know how intriguing that is to a guy like me who loves to write stories about mysteries?"

"Well, don't be tempted to do anything about that. I just need you to watch them."

"Why doesn't Kate do it?" Don sounded like he was suspicious of what was going on.

"She needs to protect Lexi. And I don't want either of them to know what I'm doing."

"Now *that's* even more intriguing." They reached Don's yellow VW Bug, and he unlocked the car door.

Ryder folded his arms. "By the way, I believe you about the wolves."

Don shook his head. "You don't believe me one bit. What time is showtime?"

"Two in the morning. Can you handle it?"

"How much are you going to pay me?"

"Two-fifty."

Don smiled. "You got a deal."

If Don kept his word and made sure the rotten thugs didn't leave the cabin, and no one followed Ryder, he might just have a chance to find the message for Lexi. More than anything in the world, he wanted to do that for her. He realized it could be dangerous for her and her father, but he couldn't imagine being separated from a family member she loved, when they were wolves which were usually cohesive as a family.

Ryder watched Don drive off, then walked back through the woods to Lexi's cabin to have dinner with the she-wolves.

Kate let him into the cabin through the front door. "They

put up two cameras. We watched them. One is around back and one out front."

"Okay, good to know. I'll have to check around my place too."

Lexi and Kate had made spareribs. "This looks and smells great," he said. "I guess we won't run as wolves after it gets dark."

"Sure we can. We'll have to take a hike in a direction away from where the message may be and remove our clothes and shift before we go for a run, but I'm not going to stop doing what I love to do when I come to the park," Lexi said.

They all sat down to eat the spareribs, corn on the cob, and a spinach and tomato salad. Ryder was glad he was able to spend more time with the ladies. He'd really thought he was on the outs with them before the thugs had come to his cabin, threatening him concerning Lexi.

"Thanks for making sure Don left our area." Lexi licked the rib spices off her fingers.

He could just imagine tangling his tongue with hers, pressing his body against hers, getting aroused all over again. Even thinking of it was making him hard. It was good the tabletop wasn't glass.

"You're welcome. He told me about the wolves stealing his camera and equipment," Ryder said, trying to get his mind back on having a normal conversation.

Lexi and Kate laughed.

Ryder started working on another rib, loving the spices the ladies used. "I'll have to get your recipe for this."

"I'll send it to you," Lexi said.

"Sounds good. So Don thought there might have been four or five of us wolves."

"He's a storyteller." Lexi buttered her corn. "I'm surprised he didn't say there were even more of us than that."

"What did you say to that?" Kate added blue cheese dressing to her salad.

"That I believed him. He told the park rangers, but they didn't believe him once they learned who he was." Ryder started to work on his corn.

The ladies laughed again.

"Serves him right for fabricating so many stories," Lexi said. "Just like the little boy who cried wolf."

Ryder still wouldn't put it past Don to continue to make up stories about Lexi's love life, and he suspected he was going to be featured as her next made-up lover. Not that he minded, since he wasn't currently seeing anyone. He just didn't think that would go over big with Lexi. "The food's great."

"Thanks. It's hard coming up with something now, knowing we have a gourmet cook in our midst," Lexi said.

He chuckled. "This is as good as I could come up with. After dinner, I'll return to my cabin, but I'm going to look for any security cameras they might have put up to observe my place. At least if they try to enter our cabins and leave bugs, we'll know it, now that we have their scents. And I have equipment that will detect them too."

"Thanks, I do too," Kate said.

"Uh, okay, good." Ryder should have known she would since she was in the same business of helping to protect Lexi's secrets.

Of course none of that would really stop them if the men decided to hurt Lexi and Kate. And that was where Ryder came into the picture—protection all the way.

CHAPTER 10

HAVING EVERY INTENTION OF LOOKING FOR HER father's message tonight, Lexi wished she could make Tremaine's thugs disappear—permanently. The sky was filling with clouds late that night, and the air smelled like rain. Lexi was glad they were going to run as wolves, despite the suited men staying at one of the cabins. She just hoped Don didn't return to find her and her companions running as wolves, but if he did, and he was taking pictures of them, she was grabbing his camera away from him again.

"I destroyed their spy cameras," Ryder said to them as he returned from his place and entered Lexi's cabin. "I brought a camouflaged field pack we can use for our clothes."

"Good on both counts, unless they retaliate," Lexi said.

"I'm sure they expected it and probably wondered why I hadn't gotten rid of them already."

"Okay, hopefully you're right. Let's go." Lexi went out the back way and in a different direction than they'd gone before.

When they thought they were far enough away from any threat, they stopped in the woods and removed their clothes, then Lexi and Kate shifted. Ryder packed their clothes in the field pack, then hid it in the ferns. He shifted, and the three of them ran off through the woods, enjoying the cool breeze ruffling their fur.

And then it started raining again. Lexi growled a little. She wasn't sure if they could find the message as wolves if it was buried under water.

Feeling no one could be monitoring their moves this far out, she suddenly stopped, and Ryder collided with her. She nipped at him in amusement, and he lightly woofed at her. She shifted, glad the rain wasn't coming down hard. "I want to look for the message. Now."

Ryder shifted. "All right. We might not be able to find it yet if the water's too deep, but I'm all for it. Did you really destroy the map?"

"I did. I didn't want them getting ahold of it. I have it memorized," Lexi said.

"I do too. I was also concerned about them seeing it."

"Okay, I'll lead the way." Lexi shifted and so did Ryder. She headed back toward the footbridge that would take them to the area near the bears' den. They ran through the rain, and she had the feeling she needed to get there before the water rose again.

When they finally reached the area near the waterfall where Ryder thought the note could be, they discovered the tangled roots of the tree that surrounded the bears' den. They waded a little beyond that, and then she began digging with her paws in the water. Ryder shifted and began digging with his hands.

She paused to watch him work. He was seriously buff. A total wolf hunk, dripping wet, which made her envision him climbing out of her swimming pool, his skin glistening with water droplets. She had a pool service that came out and cleaned her swimming pool, but Ryder would make one sexy pool boy, serving drinks, cleaning the pool, and applying suntan lotion to her heated skin.

Kate suddenly bumped into her, as if reminding her why she was there. Lexi wanted to growl at the interruption in her little daydream. She began digging again.

They had worked at it for about twenty minutes, moving around, searching new spots, but Ryder was concentrating in one area as if he knew that's where the message was buried. Still, she couldn't help feeling as though they were looking in the wrong place again.

Then Ryder stopped digging. "Hey, unless I just found trash, I think I've got it."

Her heartbeat quickened.

He pulled a tiny, sealed plastic bag from the water and opened it up. Inside was a note that he hovered over to keep it dry from the rain and read out loud for her and Kate to hear. "C3, dash, 2300, dash, 5, dash, 3. Is this it?"

Lexi shifted. "It is." She smelled her father's scent on the message and recognized his handwriting. "Now we have to decode it."

"Okay, good." Ryder tucked the note back into the plastic bag to keep it dry.

Overwhelmed with joy, she gave Ryder a hug and a kiss, tears running down her cheeks, mixing with the light rain sliding down her skin. She meant to give him a sweet, thank-you kiss. Nothing more. But she wanted more. The wolf had been there for her every step of the way. And everything he'd done for her meant more to her than he could ever know.

She wouldn't have deepened the kiss, though, if he hadn't been encouraging it. He wrapped his arms around her and pulled her snug against his naked, muscular body, warming her all the way to her toes.

Then, remembering Kate was undoubtedly observing them and that they needed to get back to the cabin, Lexi pulled away from him and he slipped the bag into the corner of his mouth. Which was a great idea. They shifted and all the way back to her cabin, she played the message back in her mind. Her dad had been in the military as an army doctor. Did 2300 mean eleven? Meet him at eleven at night? *Five-three. Five-three.* It was May 2. Did he mean for her to meet him on May 3? C3. Location? Maybe C3 corresponded to a location on the map of the park.

They finally reached the place where Ryder had hidden his field pack. He shifted, took the plastic baggie out of his mouth, and slipped it into a pocket of the backpack. He started to bring out their clothes. Lexi and Kate shifted and hurried to dress. But they were going to be soaking wet again by the time they reached the cabin.

As soon as they arrived at the back deck, Lexi unlocked the door. They walked inside, and Kate shut and locked the door. Lexi was glad they didn't smell any sign the men had been in the cabin.

"What do you think the message means?" Ryder asked Lexi.

"Not sure. But Dad was an army doctor early on. I was thinking the 2300 would be 2300 hours, military time. Eleven at night," Lexi said, giving him the towel he'd used before. "Be right back."

Kate headed for her bedroom, too, and they both changed into dry clothes before returning to the living room.

Ryder had removed his shirt, jeans, socks, and boots and was drying off. Kate was gawking at his beautiful chest.

Lexi broke the silence first. "Did you want some coffee or tea?"

"Coffee would be good," Ryder said. "Thanks."

"I'll get it," Kate said. "Decaf tea for you, right, Lexi?"

"Please, thanks." If Lexi had caffeine after two in the afternoon, she'd never be able to get to sleep.

"What do you think about the rest? May third? And C3 is the location?" Ryder asked, towel drying his hair.

Kate brought a tray out with a cup of coffee for Ryder, cream and sugar, and tea for her and Lexi. Then they took their seats in the living room. Ryder was still only wearing his boxer briefs. Lexi wished they had washers and dryers in the cabins. Though she didn't mind the view. *At all.*

"That's what I was thinking. Would C3 be a location on the map?" Lexi pulled out a map of the park. She looked it over. "No, it doesn't correlate with the area. No C3 here."

"Cabin? Would he be staying at Cabin 3 on the third?" Ryder asked.

"God, I hope not. I mean, I want to see him, but not if these men are still here. What if they got wind of it? But that's all we have to go on, so it must be."

"I could call Rafe, and he could discreetly take these guys to some other location so you can visit with your dad."

"But if they have to check in with their boss and suddenly they're not able to?" Lexi envisioned Tremaine sending an army of hit men to check it out. In fact, even now, she imagined he'd know Ryder and Don were giving the thugs trouble and might send more men to deal with them.

"We could do it before your father arrives, if that's what we think he's going to do. Would he stay at the cabin all day?" Ryder asked.

"Probably not. I imagine he'll arrive a few minutes beforehand and look for any indication that anyone's found him. If he doesn't see them, he'll go to the cabin. At least, that's what I assume he'll do."

"Then we move the guys out right before that. Their boss won't have time to send men to check it out. You see your father and then he leaves for wherever he's living now, safe and sound. Right?"

Lexi nodded. She felt tears prick her eyes and looked away from Ryder. She didn't like to show weakness. She always felt it could come back to bite her.

———∞———

Ryder reached out and stroked Lexi's arm in a comforting way, hoping she wouldn't be offended, but after she'd kissed him in a passionate manner, he wanted to show her he cared about her. She triggered carnal needs in him that he'd never felt for a woman before, but it wasn't all about that.

Her determination to see her dad despite the danger made Ryder all the more determined to help her achieve her goal. Family meant everything to him, and he couldn't imagine knowing his dad was alive but being unable to have any contact with him. He just hoped the thugs weren't aware of what was truly going on.

"Is that your father's scent on the message?" he asked Lexi.

"Yeah."

"Okay, good." Remembering he needed to call Don and tell him he didn't need him to watch the men in suits, he pulled his phone out of his pocket and called the photographer's number. "Hey, Don, forget about doing the surveillance on the men late tonight."

Lexi frowned at Ryder.

"Hell, no pay for the job? I was really looking forward to it," Don said.

"You can get some sleep instead. The mission's a bust."

"What happened? Did they leave?"

"No, I just don't need to do what I had planned to."

Ryder smiled at the inquisitive looks Lexi and Kate were casting him.

"All right. Well, let me know if you change your mind," Don said.

"I will. Thanks." Then Ryder ended the call.

"You had a mission you had scheduled to do in the middle of the night?" Lexi asked.

"Uh, yeah. A lady was looking for an important treasure, and I aimed to find it for her."

Lexi smiled warmly at him. "So you had planned on looking for the message with or without our help? *You* are the treasure. Thanks, Ryder, for planning on looking for it, even though you didn't let us know."

"I figured I could slip away to search for it alone without arousing the suited men's suspicions. Then I'd return to hand it over to you, hoping it was what you were looking for."

"But you were going to hire Don to keep an eye on the men? I know he wouldn't have done it from the generosity of his heart."

"You're right. I tried to get his sympathy for your cause, not telling him details, of course, but he wouldn't buy it."

"No surprise there," Lexi said.

"What do we do now?" Ryder asked.

"We have fun. Just do what we would be doing if we were here on vacation. Hiking, taking pictures, running as wolves," Lexi said. "The three of us, I mean. We could use your bodyguard skills and another pair of eyes, and there's no sense in you being by yourself until your friend shows up."

"That works for me." Ryder was grateful Lexi included him in their plans.

"I have to invite you to vacation with us," Lexi continued. "If I don't, you'll be watching our backs anyway—surreptitiously."

He smiled. She had that right.

"So this way, we won't be looking over our shoulders wondering where you are." Lexi smiled.

"We could go to the Little Italy Pizza Parlor in town for lunch tomorrow, if you'd like. I could call Mike to let him know to meet us there, if that is all right with you."

"Sure," Lexi said, her eyes lighting with interest. "It's owned by gray wolves, Antonio and Maria Lupo and their two daughters, Gabriella and Adriana. They've been friends for years. We always go there for a couple of meals. Best pizzas around."

"I agree. I've known them for years too. Mike and I always get pizzas there or takeout. What time do you want to go?"

"One. That way we can have enough time to hike."

"Okay, the two of you will be okay?" Ryder asked.

"Yeah, see you tomorrow."

—∿∿∿—

Lexi felt immense relief, between learning her father was going to be here soon and she could see him, and knowing she had extra help to keep them safe.

"I think you should hire Ryder." Kate put the coffee mugs in the dishwasher. "He could be our cabana boy."

"Pool boy," Lexi corrected her. "Cabana boy works on the beach serving patrons. Pool boy is the guy who works around a swimming pool."

"Right. And he could make meals and serve as a bodyguard."

Lexi laughed. "What if all his helpfulness is a ploy to court me? To win me over, but it all has to do with my money?"

"You don't have to court him. But after that kiss you shared with him? I have never seen you kiss the other guys you've been dating like that. Ryder didn't even know who you were when he so gallantly helped us with the bear cubs and finding our way back to our cabin. Sure, he was interested in you. As a male wolf is interested in a female wolf. You can deny it all that you want, but you're interested right back. Just think, you could have him model all your men's skin-care product lines. You could call on Don to model, too, when you have new products out."

Smiling, Lexi shook her head.

"Of course, you might have the hots for his friend Mike instead. So you should wait to offer Ryder a job until you see the other guy."

"I'm not hiring another bodyguard. What will Aidan think if I steal Ryder away from him?"

"He will be glad, knowing you are well protected."

"*You* protect me," Lexi reminded her.

"Aidan has four bodyguards, and from what he says, he doesn't need that many." Kate shrugged. "So you'd be giving one of them a good home."

Lexi laughed. "You make it sound like Aidan would be rehoming a pet."

"A wolf. A sexy, hot wolf, who would make a wondrous caba…pool boy. Okay, look, if you hired him, you'd get to see more of him and you'd know if he was right for you, or not. You could do a prenuptial agreement so that if something happened to you, he wouldn't get any of your estate. Though we mate for life, so divorcing him would be out."

"Exactly. Then what if he wasn't the one for me? I'd begin dating someone else and then what? Poor Ryder would be devastated, if he really loved me. He'd probably want to find another job, when he had a good one already and was very happy with it. Wouldn't it be better just to date him occasionally? See where things led? It feels like I'd be using him otherwise." Lexi couldn't believe she was talking to Kate about this. Not that she didn't talk to her about most everything, but hiring a male bodyguard? Just to see if he was the one for her in the mating department?

"He'd be working a job, just like he's working for Aidan now. I see the value of having a couple of bodyguards. Then I can concentrate on the promotion work, yet still be there for backup. He can't go into restrooms with you like I can. He can post himself outside, but you know."

"What if he's not interested in being my bodyguard?"

"Then he doesn't take the job. I just think it's something you should consider, if you're at all interested."

Lexi couldn't believe she was even considering such an option. She agreed with Kate about hiring another bodyguard. Hiring someone out of the blue like she'd done with Kate didn't appeal when Lexi considered taking on a male wolf.

Still, wouldn't it be better for them to date each other as equals, rather than as if she were the boss and he, the employee? She just didn't know how it would work. Sighing, she figured that was something she could think about later.

"I'm off to bed," Lexi said.

"But you'll consider it? I mean, just think, anytime you needed him to apply your sunscreen before you swim, he'd be right there."

Lexi laughed, mostly because she'd already considered such a thing. "Go to bed. I'll think about it."

"Yes!" Kate pumped her fist in the air and smiled broadly.

Lexi smiled. "You just want him to rub sunscreen on *you*."

"Hey, if he's not the one for you, there's always *me*."

CHAPTER 11

RYDER KNEW THAT ONE OF THE GOONS MIGHT TRY to eliminate him for getting rid of their cameras, so he was wary of the threat when he headed back to his cabin through the woods. Thankfully, it had stopped raining again. He was glad he was a wolf and able to smell scents, hear noises, and see movement humans couldn't detect in the dark.

Even so, they could be armed with guns and there were two of them. When he heard someone moving in his direction, he slipped behind a tree and waited. The tree trunks were big enough to hide three men at once. He heard a second person's footsteps, but as the people passed by the tree, flashlights illuminating their way, he realized they were just hikers, returning to their cabin, late from a hike.

Still tense, he waited, listening, then heard more movement—two people. *The men*, he was guessing. Sneakier. Slower steps. No flashlights guiding their way.

Then he saw them, both dressed in black from their boots, cargo pants, and hoodies to their ski masks, as if they were professional cat burglars, sneaking toward Ryder's cabin.

If they had been wolves, he would have taken them both out. But since they were human, he decided to wait and see what they were going to do first.

Then a car's headlights illuminated the parking area by his cabin, and the vehicle parked next to Ryder's SUV. Hell, it was Mike!

The two men paused, then ducked out of the headlights and into the darkness. They had to be wearing night-vision gear, and the headlights would have blinded them.

Ryder hurried to greet Mike at his car, shaking his hand and slapping his back in camaraderie. "You came early."

"Yeah, I figured you needed me here, so I left earlier than I'd planned. How is everything going? I assume the men dressed in black that my headlights showcased were the troublemakers."

Ryder helped Mike carry in his bags. "Yeah, and we need to get rid of them."

Mike swung his head around to look at him.

"Not permanently, unless they aim to kill us."

"Like they were about to do?"

"That was probably on account of me getting rid of their video surveillance." They entered the cabin, and Ryder locked the door. He motioned to Mike to be silent, then checked over the place for listening bugs and found none. Ryder called Rafe next. "Hey, Lexi Summerfield needs some help with a couple of thugs who aim to kill her dad if he shows up at the resort to meet with her."

"Her dad was supposed to be dead."

"He isn't. He's in witness protection."

"Hell, okay. Two guys?"

"Yeah. The meeting's for tomorrow night at eleven. We don't want to alert their handler if the guys go missing too early." Ryder explained what had happened to him, concerning the men planning to cause trouble for him tonight.

"We could helicopter her and her father to a safe place so they could visit without interference."

"I'll ask her."

"All right. Otherwise, I'll have the men take care of the thugs so they don't interfere."

"Thanks, Rafe. I knew I could count on you."

"Sure thing. Us wolves have to stick together."

They ended the call, and Ryder said to Mike, "Okay, so you heard what I told Rafe, and what we're dealing with."

"Hell, when someone is in that program, they are not supposed to have any contact with family or friends."

"I know. It must be something really important that he needs to see Lexi about."

Mike frowned at Ryder. "What's going on between the two of you? A mating in the works?"

"Not me. I'm just an extra volunteer bodyguard. I'm afraid I don't have what it takes to be the one for her." Not that Ryder didn't wish for more.

"You mean because you don't have her kind of wealth?"

Ryder knew when two wolves fell for each other, nothing would stand in their way. Still, he did feel money could be a drawback. "Maybe."

"That has nothing to do with two wolves falling in love with each other," Mike said.

Ryder thought the same. But would she even give a wolf a chance to prove he was falling for her, not her money? "It's probably hard for her to see it when she's being hounded by wolves who have only her wealth in mind."

"Yeah, I can imagine. The same thing happened to Rafe. There was always some woman trying to catch his attention. They just didn't know he was a wolf." Mike walked through the living room. "Which room is mine?"

"Second one down the hall."

"Okay, thanks. You're damn lucky you've been spending

all this time with her." Mike carried his bags into his room. "Of course, you're probably not exactly her type."

Ryder shook his head. "Right. You are."

Mike laughed. "Yeah. I can't believe you came out here without me to start the vacation and picked up two hot she-wolves."

Folding his arms and smiling, Ryder leaned against the doorjamb and watched his friend put his clothes away in the chest of drawers. "I'm glad you're here early."

"Are you sure that you don't want to deal with those men tonight? I'd rather eliminate them before they have a chance to do anything to any of us."

"I'm afraid their boss would send replacements anyway. At least now we can take turns sleeping and pulling guard duty in case they intend any mischief tonight."

"Sounds good. What's the schedule tomorrow?"

"Breakfast with the ladies. A hike. At eleven tomorrow night is when Lexi meets her dad. We might run as wolves before then. Also, Don Morgan is running around here taking pictures of wolves—us—and Lexi and Kate hiking as humans."

"Great."

"He knows about the thugs, so he agreed to help harass them."

Mike smiled. "Sounds like a good job for him."

"I'll just let Lexi know you arrived early."

"Okay, sounds good to me."

Ryder called Lexi next to give her the news. "Hey, Mike's here now, and the suited men were all dressed in black, headed for my cabin as if they intended some violence."

"What are we going to do?" Lexi asked.

"We'll all sit tight. They backed off when they saw I had

reinforcements. We're going to take turns guarding the place to make sure they don't make a move."

"I'm sorry we got you involved in this." Lexi seemed genuinely upset that she'd entangled him in her troubles.

But he was glad to assist. "Are you kidding? Mike and I live for danger."

Mike chuckled; Lexi didn't.

"Seriously, if these guys think they're going to get the best of us, they have another think coming. Human thugs against wolves? Not happening," Ryder said.

Lexi didn't say anything for a moment, but then he heard muffled talking in the background, and he suspected she was telling Kate what was going on. "Okay, we're joining forces," Lexi said.

He couldn't say enough how he didn't want Lexi in the middle of the danger, but when he opened his mouth to ask for clarification, she said, "Either Kate and I can join you over there, or we stay here and you come stay with us. If you're going to serve as my bodyguards, we need to be together."

Hell, yeah! But Ryder was surprised she'd even offered to join forces. "Okay. Do you have a preference?"

"Which place is more secure?"

"The cabins are about the same security-wise, and they're about the same distance from the thugs' cabin. If it works for you both, we'll move over to your place." He figured it was easier for him and Mike to move since the ladies were already settled into their own bedrooms. "We'll bring the food too."

"Okay, see you soon." Lexi sounded relieved, and he was glad for that.

Smiling, Mike started pulling his clothes back out of the chest of drawers and repacking them in his bag.

Ryder called Rafe. "Hey, the extra bodyguards can stay in our cabin. Mike and I are moving over to Lexi and Kate's place right now."

"They'll be on their way. I had already alerted them that they might be needed."

"Thanks." Ryder was glad Rafe was always on top of things. "Okay, Rafe's sending men and they can stay here," Ryder told Mike and headed to his room. He began to get his stuff together.

"You don't want to leave the food for the other guys?" Mike asked.

"I would, but we won't be here to protect it in case these men decide to poison it or something."

"Okay."

Ryder grabbed his bags and headed out the door of his cabin, watching, wary, making sure he didn't have unwelcome company as he packed his car.

Mike carried his bags out to his car and set them inside, then they both returned to the cabin and packed up the groceries. They hauled the bags of food out to Ryder's car.

"These guys will have more trouble than they bargained for if they try to come and give us any problems once the other guys get here." Ryder checked the cabin over once more to ensure they hadn't left anything behind.

Mike agreed. "They'll have enough trouble with us too."

"True. Kate's also a trained bodyguard. I'm heading over now."

"I'll follow you," Mike said.

Ryder drove over to Lexi's cabin and parked, and Mike parked behind him.

The women came out to help them move the bags into the cabin.

"I'm Mike Stallings, and I'm glad to meet you Lexi, Kate." Mike shook their hands.

"Thanks for coming to assist us," Lexi said, "even though you were supposed to be here on vacation."

"Anything to help a couple of wolves." Mike hauled in some of the groceries.

Ryder and Mike would be sleeping on the couch—well, taking turns guarding—while the ladies kept their separate bedrooms.

"Let's make up the couch, Mike. I'll take the first watch," Ryder said.

"I'll take second," Kate said.

Mike agreed. "All right, I've got third watch."

"That means I have last watch," Lexi said.

Ryder didn't plan on Lexi taking a turn on guard duty. She was the one they were supposed to be protecting. He gave Mike a look that said he would wake him instead. Mike nodded.

"Let's get some sleep then. We can have a wolf run early in the morning, if you all want, and then have breakfast," Lexi said.

"We've got reinforcements coming too. They'll be staying at our cabin and watching over your cabin and ours and of course the thugs," Ryder said.

"Okay, sounds good," Lexi said.

Then everyone but Ryder went to bed, and he went outside to do a perimeter check. Afterward, he headed over in the dark to check out the thugs' cabin. He'd rather be there watching for them to leave than observing their sneaky approach to Lexi's cabin. That's when he heard footfalls crunching on leaves and twigs, headed in the direction of his cabin. Checking it out? Seeing if they'd really vacated the premises?

He saw the two men peering into the cabin windows. If Ryder had listening bugs or video surveillance of his own, he would have set them up in the thugs' cabin. But he didn't think he'd have a mission like this on his vacation.

The men walked over to two different trees and removed the security videos they'd put up to monitor Ryder's activities. Then the men stole quietly toward Lexi's cabin, and Ryder followed to observe their actions. They began putting the videos on a couple of new trees. As soon as they headed back to their cabin, Ryder removed and destroyed them. They'd be pissed for sure, but he'd told them they weren't using them on Lexi. Now the thugs wouldn't know when the rest of Ryder's reinforcements arrived.

Ryder returned to Lexi's cabin and noted Mike was sound asleep on the sofa bed. Ryder watched out the window where he'd destroyed the cameras, waiting to see if the men would return to put up new ones, but they didn't. He could imagine how angry they'd be. He heard movement behind him and swung around, thinking it was Kate, getting ready to take over guard duty. But it was Lexi.

She joined him at the window. "See anything?"

"They moved the security cameras over here from my place. I destroyed them."

She smiled. "I'm sure they're happy about that."

"They'll be even happier when they learn more of our men are coming here." Ryder turned and took ahold of her hand. "I'm worried they might escalate things by attempting to grab you and trying to force you to tell them where your father is."

"I'm not leaving. And don't suggest someone else meet with my father."

"Okay, it was just a thought."

"Thanks for everything." She pulled him into her arms
and kissed him lightly on the mouth. "I mean it."

"I'm glad I could help." He kissed her back, not pressur-
ing her to deepen the kiss, just letting her know he welcomed
it. He smelled her she-wolf scent, lavender, her pheromones
sucking him in as he heard her heartbeat quicken. Their
pheromones couldn't play tricks on each other. It was the
genuine thing.

They heard movement, and he was sure Kate was coming
into the room. She was smiling at them as Lexi pulled away
from Ryder. At least it wasn't Don Morgan who'd caught
them in the act.

"I think it's my turn to stand guard," Kate said.

Ryder told her what was going on with the men, and then
he stripped down to his boxer briefs and joined Mike on the
sofa bed.

"Don't steal the covers," Mike grumbled.

Ryder chuckled. He *never* stole covers. Then again, what
did he know? He always slept alone, and all the covers were
his.

Smiling, Lexi said, "Night," and moved down the hall
toward the bedroom.

Man, Ryder wished Lexi was the one telling him not to
steal her covers.

Wishing she could share her bed with Ryder, which was just
plain crazy thinking, Lexi sighed. Yet it was the first time she'd
been interested in a male wolf like this, and she really *did* want
to take him to her bed! He'd kissed her back, but in a way that
said he was allowing her to set the limits. She appreciated that
he wasn't automatically assuming she wanted more. What

had surprised her so much was that she smelled the way their pheromones were calling to each other. And *that* had never happened to her before when she was with a man.

Just think, if she and he were alone here…then she could do what she wanted. She sighed. Thoughts like that were going to get her into trouble. She rested her head against her pillow. Despite worrying about meeting her father, she knew she had to sleep, or she wouldn't wake when it was time for her to pull guard duty.

Before she knew it, she smelled candied bacon, red velvet pancakes, and coffee brewing. She hurried to get up and dress. She headed into the kitchen where everyone was working on the breakfast.

"Why didn't you wake me?" she asked Mike, who was supposed to be the last one on guard duty before she took her turn.

"Mike woke me when he climbed back in bed. He's the one who steals the covers, so I would rather guard than sleep with him," Ryder said.

Lexi chuckled. "I thought we were supposed to run first thing this morning as wolves."

"You…slept too late." Kate smiled. "Ryder figured you needed to sleep."

Kate gave her a cup of coffee, doctored perfectly just like she liked it. They were soon eating their bacon and pancakes and drinking their coffee.

"Were there any problems last night?" Lexi cut up some more of her pancakes that were just out of this world. She knew if the guys ever wanted to quit their bodyguard jobs, they could open a first-class restaurant.

Kate pointed at her laptop. "Only that our competitor is causing trouble again."

"What's that all about?" Ryder asked.

Kate told him all about the trouble Lexi was having with the upstart cosmetic company.

"We can take care of that in a heartbeat," Mike said.

"We sure can," Ryder agreed.

"Uh, no, we're not going to do anything about it." Lexi waved a piece of bacon at the guys. "We'll deal with it if we need to. She'll probably run herself right out of business." At least Lexi was hoping she would. She didn't want to look like the bad guy and ruin her own reputation if anyone thought she was harassing the smaller company.

But she caught the looks Ryder and Mike shared with each other, and she suspected they were going to look into it. They'd better not do anything that would affect her business in a negative way!

"I mean it," she said. She'd read once that if you had to resort to saying you meant what you said, the battle was already lost.

CHAPTER 12

RYDER KNEW LEXI WAS WORRIED ABOUT MEETING UP with her dad, no matter how much she tried to hide it. She sighed again, left the dining room table, and headed for the living room window. Again. She peered out. Then she headed back into the kitchen to refill her water glass.

"You'd think I was on a hike, my throat feels so parched," she said, while everyone watched her.

Ryder wished he could alleviate her concerns somehow, but he suspected seeing her father and keeping them both safe was all that would work.

They began to clear away the breakfast dishes. Kate and Mike were cleaning the dishes, while Lexi put away the food.

Ryder was carrying the jelly and butter into the kitchen when he got a call from Edward Manning, one of Rafe's bodyguards, a Navy SEAL, and the man in charge of the six-man former Special Forces team. "Hey, yeah, you're at our cabin?" Ryder set the butter and jelly in the fridge.

"Yeah, we just unpacked our bags and did a perimeter search. A couple of our men checked out the thugs' cabin. The thugs are inside for now."

"Okay, good. We're glad you made it." Ryder turned to speak to Lexi and the others. "The other guys are here."

Mike gave him a thumbs-up. The women both said, "Good."

"Hey, how's everything going with all of you? We've got eyes on the two men over there," Edward said.

"It's been quiet here," Ryder said.

"We've seen Don Morgan out here too. What's the deal with him?" Edward asked.

"He got an interview from Lexi. I was hoping that would satisfy him. But he saw us as wolves yesterday, and he might want a story on that. Then again, I told him to bug the thugs for a story, so maybe he's attempting to harass them further."

"That could be a dangerous thing to do."

"I agree, but according to him, danger is his middle name."

"I wanted to tell him to get lost, but I was afraid that would entice him to stay," Edward said.

"It would." Ryder turned to Lexi and asked, "Since the team is watching the thugs, do you want to go for a hike this morning? We can run as wolves tonight well before eleven." They might as well do some of what they'd planned to do while enjoying their vacation since she couldn't see her father right away. And it provided a better cover story if the thugs happened to see them hiking. He thought it could also help get Lexi's mind off the meetup for a while.

"Yeah, that sounds good," Lexi said.

"I'm up for it," Mike said.

"Me too," Kate said.

"We're going on a hike, just to enjoy the park liked we'd planned to," Ryder told Edward.

"Good show. We'll do our duty here," Edward said.

"Thanks. We'll keep in touch." Ryder signed off and pulled a park map out of his backpack. "Which trail did you want to go on?"

"How about this one?" Lexi pointed to a trail on the map that was a little over a nine-mile hike. "Kate and I have never been that way, and that will be a nice half-day hike."

"Looks good to me. We'll start at a pond near the mouth of the river, climb to around eighteen-hundred feet on switchbacks taking us through the old-growth redwood forest, and see the coast from up above. It's an enjoyable hike."

"Sounds good to me," Mike said, Kate agreeing.

Carrying backpacks containing water, food, weapons, and everything else they thought would come in handy, they all started their hike and ended up at the pond. There, the land was level and mallard ducks were floating on the water. Lexi had to take some pictures of the pond and ducks, and then she and Ryder walked together on the trail, while Mike brought up the rear with Kate as they began to move into the redwoods, ferns and sorrel bordering the path. Some of the tree trunks were covered in bright-green moss, mushrooms sprouting here and there, a bright-yellow banana slug slithering over a fallen tree, purple violets and white trillium flowering all over.

Ryder knew the men who were serving as a protection team were professional enough not to say anything in front of Lexi or Kate, but when he saw the Special Forces team on his own, he would get plenty of ribbing about making a move on the billionaire she-wolf. Not that he'd known she was a billionaire at first, thinking only that she was just the she-wolf next-door kind of girl, but the chemistry between them was undeniable. Pheromones didn't lie.

Since Lexi hadn't settled down with a wolf yet, he suspected she just hadn't found a mate who was right for her. He assumed it wasn't all about her money either. One of Rafe and Aidan's friends was a billionaire, too, so if it was about that—well, hell, before Rafe and Aidan had mated even, she could have chosen either of the twin brothers or their billionaire friend. But for wolves, it had to be more than that. A compatibility and a deeper need to be with the wolf that urged them to move forward and court and take the courtship even further. A mating between wolves meant forever.

If he and Lexi ever became an item, he knew humans would consider him a gold digger; wolves would understand why they'd be together. Though it didn't mean they wouldn't give him a hard time over it. He could just see the tabloids now: Male Model Hits the Jackpot with Cosmetic Mogul, courtesy of Don Morgan.

Ryder would never live it down.

Frowning, Lexi turned to him as if she knew just where his thoughts had gone. "I mean it when I said not to go causing trouble for Silky Spring of Spring Cosmetics."

He'd forgotten all about that situation. It brought him back to reality in a heartbeat. "Gotcha." He was actually ready to go to war against the woman and had been thinking on and off about how to go about it without causing Lexi grief.

Lexi glanced at him and raised a brow.

He smiled. Of course he was going to look into the other company's practices, and he had every intention of putting a halt to them.

"You ought to invite her to a party and kill her with kindness," Kate said.

"We don't want to do anything that could backfire on us," Lexi said. "My company has a good reputation, and I want to keep it that way. There's enough room for other businesses to make it on their own if they work hard enough at it. She's just taking a lazy and mean-hearted approach."

"It sounds personal," Ryder said, "since she's not

targeting anyone else's products. Have you had a run-in with her before?"

"Not that I recall. I meet thousands of people online, not so many in person, but I host cosmetic parties about three times a year. Maybe I did run into her, but I just don't remember. As much as Kate and I have looked over the pictures and videos taken at the parties, we didn't see anyone who looked like her."

"Unless she was in disguise. Wearing a wig, maybe?" Ryder still suspected it was personal, and that's why she was only targeting Lexi's company. "What about you, Kate? Did you ever have any contact with her that you can recall?"

"Lexi and I already talked about it. I went through all the emails and texts I'd sent, but I didn't have any contact with her. It's possible she believes some perceived injustice has been done to her, but we really don't know what or why."

Ryder's phone rang, and he saw it was the bodyguard Special Forces team leader. "Yeah?"

"Do you know who we're dealing with?" Edward asked.

"Yeah, Joe Tremaine's hit men. Joe's the guy who murdered a DA and the witness testified against him, sending him to prison. No one had ever done that before. Any witness who even thought about testifying against him in other capital murder trials mysteriously vanished, even when they were in police custody and supposed to be protected."

"Right. So why are they after Lexi? Don't tell me. Her father was the witness."

Ryder glanced at Lexi, thinking how stalwart she was, despite being so vulnerable, as they continued to follow the switchbacks up the hill. "Yeah."

"Her father is on Joe's hit list." Edward sounded worried. Not about him and his team, but about Lexi and her father.

"Right."

"She's not meeting her father here, is she?" Edward asked. "I thought he was dead. He must be in witness protection. The U.S. Marshal's office will kick him out of the program if she meets up with him and they learn of it. Not to mention he'll blow his cover and could easily be murdered."

"Uh, yeah. But we'll keep the secret." They had their own way of handling situations. Her father must not have been in a pack, or his pack members would have protected him.

"Hell, Ryder. I mean, we're game, but this is dangerous for both of them no matter what."

"You just keep tabs on the men. We'll watch the women."

Edward snorted. "You don't want to switch places with me, do you?"

"Or us!" one of the other men shouted in the background.

Ryder smiled. He knew that was coming. "Sorry, no."

"You're not sorry in the least. Gloating a little, I imagine. But back to business. The thugs just started to head over to Lexi's place, but we intercepted them. They immediately called their boss and said they were having a little trouble here. Then they returned to their cabin to continue the conversation in private. One of our men put security videos and listening bugs in their place, but if they're like us, they'll be looking for them. I'm sure Joe Tremaine would like to order a hit on all of us, but they want Lexi alive in case she can lead these men to her father."

"All right. Good on the security measures. With any luck, they won't believe you've set anything up. I imagine they're wondering where all the muscle is coming from."

"She's a billionaire. I'm sure they realize she can hire all the muscle she wants. Not that she has to. Rafe is footing the bill on this one. He likes to keep his friends safe."

Which reminded Ryder that he'd never met Lexi at any of Rafe's shindigs that he and Mike had to attend while protecting Aidan and Holly. Then again, they were fairly new on the job, and Lexi could have been visiting with the brothers before he and Mike started working for Aidan.

"Keep up the good work. If we run into any trouble at this end, we'll let you know. We're headed up to the ridge with a view of the ocean," Ryder told Edward.

"Know it well. Talk later."

Ryder slipped his phone into his pocket and turned to speak to Lexi. "Mike and I just started working for Aidan about a year ago, but I was wondering why I'd never met you before."

"If you *had* seen me at one of Rafe's parties, would it have changed the way you viewed me when you met me here at the park?" Lexi paused to take a picture of a banana slug peering at her from a tree. Then she saw a blue jay settle on the path way up ahead, and she snapped a shot of it.

"While we were rescuing the bear cubs? If I'd met you in some other setting first, it would depend. If you were rescuing seal pups on the coast where Rafe lives, I'm sure I would have viewed you in the same way I did while you were handing a bear cub off to me. But if you had been all dressed up, sipping tea and eating fancy little cakes the first time I saw you, it might have been more of a shock to see you all muddy, scraped up, with your hair, shorts, and T-shirt soaking wet and plastered to you in the pouring rain."

Lexi laughed. "Yeah, I'm sure Kate and I were a sight." She snapped some shots of fungi on one of the trees.

He smiled. He had been too. Naked, muddy, dripping with rainwater. "You looked like a rugged naturalist, a heroine in bear-cub-rescue mode, and were a beautiful sight."

She only smiled back but didn't comment on how she'd perceived him at their first meeting. He didn't want to ask while Mike and Kate were tagging along after them.

"How do the others feel about protecting us when my father and I are not supposed to meet?"

"You're a wolf. They feel as protective of you as Mike and I do."

"Are you sure? They don't need to be here."

"Yeah, I'm sure. The more there are of us, the more we can protect you and your dad."

"All right. And thanks. So what do your mother and father do?"

"They retired from the Air Force. Dad was a navigator, and Mom was a pilot. But they own a gift shop on the California coast near the Oregon border now. I went into the army because I wanted to be Special Forces."

"A Green Beret, cool," Lexi said. "My father had been a family physician in the army. Mom was a pediatrician, both stationed at Fort Sam Houston. When they retired, they worked at a civilian hospital there. I didn't want to join the military, despite all the benefits."

"Or be a doctor."

"No. I went in a completely different direction in life. Do your folks accept what you do now?"

"Yeah. Of course they worry about me, but they worried about me when I was in combat zones while serving in the army too."

"How far away do they live?"

"About an hour. Mike's parents are their next-door neighbors now. They have a little café next door to my parents' kitchen, wine, and cheese gift shop. They're good friends and have cooking parties once a month."

"Aww. That's where you and Mike picked up the cooking business."

"Yeah. Mom and Dad loved to cook when they retired, so they opened the gift shop. They couldn't believe it when Mike's parents opened the café next door and learned they were wolves. Anyway, they ended up getting a house near my parents so they could run as wolves on the combined acreage. They went on a Caribbean cruise together last Christmas."

"Oh, how nice. My folks have been lone wolves mostly because they never met any wolves while they were in San Antonio. Oh, except one time while they were at Fort Sam Houston, a CID agent came in with strep throat and my dad treated her. She returned to Denver that year, or they would have invited her to their home for Thanksgiving. You know how it is when we meet fellow wolves."

"Absolutely." Except when she'd first met Ryder! He knew she'd had issues with male wolves then.

Two and a half hours later, they finally reached the point where they could see the coast from the cliffs. The ocean waves were crashing against the beach, sea lions barking on the rocks, and behemoth stones pointed toward the sky, some surrounded by the turbulent water and some standing tall on the rocky beach. Lexi began taking pictures of the water and rocks, but she stayed far away from the edge of the cliffs.

"Did you want to get a little closer to the edge to see the baby sea lion down there?" Ryder asked, holding his hand out to her.

Lexi was so far away from the cliff's edge that Ryder knew

she couldn't see the sea lion calf. "I can see it just fine from here," she said.

Ryder was eyeing her with suspicion. "Do you want me to take a picture of it?"

Lexi finally inched closer to the edge, and he could smell her fear. He was surprised because she'd climbed down the other cliff to reach the bear cubs, and this one was perfectly stable. Unless she'd had a tumble when she climbed down the cliff to rescue the bear cubs and it had unnerved her.

Mike and Kate were peering down at the sea lion calf. Kate had her camera out and was taking some pictures. Ryder offered his hand to Lexi again, and she finally took his hand, but he didn't pull her closer to the edge. He let her decide how close she was going to get, but he was holding on to her so she wouldn't be quite so afraid. She was trembling, though, and he finally pulled her closer, offering his strength. "Do you see the calf down there?"

She finally trusted him enough to keep her safe and moved close enough to the edge to see the calf. "Aww, she…or he…is adorable."

He wrapped his arm around her waist so her hands were free to take several pictures. He was glad she felt safe enough with his help to see the sea lions.

"The view of the ocean is beautiful from up here. And it's always fun when the sea lions are sunning on the rocks." Ryder was glad he and Mike were able to enjoy the hike with the ladies too.

"It's lovely," Lexi said, but she was still trembling a little.

Her brows furrowed, Kate watched her and appeared to be worried too.

"If you're done with your picture taking, we can move over there and have something to snack on and drink,"

Ryder said, taking Lexi's hand again and moving her further away from the edge.

They removed their backpacks and pulled out their protein bars and bottles of water.

"This is truly beautiful," Lexi said. "We had seen the reviews and thought it would be a nice hike. It really is great." Now that Lexi was away from the cliff's drop-off, she took a deep breath and let it out, looking much more relieved.

"Mike and I always have to come up here when we visit. There's another longer hike that we do, but we take a tent and sleep overnight on that one," Ryder said.

Lexi sighed. "You were supposed to be here to enjoy yourself, not have to be a bodyguard."

"We're enjoying our time with you," Ryder assured her.

"Hell, yeah. A couple of beautiful she-wolves with us on a hike? Much better than just the two of us roughing it on our own up here," Mike said.

Ryder appreciated Mike speaking up to reassure Lexi that this was better than just spending all his time with another male wolf. He'd thought maybe Kate and Mike would hit it off, but she seemed a little aloof with him, as if she were afraid he might think she was interested in him and she didn't want to give him the wrong impression. Mike must have sensed it, too, so he was strictly being a friend and not showing any interest in the she-wolf. It made Ryder curious whether Kate was interested in another male wolf but nothing had come of it—yet. He couldn't help himself when it came to showing his interest in Lexi.

She didn't seem to be pushing him away either.

After they finished their snack, they began the hike down. On the descent, the trees were smaller, the bark lighter on the ocean side, the huckleberry shrubs larger and denser. It was an easy path bordered by trees all the way down. Even lower, the trees turned to red alders and small spruce, the understory now lush ferns and sorrel.

Ryder was glad they'd had this diversion before they met with her father and did what they could to safeguard him. But he was still curious about what made Lexi fear the cliff's edge.

CHAPTER 13

AFTER SHE AND MIKE, RYDER, AND KATE HAD returned to their cabin and washed up, Lexi wasn't surprised when Ryder brought up the business with the cliffs. He and Kate were too curious for their own good. Mike was not as inquisitive, though Lexi imagined he was just as interested in learning about it as they were.

"Did you fall from the cliff when you went to the rescue the bear cubs? You don't seem to be afraid of heights except when you didn't want to get close to the edge of the cliff to see the sea lions." Ryder asked.

"Yes, I fell. So did Kate. But that wasn't why I was so reluctant."

"Oh, okay. Sorry to bring it up. I just noticed your scratches and bruises and worried that was what it was all about."

"It had to do with an earlier incident, five years ago. I was angry with a boyfriend. He told me I would never be successful at what I do, and I needed to get a real job like my mom and dad had. He really admired them, but not what I was trying to do. Ironically, he didn't work, so he really had no business telling me what to do."

"You're not seeing him any longer, are you?"

Lexi frowned at Ryder. "Of course not. I needed positive influences in my life, not negative."

"Like me."

She chuckled. "Anyway, I got angry and went for a hike

as a wolf in the woods along a cliff I'd never been to because it was off-trail and isolated. Mom and Dad were busy working at the hospital. I didn't figure I'd be gone very long. I could run through more rugged wilderness as a wolf, far away from the human population. My mistake was not telling anybody where I was going. I didn't see my parents all the time. They were working long hours, and I didn't live at home with them any longer. So they didn't realize I was gone right away.

"I felt some of the pebbles give way near the cliff's edge, and I should have been more careful and put some distance between me and the cliff. But I was angry at Wayne and not really paying attention to my surroundings, fuming about what he'd said. You know how it is. You keep thinking about everything the person said or did, wondering if they're right or wrong. I was trying to see his point of view, but he had rich parents who were still paying his way while he did whatever he wanted."

"So you hadn't made a success of your business yet," Ryder said.

"I hadn't gotten off the ground floor with my company yet, no."

"When you became famous, did he come around?"

She smiled. "About a year after I'd made my first million, I saw him with a woman and a couple of babies—he was already mated. I wanted to say something to him about how helpful he hadn't been, but who cares? It was just better to get rid of a toxic relationship. Anyway, while I was running in the park, I stayed near the cliff edge and I heard a dog crying way down below."

"Oh, not unlike the bear cubs."

"Yeah. Weak, starving, trapped. There was no easy way

down the cliff, but then I saw what looked like a deer trail so I tried to go down it. I was a wolf, after all. But we'd had a lot of rain and the narrow ledge crumbled. I slipped off the edge and fell into the ravine. I was fortunate I didn't kill myself as I banged against the rocks on the way down. I landed at the bottom, breaking my left hind leg. I couldn't climb or crawl or do anything, and I had no water with me—naturally. Plus, I was a wolf."

"Right, so either rescuers would find an injured wolf—"

"And put me out of my misery, or they could find a naked human woman. I still had to rescue the dog. Which I figured wasn't going to happen in the shape I was in. I woofed at him to let him know help was coming. Afraid howling would scare him, I woofed and woofed, hoping someone would hear me and come to help us. In considerable pain, I finally managed to stand on three legs and hopped over to the tunnel of the cave where he had fallen. I woofed at him, reassuring him I wouldn't leave and would stay there with him until help came. I stayed in my wolf form for as long as I could because at least my fur kept me warm when temperatures dropped at night and protected my skin from sunburn during the day."

"Hell, Lexi. I wish I'd been there for you."

"We both might have fallen off the cliff then."

"At least you wouldn't have been alone."

She smiled at him.

"Somebody must have seen your car," Ryder said.

"The police did. And my parents had dropped by the apartment when they couldn't get ahold of me to see if I wanted to go to a movie with them. It wasn't like me not to respond to their calls. Of course my phone was in my car while I was running as a wolf. The police told them they'd found the car. My parents had checked with my boyfriend, too, and he said we'd broken up. My parents worried I was off hiking, upset, and they knew I'd be alone. They joined the search party. Unfortunately, someone else found my clothes hidden in the woods.

"My parents wanted to locate me first, and with their sense of smell they could. I'd been gone for two days, lucky enough to catch some water when it rained. I finally decided to shift and crawl into the tunnel to reach the dog, hoping I could get him to where he could get some water too. It nearly killed me, shooting pains shot up my leg every time I bumped it, but I finally managed to get down into the cave where the dog had fallen.

"He turned out to be a she, and she was afraid of me at first. Shy. I talked to her and held her, comforting her. Then she licked my face, and I hugged her to my chest. I made the torturous climb back out of the tunnel with her in my arms. She wasn't injured, just starving and dehydrated. We had a welcome rain and deep puddles formed, giving us something to drink.

"My parents were able to track me, but others followed their lead. My dad said I usually took that path to give a reason why he was so sure I headed that way, when in truth, I'd never hiked in that direction before. They asked why he hadn't told them that in the beginning, but he had to find my scent first. He said he'd forgotten about it.

"When they saw me at the bottom of the cliff with the dog, a helicopter was sent to my location to pick us up. No one could climb down the cliff and get me out of there fast enough."

"No wonder you're afraid of getting too close to the edge of a cliff. What did they say about you having no clothes?"

"I was dehydrated and disoriented. I just told them I didn't remember what had happened. Except I heard the dog crying and tried to reach her, and the cliff gave way. It didn't explain why my clothes were so far away, but I just stuck to my story. My parents were so upset with me and furious with the ex-boyfriend."

"And the dog?"

"Sandy had a collar on her with her family's name and phone number on her tag. They were reunited right away. You should have seen her with me and the other rescuers when they fussed over her. She rolled onto her back and wanted her belly rubbed. Her family was so grateful to me and were so sorry I had been injured trying to rescue her. They sent me flowers and chocolates. Anyway, I try to fight the fear when I'm near a cliff. Sometimes I don't have any trouble, but sometimes I just can't fight it off."

Ryder said, "If we ever have a fight, we'll work it out. No running off to fall down cliffs."

"But I saved the dog."

He chuckled. "Yeah, and if that happens again, I want to be there with you, helping out again."

"And me," Kate said.

"Me too," Mike said, smiling.

"Pizza after this, right?" Lexi asked, wanting to get off the topic of cliffs.

"Yeah, we're still on for pizza," Ryder said. "We couldn't come here without a visit to the pizza parlor."

"I'll drive," Mike said.

"I'm famished," Kate said, her stomach growling.

Lexi laughed. "I can hear that you are all the way over here."

"That makes two of us," Ryder said as they all piled into

Mike's truck and he drove them over to Little Italy Pizza Parlor in the small town nearby. The restaurant owners, Antonio and Maria Lupo, and their two daughters, Gabriella and Adriana, greeted them as if they were all family. Which, in a way, they were—considering they were all gray wolves, like members of a secret family.

Statues of maids wearing togas and men wearing loin cloths poured pitchers of water into mosaic-tile fountains. Flowers filled tall mosaic-tile planters, and blue glass vases sat on each of the tables. Pictures of vineyards in Italy, where the family had come from, hung on the stucco walls, the brick exposed in part to make it appear to be an old-world restaurant. They were Apennine wolves, native to the Italian Peninsula.

Lexi loved the ambience as a couple of men tossed pizza dough in the air behind a counter, the Italian music of love played overhead, and the scent of cheeses, pepperoni, wines and spices filled the air. Everyone was enjoying the conversation, food, and drink, when several more people entered the restaurant.

Lexi and her party all watched the new arrivals, but none looked like trouble. They ordered a large pizza with mushrooms, pepperoni, extra cheese, and black olives, and a bottle of wine.

Ryder got a call and answered his cell. "Hell, okay. Thanks, Edward." He ended the call and told Lexi, "The thugs left the cabin. He suspects they want to see where you went, not because they feel the heat's on and are leaving for good."

"Too bad it wasn't for the latter reason." Lexi settled against her chair.

"I agree, but then we'd worry about what they were up

to. Like if Tremaine had sent new people we didn't suspect because these guys had blown their cover," Ryder said.

Their pizza finally arrived, and the server poured each of them a glass of wine. When she left, Lexi glanced at the door and saw two men arrive wearing suits. Why they would wear suits was beyond her. They looked like they were FBI or CIA or from some other governmental agency. Not someone working for a crime boss like Tremaine.

"They're here," Lexi said to the others.

They all glanced in the direction of the door.

The two men working for Tremaine looked around the restaurant, then spied the table where Lexi and her friends were sitting. They grabbed a table near the door so they could watch them and not lose sight of them.

Mike was about to get up from the table to say something to them, but Lexi took ahold of his arm and shook her head. "We don't want to make a scene here. We wouldn't want to anywhere, but especially not in our friends' establishment."

"You know if we told the Lupos what this was all about, they'd make them leave," Ryder said.

"I'd just as soon the thugs be here so we can keep an eye on them." Lexi took a bite of her slice of pizza.

"Like they're keeping an eye on us." Kate cut into her pizza.

"Why don't you just eat it with your hands?" Mike asked.

"Because it's messy." Kate motioned with her fork to the tomato sauce, melted cheese, and pepperoni grease dripping on his hands from his slice of pizza. "See? Look at your hands."

Mike smiled. "This is the only way to eat a pizza."

Ryder and Lexi were both eating with their hands as well.

"You will take so long that we'll eat your slices." Lexi smiled at Kate.

"Ha. I can cut up my pizza just as fast, and I do have a fork, you know, so hands off my slices," Kate said.

They all laughed. They were having fun, even if the thugs were there to put a damper on their lunch activities.

Lexi glanced at the pizza makers. "I tried that once. The pizza ended up on the floor."

Mike chuckled. "Ryder and I did too. Right after we ate here, in fact. We were headed home, and Aidan dared us to make that kind of pizza—tossed. He said it's the best and he wanted the best, if we were to make it."

"So what happened?" Lexi wondered if they had mastered the ability. She'd love to have a party where Mike and Ryder could entertain them by making the pizzas.

"Well, each of us had to make our own pizza," Ryder said. "We were doing really well at first. Not sure what happened, but we figure we got too close to each other, and the next thing we knew, it was like two airplanes colliding midair, total disaster."

The ladies laughed; Mike smiled.

"What did you tell Aidan about the pizza disaster?" Lexi asked.

"That we'd take another trip to the redwoods and have pizza here," Ryder said.

Smiling, Lexi shook her head. "I can't believe you'd give up that easily."

"We haven't," Mike said. "But we wouldn't let Aidan know we're still trying to perfect it."

"That's good to know. I could have quit so many times when things weren't working out for me with my business, but I didn't. I wouldn't."

"What kept you going?" Ryder asked.

"Me, stubbornly refusing to let go of my dream. It wasn't just that I didn't want to fail. I didn't want my parents to see me fail. They're successful in their chosen professions. I just floundered, not sure of what to do. But you know what? I began to learn about the issues of carcinogens—substances in cosmetics, hair products, nail products, deodorants, and all kinds of products we use daily that have been linked to cancer. So I don't do this because I think women should wear makeup to look more glamorous, but because women will wear makeup whether I tell them to do so or not, and while Europe has banned a thousand carcinogens that were being added to makeup, the United States has only banned eleven! Why? You'd think we'd care about our people. But nope!"

"Big business," Ryder guessed.

"Yep. Government cracks down, manufacturers put on pressure to keep producing unhealthy makeup, and voilà, it's perfectly legal and the FDA gives in and doesn't regulate it further. I mean, why bother? If the manufacturers can get out the big guns and the government can't fight it? Something's really wrong there. In one case, an American cosmetic line had asbestos in its cosmetics. So what did the government do? Same old thing. They tried to put a stop to it. The manufacturers put an end to the government's attempt to do anything about it. *But* the word had spread online, yay! And the stores pulled the cosmetic line from their shelves. It took the retailers doing something about it before the company finally changed the manufacturing process.

"There are sites online where women can go to check out what products are known to contain carcinogens. Armed with information, we can make our own choices. But so many don't know there's a problem. Heck, I didn't know

Europe was so much better at keeping their people safe than our country is. It's disgusting that big business has such a stranglehold on product regulation. I was thinking about those gray-haired old men with their huge manufacturing businesses, making billions of dollars, while their wives, daughters, and friends are using unhealthy products."

"So Lexi started her product line based on how the European cosmetic markets create theirs, cutting out so many of the carcinogens in American products. The thing is, it can be done," Kate said.

"Like I said, if women are going to wear it, I can at least offer something that is safer." Lexi drank some more of her wine. She noticed the thugs were having spaghetti and meatballs. Though the pizza parlor was best known for its pizzas, they served pasta dishes too.

Lexi glanced up at the wall to see the time. Then she pulled her cell phone out and checked the shows at the movie theater in town. "How about we see a movie after we finish eating? Kate and I were going to do that if you guys hadn't shown up." She hadn't seen a movie at a theater in forever, and going on a "guy date" really appealed. Not to mention she was feeling super anxious about seeing her father and thought it would help to take her mind off it before that happened. She wasn't one to sit still and do nothing, pace, and stew, so she figured this would be perfect.

Kate looked at her phone. "Yeah, there's a thriller, a comedy, a kids' movie, a sci-fi thriller."

"Sci-fi thriller?" Ryder started to play the trailer.

"That one looks good to me," Lexi said, looking over his shoulder at the trailer.

Everyone agreed. Once they'd eaten, Ryder and Mike were going to get the bill, but Lexi said, "I already got it."

"Then that doesn't count as a date, right?" Ryder asked.

Lexi thought he almost looked serious.

Mike was smiling at them, probably wondering what that was all about.

"It's a date. And hiking earlier was a date. Didn't I mention the other one was too?" she asked.

"Then we're beyond three dates." Ryder smiled. Genuinely smiled.

He was cute.

"Yes, we're beyond three dates. They're my rules, so if I want to break them?" She lifted her shoulder. "The movie is a date too. You're still safe." Lexi paid the bill, and then they said goodbye to the Lupos and headed outside. They piled into Mike's truck and couldn't help but notice the thugs hurrying out of the pizza parlor to tail them.

Mike drove off and soon parked at the theater, where Ryder paid for the tickets before Lexi could. She smiled and took his hand. "We just had lunch, but I need dessert."

He smiled down at her as he walked her to the concession stand. "No popcorn, I take it."

"Nope." She pointed at a box of chocolate candies. "That's what I'll have."

"What about you, Kate?" Ryder asked. "Mike?"

"I'm fine," Kate said. "Lexi always has to have the chocolate mints when she goes to the theater. Which she rarely does. I've been working for her for a year, and we've gone one time. But she said that was her vice—the chocolate mints."

"If that's your only vice, you're doing good," Ryder said.

"I'm good," Mike said, though he bought himself a soda.

Lexi saw the thugs enter the movie theater, but Edward and two other men came in right behind them. She took Ryder's hand. "They're here."

He glanced back at them. "And so are Edward and the others. So we're good. I'm surprised Tremaine's men haven't tried to strong-arm you before."

"Not these guys. The other one who did is no longer among the living." Lexi smiled at Ryder with the sweetest smile she could offer.

"Hell, I knew you were a wolf." He smiled back at her, squeezing her hand in approval, but she suspected he'd want to know the whole story when they were alone.

Mike and Kate were studying her, and she figured they both wanted to know too.

"All right. I'll tell you after the movie. No one but Rafe knows about it. And some of his men. Not even my dad knows, and I want to keep it that way."

"Yeah, sure, we understand." Ryder walked her into the theater, the others following behind them.

She'd hated that the hit man had come for her at her home and she'd been forced to kill him.

When she and the others took their seats high up above in the auditorium, the thugs found seats a few rows behind them, but Edward's men did too.

Ryder put his arm around Lexi's shoulders, and she leaned her head against him, trying to relax. The movie started, and once the aliens landed on earth, she was caught up in the story, almost forgetting she was meeting up with her father later. Feeling the warmth of Ryder's shoulder and surrounded by his wolfishly delectable scent, she snuggled closer against him. He pressed his mouth against her head, and she felt like she was really on a date, a good date, and she hoped they survived to have many more.

CHAPTER 14

AFTER THE MOVIE, LEXI WANTED TO GO FOR ANOTHER hike, hating that she felt so anxious. She wanted to just go and go and go until she had to meet up with her father.

"Yeah, let's go," Ryder said, and she appreciated that he didn't mind.

"Time to work off the pizza," Kate said. "Hey, do you guys know some martial arts? Lexi and I were going to practice some while we're here."

"Not now," Lexi said, gathering her water for her backpack. She wasn't going to take her camera, but she knew if she didn't, she'd miss the perfect photo op. "There are too many of us." And she didn't want to practice in front of Ryder and Mike.

"Okay, fine. It was just on the agenda," Kate said. "We'll wait until we get home. But you're getting so good at this, I figured you were ready to go up against a male opponent."

"Only if he didn't know martial arts," Lexi said.

Ryder smiled, but then called someone. "Edward, we're taking the southernmost trail, which is about a two-hour hike... Yeah, we'll be okay."

"Oh, and I was thinking we could plant Don's camera equipment in the thugs' cabin somewhere they wouldn't find it, and your men could call the police about these guys causing trouble, and then the cops could find it and hand it over to Don." Lexi couldn't just leave it out in the weather and chance someone random finding it and not handing it over to the rangers, but she did want to give the equipment back to him.

"That's a great idea." Ryder sounded proud of her for wanting to do that. He got on his phone and sent a text message.

She'd only wanted to keep Don from discovering what she was doing and reporting on it. Since they'd found the message, she had no need to keep his equipment any longer.

They'd been hiking for about an hour, talking about everything under the sun, from what their favorite foods were to their favorite dream vacations, all while watching for black bears and Tremaine's men when they heard someone running to catch up to them. Since the person wasn't trying to be stealthy, Lexi didn't think he could be a threat, but they all had their guns out just in case. Then they saw it was Don, huffing and puffing as he closed the distance between them. He appeared to be in good physical shape, but between running, and carrying a camera and a camera bag, he was short of breath.

"What are you doing out here?" Lexi couldn't help but be annoyed.

"Now Tremaine's men are after me." Don joined them as if they had invited him to hike with them.

"I doubt it," Lexi said.

"Yeah, for real. The bastard's got two men watching my room at the hotel. I slipped out through the laundry room to make my escape. They never knew I'd gotten away." Don smiled, proud of himself.

"Those are more of *our* men." Ryder got on his phone right away. "Hey, if our men realize they've lost Don, he's here hiking with us… Yeah, okay. Talk later." Ryder put his phone away. "Hell, Don." Ryder gave him a scowly look, but Lexi swore Ryder was fighting a smile.

The men hadn't been there to provide protection for Don as much as they were trying to stop him from harassing Lexi further and discovering what her true purpose was here. So he'd bested some of Rafe's men at the game.

"Protecting me?" Don frowned. "I don't need any protection."

"Sure you do. We'll help chase the wolves away," Ryder said.

Now Lexi was fighting a smile.

"I knew you didn't believe me," Don said.

"What are you doing here?" Lexi asked again. "Go home or find another celeb to target for a story. You won't need any protection from wolves, bears, or Tremaine's men then."

"I know there's a story here. That's why Tremaine's men are here. And I want the exclusive," Don said, keeping up with them.

No one said a word. Lexi knew it was because they didn't want anything they discussed being picked up in a tabloid, even if it was just about their favorite hikes.

"Aren't we supposed to talk to scare off the wild beasts of prey?" Don asked.

"Talk all you want. We'll listen," Lexi said. *Not.*

"Why didn't you tell me you had a couple of guys staking out my room at the hotel for my protection? What if I'd called the cops on them? Or what if I'd hurt one of them? I know martial arts, you know."

"Do you have a gun?" Ryder asked.

Lexi suspected Don didn't.

Don didn't say anything for several heartbeats as they continued to hike along the trail.

"They have guns," Ryder added for Don's benefit.

"Hell, you weren't trying to protect me," Don finally said. "You were trying to keep me from learning Lexi's secret."

Lexi had to admit the guy was smart. She turned and stopped to face Don down. "We are hiking on a vacation. Just the four of us. Nothing. More. You already know why Tremaine's men are here. I don't have to spell it out for you. And I won't. We thought it might be a good idea to have our own men watch your back since we were the ones who asked you to harass them. But, hey, if you don't want our protection? Fine. I don't want you harassing me while we're just trying to enjoy our vacation."

Don looked glum.

Lexi wanted to roll her eyes. What? Did he feel he'd become her friend, and now she was angry with him? He wasn't her friend. Friends didn't share secrets with the world. "All right. Hike with us if you want. But if someone starts shooting at us, we can't guarantee your safety." She turned and started hiking again, and the others picked up their pace.

Except for Don, who seemed to be considering whether to go with them or not, and then he hurried to catch up to them. "I don't have any protection if I return through the woods to my vehicle. I'll stick with you guys. I thought the other guys were Tremaine's men and I had to get the word to you."

"You don't have Ryder's phone number?" Lexi glanced back at Don, knowing damn well he did since they'd talked on the phone at her cabin.

"Uh, yeah, I guess I do."

A shot rang out and hit a branch near Ryder with a thwack. All of them rushed off the trail and crouched down among the ferns. Ryder called it in. "Shots were just fired at us. We're an hour along the trail."

Don was sweating like crazy, and Lexi thought he didn't look happy about being in danger like this, despite saying he was good for it. She wasn't happy about it either. Why would Tremaine's men be shooting at them now? She suspected they figured that she was trying to meet her dad. Why else would she stay here, pretending they were having a vacation, bringing in more guns to ensure she was safe?

"I know you think I should just give up my vacation and return home, but I'm not going to do it, Kate. I haven't had a vacation in a year," Lexi said loud enough for the thugs to hear.

Ryder glanced at her. She didn't believe she'd convince the thugs she was here for just a vacation, but she had to make up the story anyway, just in case. But then she worried. What if her father had arrived early and they were shooting at him?

Not wanting Don to hear what she had to say, she whispered to Ryder, "What if they're after someone else?"

"I wondered," he whispered back.

"Can't we go after them?" she entreated.

"No. We have to safeguard you and Don."

She hated not going to her father's aid, if he was out here on his own. But she understood Ryder's concern. Suddenly, someone made a mad dash in their direction, and she was certain it had to be one of the thugs. Rafe's people wouldn't make a move like that, crashing through the underbrush as if a wild boar was out to gore him.

Don was wild-eyed and looked like he wanted to run, but Lexi grabbed his arm and shook her head slightly, telling him to stay put. They were well hidden in the ferns, and then the man appeared, his head turned back to watch who was following him. Ryder jumped up, lunged forward, and slugged the guy in the head. The thug, dressed in camo and carrying a rifle, dropped to the ground, out cold, and Ryder quickly put a plastic tie around the man's wrists. Lexi needed to be able to knock out someone like that who was out to do her harm.

Ryder got a text and responded to it. Then he returned to where Lexi and the others were. "A couple of men are coming for this guy. They picked up two others, and they'll turn them over to the police."

"Just how many bodyguards do you have?" Don asked Lexi.

"More than enough to escort you back to your car," Ryder said.

Unlike the thug Ryder took down, the two men who approached them were cautious and quiet, and if the wolves didn't have such excellent hearing, they wouldn't have known they were approaching.

"Hey, Edward," Ryder said to one of the men. "We got the other one, and from the smell of his gun, he's the one who fired the shot. Can you escort Don back to his car too?"

"Yeah, sure thing." Edward and the other man who worked with him got the thug to his feet, confiscated his gun, and motioned with their heads to Don to come with them.

Don glanced at Lexi as if he was waiting for her to tell him he could stay with them, and she motioned to the other guys. "Go on. If we run into any more trouble, I don't want to worry about your safety too."

"Hell, if Ryder hadn't taken down that guy so quickly, I fully intended to protect you." Don brushed off his clothes. "Gotta be Special Forces." Then he said to Ryder, "Right?"

Ryder said, "Keep yourself out of trouble. We don't want to be the ones reading about *you* in the tabloids."

Don snorted. "That would be the day."

Lexi thought Ryder was right.

"Oh," Edward added as he and the others began walking back down the trail, "others are up here watching your back. Just in case. You shouldn't have any more trouble. The guy that shot at you was aiming for Don, according to his buddies. He figured if they didn't take him out, *they'd* be in all the tabloids."

Lexi appreciated Ryder for not asking if she wanted to continue with the hike as if she was too rattled to go on. "Do you think the other guy was really shooting at Don?"

"Yeah, I do," Ryder said.

"Maybe Don will heed our warning next time," Lexi said, climbing to the top of the cliff to see the waterfall.

"I doubt it," Kate said. "That guy can't stay away from causing or finding trouble."

Without any further issues, they finished their hike and returned to the cabin. They washed up and began making dinner—spaghetti and meatballs, garlic toast, and salad, while Ryder served glasses of wine and they discussed the movie they'd seen earlier. "I loved how the aliens turned out to be the good guys." Kate sprinkled garlic salt on the buttered bread before she put it in the oven.

"Yeah, they reminded me of us. We're the good guys, but I suspect if anyone learned about us, they'd think *we* were the aliens." Lexi added mushrooms and tomatoes to the salad.

"Speaking of wolves, you promised a story about the bad guy who was after you that ended up dead," Ryder said.

"Uh, yeah, nice bedtime story. Are you sure you want to hear it?" Lexi set the bowl of salad on the table.

"Yes!" everyone said.

"Bloodthirsty wolves." Lexi meant it in a loving way. She set her wineglass on the table. "Okay, so as soon as my dad was put in the Witness Protection Program, I was on my own, by my choice.

"Tremaine sent a hit man to my house, and he managed to disable my alarms and intended to torture me to learn where my father was in hiding. I had no idea where my father was, and I wasn't going to let the hitman get the drop on me. Thankfully, with our wolf hearing, I heard him moving as quietly as he could toward my bedroom. It was two in the morning, and I stripped off my nightshirt and shifted. I waited for him to open the door to my bedroom."

Kate put the garlic bread on a platter and set it on the table. "I was not her bodyguard at the time, or I would have stopped him before he reached her door."

"Right. I hadn't looked into getting a bodyguard at the time. I knew the risk, but I was so busy with my business, all I thought of was getting a personal assistant, and that was something I had planned to do within the next couple of weeks. So it wasn't Kate's fault."

Mike served up the spaghetti and meatballs, and Ryder brought over the bottle of wine.

"He wouldn't have gotten past me either." Ryder took his seat at the table.

Mike did too. "Me either."

Lexi sighed. "Well, you weren't there." She forked up some of her spaghetti. "The hit man came into the room. I attacked and killed him. I was angry that he'd disabled my security system and broken into my home, furious he was planning to torture me—I found his torture kit at the front door where he'd let himself in—and livid that he'd forced me to kill him. I'm all about helping others out in a crisis.

Not killing someone. Once I shifted back, I was sort of in shock, upset over everything, not sure what to do. I'd only just met Rafe when he'd invited me to one of his socials, glad to meet another billionaire wolf and take me into the fold. Now I had to call him and tell him I'd murdered a man?"

"You did it in self-defense." Kate slipped another piece of garlic bread onto her plate.

"Knowing that didn't make me feel any better. Of course Rafe was furious that the hit man got into my home in the first place and that I didn't have an army of bodyguards at my disposal."

"That sounds like Rafe," Ryder said. "He's a big fan of having bodyguards."

"I really didn't think they'd come after me. Rafe gave me a list of names of wolves he trusted who could be my personal protection, but I wanted someone who could be my personal assistant too."

"Me," Kate said. "Only I would do."

Lexi smiled at her. "You were perfect for the job. So Rafe had his men clean up the place, put up new and better security devices, and while that was going on, he took me out on the yacht to help me get over the trauma."

"Did it help?" Ryder asked.

"I got seasick."

They all laughed.

Lexi smiled. "But yeah, it helped me forget as I was heaving my lunch into the toilet. Kate hasn't been on his yacht yet, but it's beautiful."

"You haven't had any other trouble since then?" Ryder asked.

"I had more trouble after that. When Tremaine couldn't get ahold of his hit man, he sent two men the next time. Except they didn't try to get into my home that time, or I would have been alerted. When I reached the road from my long driveway, intending to go into town to grocery shop, a pickup truck hit me from behind and rammed my car into a pine tree. Remember, they didn't want to kill me. They wanted to learn where my father was. Then they would have killed me."

"Ohmigod, Lexi. You didn't tell me how much trouble you'd had all on your own. How did you manage to get yourself out of that one?" Kate asked.

"Luck. Two of my neighbors were headed into town and came upon the wreck. I was afraid the hit men would kill them and still try to get me out of my car, but my doors were jammed, and they couldn't get to me, so they drove off. Lucky for me. One of my neighbors called in the truck's license plate number, and the police picked them up and found all kinds of guns and torture tools in the cab. They tied their own nooses. Tremaine had the men murdered while they awaited trial."

"Good," Kate said.

"Right. I was really lucky that time. Then Tremaine left me alone. He was having other trouble about then. It was in the news that one of his lieutenants was trying to take over his operation and eliminate him."

"Too bad that didn't happen." Ryder dished up more spaghetti.

"Tremaine still had too tight a hold on things. He got rid of the lieutenant and a couple of the men who sided with him. Tremaine was really busy for a while, but then I noticed men following me. And Rafe told me he was having men watch me, to protect me until I hired someone. I think he was afraid I would object, but he didn't want me dead. I appreciated him for doing that."

"Then you hired me, and I protected you." Kate scarfed up another piece of garlic bread.

Lexi laughed. "Yes, and then I hired you. We haven't had any trouble until we were here, but I think the men were told to just watch me to see if my father showed up. Then here are Ryder, Don, Mike, and Edward and his men. Tremaine can't win for losing."

"We want to keep it that way," Ryder said, his tone of voice dark and serious. "How are you feeling about seeing your dad?"

"Anxious." Lexi sipped some more wine. "What if, despite all the extra muscle here, things get out of hand and my father is put at risk?"

"If you'd been here just with Kate, it could have been worse," Ryder said.

"What are we going to do about Don?" Lexi didn't want him to be at risk either.

"Edward's got some men over at his hotel, and they're watching to see if he leaves. If he does, they'll tie him up so he can't come here and get himself into more trouble," Ryder said. "We have about three hours to go before it's time to see your dad. I think we should get some rest. No telling how crazy it's going to get."

Lexi agreed, though she knew she wasn't going to be able to to sleep.

~~~

Stretched out on the sofa bed, Ryder was trying to rest up before they saw Lexi's dad, thinking over what Lexi had told him about killing the hit man. He knew what it was like to eliminate someone for self-preservation and how it could continue to haunt him. He was glad she'd at least had Rafe to confide in and that he'd taken her on a cruise to help her deal with it. Ryder wished he'd known her then and had been there to protect her instead. Now that Kate was her bodyguard, it made him wonder if she had ever had to kill anyone.

"Hey," Mike said, sitting on the edge of the sofa bed, tense like Ryder was. "I'm sure this will all work out tonight."

Ryder sure the hell hoped so. "Well, we'll have to make sure it does."

CHAPTER 15

IT WAS NEARLY ELEVEN WHEN EDWARD CALLED RYDER. "I suspect you're heading over to the cabin soon. The thugs are sound asleep, courtesy of a tranquilizer. They won't be waking up until late tomorrow morning. We've got a man babysitting them just in case, and the rest of us are set up at different locations to watch for any other sign of trouble. We left Don's camera and equipment under one of the beds. We'll report the men to the authorities once we know Lexi has visited her dad and he's safely away. We've been monitoring her dad's cabin, too, but we haven't seen any sign of him," Edward said.

"Okay. We're headed over there now, and we'll wait for him." Ryder glanced at Lexi, who was wringing her hands, frowning. He prayed her father would make it okay and everyone would be safe.

Lexi took a deep breath and let it out. He hated to see how anxious she was. He didn't blame her. Between worrying that something might go wrong and her father could be killed, or that the U.S. Marshals learned he was seeing her and they'd kick him out of the program, she had a lot on her plate. But he thought he could help settle her father with a pack that could look out for him, better than just changing his identity and where he lived. Then Lexi could see her father, as long as they took precautions not to alert Tremaine's men.

"Let us know how it goes," Edward said, though Ryder

assumed he would be on point the whole time and have some idea of what had transpired while it was happening.

"Will do." Ryder ended the call and was ready to escort Lexi to her dad's cabin, but she held up her hand and shook her head.

"I'm going to do this on my own. None of you are supposed to know anything about this."

"No way," Kate said. "If Tremaine sent other men we're unaware of, particularly since you 'hired' other men to protect you, they may hit you and your father as soon as you reach his cabin. You're not going alone."

"Kate's correct. We can't risk you and your dad's safety by letting you do this on your own. We can keep out of sight," Mike said. "But we'll be watching your back closely."

"I'm going in with you, just in case." Once Ryder learned she'd intended to meet with her dad who was on a hit list, he'd planned to stick to her through the whole ordeal.

"You weren't supposed to know about any of this. Kate either. It was supposed to be strictly on me," Lexi said, tears in her eyes.

"We're not letting you risk your life unnecessarily, and we'll keep your father safe too." Ryder wasn't backing down on this. He ran his hand over her arm, hoping she wouldn't be annoyed with the intimacy. He wanted to pull her into a hug and hold her tight, to know for now she was perfectly safe. Who knew how it would go down when she headed for the cabin? After she met with her father, Ryder wanted to send some men with him to wherever he lived to ensure he wasn't followed. Then Ryder proposed something he'd been thinking about ever since he'd learned her dad was in witness protection. "Listen, what if your father joined a wolf pack? I believe he would be safer."

"But the people he joined wouldn't be. And why would they want to take him in when he could bring danger to the pack?" Lexi asked.

"He's a wolf who did a good deed—putting a murdering bastard behind bars. I can name half a dozen packs that he could join, and he'd find good protection. Two packs in Colorado, one in Montana, our pack here, to name a few. We've got a number of bodyguards between Rafe and Aidan, and more to call on. Your dad was in San Antonio when he was a witness to the crime, living and working there as a family physician, right?"

"Yes."

"All right. You couldn't go there, since Tremaine may believe your dad would return there. He could join us, but you live here. They'd make the connection too quickly. Then Colorado or Montana, where he hasn't lived before, would be the best choice, right?"

"True. But he's never belonged to a pack. I don't know if he'd want to do so now or put others at risk." Lexi was frowning, not appearing to believe it would work. Then she stiffened her back. "We need to go. Now. Before my father leaves because he doesn't think we'll get there in time."

"He's not there yet, according to Edward."

Her face paled a little. "All right, let's go, and we'll wait for him."

Ryder was concerned too. What if Tremaine's men had intercepted her father on the way here already? And he wasn't ever coming? What if C3 didn't mean Cabin 3?

They walked out of the cabin, and Mike and Kate split off from them. Ryder took hold of Lexi's hand as if he were strolling with her through the woods. The moon was covered in fog, making it appear spooky. The shadows of the trees wavered across the forest floor, the cabin lights on, as if they were still at home. He knew some of the team members would be hidden in the woods, safeguarding them, but he saw no sign of them.

The cabin where they thought her father was supposed to meet them was dark and unwelcoming. She knocked on the door, but there was no answer. "It's me, Lexi, and my boyfriend."

Ryder smiled at her, but he suspected her father wasn't here yet.

Then her phone rang, startling her, and she answered it. "Hello?"

He hoped it was her father and he wasn't in trouble.

"Meet me where you found the note. I'm waiting there for you. If you don't come within half an hour, I'll be gone," Lexi's father told her.

She was elated to hear his voice, rough and gruff, warm and familiar. She missed his voice, missed seeing him, and now her heart was already beating a million miles a minute while she rushed off to meet up with her dad at the location. "I'm on my way. I've got bodyguards. They're for our protection." She couldn't wait to see him, still fearful things would go topsy-turvy.

Her dad ended the call, and she hoped he trusted in her instincts and didn't leave before she reached him.

She whispered in Ryder's ear to tell him they had to return to the bear den.

"Are you sure it's him and he's not being coerced?"

"Yes. He's anxious, but he would have warned me if he was putting me in danger."

"All right. I'm letting everyone know what's up. They'll have to spread out and follow us because they won't know the place we're going to." Ryder texted everyone as he and she booked it on the path to the footbridge that would take them to see her dad.

Thankfully, they could see well enough in the dark with their wolf's vision that they didn't need to run around with flashlights and make themselves moving targets, in the event more of Tremaine's men were sneaking through the woods.

Lexi was glad she had all this muscle behind her to help protect her, but she wished she could clue them in on where her father was exactly so they could be there to protect him too. Still, she was certain her father would be armed, and he wouldn't know they were some of the good guys.

She and Ryder finally made it to the bridge, and she heard someone behind them. Guns in hand, she and Ryder whipped around, but she saw it was just Kate and Mike. Lexi let her breath out in relief. If any of the men Rafe had sent were following them, they were staying out of sight. If so, the men were truly good at this game.

Because it was so exposed, she and the others rushed across the bridge and then she and Ryder continued to lead the way on the trail. No one was talking, not wanting to give their positions away in the dark.

Mike and Kate disappeared into the woods. If they tried to go through the underbrush, it would take them longer to get there. Unless they were stripping and shifting into their wolves. That would be perfect. They would be lower profile, and if any of Tremaine's men were on to Lexi and her father, they wouldn't think wolves were in on this. Plus, if her father saw the wolves, he'd know they were some of Lexi's backup, not Tremaine's hit men.

They continued the long hike to where the bears' den was, and she was glad it hadn't been raining constantly since the last time they were here. Hopefully, more of the rainwater that had flooded the area would have receded by now. The path on this side was above water. Had her father crossed the swollen creek to the other side like they'd had to do to find his note? She imagined so. He'd be more protected from anyone who might have come after him. The bad guys might not be expecting him to cross the creek to avoid them.

When they reached the area across from where the empty bear den was, she and Ryder made their way across, hand in hand, which she was thankful for because she slipped. He held her steady until she could get her footing. Only a few steps further, and he slipped this time, and she threw her arms around him, holding tight. She would have laughed if they'd just been doing this for fun, but she did smile up at him and he shared a smile. Then they continued on their way, his hand on hers, his grip strong as he kept her from slipping further. He seemed to have better footing the rest of the way. Two wolves suddenly appeared on either side of them, paddling across the creek. She smiled, glad to see them. Kate, and the other wolf she assumed was Mike, would help to convince her father Ryder was a good guy, not a hostage-taker. Her father would know Ryder was a wolf, too, once he could get a whiff of Ryder's scent.

Once they reached the shore, Lexi was about to start walking north to the spot where Ryder had found the note, not seeing any sign of her dad. She was afraid they were too late, and she felt tears pricking her eyes. But then her father poked his head out of the bears' den and crawled out on his hands and knees. Ryder immediately moved forward and grabbed his arm and helped him to stand.

Her father's jeans, blue-and-black-plaid shirt, and hiking boots were muddy. She thought he was going to meet her as a wolf, but he must have changed his mind.

He was as tall as Ryder, six foot, and wearing a dark beard. She'd rarely seen her father wearing a beard, and it took her a minute to adjust to the look. Then he rushed forward at the same time she did, and they hugged. She'd missed his scent, wolf and man, though he also smelled of the woods and earth now.

"These are Ryder Gallagher and Mike Stallings, Aidan Denali's bodyguards. And Kate Hanover, my personal assistant and bodyguard. They're all here to protect me. You know the real estate mogul, Rafe Denali? He sent a Special Forces team too."

"Good. I worried for your safety," her father said.

Not for his own safety. He never worried about that, when he should!

"I have news, which is the only reason I had to contact you, or I wouldn't have put you at risk in such a way," her father said.

"I wanted to see you. No matter what the news was. I had to see you." They were still hugging each other. She couldn't let him go, even though her father seemed to have the same need. "What's the news?"

"Your mother is alive."

"What? No. Where?" Lexi couldn't believe it. After all this time? She felt light-headed, her stomach queasy, and she was glad her father still held her or she might have collapsed, her legs felt so weak. "How did you learn of it? Where has she been?" She was guardedly thrilled. She couldn't truly believe it until she saw her mother and was able to hug her, to know that she was real.

"She's had retrograde amnesia. She couldn't remember what had happened to her, and she couldn't remember her past. She began getting her memories back. She remembered me, but she said she doesn't remember you."

Lexi sobbed against her father. She was glad her mother was alive but devastated she'd lost all her memories of Lexi. "Where is she?"

"She saw the news about my testimony, and that I had died. She contacted the district attorney's office, wanting to know the whole story. After she proved who she was, they told her I was alive, but they couldn't let her see me. When they mentioned you, she said she didn't remember you. She's been living with a man in Brazil all this time, and she started recalling how she was mated to me. She finally made her way back to the States."

"Where is she now?"

"She's back in San Antonio, but I can't go to see her. You need to. You need to bring her home. She's at risk if she stays there and Tremaine learns she's there."

"We'll do it," Ryder said, then looked a little chagrined that he'd said anything without seeing what Lexi wanted to do about it first.

Her father turned to study him for a moment. "Yes, you'll do. As Aidan's bodyguard, I know you'll do right by Lexi."

"Mom has to see you," Lexi said, still holding her father tight. "She needs to see you. Not just me. Especially when she doesn't even know me."

"She can't be with me. Not when her memory comes and goes. She could put us all at risk."

Lexi couldn't believe that. Yet, maybe he was right. It didn't change the fact her mother and father needed to be together. "Okay, then you get out of the Witness Protection

Program. You and Mom join a pack. One that will protect you both. Ryder knows of several that could help."

They heard shooting in the woods and men shouting.

"I've got to go," her father said, pulling away from Lexi, but she held on to his hand and wouldn't release him.

Lexi hadn't realized how much seeing her father again would affect her. She didn't want to let go of him. "We can get him out of here, can't we?" Lexi asked Ryder, tears running down her cheeks.

"Yeah," Ryder said, getting on his phone and texting Edward.

"All right. If we can do this safely." Her father waited with Lexi as they crouched down next to the wolves, making for less of a target.

Ryder soon joined them, crouching down beside Lexi. "Okay, Tremaine sent a handful of men to learn what was going on, most likely assuming that with all the men we have here, you must be meeting with your dad. Edward said they killed one of the men, but they're trained survivalists, and the rest have scattered. We need to get you both out of here safely now."

"But how?" Lexi asked, her voice low. She was desperate to get her father out.

"We need to go another direction, back up to the place where we hiked earlier. They'll pick us up at the campground there. They'll pack up our things, but they're taking us to the airport and Rafe has a helicopter standing by. Let's go," Ryder said. "Our vehicles will be driven back home."

"What about our car? It's a rental," Lexi said. "We flew here."

"The guys will turn it in for you."

"The campground is a long way to hike," Lexi said, given their current circumstances.

"Not as wolves. The men will get our stuff once they take care of the loose ends. We can leave everything in the bear den. I'm taking my cell phone with me."

"Like a wolf with a bone," Lexi said. "Me too."

"Exactly."

The three of them stripped off their clothes, and then Lexi and her father shifted into their wolves and Ryder tucked their clothes in the bears' den, then shifted. He led the way in a different direction, and the rest of them followed him up another way to the campground.

If they'd walked as wolves, it would have taken about two hours. But they were in a hurry, so they reached it within an hour. This part was tricky. They were still wolves and had no clothes. She hoped the campers at the campground were all asleep—they should be, as it was three in the morning. Then she saw three men dressed in paramilitary uniforms heading into the woods with backpacks. She hoped they were Rafe's men and had clothes for them. Lexi and the others moved around quietly as wolves.

A few people were sleeping in their vehicles in the parking lot, having come in too late and being unable to sign in to get a camping space for the night. Two of them lifted their heads to see what was going on.

Rafe's men had brought some of Lexi's and her companions' clothes from the cabin. They quickly shifted and changed and then moved quietly toward the parking lot to a waiting Humvee. There, they loaded into it, and two of the men went with them.

"I'm Edward," the blond-haired, bearded man said, his blue eyes considering them as he inclined his head to Lexi and her father.

"Thank you for coming to our aid. Where are we going from here? I need to get to San Antonio," Lexi said.

"We're going to the Crescent City Airport first. What does the good doctor want to do?" Edward asked.

Lexi glanced at her father to see what he would say.

"I want to see Adelaide. My wife. My mate. She's in San Antonio. Can you guarantee a pack can protect us?"

"No one can guarantee that, not the U.S. Marshals either, but at least you can be a wolf. You can be with our own people," Edward said.

"But we'll put others at risk," her father said.

"Other wolves could use your expertise. Wolves can always use wolf doctors in their packs," Ryder said. "You could at least give it a try. Especially if the government won't let you be with your mate. If she lived with Lexi, Tremaine might learn she was your wife. If she was to live with a pack without you, then all three of you would be apart."

Lexi's father nodded. "I'd have to find a pack willing to take us in."

"There's a pack in Montana. It's run by a couple of Navy SEALs. They do have a doctor, but they could always use another. There's a pack in Silver Town, Colorado, that runs the town. They have a doctor and a clinic, and also a whole sheriff's department," Ryder said.

Her father's eyes widened.

"The whole pack would protect you. They watch for humans who could cause trouble. It's a ski resort town, used to be a silver mining town. But all the businesses are run by wolves," Edward said.

Her father rubbed his beard in thought. "Do you have any way for me to contact the leader?"

"Yeah." Ryder handed over his phone. "You can call Lelandi

or her mate, Darien Silver. See what they have to say about the situation."

"Thanks." Her father took the phone from Ryder, then called the contact number for the Silvers. "Hi, I'm Kurt Summerfield, a wolf doctor who's in the Witness Protection Program, and they won't take my mate into the program. I'm on my way to collect her in San Antonio. Ryder Gallagher said you might be able to take us in. But we don't want to cause your pack any trouble." He smiled. "Yes, a family physician, and my wife is a pediatrician. But she was in a bad accident and has suffered from retrograde amnesia. She remembers me, but not our daughter… Thank you. We'll come see you as soon as we can. Thank you." Her father was smiling when he handed the phone to Ryder. "Thanks. They said we'd be welcome. We'll have to see. It might not work out, but we'll give it a shot." Her father took a deep breath. "What about you, Lexi?"

"I'll visit anytime that I can, but I'll have to be discreet. Maybe I'll take up skiing."

Kate sighed. "I don't ski either. I'll have to come with you, and we'll stick to the bunny slopes. But maybe we'll get lucky and catch a couple of cute ski instructors."

Lexi chuckled, but then she glanced at Ryder to see his take on it and he quickly said, "No need. I can teach you how to ski."

"Sounds like he's a man for all seasons," her father said.

She was thinking the same thing as she smiled at Ryder, his ears tinging a bit red.

Now they just had to reach her mother before Tremaine's men did.

CHAPTER 16

SUSPECTING THEY HAD A TAIL ON THE WAY TO THE airport, Lexi said, "Do you see—"

"Someone's following us." Edward called one of his men on his cell phone and said, "Hey, I believe we've got a tail. If you can intercept him, that would be great."

The black SUV behind them sped up to reach them, but another car, a little yellow Bug, tried to pass him.

"Hell, that's Don's car," Ryder said.

"I hope he didn't discover my father is with me." Lexi was annoyed with the paparazzo. There was no such thing as just being friends with the guy.

"He's making a bad move," Edward said. "If Tremaine's thugs are driving the SUV, they're sure to believe he's pulling up alongside them to take them out."

"We've got to do something then." Lexi didn't like that Don was still trying to get a news story out of this, but she didn't want Tremaine's men injuring him or worse.

"Slam on your brakes," Edward told the driver. "Everyone brace for impact. If this goes sideways, we might not reach the airport on schedule."

"If they're Tremaine's men, we might not anyway," Lexi said.

Ryder reached over and held Lexi's hand. She took a deep breath and glanced at him. He was frowning, a gun in his right hand, ready for whatever came next. Shots were fired at Don's car, and he swerved into the SUV. A Bug against an SUV didn't stand a chance.

The driver of the SUV was so busy concentrating on Don that he didn't have time to react when Lexi's driver slammed on his brakes and the SUV rammed into the back of the van. Both vehicles stopped, and the Bug caught fire. Edward grabbed a fire extinguisher from the van. Mike and Ryder and the other men jumped out of the van to assist.

"Stay with Lexi and Dr. Summerfield," Ryder said to Kate, then hurried after the others. He just hoped no more of these guys showed up.

He and Mike and the driver made their way to the SUV, while Edward put out the fire in Don's car. Ryder and the others had to ensure the thugs didn't come out shooting, so that was their priority—taking them into custody and calling the police.

Ryder tried the driver's door, but it was locked.

"They've got bulletproof windows," Mike said. "Look at the thick black frame around the dark windows."

"Fine. We'll wait for the police to get here and arrest them then." Ryder called the police and told them the situation. While Mike and the other man helping them kept an eye on the SUV, Ryder stalked off to assist Edward in opening one of the Bug's car doors.

Both were putting their backs into it, trying to open the jammed driver's door to reach Don. As soon as they tore it open with a crunch, Ryder and Edward pulled Don from the smoke-filled car.

"Told you it was dangerous messing with this bunch," Ryder said, while Don was coughing his lungs out from smoke inhalation. They moved him to an area away from the smoke still billowing out of the car's engine where he could breathe in the clean air. "The police and an ambulance are on their way. Just keep taking deep breaths of the fresh air and lie still." Ryder pulled off his T-shirt and rolled it up so Don had a pillow for his head.

Don's skin was a little gray and his dark eyes red from the smoke. He opened his mouth to say something, but all he could do was cough some more. Ryder thought that was the first time Don couldn't have the last say.

Ryder glanced at the van and saw both Kate and Lexi peering out the back window. "I'll be right back," he told Don and Edward.

"Not going anywhere," Don said, his voice hoarse and he coughed again.

Ryder opened the van door. "Hey, as soon as the police and EMTs are here, we're heading to where we were going until all this happened."

"Can we see Don?" Lexi handed Ryder a blanket from the van.

"No. We can't get the thugs to open their door, so we can't confine them. If they suddenly come out shooting, I don't want you at risk."

"I should tend to the man," the doc said.

"There's nothing you can do, short of giving him some oxygen. He's fine." Ryder thought he heard the faint sound of sirens in the distance. "Sounds like everyone's on their way. We don't want Don to see you in any event, and the same thing goes for you as far as Tremaine's men coming out shooting. Particularly since you're their real target." Ryder took the blanket from Lexi. "Thanks." Then he took it to where Don was lying down, and Ryder and Edward moved him on top of it. "Courtesy of Lexi," Ryder said. "She wanted to check on you, but we couldn't risk it because the other guys are holed up in the SUV and still armed. What the hell possessed you to try to take out Tremaine's men?" Ryder assumed Don was just trying to pass the other vehicle to make sure he didn't lose the van. He probably hadn't realized Tremaine's men were in that car, unless he had a death wish.

Don gave him a big smile, then had another hacking cough.

Ryder smiled back and patted his arm. "Hang in there, man. The troops are on their way."

As soon as the police verified who everyone was, they took Don away in an ambulance, but not before he pulled the oxygen mask off his face and thanked Ryder and the others for saving his ass. "I owe you, man."

"Do right by Lexi," Ryder said, "and we'll be even." He shook Don's hand, and then he left with the others. Tremaine's men had a standoff going with the police, but law enforcement didn't want Edward and the others to help out. At least Ryder and the others hadn't been involved in a shoot-out, so they were able to keep their guns after showing the police they had licenses to carry.

"Is Don going to be all right?" Lexi asked.

"Yeah. We can call him later to see how he's doing."

"The question is, did he see my father and was that why he was trying to catch up to us?"

"I don't know, but I suspect he thought he was going to have a story one way or another. Tremaine's men might have figured you were meeting with your dad or that he was already with you. They weren't the two men our guys knocked out with tranquilizers at the cabin."

"Were they injured?" Lexi asked.

"The driver had blood on his forehead. The passenger had a bloodied nose."

"But they still wouldn't leave the vehicle."

"No. I'm sure they know they're going to jail, and they're waiting out the inevitable. They're only making it worse for themselves. Maybe they thought we'd kill them if they exited the vehicle. I don't know. Anyway, the police have control of the situation now, and though I didn't want Don injured, now he's off our backs. He won't know where we went." Ryder squeezed Lexi's hand.

"That's good."

They kept watching for anyone else to follow them, but they didn't see anyone, and they were glad for that. They finally reached the airport and headed for the helicopter and boarded it. None of them had any luggage, but at least onboard there were bottles of water for everyone. Glad they were going to be on their way and away from the trouble here, they settled down to sleep for the four-hour flight to San Antonio, including a refueling stop along the way.

$$\sim$$

They were so exhausted, they didn't wake until they landed at the airport in San Antonio. There, they took a van to the hotel where Lexi's mother was staying. Lexi was apprehensive, worried her mother truly wouldn't recognize her. Trying to get her mind off it, she asked her father, "What was your job when you were in the Witness Protection Program, Dad?"

"Well, you know how much I love to bake, so I went to work at a bakery." Kurt patted his stomach. "Gained a few pounds too."

"And a beard. I almost didn't recognize you."

"There's some advantage to not having to shave, but in the summer, it's hot."

She smiled at her father.

They parked at the hotel and everyone got out.

Edward escorted them to Adelaide's room. "We'll stay at the hotel until our reinforcements arrive, and then we'll take all of you to the airport."

Lexi was hoping they could just get her mother and leave, feeling the only safe place for her parents was in Silver Town right now. But Edward knew better how to manage their safety, so she just agreed.

As soon as Lexi's father knocked on the hotel room door, her mother answered it looking just like she had before she left for Brazil, her dark hair tied back into a ponytail, except that her green eyes were now filled with tears. Her father hurried to embrace her mother, and she hugged him back. "Once I remembered who I was and that you were my mate, Kurt, I missed you so. It took me a while to make it back here though."

"Momma?" Lexi hoped her mother would recognize her, too, but she didn't want to upset her by hugging her if she didn't remember who she was.

"I don't know who you are," her mother said, but Lexi knew by the way her mother's voice hitched that she was telling a story.

Why? Because her mother was afraid if she let on that she knew her, Lexi would be more at risk?

Her mother glanced at Kate, and Lexi said, "This is Kate, my personal assistant and bodyguard. I hired her soon after I was living in California—"

"California?"

"Yes, and after Dad witnessed Joe Tremaine murder the DA."

Her mother looked at Ryder, Mike, and Edward and

two other men on the team who were setting up perimeter watch. She probably hadn't ever met them before. "Who are *you*?" she asked the men.

"Protection, ma'am. This is Mike Stallings," Ryder said, motioning to his partner. "I'm Ryder Gallagher. We work for Dr. Aidan Denali as his bodyguards, and Edward and his men work for Rafe Denali. But for now, we're here for you, your mate, and Lexi. I ran into Lexi and Kate at Redwoods National Park while I was vacationing there. Let's move this inside, okay?"

"Is that how you knew about Lexi and me meeting?" Kurt led his wife back into the hotel room.

"Yeah. Not at first. Not until some of Tremaine's men started causing trouble for her. Not to mention Don Morgan was there," Ryder said.

"The paparazzo?" her mother asked. "Did he know about Kurt?"

"No, he didn't know Kurt was coming to see Lexi," Ryder said.

"Don was after me. Mom, you don't remember me?" Lexi asked, shutting and locking the door.

Her mom looked at Kurt, as if she was waiting for him to tell her it was okay to speak the truth.

"They're after Lexi, too, watching to see if she tries to meet up with me. If you recognize her, let her know, Adelaide," her father gently said.

"Mom, you're denying you know me because the man who is after Dad will come after me too? I didn't go into the Witness Protection Program. I couldn't because I didn't want to give up my business. It's too successful now. I would have had to give it all up. And I couldn't. It's something I always dreamed of having."

"How is it going?" her mother asked, reaching out to hug Lexi.

Lexi smiled and hugged her mom. "Basically, I'm a billionaire. I couldn't have done it without your and Dad's support."

Outside the room, Edward and his men continued to keep an eye out for trouble.

"You've really made that much?" Her mom put her hand over her heart and let out her breath. "You can support your father and me now."

Lexi laughed. "I would, too, if Dad would let me."

"I'm so proud of you. After all the fretting and thinking you couldn't do it, I knew you could," her mother said.

"I did have my doubts, you're right." Lexi glanced at Ryder. He was smiling at her. She hadn't wanted him to know how stressed out she'd been to make this work.

Her mother sat down on a chair, and Lexi wondered about the ordeal she'd gone through to return here, and about the memory loss. But she was thrilled her mother recalled who she was.

"What happened?" Lexi asked. "We were devastated when we received word that you had to have drowned. We always held out hope that you hadn't, and Dad and I were there for weeks talking to people and looking for you. We hired more people to search for you, but we couldn't find any leads. It was as if the Amazon River had swallowed you up and you were gone." Lexi sat on the edge of the bed.

Her dad sat on a chair next to her mother, a small table between them. Kate sat on the bed with Lexi. Ryder and Mike stood nearby and waited to hear her mother's story.

Her expression weary, her mother slumped in the chair. "I nearly died in the river. A man rescued me downstream from the accident, but I didn't remember who I was or where I was from at the time. He was a good man, but he wanted me to stay with him to take the place of his wife who had died the year before. When I began to regain my memories, I remembered I had a mate and a grown daughter. I knew I was a wolf, but I couldn't shift. I'm sure it had all to do with the head trauma. Still, it was better than shifting and not being able to return to my human form or shifting at the wrong time.

"I couldn't remember what had happened. Only bits and pieces. Then I remembered flying to Brazil, taking care of the sick Mexican wolf pup shifters, and living with a pack there for two months. I recall the pack's children recovering from their illness and then leaving when they were well again. I don't remember anything about the bridge or the car plunging into the river. I only recollect being pulled onto the shore, soaking wet, and there was no bridge in sight. No matter how hard I tried, I couldn't even dredge up my name or where I was from or why I was in the water."

"The authorities said they couldn't find your body or the passengers from the other car that fell from the bridge. But everyone on the ferry survived," Lexi said, her father holding her mother's hand, giving her comfort.

"I...I don't remember anything about that."

"The man who rescued you had to have assumed you had family. That your car was one of the ones that had crashed into the river when the bridge collapsed," Lexi said, irate. "Why didn't he call the authorities? For a year we thought you were dead."

"I believe he needed me in his life. He thought I was an angel sent to him to bring him out of his depression. It took me a long time to figure out I wasn't his wife, that I didn't belong there. Because of being a wolf, I was confused about having a human husband. At least I remembered being a wolf."

Lexi couldn't believe that the man who had rescued her mother had lied to her. What a horrible thing he'd done to all of them—her mother, father, Lexi, and everyone in her mother's life. Lexi glanced at her dad, hoping he wouldn't be upset with her mom for being with another man for the past year when wolves mated for life and stayed true to their mates. But her dad patted her mother's hand comfortingly. Her mother smiled at him.

"How did you get away?" Lexi asked.

"We heard a Jeep pulling up to his house a few days ago. Smelling of rampant fear, Miguel urgently told me to hide in the jungle. I worried about him and wanted to stay, but he forced me out of the house, telling me these men were dangerous. As much as he feared them, I assumed they had to be. They knew him, and from the heated conversation they were having with him, he owed them a lot of money. Four men entered the house and the shouting began. 'Pay me what you owe Tremaine, Miguel. He ordered us to kill you if you don't pay up this time,' one of the men said. 'I don't have it,' Miguel said. 'Hey, Miguel, we know your wife died and you took a new wife, but we heard she's an American. She wouldn't be the woman missing from the bridge accident, would she? Adelaide Summerfield?'

"I nearly died when I heard them mention my name. It was as if an electrical shock forced the memories to flood back through my mind—who I was, who I was married to, why I'd been in Brazil. The men were so vile. I was confused. I knew who Tremaine was. Your father had saved his godson's life when he'd had an asthma attack. I wondered if his men wanted to rescue me then. I felt numb that Miguel had lied to me all that time. I understood the grief he'd been through, but he'd helped to cause more grief for us as a family.

"I heard Miguel praying, and they said prayer wasn't going to get him out of this. 'If you hand her over, Tremaine can use her for leverage and will forgive your debts.'"

"The bastard," Lexi's father said.

"I agree. I couldn't understand how I could be used for leverage. I was afraid Miguel would give me up. But he didn't. 'Last chance,' the man said. I knew they were going to kill Miguel whether he told them I was there or not. If I could have, I would have stripped off my clothes and shifted and attacked them, but I hadn't been able to shift since the accident. Then shots were fired. One. Two. Three. I felt terrible, because even though I knew Miguel had kept me at the house under false pretenses, he had saved my life, and he had been kind to me. He had taken care of me until he died. The men began ransacking the house, but then they got into the Jeep and tore off.

"Relieved they were gone, I was still afraid they might come back to search for me. It was nearly dark outside by then, and I went inside to see to Miguel, in case there was any chance I could save his life. He had died of the gunshot wounds. I grabbed a backpack, food and water, and lifted the floorboards underneath a rug to get the money he had hidden in his house."

"That was the money those men wanted?" Lexi asked.

"Probably. He could have told them the money was there, but I suspect he knew they would have killed him anyway. He could have told them I was there, too, but he kept silent.

"Miguel didn't have a vehicle, so he walked everywhere. And he didn't have a phone. I walked as fast as I could to the nearest village, found a café, and asked the people there if anyone could contact the leaders of the pack where I'd nursed several of the children back to health. Of course, these people didn't know they were wolves, though I'd heard rumors from some of those living in the region that they knew wolf shifters were real."

"Oh wow. But then anyone who heard them talk about it probably figured wolves were just legend and myths, don't you imagine?" Lexi asked.

"Yes, for visitors to the area, I'm sure of it. Some of the locals believe it's real."

"So you got ahold of the pack?" her dad asked.

"Yes. I had Miguel's money, but I needed a passport to leave the country. The pack members were thrilled to learn I hadn't drowned, but horrified Miguel had kept me hostage. They helped me get a passport and an airline ticket to San Antonio, the last place I remembered I'd lived with you, Kurt. But then I learned all about the trouble you were in with Joe Tremaine. I can't believe that after you saved his godson's life, he ordered your death."

"It didn't matter. To him, I was only doing my job when I saved his godson, but when I testified against him and sent him to prison, that's all it took to turn him against me. I had to do it. I've gone over it in my mind a million times, thinking you were dead, and you wouldn't be in any danger, but Lexi was another story. Still, I couldn't let him get away with murder. The district attorney had a family too. And no matter how hard I tried to convince Lexi to stay with me, I couldn't."

"I wouldn't let Dad do anything else," Lexi said. "He

would have to have gone into hiding no matter what. If he hadn't testified against the drug lord, Tremaine would still have been out for his blood, afraid Dad still might testify against him. As for me, I couldn't give up what I had worked so hard to build up. It's taken me years to get to where I am in my business. For the most part, Tremaine has left me alone, though I suspect that's only because he's had men watching every move I make to see if I reconnect with Dad."

"You both did the right thing, and I'm so sorry I couldn't let you know sooner that I was alive," Adelaide said.

Kurt shook his head. "That's not your fault. All that matters is that you *are* alive and well, and you're here with us now."

"I agree. Dad will court you all over again to help you regain any memories you've lost, or at least give you great new ones," Lexi said.

Kurt smiled at Lexi. "I will at that."

"I...I would love that. I remembered working as a doctor at the same hospital where you worked, Kurt, and that's where we ran into each other literally, the first time we met." Adelaide smiled at him. "I was carrying a stack of records, and you knocked them out of my hands and all over the floor."

Lexi had never heard this story before. "Because he was in a hurry to see his patients?" she guessed. He was really dedicated to his patients.

"He was in a hurry to see a wolf girlfriend, and he was late for his date. I was so annoyed with him. He hurried to help me pick up my files, apologizing, but he offered to get me a coffee, then lunch, then dinner. He wouldn't leave me alone after that."

Kurt gave Lexi's mother a wolfish smile.

"What about the wolf girlfriend?" Lexi asked her father, not knowing he'd been dating some other wolf when he'd met her mom.

"She was totally forgotten," her mother said, lifting her chin, her father still smiling.

Lexi loved her mom and dad. They made the perfect mated couple. "Good thing for me."

"I wouldn't have had it any other way," her father said.

"But what do we do now?" Adelaide asked.

"Ryder mentioned that we might do well to join a wolf pack. They convinced me to come with them to pick you up. We haven't lived with one before. Would you consider it?" Kurt asked.

"How that would affect the pack members? What if, in protecting us, some of them are targeted?" Adelaide asked.

"As wolves, we protect our own," Ryder said. "Some of the wolf packs have a lot of muscle. You'd need to meet up with the packs, but a pediatrician and a family practitioner are always welcome. If you moved to the wolf pack in Silver Town, they'd be able to hide your identities because they run the whole town. In other words, you could work there, but they'd keep you off any published lists indicating you are medical personnel. You could change your names again, and you'd have a whole pack to watch your backs. Much better than the Witness Protection Program where your identities are changed and then you are out there on your own and can't continue to work in your trained profession. They do have a good track record of keeping many of their witnesses alive. It just wouldn't be viable if the two of you want to be together on your own."

"Which we do," Kurt said. "I wanted to see how you felt about it, Adelaide, and I've already talked to the Silvers who are the pack leaders of Silver Town, since they have a sheriff's department too. They said we are welcome to join them."

"What about you, Lexi?" her mother asked.

"I've got a business to run, and I'm not leaving it behind." Lexi wasn't giving it up for anything.

Her mother looked at Ryder, as if he was supposed to straighten her out.

He lifted his hands in resignation. "I'd be willing to join Kate in protecting Lexi."

"You said you are working for Aidan Denali now?" her mother asked Ryder.

"Yes, ma'am. But he's got several bodyguards."

"And Ryder's a fantastic cook," Kate said, winking at Lexi.

"I guess if you go, I'll have to be Lexi's bodyguard too," Mike said. "We compete in cooking contests with each other, and Aidan always says he has too many bodyguards now."

"And you could be the pool boys." Kate rubbed her hands together.

Lexi rolled her eyes. She couldn't believe Kate had brought that up in front of the guys and her parents. Then again, she could. Both Mike and Ryder smiled.

"Pool boys, eh?" Ryder asked. "Sounds like that could be interesting."

Her mother's mouth was gaping. Smiling, her father didn't seem surprised.

"So you'll be okay then," her father said to Lexi.

"With three bodyguards, sure. And if we think it's safe enough, I can come and visit you and Mom when you live with a pack. But you can't visit me."

"Agreed," both her parents said.

Her parents hugged each other again and looked so happy to be together, Lexi was thrilled.

Suddenly, there was a banging on the hotel door, and Ryder and Mike went to see who it was, their guns readied. "It's Edward," Ryder said, then opened the door.

"We've got to move. Our intel says Tremaine has men headed this way."

Despite how tired everyone was, once they knew Tremaine's men were bearing down on them, everyone perked up, and those with guns had their weapons ready. Everyone hurried to leave the hotel and head down the stairs to the parking lot and the two vans Edward and his men had waiting for them.

"How many of them are there?" Ryder asked Edward.

"They're driving two pickup trucks. We're not sure how many men are involved. Normally, we'd have the Summerfields split up, two in one van, one in the other, but it's up to them," Edward said.

"We stick together," Lexi said. "We'll fight this out as a family."

"Right, we stay together," Kurt said. "We are finally back together as a family."

"We remain together," Adelaide agreed.

The family climbed into one of the vans, and Kate, Ryder, Mike, and Edward joined them. Another man was driving the van.

"Where did you get the intel?" Adelaide asked Edward.

"We planted a bug in the men's cabin in the redwoods, ma'am," Edward said. "We learned they had gotten word you were here, and they have men in the area who are on their way to grab you. They don't know the doc and Lexi are here too. Or that we are."

"Where did you want to go?" Ryder asked Lexi.

"With my parents for now. I want to see the pack in Silver Town. After that, Kate and I will return to California."

"Mike and I will be with you every step of the way. That is, if you're hiring us. I guess we should make sure that really works for you." Ryder smiled at Lexi. "If you're agreeable, we'll be on pool duty too."

Lexi felt her face heat, certain it was crimson.

"You bet," Kate said.

Lexi said, "If you'll cook gourmet meals and model for the line of male skin-care products we're now selling, you're hired."

"Wait, male skin-care products?" Frowning, Mike looked like that additional chore was going way over the line.

"Yeah, you'll do great." Ryder slapped him on the back.

"Hey, if I have to do it, you have to." Mike sounded resigned to his new circumstances.

"Been there, done that," Ryder said.

Mike's eyes widened, looking shocked.

Lexi chuckled.

Her mother smiled. "You did create a skin-care line for men, just like I suggested."

"Yeah, Mom, all your suggestions were great. I'm sure you can continue to advise me from Silver Town. We just need to have a plan on how to do it so no one is the wiser."

"We'll figure out something." Ryder sounded determined to make this work. "As many wolves as there are in the Silver Town pack, and in our own small pack, we'll be able to get messages back and forth between the packs and you. Tremaine and his goons will never know you're corresponding with your parents." He got a call and answered it. Then he smiled. "Yeah, Don. How are you doing? Good.

I'll let Lexi know." He glanced at her. "Yeah, she'll be glad to hear it." He paused. "I'll tell her. Talk later."

"Did he know my father was with us?" Lexi asked.

"No. But he wanted you to know he was only trying to catch up to you and protect you."

She scoffed. "Yeah, right." No way was Don attempting to protect them. In a VW Bug? And he wasn't even armed with a gun!

Ryder squeezed her hand and smiled. Then he frowned. "I was only concerned how he was doing, but I probably shouldn't have answered my phone."

"He doesn't know where we're going."

"Right. And he's staying overnight in the hospital. He wanted you to know he's fine."

"Good. I'm glad to hear it." Even though she felt it was partly her fault he was injured—since Tremaine's men were after her—it was also Don's fault for stalking her. But she was relieved he'd be all right.

Since most of them had only four hours of sleep in the helicopter on the flight to San Antonio that night, Lexi ended up snuggling against Ryder, figuring he'd make a good pillow for the half-hour drive to the airport. He leaned against the window and closed his eyes. Kate and Mike stretched out in the back. Lexi's mother and father cuddled with each other and closed their eyes.

All Lexi could hope and pray for was that her parents made it to the airport and took off in the helicopter before Tremaine's men figured out where they were headed.

CHAPTER 17

WITH THE BAD GUYS TRYING TO CHASE THEM DOWN, Ryder figured the honeymoon wouldn't last long before they'd be in the thick of danger again.

"We're doing evasive maneuvers while a couple of vehicles are headed our way to take them out. We don't want Tremaine's men to know we're taking a private flight to Colorado. Once the family is in Silver Town, they should be well protected," Edward said. "We put out an alert to the police, saying the two vehicles were involved in breaking into a home south of here. We have their license plate numbers and vehicle descriptions. Hopefully, the police will pull them over before Tremaine's men reach us."

Ryder sure the hell hoped so, but the way things were going, he suspected they weren't going to get out of there without some trouble.

They hadn't driven but about fifteen minutes when Edward said, "There's a truck following us. It's not one of our own."

Ryder knew it wouldn't be good.

"What's the plan?" Ryder and Mike asked at the same time.

Edward was in charge of getting them out of there safely, but he was always open to suggestions.

"If we continue on our way to the airport, they're probably going to assume that's where we're headed," Edward said.

"If we go somewhere else, we might never make it there," Mike said.

"Sure we will. We just have to give our other men time to reach us." Edward called in the coordinates to the other members of the team. "Okay, that's even better." He turned to Ryder and Mike. "We're driving to a small heliport that has only a thousand-foot runway—perfect for a helicopter. The other van is heading to the airport to throw these guys off track." Edward got another call. "Good, thanks." He still didn't look happy about the news, but he said, "The police pulled over one of the trucks."

"That's good news," Ryder said, glad at least one of the trucks would be stopped for a while. If all the men were armed, which he was sure they would be, they'd have some explaining to do to the police.

They pulled off on another road. "We're almost there," Edward said, and then he got another call. "Hell, okay." He told the rest of them, "The men they pulled over started a shoot-out with the cops. We told them they were armed and dangerous. They're still having a showdown."

"I hope the cops aren't injured in this," Lexi said.

"They have several more patrol cars on the way," Edward said. "But I agree. At least it shows that we didn't call in a false alarm, and some of the men will most likely serve jail time."

Ryder reached over and squeezed Lexi's cold hand. He was trying to ease her concern, but he knew no amount of reassurance would mean anything until they were safely away.

They finally reached the heliport and parked, and then everyone hurried to get out of the van and into the waiting helicopter.

Edward spoke with the other men, and two of them returned to the van and drove the vehicle off. "They'll also be our decoy. Let's move it."

They all got into the helicopter, which seated seven passengers and the pilot, and were soon airborne for Colorado.

"It'll take us four hours to get there, and we'll need to refuel once on the way," Edward said. "Everyone just get comfortable. Relax. Sleep if you can. We're in the driver's seat."

Everyone was tired, and they all dozed or slept during the flight, waking for the refueling and then sleeping again.

Every time Ryder drifted off, he woke again. All he could think of was getting Lexi's parents safely to the Silver Town pack and making sure they liked it well enough to stay there. Otherwise he would be escorting them to another pack and continuing the process until they found the one they'd be happy with. Then Ryder planned to take Lexi home and prayed she'd be safe in California.

He still couldn't believe she'd really hired him. He hadn't given notice to Aidan yet. He enjoyed working for him and for Holly now. But he really felt this was his new mission, taking care of Lexi. He just hoped it would work out well and he'd truly keep her safe and that more could come of their relationship. Though he was afraid the issue of her being his boss could still be a problem.

Four hours later, they finally landed in the meadow near the woods surrounding the pack leader's estate. Everyone was waking and looking much more refreshed.

"I've notified Lelandi and Darien that we've arrived. They're on their way," Edward said.

They expected to see just Darien and Lelandi, but when everyone exited the helicopter, several vehicles pulled up and parked. Ryder noticed how anxious Lexi and her family were, and Kate too. But Darien and Lelandi hurried to greet them.

"Welcome," Lelandi said, with her arms open wide as she gave each of them, Lexi's family and bodyguards alike, a warm embrace.

Smiling, Darien shook the men's hands and hugged the ladies. "We're happy to have you join our pack," he said to Adelaide and Kurt. "We've got a rental house you can use free of charge until you know what you'd like to do. It's my cousin Sarandon Silver's home, but he's moved out of town to join his wife and her family in another city."

"Thanks so much," Kurt said, Adelaide thanking them too.

Other people left their vehicles and joined them to welcome them.

"I'm Doctor Weber," one of the older men said, shaking Kurt's hand and then his wife's. "I understand you're a family physician and your wife is a pediatrician. I sure hope you will take over the clinic in about a year or so. Then I can retire."

Kurt smiled. "I hadn't expected that, but I'd be happy to work with you until you want to retire."

"I'd be delighted to work there too," Adelaide said.

"We couldn't be happier to have both of you join us at the clinic," Dr. Weber said.

Lexi and Kate were welcomed as well. Ryder and Mike stood back, arms folded across their chests, smiling. Edward and his men were still watching, cautiously aware of their surroundings.

Sheriff Peter Jorgenson introduced himself and his deputies, Trevor Osgood, CJ Silver—Darien's cousin—and Michael Hoffman, a retired army Green Beret. "We also have half of the pack deputized. Everyone will be on the lookout for Tremaine's men. We've all been briefed on him and the crimes he's been involved in. We always keep an eye on people who come and go in Silver Town. It's not like human-run towns where you have so many people coming and going that no one knows who they are. Most of us have been here for eons. Literally."

"That's good to know. Thank you for taking us in," Kurt said, his wife nodding in agreement.

"You're welcome, and you're doing us a big favor in bringing the kind of skills you have to the pack. Come, we want you to have breakfast with us. We have a loaner car for you, and we'll set you up in the house right after we eat," Lelandi said. "That goes for all of you." She motioned to the rest of the party. "I'm sure you want to rest after being up most of the night."

"We managed to get some sleep on a couple of long helicopter rides," Kurt said.

"Okay, that's good," Lelandi said.

They all headed into the house, and Ryder was surprised to see the dining room table was already set and other tables were set up in the living room.

Two more men arrived at the house and said they were Jake and Tom Silver, Darien's brothers, and that they served as subleaders of the pack. Then several of the men pitched in to help cook the breakfast, including Ryder and Mike.

Lexi came over and joined Ryder and smiled at him. "You *are* going to work for me, aren't you?"

"Hell, yeah. I was worried you weren't serious."

"Oh, I'm serious."

"Pool boy, eh?"

"Yeah, and other duties as assigned."

Mike was smiling as he cooked the sausages.

Dr. Weber was talking to Kurt, and Lexi's dad was smiling. "I've never had a practice where I worked on mostly our kind."

"That's one of the real benefits of working here," Dr. Weber said.

Adelaide agreed. "What if the women are in their wolf form when the babies are born?"

"We've delivered them both ways at the clinic. We also have Doctor Mitchell, who is our vet, but he's delivering a colt this morning at his ranch. Otherwise, he would have come to meet you both."

"I'm sure we'll have plenty of time for that," Kurt said.

Lelandi began to talk to Adelaide about all the things going on with the pack. The parties, the holidays, the festivities.

Lexi watched her parents and smiled. Ryder stole a kiss from her, and she smiled up at him. "I think they'll be good here."

"I think so too. There's a world of difference between living in a strictly human world and one where the wolves rule." He rubbed her back. "If they decide they're unhappy here, there are other packs they can join. It's up to them. I'll take them to wherever they'd like to go if this doesn't work out for them. How do you feel about returning to California? Do you feel you'd be safe enough with just Mike, Kate, and me protecting you?"

"Yeah. And I'm not a wilting flower either. I'll watch everyone's backs too."

He smiled down at her. "Yeah, I agree, but we're supposed to be protecting you, primarily. I'm ready to get in some martial arts practice with you when Kate wants to take a break."

Lexi sighed. "Oh, all right. Remember to go easy on me. I'm just learning. When are you going to tell Aidan you're working for me?"

"I'll call him right after we finish our breakfast. I wanted to make sure you were serious about the offer."

"Oh, I'm serious. I don't think Tremaine is going to stop trying to get to my father through me."

"He'll have a fight on his hands if he comes here." Ryder was confident the Silver pack would keep her parents safe.

"I think you're right. I feel comfortable with my parents living here with the pack. Even so, I'm afraid if I try to see them, it could cause trouble for them and everyone else here."

"We'll work out a plan. Tremaine and his men will never learn the truth." Ryder was thinking he needed to destroy Tremaine. That was the only way her family would truly be free. Someone else would take over Tremaine's criminal businesses, but he was the one who had ordered the hit on her dad. No one else. And when other crime lords were taken down, permanently, they were relegated to the annals of the past.

Lexi was thinking Tremaine would never give up in his attempt to murder her father. And now he knew her mother was alive too. If only Lexi could hire a hit man to take Tremaine out! Not a wolf though. It was one thing to have to fight the bad guys when they were out to kill them. Another to kill him in prison when he was defenseless.

"How long did you want to stay here?" Ryder asked Lexi.

"I've got engagements when I return. So I was thinking I need to leave in a couple of days."

"One of your engagements is at Rafe's house."

"Yeah. Instead of you being there to guard Aidan and Holly, you'll be there to guard me. Do you think anyone will have hard feelings about it?"

"Not at all."

Then they all sat down to eat breakfast and talked about the pack fun coming up—a summer festival. Lexi's parents looked delighted to take part in all the activities the pack had. This was so different from their lives the last few months. At least working in a bakery wasn't too trying—her father loved baking and had taken it up as a hobby years earlier. But he loved doctoring people even more.

Lexi knew he would be happy to be back to work, and as old as the red wolf Dr. Weber looked, she suspected he might be ready to retire soon, like he talked about. It could be good for everyone: her parents, the pack, and the doctor. Everyone seemed to enjoy her parents' company, and they seemed to enjoy being with others of their kind.

Lexi was surprised Lelandi was a red wolf too. They were rarer than the gray wolves.

"What about seeing Lexi?" her mother asked.

"We'll make arrangements to get her here without Tremaine knowing she's coming here to see you," Ryder said with surety.

Her parents smiled. "We're so glad you helped us with all of this," her mother said.

Kurt agreed. "We couldn't have done it without you."

"We'll have a pack gathering later this afternoon here.

We have a building where we have large gatherings. That's where you'll meet the rest of the pack," Darien said.

Her mother smiled. "That will be nice."

"In the meantime, Jake will take you to your home and help you get set up. We'll make sure you have everything you need to start out here again," Lelandi said.

"I can pay for anything you need." Lexi didn't want the Silver pack to have to pay for anything. They were doing enough to keep her parents safe and make sure they felt like they were part of the pack.

"We can help out with anything you need too," Lelandi said.

Lexi would help her parents build or buy a home. She had enough money if her father hadn't been able to get to the money in his investments before he went into the Witness Protection Program.

After they ate breakfast, Jake drove her parents and Mike to the rental house, while Tom took Edward, Kate, Lexi, and Ryder there.

The home was sitting in the woods near town, so it was the perfect place for her parents to live for now.

"My cousin and his wife said you can buy the house if you want," Jake said.

"Thanks," Kurt said. "We'll sure consider the possibility."

The house was furnished, and it was just the right size for her parents and for Lexi to visit them when she could. They could run as wolves when they had time off, and they could run with other wolves, which was really nice for them and safer too.

"We'll take you to the grocery store to stock up your kitchen," Jake said.

Lexi thought the world of the Silver pack for doing so much for her parents.

Tom said, "We have a loaner car being delivered that you can use until you can pick up a couple of cars of your own."

Lexi was glad for that because she figured her parents wanted some alone time. But they took them to the grocery store, and picked up items for the bathroom and kitchen, and dropped by a couple of clothing stores to buy some things to wear for the week. Jake was going to pay for everything, but Lexi did instead.

"I do have the money from the sale of the house, thanks to you. I was able to transfer my investments and cash into new accounts," her dad said. "But I'll need it for buying the cars and buying a home."

"Dad, I said I'd help."

"You can, if we get strapped."

Then they returned to the house and found that the loaner mini SUV had been delivered.

Jake said, "All right. We'll see you at the gathering at noon. We'll let you get settled and have a chance to visit with each other. We understand how you just were reunited."

"Thank you." Adelaide gave him a hug. Then she hugged Tom.

The brothers both smiled at them.

Jake said to the others, "Did you want to come with us? Or stay here?"

"Even though I'm sure it's safe here, I'm staying with Lexi," Ryder said. "If she's staying with her parents, I'll need to remain here."

"Me too," Kate said.

"And me," Mike said.

Edward got a call. "Okay, good news. They arrested the men in the two trucks. All five of them had illegal handguns, the serial numbers removed. Three of them had warrants out for their arrest, the other two were on probation, so they're all sitting in jail."

"Tremaine's going to be pissed," Ryder said.

"Yeah, he is. I'll return with you, Jake, to check on my men." Edward went with Jake and Tom, and they left the Summerfields there to visit.

"Will you change your name here?" Lexi asked her parents as she helped them put away the groceries.

"I was going by Hershman, but I think Grayson will work for us." Her father smiled. "We'll fit in with the Silvers that way."

"I can live with the name Grayson," her mother said. "I guess I can't tell the Brazilian pack where I ended up, and I can't return there to help them out if they need it again."

"No," Kurt said. "You would be at too much risk."

Lexi knew her father well. He said it out of concern, not to be controlling. Her mother had to know that if Tremaine's men located her, they could potentially force her to tell them where Kurt was. Then the pack would have to deal with the fallout too.

Her dad was supposed to have died. At least as far as the world knew. Lexi suspected Tremaine must have figured the Witness Protection Program had created the fictional tale and Kurt was still very much alive. But if Tremaine had tried to find her dad working as a doctor anywhere, he wouldn't have located him. Which meant he had to find him by watching Lexi. She hadn't seen any sign of anyone observing her after the first two confrontations she'd had with his men, though she'd always been mindful of it. She hadn't thought she'd see her dad again anyway, but still, she'd been wary, just in case. Ryder was the one who had brought Tremaine's thugs out of hiding, when they confronted him to leave her alone.

She gave her mom a hug again, tears in both their eyes. She still hadn't accepted the fact that her mother was alive. "I still can't believe I'm holding you. I love you."

Her mom hugged her back. "When I remembered you and your dad, I couldn't quit thinking about how I was going to get out of the jungle and return to you both. I couldn't believe the trouble your father had gotten into when I learned he had witnessed the murder and was no longer practicing medicine in San Antonio. That our home was no longer ours. That he was supposed to have died in a bad car accident, and everyone had thought I had died too. I saw you had what looked like a successful online cosmetic business, but I believed that either Tremaine had killed Kurt for putting him in prison or the government had put him in the Witness Protection Program. I was counting on it. And then I learned the truth. He was alive, only they didn't want me to join him for his sake, fearing I would make a mistake and he would be killed. I'm glad we're here instead."

"I am, too, Mom. And you'll be great at taking care of the children of the pack."

"I'm glad we're here too," her father said.

Lexi gave her father another hug. "Dad, I'm so thrilled we can see each other again when we have the time and that you want to be with the pack here. They'll love you, just like your other patients did."

"I'll be glad to be working as a doctor again." Her dad patted his stomach again. "When I was working in the bakery, I was eating a few too many baked goods."

Her mom gave him a hug. "You're just perfect. But we can run it off in no time, if it bothers you."

"Speaking of that, did you want to go for a run as wolves here? Check out the woods?" Lexi knew that was part of the whole business of settling in as wolves. To learn about their surroundings where they could enjoy their other halves.

"Sure. We haven't run in a year as wolves, and I'd love to check out the clinic," her dad said.

"Me too," Adelaide said. "I haven't had the opportunity to shift since I regained my memories, but hopefully I can now."

"We'll see the clinic afterward," Lexi said.

"You're coming with us, right?" Lexi's mom asked the guys and Kate.

"Absolutely," Ryder said.

Her mom and dad went into the master bedroom to strip off their clothes and shift. Lexi and the others stripped and shifted in the living room. She noted the back door had a wolf door, another really nice thing about living in a wolf community. She imagined a lot of the wolves had them, which made it great for coming and going without having to shift again.

As if he was protecting them, Ryder headed out first. She smiled and ran out the door after him, wanting to play with him instead.

CHAPTER 18

THE SUMMERFIELDS AND THEIR BODYGUARDS TOOK off through the woods. Ryder was having second thoughts about working for Lexi as her bodyguard. He wanted to be with her to protect her, but he was afraid he was falling for the wolf, and he sure as hell didn't want others to see him as a fortune hunter. He knew everyone would. Maybe those close to him wouldn't, but he didn't want to be seen as Mr. Summerfield, cosmetic billionaire, gold-digger husband.

It reminded Ryder too much of one of his human friends growing up, whose stepdad worked as a mall security guard, but as soon as he saw the opportunity to marry a woman who was wealthy through her real estate work and investments, he did and quit his job, saying he had to be his wife's personal protection. Which would have been fine if he'd contributed to the marriage somehow, but he hadn't. When a burglar killed her, the husband took off to save his own skin and inherited all the money. Ryder's friend was kicked out of the house because he'd been furious with the stepdad for not protecting his mother, the only job he had.

Ryder swore he'd never take advantage of a woman like that. Still, he felt it was similar, except he wouldn't run off to save his own skin. Yet, what if he lost Lexi because he couldn't protect her well enough?

As soon as he was thinking that, Lexi made the move to rub up against him on the wolf run, and that surprised and pleased him. He returned the affection and rubbed her cheek with his.

He was worried his interest in her could jeopardize her safety, yet he had no control over the way he felt toward her and the way she stirred up his pheromones. It wasn't something that had ever happened between him and another she-wolf, and the feeling was exhilarating and surprising.

Her father and mother were enjoying the time together, playing, biting, licking, and rubbing each other like two young wolves in love. He was glad Adelaide had been able to shift all right, and she looked like she was really enjoying being a wolf again. Lexi looked over at them and smiled in a wolf way. He was as glad as she was that they were together again and had a pack to watch out for them. He was also grateful Lexi wouldn't have to worry about them. They would be in good hands.

Kate and Mike were playing with each other like wolves would who were friends, not in courtship. Switching his attention to Lexi, Ryder nipped at her, and she bit him playfully back. Then she turned and ran off to tackle Kate. Ryder woofed at her, and Mike chased after Ryder.

He and Mike often play-fought, both for fun and for training if they should ever need it for a real wolf fight, which they did on occasion. It looked like Kate and Lexi were doing the same thing. His distraction meant Mike tackled him to the ground. But if Lexi and Kate really wanted to do some good tactical wolf training, the she-wolves needed to pit their tactics against the males.

Ryder woofed at Mike to let him know his plan, and then the two of them took off for the she-wolves. For an instant, the ladies were surprised, their eyes wide to see the two male wolves coming at them. But then they rounded on the guys and had a rousing good time.

They'd played for some time when Kurt and Adelaide joined them and urged them to return to the house. Ryder figured they wanted to see the clinic now, but he appreciated the time he'd spent with the ladies and Mike as wolves.

He hoped the clinic was someplace that Kurt and Adelaide would enjoy working since they would be spending a fair amount of time there. He also hoped he would be comfortable living in Lexi's house as a bodyguard when he wanted to be her lover instead. He wasn't giving her up for anything!

When they returned to the house, they all shifted and dressed, then met in the living room. Everyone looked well pleased to have gone for a run, and Lexi was glad her parents had been so cute and playful and loving toward each other. They needed that—to feel the bond, to feel safe again, to be with each other. She knew she shouldn't be nipping at Ryder as if he was her wolf lover, but she felt such an urge to do it that she couldn't help herself. Maybe it was seeing the way her parents were with each other. Maybe it was because she couldn't quit thinking of the hot wolf, naked in the creek, carrying the bear cub to safety, or remembering the way he kissed her back when she wanted to thank him for finding her father's message.

Maybe it was because she was so relieved her parents were safe and together again that she felt so much more lighthearted and freer to have fun with another wolf. Not just with Kate, but with a male wolf she was wholly interested in.

"Are you sure you don't want to at least stay the night?" her father asked Lexi before they drove over to the clinic to see the facilities.

Before she could answer, Kate reminded her, "Your schedule for your vacation is clear for three more days, if you don't feel we have to get back right away. I could probably borrow someone's laptop to keep up with emails and other business."

"Thanks, Kate. Yeah, Dad. I'd love to stay and visit with you and Mom." But she also wanted them to have their time together alone without Lexi and her three bodyguards imposing on them. Then again, when they left, her parents would have all the time in the world to get reacquainted.

As if someone had heard Kate's comment about the laptop, there was a knock at the door, and when Ryder checked to see who it was, Edward had her laptop and a bag in hand. A couple other team members were carrying more bags. His, Mike's, Lexi's, and Kate's.

"My team gathered all your things right away, but we didn't have time to bring them here until now. The bags were with the other guys," Edward said.

"Thanks, that's just what we all needed." Lexi really did want to visit with her parents a little longer. She didn't know when they could do this again, between her work and theirs and all the trouble with Tremaine. "What do you think, Mom? Did you want to get back to work right away?" She knew her mom loved what she did, so Lexi didn't want to make her feel she had to stay at home and visit with her daughter.

"Heavens no. I mean, I love my work, but after being away from the two of you for so long, I want us to be together. Besides, even if you don't join the pack because you don't want to give up your business, this will give you a chance to meet the people we're going to be living and working with. You'll be a pack member, too, though mostly in absentia. Oh, oh, can you do a makeup party? That would really make a splash. I miss doing those with you."

Lexi smiled. "I would love to."

Kate pointed at a big bag. "Samples galore. We take them with us everywhere. It would be fun. I'll set it all up."

"We all will." Lexi smiled at Ryder and Mike.

They smiled back, nodding.

She was glad she'd hired them. They seemed to be good sports about anything she wanted them to do.

"When did you want to return to California?" Edward asked.

Lexi saw her parents' expectant faces, and she took her mother's hand and squeezed. "Three days from now. I have commitments back home after that."

"Okay, great. We'll come for you then and transport you there," Edward said.

"Thanks so much for everything," Lexi said, and everyone agreed.

Then Edward and his men told them goodbye and left.

"Let's head over to the clinic, and after that, we can visit a while and then go to the pack celebration." Her father put his phone in his pocket. "I've already texted Doc Weber to let him know we're on our way."

They headed over to the clinic, where Dr. Weber came out of an exam room and welcomed them to his domain. He was cheerful and seemed thrilled to be getting some additional wolf staff. Kate and Mike stayed in the lobby that featured a sitting area with a section for kids to play in with a TV, aquarium, and tables for building puzzles. The rest of the lobby consisted of the reception area and seating for adult patients and their families.

The clinic's color scheme was a cheerful mix of purple, orange, and blue. Photos of the mountains and flower-filled meadows were displayed on the wall, making it a pleasant place for both patients and the staff working there. Lexi noted the photographer was Jake Silver, one of the sub-leaders of the pack that she'd met when her family arrived in Silver Town. She could use some tips from him on photography!

She and her mom and dad, and of course, Ryder—who was still serving as her bodyguard no matter what—checked out the rest of the clinic: six rooms for overnight patients amounting to twelve beds, six exam rooms, three operating rooms, a nurse's station, and a break room outfitted with a kitchen.

"Lots of room for lots of patients," Lexi said.

"We don't get a lot yet, unless we have an avalanche or bad weather and we have a lot of vehicular accidents. Though we've had multiple deliveries at one time, and they're usually multiple births," Dr. Weber said. "But we wanted to plan big for our growing *lupus garou* population." He showed them his office. "I have a room off my office for sleeping, when I need to be here all night. The nurses' office has a bed for when they have to stay on call overnight too.

"We have an extra-large room we use for storage, which we planned to turn into another doctor's office if we had anyone join the staff." He smiled at Kurt and Adelaide. "Looks like we now have a need. If you don't mind shar-ing an office, it's big enough to support two doctors." He motioned to the bathroom. "Staff restroom. In the waiting area are the patient restrooms."

He took them to the break room where the nurses were grabbing some coffee since they had no patients at the moment. "The nurses, Charlotte Grey and Matthew Adams, work here." Dr. Weber introduced the nurses to Kurt and Adelaide. "They'll be working here as soon as they are settled in and ready."

"Welcome." Nurse Grey was an older woman with a pleasant smile.

Matthew inclined his head to Lexi's parents and then smiled at Lexi and Kate. "And you ladies are joining the pack?"

"Uh, no," Lexi said. "Kate and I live in California. We'll be returning there but visiting my parents when we can."

Matthew appeared disappointed. Ryder was smiling a little. Lexi could just see Ryder chasing off any wolves who were interested in dating her. Which could be a good thing, she supposed, if some of the fortune hunters continued to plague her.

"Our receptionist is Carmela Hoffman, retired army lieutenant colonel, mated to Michael Hoffman, also retired army lieutenant colonel, now a deputy sheriff. You met her mate when you first arrived," Dr. Weber said.

They took the elevator to the basement level, where the door opened to reveal a lounge area, a testing lab, a laundry room, and a snack room.

"And down this hall is the morgue. Doctor Featherston is our medical examiner. He's off in Hawaii on a vacation at the moment." Dr. Weber got a text. "Looks like I have a patient I need to see. Human hiker, broken leg. I'll set it and send him to the nearby hospital at Green Valley. When we can," he said as they all climbed into the elevator, "I send human patients there. Oh, and our vet sometimes pops in to assist with wolf pup deliveries if we've got a full patient load and the momma wants to shift into her wolf."

"Now that's something I never get to do. Deliver wolf pups," Kurt said.

"Or take care of kids who are wolves in a hospital setting," Adelaide said.

Lexi heard the pride in their voices, and she was thrilled they were happy to cater to their own kind for a change.

Dr. Weber agreed. "You'll love living here."

"A lot different from working in a human hospital," Kurt said. "I *am* going to love working here. Do you need any help with the new patient?"

Dr. Weber smiled. "Yeah, sure. Come with me and we can get this taken care of."

Lexi was glad her father offered to help with his first patient case.

"We're going home," Adelaide said. "I want to visit with Lexi."

"Sure thing."

"And if you don't make it back in time, we'll pick you up on the way to the pack celebration," Adelaide said.

Knowing her father, he wouldn't make it home before the celebration started.

When they returned to the house, Ryder said, "We'll give you some private time to spend with your mother."

"We'll sit out on the back porch." Lexi appreciated that Ryder and Mike wouldn't be hovering over her the whole time. She really did feel safe here. "I'm going to have to get used to having you around."

Ryder smiled.

"In a bodyguard capacity," she clarified.

His smile broadened.

"If you don't mind, I'll join you," Kate said to Lexi and her mother.

"Absolutely," Lexi said. Kate was a friend and confident, and she never felt the need to exclude her.

"Would you like some iced tea or lemonade?" Ryder asked the ladies.

Wow, Lexi could really get used to this. "Iced tea sounds good. No sugar."

Her mother and Kate asked for the same.

"I'll help you make them," Mike said, and the two men went into the kitchen.

Once Lexi, her mother, and Kate were settled on the back porch looking out at the woods, iced teas in hand, Lexi asked, "Are you all right, Mom? After all you went through, all that you had to survive, coming home to this chaos, are you all right?"

"It was all a shock. I have to admit I felt panicked when I took a taxi from the airport to our house, expecting everything to be the same as before. The new owners told me that you sold it. I didn't know what to think. They didn't have a forwarding address for Kurt, and you were gone too. I assumed he'd pulled up stakes, figuring I was dead and not coming back. But he would have sold the house, not you."

"Yeah, I had to because he was declared dead and you were gone, so I 'inherited' it. I wired the money to him when I could safely do so."

"Okay. I was so upset, confused, thinking I wasn't remembering things clearly. Then I went to the hospital where we both worked, and the staff members I ran into there were aghast I was still alive. Not surprising. They said Kurt testified against Joe Tremaine and he disappeared. I was frantic that Tremaine had murdered him. Then I went to the DA and they waffled for a bit, then finally told me he was safe. When they learned I had suffered memory loss, they wouldn't give me any information on how to get in touch with him, afraid I'd put him at risk. I didn't want to put him at risk either, but he had to know I was alive. We needed to be together."

"Humans wouldn't understand."

"I agree. Being with a pack like this couldn't be better. You know, your dad and I were stuck in a rut. That's why I went to Brazil. Well, to help out too. Those kids needed me. You had moved out, and I was helping you with your business online when I was off from work, but your dad and I weren't going anywhere. Same old thing, day in, day out. Work, eat, sleep. Nothing new and exciting. We loved each other, but we needed some excitement in our lives again."

"You sure got that."

Her mother laughed. "Even just living here will do the trick. I'll have wolves to socialize with."

"And Dad. I mean it, Mom. If he doesn't have some date nights, you call me, and I'll set him straight." Lexi was serious.

"It looks like the pack has a lot of activities going we can participate in throughout the year, which should be fun. I hope you can join us for some of them."

"I will."

"So what's the deal with this Ryder?" Her mother sipped some of her tea.

"He's protective and helpful and fun to be around and—"

"Hot," Kate said. "Real hot."

Lexi smiled, but gave her a look that told her to watch what else she said. She was afraid Ryder, and Mike, might hear them.

"He helped Lexi rescue two bear cubs and return them to their mother. He's got a tender heart when it comes to animals in peril. He didn't know we were down at the bottom of the cliff trying to take care of them ourselves. He had planned to do it all by himself," Kate said.

Lexi's mother frowned at them. "You could have been badly injured. But I know no one could have changed your mind about it."

"Not only that," Kate continued, having the floor and making the most of it, "but he's really a good sport. He modeled for Lexi's men's skin-care line for a promo video."

Her mother laughed. It was good to hear her laughter. "Ohmigosh, he's a keeper."

"He was good about that," Lexi agreed.

"I'll say. He seems to be a real macho wolf." Her mother frowned. "He's not interested in your money, is he?"

Lexi didn't think so, but what did she know? "He didn't know who I was when we first met."

"And they still had the hots for each other," Kate offered. "You should see the chemistry between them. Sparks fly. I can just imagine what will happen when he serves as her pool boy."

"Okay so what's all this about him being your pool boy?" her mother asked.

"He can serve drinks, apply sunscreen, and whatever else the lady needs," Kate said.

"Aww. What about you and Mike?" her mother asked Kate.

"He's really hot, too, but I'm interested in someone else." Kate drank some of her iced tea, her cheeks suddenly a little flushed.

"Who?" Lexi and her mother asked at the same time. That was news to Lexi, and she was more than curious. Kate had never mentioned wanting to date someone. Unless the guy wasn't interested in her. Or was dating another wolf already.

"I'd rather not say," Kate said, dismissively.

Now Lexi was dying to know just who *Kate* was interested in.

CHAPTER 19

RYDER AND MIKE HEARD KATE TALKING ABOUT THEM to Lexi and her mom about how hot they were. They were chuckling about it when someone drove up in the driveway. They both checked it out and saw Nurse Matthew dropping Kurt off.

Ryder had suspected Kurt would still be at the clinic and waiting for them to pick him up for the celebration, so he was surprised to see him return home before that. Ryder opened the door for him. "The ladies are on the back porch visiting."

"I'll sit in here with you and talk then before we have to go." Kurt took a seat on the sofa.

"Sure." Ryder suspected Lexi's father wanted to make sure he and Mike could protect Lexi. "Did you want anything to drink?"

"Water would be good. Thanks."

"I'll get it." Mike hurried off.

"Are you certain you can protect Lexi in California?" her father asked them as he took the glass of water Mike handed to him.

"Yes, sir," they both said.

"She's headstrong. If she wants to do something, she'll do it, even if it means risking her neck."

"Uh, right. I've seen that firsthand." Ryder was thinking of the bear cubs' rescue.

"What else is going on between the two of you?"

"I won't deny I'm fascinated with Lexi."

"She has a lot of money." Her dad raised his brows.

"I make a good salary, and I have a lot of money saved up. I may not have Lexi's wealth, but I'm not a spendthrift and I'm good with my own money. And I'm not looking for an easy setup."

Her dad smiled a little. "Hell, if Adelaide had money like that when I first met her, I would have been tempted."

"You love Adelaide. That much is evident. Money or no." Ryder had known this would happen. Even her parents would be suspicious of his motives. And he didn't like it.

"Lexi's had a lot of male suitors. Wolves and otherwise."

Ryder wasn't surprised. "I'll keep them at bay, unless she's interested in seeing one of them."

"I'm surprised you'd agree to that." Kurt raised a brow.

"We're not courting." And that was also the problem. Ryder was just her hired hand, even though she had said they'd been on dates already. "I'll be working for her." Possibly nothing more. He didn't think he could watch her court someone else, though, and continue to work for her.

Kurt smiled. "I think there's more to this than you're willing to admit."

"Your daughter is a wild card," Ryder said quite frankly. He really didn't know how he stood with her in the long run.

Her dad chuckled. "Yeah, she is at that."

The ladies joined them, and Adelaide said, "It's time to party."

⁓

At the Silvers' estate, the outer building and surrounding grounds were already set up for a party. They had food and drinks sitting on long tables and barbecued ribs, brisket, and chicken were cooking on a couple of grills. Ryder was impressed. If he didn't love working with Aidan's family and living on the West Coast, he would have loved to be part of a pack like this.

Everyone came to meet their new doctors. Wolves with young children were delighted to have a doctor who was trained in pediatrics.

The word had spread through the pack about Lexi's cosmetics business, and Kate was already organizing a party to be held at the pack leaders' estate the next day. Lelandi was delighted to offer her home for the party since it was so much bigger than the Summerfields' rental house and set up for pack functions.

"We'll have it in the sunroom. A wine and cheese and makeup party," Lelandi said.

Lexi was delighted. "I wish we could videotape it, but we can't." Lexi didn't want to do anything that could expose where her parents would be living. It would have made for a great promo opportunity. "That's so generous of you to turn it into a real party. We'll have free cosmetic samples for all the ladies who come and extras for anyone who couldn't make it but would like some."

"It's not just a cosmetics party. It's important to show our pack members how one of our own can be such a success," Lelandi said. "You see, I have an ulterior motive."

Lexi smiled. "A lot of hard work, a lot of stubborn determination, a lot of failures before I truly made any real successes."

"And that's what I want you to impart to the other women while we have the party."

Lexi had learned Lelandi was a psychologist, not just a leader of her wolf pack, and she admired her for it. "I would be happy to."

"Don't worry about your parents living with us. They'll be in good hands. The whole pack will look after them. We worry about you, though, living on your own."

"I'll be careful. And I'm sure my extra bodyguard detail will ensure I'm safe. I just worry about returning here to see my parents and alerting Tremaine and his men at the same time. I probably won't be able to return for a long time. I know my parents hope I can enjoy some of the activities you put on, but I'm afraid Tremaine's people will be watching me to see if I'll lead them to my parents. Right now, we lost his men, and he doesn't have any idea where we are."

"Ryder will find a way to get you here safely without alerting them. I'm confident of it," Lelandi said.

Lexi sure hoped so because she didn't want to give up her family, but she didn't want to endanger them either. She knew the holidays would be the hardest, if she couldn't see them. And she was certain Tremaine's men would be watching her like hawks when it came to the holidays. Which was another reason she'd love to eliminate the cause of all their trouble. *Tremaine.*

She glanced around at everyone enjoying themselves at the celebration and was really thrilled her parents were together again. Her father leaned over and kissed her mom's cheek and placed his arm around her waist. Lexi was thinking they should be alone tonight to enjoy their time together after being separated for so long.

But she knew they would want to have her at home for as long as possible until she had to leave. Still, she was glad to see them together, loving each other, and she figured her father would court her mother again, just as he'd promised.

Ryder was speaking with Jake and Darien. She wondered if he was talking business. He seemed to focus so much on her family's safety that she suspected he might be talking to the leaders about that.

"Any possibility between you and Ryder?" Lelandi asked.

Lexi laughed. Wolves were always curious about relationships. She suspected if her mother hadn't survived her accident in Brazil, her dad would have had numerous widowed ladies interested in him in the Silver Town pack.

She still couldn't believe their good fortune to learn her mother was alive and well.

After two hours of eating and visiting, the Silvers welcomed Lexi's parents again to the pack and told them to rest up from their ordeal. Lexi was glad when they could return to the house and just relax. Even though it had been fun, it had also been a strain to meet so many new people and they just needed to chill.

"What do you think of your new pack?" Lexi asked her parents as they drove back to the house.

"I will never remember all the names and faces I met today," her mother said, "but I'm thrilled to be with a wolf pack that's this welcoming."

"I agree," her father said. "Not that I wished this business of Tremaine, but I think this new start is going to be just what we needed in our lives."

"And you're courting Mom all over again, right, Dad?"

He chuckled. "Of course. Didn't you see that I returned home from the clinic before you went to the pack party?"

Lexi sighed. "Yes, but that's not courting."

"It's a start."

Everyone laughed. But her father was right. Normally, he'd be so wrapped up in taking care of patients, he'd miss meals and stay at the hospital way past when he could have been home. Of course, her mom did, too, on occasion.

"I was thinking this afternoon we could decide on the cars we wanted to buy. Darien said the closest car dealership is in Green Valley. He doesn't want us leaving town right now, for our own safety. He said if we could pick out the cars we want online, he'll have someone give them an offer they can't refuse and purchase them. Then they'll deliver them to the house. I want to feel like something is ours and that we're not borrowing everything," her father said.

"That's sounds good to me," her mother said.

"Tomorrow, when you're having your makeup party, did you need my help with anything?" Kurt asked.

"I think we'll manage all right," Lexi said. "I assume Ryder and Mike will be with us. You can come and visit with the guys while we're putting on our party or get together with some others in the pack if you'd like, Dad."

Her father smiled. "Good. I'm going fishing then."

They laughed.

"You have some fishing buddies already?" Lexi asked.

"CJ Silver, one of the deputy sheriffs, and four other men said they'd take me fishing while you ladies were having fun with your makeup session. If anyone gets a hook someplace it shouldn't be, I can remove it with finesse."

Smiling, Lexi shook her head. This was just the place for her parents to be. She was glad CJ was going with him, too, just in case there was trouble, but so many of the pack members were deputized that she figured some of them might be going fishing with him too. She was thrilled they were making him feel like part of the pack by keeping him occupied at something he loved to do. She hoped they'd take him out fishing every once in a while. She suspected they might, while her mom participated in women's socials.

When they arrived at the house, her mother and father

sat on the couch next to each other and discussed the cars they wanted to purchase. Mike was looking on, giving advice about each of the cars. Kate was getting iced teas for everyone.

Ryder said to Lexi, "I talked to Aidan about my employment, and he's surprised, yet not surprised that Mike and I are going to work for you. He's told Rafe all along that he didn't need that many bodyguards, and he's glad we're working for a friend of his. But he said you could have taken a couple of the other guys who aren't gourmet cooks instead."

Lexi smiled. "That's why I chose you. Um, two. Both of you."

"I didn't mention the pool-boy part. The other guys will be trying to convince you that they need to be guarding you, not Mike and me."

She laughed, then took his hand and led him onto the patio and shut the door. "I feel ashamed to even talk to you about this, but I wish there was a way to eliminate Tremaine in prison. Don't you think if he was gone, the contract on my parents would go away?"

"Yeah, because whoever's in charge won't care about anything that had to do with Tremaine. He has no family. His brother and two sons were killed earlier in shootouts with either the police or rival criminal elements. So no family is left to avenge his death. I'm sure several criminals would be pleased to see him buried six feet under. So no, I don't think ill of you for feeling that way. I was thinking the same thing myself. It's just not something we usually do. In self-defense, we have every right to protect ourselves. Trying to eliminate him in prison? That's another story."

"That's what I was thinking too. I just wish there were

some way to stop this. I don't want to always have to look over my shoulder or worry about seeing my parents and putting them at risk."

Better to kill Tremaine herself before he got to her parents.

CHAPTER 20

THE NEXT DAY, LEXI, HER FAMILY, AND BODYGUARDS arrived at Lelandi and Darien's home, and she was thrilled at how excited Lelandi was to have the makeup party at her home. She'd decorated the sunroom in ribbons, bows, balloons with paw prints on them, vases of roses and babies' breath, lacy tablecloths on all the tables, and jasmine candles scenting the air. Some of the ladies served up wine and cheese and petit fours, and music was playing in the background for additional ambience.

Her dad cheerfully went off with CJ and the other men.

Lelandi announced, "We're pleased to have Lexi Summerfield come to Silver Town pack and present her Clair de Lune Cosmetics products. She'll show us how to apply makeup and tell us about how she got started in the business and more. She's open to any questions. Thanks, Lexi, for being here. Some of you already know Kate is her personal assistant and also serves as a bodyguard. She was the one who set up the party."

Kate laughed. "With all your help."

Lexi had thought she, her mother, Kate, and the guys would have done all the work, but other than Lelandi asking what Lexi's favorite colors were—purple, blue, and green—the flowers she liked best, and her favorite wine, cheese, and desserts, Lelandi had the pack set things up. Kate and Lexi only had to set up the makeup stations while her mother left the sample cosmetic bags on each of the chairs.

"I want to thank Lelandi for making this so special," Lexi said, tears clouding her eyes. She hated getting emotional like this in front of all the women, but this meant the world to her. She'd never been around other packs, and if they all were like this, she realized how much she'd been missing out. "And thanks to everyone for their assistance with the party and for showing up."

She usually had big parties, but she hadn't expected to have this many from a pack turn up. There were about twenty ladies. Everyone looked so eager to get started that she said, "All right. Let's start with Lelandi. My mother, Adelaide, and Kate will be the makeup artists for another couple of ladies."

Alicia Silver sat at the table where Kate was going to work. She was the subleader Jake's wife and a bounty hunter by trade. Elizabeth Silver, Tom's mate, took the seat where Adelaide was set up.

Lexi could see that there was a definite pack order of leadership, but everyone seemed to respect it and enjoyed the food and wine while she explained about the makeup process.

"No matter what your job entails, whether you're a psychologist or a bounty hunter, from young to old, or dressy to casual, a little touch of makeup can make you feel like a success."

"Are you sure you're not giving the wrong message?" one of the ladies asked. "I mean, aren't we all beautiful just the way we are?"

Lexi had heard that argument before, and she agreed with it, to an extent. Guys didn't have to wear makeup to be hugely sought after. Wouldn't it be nice just to roll out of bed and get on with the day's work without worrying about putting one's face on?

"Sure we are beautiful just the way we are. And we're wolves, so it's a little different for us. Makeup vanishes when we shift into our wolves. Just like wearing nail polish or dyeing our hair does. Would I ever wear false eyelashes? No. Not because I don't care for them. I think they have their place. But if I have a sudden urge to shift, that would concern me." Lexi added eyeliner to Lelandi's eyelids that was similar to her red eyelashes, but a little darker. "Have any of you worn false eyelashes and then had to shift?"

Smiling, Alicia raised her hand and the others laughed. "Luckily, I wasn't caught in my wolf form and my mate hadn't shifted, so he removed them for me. Being the photographer that he is, he had to take a picture first. A wolf with false eyelashes? Everyone else knows I am fairly newly turned, so I didn't realize what a problem it would be, and Jake hadn't told me about it."

The women laughed.

Lelandi said, "He probably wouldn't have realized there could be a problem with it."

"That's what he said." Alicia pulled out her phone and showed the picture to Kate and then passed it around the room. The ladies were all laughing, and Lexi thought it was a great shot for posterity's sake. A beautiful wolf with long, curling eyelashes. "I'm always learning the do's and don'ts of what we need to know as *lupus garous*. I could have used your advice earlier."

Lexi smiled. *Men.*

"What's your most popular cosmetic line?" one of the ladies asked.

"Usually, it's my newest line, and customers are eager to try out the new product. The key is to not only have the standard products customers grow to love, but to have new products each year too. It means a lot of work, but it shows in sales in the end."

"Do the paparazzi cause trouble for you because of your wealth?" one of the women asked.

"Yes. Mainly, they're watching to see if I'm involved in any scandals. I'm not. Being a wolf, I keep to myself a lot. There's a lot of speculation in the tabloids about who my Mr. Right will be. Of course, they often get it wrong because my mate will have to be a wolf."

"Like Ryder Gallagher?" one of the women asked.

Lexi only smiled. "Okay, what do you think?" she asked Lelandi, handing her a mirror.

"I love it. Darien will have to take me out now."

The ladies chuckled. "You look beautiful," several of them said.

"But it's nice and natural." Lelandi admired herself in the mirror. "That's what I like."

"Me too," Alicia said, when Kate finished her makeup. Elizabeth was just as pleased with what Adelaide had done for her.

"We have some extra samples we'll leave for the ladies who couldn't make it to the party," Lexi said.

"Thank you," Lelandi said. "Some were running their businesses, so they couldn't make it. They'll be thrilled."

Then Lexi, her mother, and Kate began working on the next three volunteers.

"You'll have to come back and do this before our Christmas party and spend the holidays with your parents," Lelandi said.

"Oh, yes," one of the women said. "We have so much fun during the holidays. You have to come back and spend some time with us."

"Yes!" Lexi's mother said. "You have to."

"I hope to, if I can do so without endangering my parents."

"I wish we could find a way to just get rid of Tremaine," one of the ladies said.

"Yeah, lure him here and take care of him," another said.

"Then the police could think your pack had something to do with it," Lexi said.

"The pack sticks together. No one would ever know. We take care of our own. If Tremaine sends men after your father, they're going to vanish into thin air." Lelandi snapped her fingers to emphasize her point.

"Do you have a lot of male suitors because of your wealth?" one of the ladies asked.

"Yes! Too many. You know how we can smell a wolf's interest. A human's too. Humans don't have a clue that we can. Wolves know better, but I think the ones interested in me are so determined to convince me that they overlook that part of our true nature. Or they think with all their smooth talking, they'll talk me into it. I get tired of all the phony compliments."

"I'd love it if I had tons of suitors," one of the teens said, her hands over her heart as she looked heavenward.

"Not like she has, you wouldn't," Kate said. "These men are fortune seekers. They're cads, rogue wolves, just looking to hook up with a woman for her wealth. We need someone who truly loves us. Since we mate for life, it's the only way."

"Amen to that," Lelandi said.

Several of the women agreed, including Lexi's mother.

"So why would wolves do it? They know they can't convince you they love you for real, so why try?" one of the women asked.

"I'm sure they think if they act sincere enough, I will believe what they say is true." Lexi shrugged. "Who knows? If I find the right mate, I suspect I'll still have trouble with some human males who think they can change my mind. Hopefully, the wolf suitors will give up."

"We've heard Rafe has a bachelor friend who is a billionaire too," Lelandi said. "That Derek Spencer? Any possibility there? At least you wouldn't have to worry about him mating you for your money."

"No possibility. For the right woman, he'd be perfect, I'm sure. Not for me," Lexi said.

"What about Ryder?" one of the women asked.

Lexi's mother stopped applying makeup and looked over at her, waiting for a response. Kate was wearing a smile as she applied lipstick to her volunteer's lips.

Lexi laughed and started applying makeup to the next volunteer. She wondered how many more times she was going to be asked about her and Ryder. Was it that obvious she really liked him? "I thought you'd want to know more about how to apply makeup."

"We're wolves," the lady said. "Finding a mate is what really intrigues us. Though this is fun and we're eager to learn how you started your business and became so successful at it."

"My mother and father were very supportive of my venture. They helped back my research into the kinds of products I could develop. Without their money and backing, I would still be trying to reach my first goal."

Adelaide started working on another volunteer. "Lexi was driven to make a business of this. She had the drive to do it, and you need to have that more than anything else."

"True. I probably drove my mother and father crazy

when I was trying to figure all of this out to begin with. Once I had my first cosmetic line, I had to find a way to better market it. Rafe and Aidan Denali helped to promote me to their circles of friends. Especially Rafe, because he's much more social. He introduced me to several important people through his social gatherings. Aidan was more help to me in my research. He even did some tests on products. I was already starting to bring in money. But then I began to get a lot of males interested in dating me. Rafe was concerned about my safety, but I also knew I needed to hire a dedicated personal assistant and Kate was a godsend. Not only is she a marketing guru, but she's the perfect bodyguard. When Ryder and I were rescuing bear cubs, she was facing down the mother bear."

Kate laughed. "Well, I have to earn my pay some way. And Lexi's fun to work with."

"Wait. Back up to the business with the bear cubs," Lelandi said.

Lexi had to tell her and the others the story, but of course Kate had to tell the part about Ryder showing up as a wolf and getting naked to help Lexi with the cubs. The women were all smiling.

They continued doing makeup, and some of the ladies who were following along on how Kate and Lexi were applying it began to help out. Lexi was delighted. Once they were all done, they thanked their hostess and all the ladies who had participated.

Then Lexi, her mother, and Kate gathered their two bodyguards, who had been visiting with some of the guys in the pack, and headed back to the house.

No one had tried to buy any cosmetics at the party, and Lexi was glad about that. She had meant for it to be a way to say thank you to the pack for taking her parents in and being so good to them.

She was glad they were heading back to the house though. She needed to just relax the rest of the day. She hadn't expected Ryder to suggest cooking on the grill, but that really appealed. They decided on beef ribs and corn on the cob. Her father slapped Ryder on the back in a show of camaraderie, and then Mike, her father, and Ryder headed out to start cooking the meat.

"You do realize Ryder is earning your dad's favor," her mother said.

Lexi smiled. Yeah, she did. But that didn't mean they were right for each other. At least that's what she kept telling herself.

Ryder and Mike joked with Kurt about him not catching any fish.

"Hey, the younger guys had better bait." Kurt seasoned the ribs.

The guys all laughed.

"Is that all it takes?" Ryder asked.

"Yeah."

They laughed again. Ryder really liked her dad. He reminded him of his own.

"I haven't been fishing in years. I think I'm out of practice."

"I usually fish as a wolf," Ryder admitted.

"Yeah, me too. Lazy. We catch them, then cook them," Mike said.

"Ha! Now *that* I could do. I'd never miss my catch then. It was nice of the other guys to offer me their fish, even if I declined."

"It seems like a really good pack to belong to," Ryder said.

"Yeah, too bad you and Lexi and the others can't join the pack."

"We're part of Rafe and Jade Denali's pack. Not as organized as this one, but we enjoy being with them," Ryder said. "And Lexi can't join you until Tremaine is out of the picture."

Kurt turned the ribs over. "That's just what I was thinking."

Ryder shook his head. "The bastard's in prison for forty years."

"He'll most likely die there, unless they release him early," Kurt said.

Ryder wished Tremaine would die early—in prison.

Mike served up the ribs and the corn on the cob. "The problem is he still has control over the criminal organization."

The problem was the guy was still alive.

Two days later, Kate, Mike, and Lexi boarded the helicopter to return to her home in California, but when Ryder shook Kurt's hand, he pulled him aside. "Let me give you a piece of advice before you go. Lexi has a mind of her own, but don't let that stop you. She needs more than just work in her life."

"Are you saying you approve of us getting together if it works out?" Ryder had always hoped if he found a mate, her parents would be family too.

"I'm just saying don't worry about the differences in your income. If the two of you are meant to be together, let it happen. I've had you checked out, naturally. I always check out the wolves interested in my daughter. You're the first one she's shown any interest in and the only one I approve of."

Ryder shook his hand. "Thanks, Doc. That means a lot to me." Even if Ryder and Lexi didn't end up mating, he was glad her father believed he was all right.

Then he climbed into the helicopter and saw everyone watching him.

Lexi's brows rose in question. Ryder just smiled. Her father's approval was their secret.

CHAPTER 21

IT WAS LATE AFTERNOON WHEN RYDER AND THE others arrived at Lexi's home, and his first thought was of securing the place. But when she took them through the locked gate in the stucco wall topped with motion-detector lights, he had to take a moment to admire the vista. The two-story composition-and-wood home sat on a bluff, featuring a large veranda with a stunning view of the Pacific Ocean. Virtually every room of the house had floor-to-ceiling windows. The edge of her property was just fifty feet from the ocean. Coastal trees like pine and beech gave her wooded front acreage lots of privacy, but the focal point of her home was the backyard and the ocean view.

"This is beautiful," Ryder said. "Rafe's home is above a beach, too, but his beach isn't private like yours, and it's filled with beachgoers. I love your rocky cliffs and the privacy you have here. Can you get to the rocks down below?"

"Um, no, not unless you want to break your neck. Maybe someday stairs could be constructed. Don't get too close to the edge. The place is great for indoor and outdoor parties, when the weather is good." Lexi showed them the patio and grassy lawn where they had a stone firepit for roasting marshmallows and hot dogs and staying warm on a cold night, a gas grill under the patio cover, an outdoor bar, a whirlpool bath, and a swimming pool. "And it's perfect for whale watching. With two acres covered in coastal trees, we are able to spend some time as wolves out here without being seen. We have no neighbors for a couple of miles."

Seagulls cried out above as a squadron of pelicans flew by. A flock of geese was flying off in the distance as the waves crashed down below.

"This *would* be perfect for parties." Mike folded his arms over his chest as he looked at the waves cresting and breaking on the rocks, standing rocks in the surf adding to the artistic view.

Ryder could spend his days sitting out here, just enjoying the breeze and salt air. "We need to check out the house."

Lexi gave him the security code.

"Kate, if you would, stay outside with Lexi to protect her. Mike and I will check over the home to make sure she doesn't have a welcoming party."

"There better not be," Lexi said.

"I agree." Kate pulled her gun out just in case.

"We'll be back in a little bit." Ryder turned off the security alarm, and then he and Mike searched the place, both of them armed with guns.

They checked out most of the rooms, including the large sunroom and kitchen having winning views of the ocean and the swimming pool, and the basement set up for exercising. Even the guest rooms had views of the ocean and pool, and they each had individual decks. One of the rooms had more of Kate's scent and the closet was filled with her clothes. The next room was the master bedroom suite with another beautiful view of the ocean. Then Ryder checked the closets and underneath the bed, and the opulent bathroom with a whirlpool tub and glassed-in shower.

Relieved no one was in the house but him and Mike, he rejoined his friend in the central living area.

"I couldn't find any sign of anyone here. Lexi and Kate will have to smell for scents to double-check," Ryder said as they went to the back-patio door to let the ladies in. "It's all clear. Come on in."

Her posture relaxing, Lexi looked relieved. "Thank you, Ryder, Mike, for keeping me safe."

Holstering her gun, Kate shook her head. "What am I? Chopped liver?"

They all laughed.

"You had the most important role. You were protecting Lexi. We were just cleaning house," Ryder said. "We need you ladies to see if anyone has been in the house who shouldn't have been."

"We can do that. Kate, can you show Mike the room he'll be staying in?" Lexi asked.

"Yeah, sure." Kate took him upstairs to one of the guest rooms. "You can put your bags in here, Mike."

Lexi took Ryder to another room upstairs. He'd had the idea she might put him up in her room, which was a crazy notion, but he couldn't help thinking about it. He set his bags down in the guest bedroom. He was glad to be here for her, no matter what room he ended up in. Kate's room was right next to the master suite, so he was certain she could protect Lexi, if anyone got that far in the house. But he planned for Mike and him to be the first line of defense.

Lexi said, "I'm going to take a swim after I check out the scents in the house. Tomorrow I have a busy day. We're having a promotional party for the women's new gold line. We have reporters from print magazines and e-zines, and store owners and reps from the different high-end stores who will be here to help sell or sink the line. We'll also have actresses and models to add to the fun. We'll have a makeup party similar to what we had at Lelandi's home. We'll have finger foods, champagne, and probably some swimming."

"You're sure they're all vetted?" Ryder asked.

"Yes. I've been doing this for a year now, and it's really helped to push sales on the newest products."

"But you weren't having trouble with Tremaine's people before."

Lexi gave him a look that said to give it a rest.

He let out his breath. "I just want to make sure you stay safe."

"We will be." She patted his chest. "Because you will make sure of it. Anyway, I want to enjoy the rest of the day off. Tomorrow morning, we'll set up for the party. I have a couple of ladies who serve the food and drinks."

"Does that mean it's time for me to be the pool boy?" Ryder arched a brow.

Lexi smiled. "It sure does. See you at the pool. Be sure to wear your bathing suit, and I'll have the sunscreen."

"I guess you have drink detail," Kate said to Mike as they left his bedroom.

"And you?" Mike asked.

"I'm on guard duty." Patting her holstered gun, Kate laughed.

After Ryder had changed into his board shorts, he headed down the stairs, gun in hand and not feeling like a bodyguard. Lexi was wearing a pretty green bikini and a smile for him, a summer floral cover-up slung over her arm. A knock sounded on the door, and Kate went to answer it, dressed in shorts, flip-flops, and a tank top, and armed with a gun. Mike joined them wearing shorts, tennis shoes, and a muscle shirt, his gun holstered at his waist. The bunch of them looked like they were ready for business in a beachy sort of way.

Kate pulled open the speakeasy door that had an iron grate over it, which made it perfect for telling solicitors to get lost without having to open the whole door. "It's Benjamin." Kate sounded resigned.

"Let him in." Lexi also sounded as though it was a necessary evil, and that she wasn't eager to hang out with him, which Ryder was glad for.

He was ready to send the guy packing.

The redheaded, bearded man walked into the house and smiled brightly at Lexi, who hadn't moved from her position near the sofa. She was smiling slightly. Benjamin had eyes only for her. He brushed past Kate as if she were a minor impediment and headed for Lexi.

Ryder strode from the stairs to join Lexi, then realized he was being a little territorial and stopped in his tracks, but he caught Benjamin's eye. Benjamin swung his attention in Ryder's direction and saw Mike, too, both armed, except Ryder was dressed in a swimsuit like Lexi. The guy only had to put two and two together to figure out something more was going on between Ryder and Lexi. Both Mike and Ryder were wearing growly expressions.

"What's with all the guns? I came to see you because I just returned from Italy. Well, four days ago. I told you I would, but I wanted to surprise you," Benjamin said, his attention back on Lexi as he stood before her.

He looked like he wanted to give her a kiss. He'd better not do it.

"If you know what's good for you, you'll leave," Ryder said before Lexi could say anything to Benjamin.

Kate's mouth gaped, and Lexi's jaw dropped. Mike's growly expression turned into a smile.

"Excuse me?" Lexi said, and Ryder clarified what he meant.

"For your own protection." Ryder motioned to the guns they were all carrying. "You asked what was up with all the guns. Some men want Lexi, thinking she can provide important information to them. It's not safe for you to be around her."

"What about you?" Benjamin asked. "It looks like you're more dressed for playing than for protecting."

"It goes with the job." Ryder noticed Kate wasn't smiling but glancing at Lexi to see her take on it.

"I'm not afraid of anyone." Benjamin wasn't getting the message.

Lexi said, "Let's go to the patio and have a drink, shall we? Mike, can you get us some drinks?"

Ryder wanted to growl. Lexi looked sharply at him, and he realized he had growled a little. He smiled at her. He couldn't help it, but he wondered how many dates this joker had gone out with her on. She gave Ryder a look to mind his manners.

"Yeah, sure thing." Mike followed them out to the patio.

Kate patted Ryder's arm. "Don't worry. She's getting ready to dump him."

"Three dates and he's out?" Ryder felt less annoyed, thinking Lexi was going to give Benjamin the boot. At least he was hoping she would.

Kate smiled. "You know, if you hadn't gotten all growly over it, she would have just told him she wasn't seeing him anymore. But then she had to prove to you that you weren't running the show."

"That I'm just the bodyguard." Ryder hadn't meant to sound so disgruntled over it.

"No. Not at all. She hasn't shown this much interest in a guy since I've worked for her. And I'm not talking about Benjamin. You are the one she's set her sights on."

"So I screwed up."

"Yeah, but I'm sure you can come up with a way to make it up to her. I wouldn't leave her alone out there on the patio with that guy for too long."

"Thanks for the advice, Kate." Ryder headed out to the patio where Lexi and Benjamin were sitting at one of the tables under an awning.

After setting his gun down on a table next to one of the chaise longues, Ryder walked over to join Lexi. Since his business was protecting her, he interrupted Benjamin, who was telling all about his trip to Italy. "Excuse me, Lexi, did you smell any sign of trouble in the house?"

Lexi smiled at him. Ryder thought that was a good sign. He even wondered if she had been waiting for him to rescue her.

"No. They didn't enter the house while we were away." She took a sip of what looked to be an iced tea. Benjamin was drinking a beer.

"Good." Ryder was still concerned about her having her parties here at the house. Then again, keeping her safeguarded at some other location could be a problem too.

A full bar was set up on the deck, and the sauna looked as inviting as the pool. He was ready to start applying her suntan lotion.

"As I was saying, the Venetian glass art was spectacular. Every piece handmade, just beautiful," Benjamin said, focused on Lexi, his scent turning annoyed.

Good. Ryder was annoyed the guy was here bugging Lexi.

"And you got something for Lexi from one of those shops?" Ryder folded his arms as he hovered over them, not about to move unless Tremaine's men intruded, or Lexi wanted him to do something else.

Lexi smiled at Benjamin, waiting expectantly to hear his response.

Benjamin glowered at Ryder and looked him up and down. "What are you, anyway? The hired help? Go clean the pool and butt out of our affairs."

"I take that as a no, you didn't get Lexi anything from Italy," Ryder said. "Now if I'd been there, well, I would have taken her with me, for one thing." He smiled at Benjamin. "I think you might be getting a little sunburned, Lexi. Did you want me to apply your sunscreen while you're talking to this guy?"

"I think we're done here. Benjamin, I had fun on our last three dates, but as I told you before, that's all I allow myself before I call it quits with a wolf."

"We've only had two," Benjamin said, frowning at her.

"Today makes three."

"Yeah, she counted the seven or eight times I've been with her as a date, even when I hadn't thought they counted," Ryder said, as if he were part of the conversation.

Lexi looked like she was fighting a smile. Mike was wiping off the bar counter, as if he was the permanent bartender, listening in on the conversation. Kate headed outside with her laptop, giving Ryder a wink.

Benjamin couldn't have looked any frostier. "Is this all because I didn't get you a present from Venice, Lexi? Why should I, when you make a lot more money than me and you have this crazy system of dating a wolf only three times?"

"More dates with me," Ryder reminded him. "I still would have gotten her a gift, just to show she meant something special to me while I was away and that I'd been thinking of her. But we've already had a lot of life experiences together: rescuing bear cubs to begin with and protecting her from paparazzi and thugs. That was just the beginning of the fun."

"I told you why," Lexi said, ignoring Ryder. "There's no connection between us."

"It's because of the money you have, isn't it?" Benjamin finished his beer.

"I'm sure that has all to do with it," Ryder said. "Her money draws people like *you* who are eager to meet up with her."

Benjamin rose to his feet. "I meant because I don't have the kind of money she has, wiseass."

Ryder smiled. "Exactly. Because you don't have the income she has, and you're drawn to her wealth."

Benjamin took a swing at Ryder, but he was expecting it. Instead of knocking the guy out, he dodged the blow, and Benjamin took another swing.

"Give it up, man. She's not interested in you, and you need to take it like a man and go home. Hell, you're not upset she's dumped you because you care so much about her, but because you lost a chance to be with someone who makes so much money." Ryder knew just the type.

"What about you?" Benjamin was still swinging at Ryder. And missing.

"What *about* me? I met Lexi before I knew who she was, and I was totally under her spell. It had nothing to do with her wealth." Ryder thought about maneuvering over to the pool and giving the guy a good dunk, but he was trying to get Benjamin to listen to reason first. He didn't want to hit him when he needed to be fresh for a real fight with the bad guys, and he didn't want to give Lexi a new list of enemies. Though he supposed if he'd thought about that beforehand, he really should have stayed out of it and let her handle it.

"Ryder's right," Lexi said. "We have no common interests."

"We're wolves." Benjamin was red-faced, but at least he gave up trying to hit Ryder.

Ryder was wary he might try to sucker punch him.

"That's not enough of a connection. I'm sorry it didn't work out between us, but I really need to get on to other business, Benjamin." Lexi smiled in an amiable way.

"I'll walk you to the door," Kate said.

"Thanks, Kate." Lexi got up off her chair, handed the sunscreen to Ryder, then walked to one of the chaise longues where she stretched out on her tummy.

That was Ryder's cue to slather the sunscreen on, but he didn't like that Kate was walking Benjamin out by herself.

"I'll go with you," Mike said to Kate.

Relieved, Ryder nodded to Mike and Kate as they headed inside the house. Mike cast him a smirk. Ryder joined Lexi at the lounger and took the cap off the sunscreen. The smell of the sea filled the air, and the salty breeze blew her hair about. Then they heard Benjamin and Mike arguing in the house.

"I was going to handle him on my own just fine, you know." Lexi sounded more relaxed now, and then they heard the door shut and Mike and Kate talking as they returned to the patio.

"Sorry, Lexi. He just annoyed me," Ryder said.

"Thanks for not fighting him back."

"I wanted to save up my strength for the really bad guys." She chuckled.

She was beautiful, and he was amazed at how she'd built up such a successful business. It made him feel like a bit of a slacker. But he also felt privileged to work for her.

"Did you have any trouble sending Benjamin on his way?" Lexi asked Mike and Kate.

"No. I think he thought he could try something else to win you over, and I'm sure he was really frustrated that he wasn't able to knock Ryder out," Kate said.

They all laughed.

"I was trying to be the nice guy. He didn't want to see me in a real fight," Ryder said.

CHAPTER 22

RYDER BEGAN APPLYING THE COCONUT-SCENTED sunscreen on Lexi's soft skin, massaging her legs with a relaxing touch. He made sure he covered every inch of her skin so she wouldn't burn, but also continued to gently knead her muscles, working his way up. Then he rubbed it onto her back and shoulders, neck and arms. She turned over and smiled up at him. "I've never had a pool boy before. You sure do a great job of applying the sunscreen."

"I've never been one before." Ryder smiled at her. "But I always try to do my best at any job I do."

"Well, you're doing great."

Mike brought her a mai tai. "I thought you might be ready for a fancier drink this time around. Enjoy."

"Thanks." Lexi sat up and took a sip. "Wow, this is great. I bet Aidan's missing the two of you already."

Ryder smiled. "Yeah, one of the guys said Aidan has been after them to get some cooking and bartending lessons from us."

"I bet."

Kate sat down at the umbrella table where she'd set up her laptop and began to tap on the keyboard.

Ryder motioned to Lexi's front. "Did you want me to do more?"

"All of me can burn. So sure."

He began to work on her feet, then shins and thighs, loving how she purred while he massaged the sunscreen

onto her skin. He smiled when he smelled her pheromones
kicking into first gear, something Benjamin hadn't done for
her. He massaged her stomach and the swell of her breasts.
Her nipples were already poking against the green fabric of
the bikini top. He was trying not to notice too much. He
slathered her arms and throat. "Did you want me to put
some on your face?"

"Yes, thanks."

He carefully applied it to her face, making sure not to get
it too near her eyes, and she sighed.

"Just perfect," she said when he finished up.

"Yeah, I agree."

She chuckled, left the lounger, and patted it. "Lie down
and let me put some sunscreen on you now."

He was really surprised she would offer, since that was
his job. He felt like he should object because he was the
hired help. He realized how much that bothered him. He
finally willed himself to lie down on the lounger and let Lexi
pamper him a bit. He wouldn't have had any problem with
this if Kate and Mike hadn't been there. Then it would have
been just the two of them. Even though Kate and his friend
weren't watching them, they could hear what was going on.
Though he was glad they were here to protect Lexi should
anything go wrong.

Once Ryder was stretched out on the lounger on his
stomach, she began applying the sunscreen. Immediately,
he fell under her spell, her hands sliding all over his skin:
first his legs, then moving to his arms, shoulders, back,
and neck. She was giving him the same treatment, not just
applying the lotion, but gently massaging his muscles too.
"Man, I've never had a massage before, but I'd hire you in a
heartbeat to do those daily."

"You and me both. I was afraid I was going to fall asleep on you. Okay, flip over," she said.

This was the hard part. His arousal was tenting his board shorts, and he really didn't want her to witness how much she had turned him on with her touch.

"Come on. I want to swim." She tugged at the back of his board shorts.

"I can get this." He knew she realized why he was reluctant, but she was having fun playing with him.

"Yeah, you sure can. So, turn over."

"How often do you lather up the guys you're dating?"

"Just Benjamin, but don't worry. I asked him to put some sunscreen on my back, and he did. Nothing more than that. Then he asked me to put the lotion on his back. And that was that."

"Okay, but don't laugh." Ryder rolled over and she smiled, taking in his appearance. She seemed to be enjoying herself, so he smiled too.

"Hmm, all these strong, beautiful muscles." She continued massaging him—his arms and hands, his legs and feet, his torso and neck, all of which kept his erection firm and wanting. She finally applied some sunscreen on his face and sighed. "You are so firm all over." Lexi offered her hand to him. "Come swim with me."

Ryder wanted so to pull her into his arms and kiss her like there was no tomorrow. "Is that what a pool boy does?"

"This one does."

Ryder wasn't going to be asked twice. He took her hand, then rose from the chaise longue. He walked with her to the pool, and when she released his hand, he dove in. The water was warm and silky, and he surfaced to see where Lexi was. She was sitting on the edge of the pool and slipped into the water. He swam over to join her and caged her against the side of the pool, wanting the intimacy after she'd gotten him all worked up. Her pheromones were just as wild.

"My biggest fear, you know," he said, nuzzling her cheek, "is that I'll be so busy wanting you, I won't be able to protect you like I should."

"I want you here for me. I know it's crazy"—she rested her hands on his hips—"since we haven't known each other that long. But I want you for more than just a bodyguard. I hope you know I'm teasing you about the pool-boy part."

He kissed the water off her cheek. "I love that part of the job."

She chuckled and kissed his chin. "Good, because during the summer, we'll be spending a lot of time out here."

"I know you're really interested in me as a model for your product line."

She smiled. "Yeah, well, there is that." Lexi kissed Ryder's cheek and pressed her body closer to his arousal.

He had to admit he was doing a lot of things he wouldn't normally be doing. He wanted to be with Lexi, even if he stepped out of his comfort zone a bit. He was thinking they needed some alone time. As long as Mike and Kate could protect them. Ryder glanced at Mike and Kate. She was busy on the computer, ignoring them. Mike was still at the edge of the bluff, watching the boats.

Ryder wanted to share Lexi's bed with her. Wouldn't she be safer if he was right there? Even with Kate in the room next door, she wasn't close enough if someone should break into Lexi's room from the backyard.

He kissed Lexi's lips, and she encircled his neck with her arms. "I think you're working your way into my bedroom."

"Bed," he corrected, smiling.

She laughed and kissed him on the mouth, then parted her lips for him. He slipped his tongue into her mouth and stroked hers, and he groaned, wanting to take this to her room where they could really have some privacy. He was so ready to come.

"Can you make it out of the pool without too much discomfort?" She kissed his mouth again.

He chuckled. "Hell, yeah. What do you have in mind?"

"Let's take this to my bedroom."

"Now you're talking." He boosted her out of the pool and then climbed out, his wet board shorts molded to his erection.

She smiled as she looked down at his swimsuit. "Sorry I made you wait so long to do something about that." Lexi grabbed a towel from her lounger.

Ryder grabbed his towel and wrapped it around his waist, but then he reached out to take her towel and dry her first.

"You're offering to dry me off?" Lexi asked, then handed him her towel.

He smiled. "Yeah, I figured that's part of the job." He began drying her shoulders and then her back and legs.

She turned so he could dry her front and himself, and then pulled the floral cover over her bathing suit, took his hand, and headed for the back door. "Going inside for a bit," she told Kate.

Kate didn't even look at her and just said, "Okay, yell if you get into trouble. Mike and I will come rescue you."

"Thanks."

"I'll be there as her first line of defense," Ryder promised.

"You sure will be," Kate said smiling.

Then Lexi and Ryder headed inside the house and she hauled him down the hall toward her bedroom, appearing eager to have her way with him. Just as eager as he was to be with her.

"Do you still want me to stay in the guest room tonight?" He was hoping she'd change her mind.

She just smiled. "We may be rethinking the room arrangements."

He sure liked that idea. Not only because he thought he could protect her better, but because he wanted this to go much further between them.

Once they reached her room, she closed the bedroom door and smiled wickedly at him. This was a side of her he had rarely seen, and he was ready to explore. He rested his hands on her shoulders and kissed her mouth, his hands sliding to her breasts, her nipples fully extended, poking at the damp bikini top. His board shorts were just as damp, and he was eager to dispense with the wet garments right away.

He slipped her bathing-suit straps down her shoulders, kissing one shoulder, then the other. She sighed with pleasure, her hands caressing his waist, her touch sizzling. She shivered and he removed the wet bikini top, dropping it to the floor. Her breasts were full, her nipples fully erect, enticing him to lathe them with his tongue. When he ran his tongue over them, she gasped and tightened her hands on his hips. "Oh…my…god."

Smiling, he slid her bikini bottoms over her hips, pressing warm kisses on her cool skin all the way down her legs. She rested her hand on his shoulder, pulling her feet out of the bottoms. He nuzzled her neck and felt her pulse leap, his body still hard with need. He leaned down to kiss her mouth, and she began to slide his board shorts past his hips.

"We have kind of an obstruction to our progress here."

She slid her hand over his steel-hard erection and curled her hand around it, firing up his blood.

He wanted her on the bed now, in his arms, feeding into her desire like she was feeding into his. "You'll have to take care of it."

"I will." She pulled his board shorts down and released his cock, which was boldly stretching out to her. "Magnificent."

He took her in his arms and they began kissing, naked, their aroused bodies melding together, his cock rubbing her mound. Caught up in the heat of the moment, he covered her mouth with his. She licked his lips, and he opened his mouth to her, inviting her to join him, his cock twitching with need. Everything about her felt right to him—her scent, her touch, the pleasurable sighs she made. Tongues connected, he tasted the mai tai Mike had fixed for her earlier. The pineapple, oranges, lemon, lime, hint of almonds, and light rum made her taste like a fruity delight.

"Delicious." He moved his hands over her breasts, loving the way her skin was soft and warm and her breasts firm and high.

"Hmm, you are," she whispered against his ear, her hands roaming over his shoulders, down his back, and over his bare ass. "I thought so from the moment I saw you rescuing the bear cub—all naked and muscular and determined."

Then they were kissing again, and they ended up on the bed. He was on his back, her straddling him. It was as if she was claiming him, and he liked the notion. She pressed her breasts against his chest, and he drew his fingers through her silky strands of hair.

Ryder had been waiting for Lexi all his life. He knew she was the one for him. He wanted to mate her right then and there. No waiting. Yet, he felt Lexi might need more time to get to know him, and so he would hold off asking…for a little while. He didn't think he could hold out for long though.

———∿∿———

Lexi was certain Ryder wouldn't ask him to mate her. She had to tell him in no uncertain terms that she was ready for this if he was, and she had every intention of doing so, right now.

Ryder stroked her hair, and she felt swept up in his touch. She was glad to have him, Kate, and Mike all working for her but being her friends too. She couldn't believe how much they meant to her, and she didn't want to ever go back to the way it was when she couldn't see her father and she was all on her own. It didn't matter how many dates she went on, she wasn't giving him up for anything. Ready to go all the way, she just hoped he didn't want to make her wait.

She cupped his head with her hands and kissed his cheek and then his lips. He sank his tongue into her mouth and stroked her tongue in a sexy way.

She slid her fingers down his beautifully sculpted chest and licked his chin, tilting hers up to kiss him deeply again. He was magical—his touch, his kisses, the heat, and his pheromones. When they came up for air, she hit him with the proposition. "I want you for my mate."

"The catch is I have to work at it," he said, smiling down at her, looking like the happiest wolf in the world.

"Oh, yeah, starting now."

He began to kiss her again, slowly, building up the heat and then passionately filling her with overwhelming emotions—of lust and desire and need and want. He wasn't holding back, and she was so glad for it.

She felt intoxicated with his strength and gentleness and kissed him fervently back.

"I love you, you know." Ryder paused to run his hand over her breast.

"Yeah, I know. Just as much as I love you. That's why I wasn't waiting any longer for this." She loved his hard body, his aroused cock, the lustful look in his eyes, and the way he stroked her breasts in a way that said he loved caressing her. Her nipples erect and aching, she soaked up his touch.

He nipped her earlobe, and she nipped his in return.

She felt sexy and frisky when she was with him, both as a human and a wolf. She loved being with him. His hand swept down her stomach, and he ran his fingers between her legs, touching her mons, stroking her into the next world. He nuzzled her breasts, and she couldn't have stopped the hot desire flooding every cell as he carried her off, making her come. She cried out, not caring if the whole wide world heard her.

"Are you ready?" Ryder had hoped it would come to this eventually, but he thought it would take longer to convince her. He was glad she had a mind of her own and didn't waste time deciding.

"Yeah, let's go."

He smiled and pushed his cock into her, slowly at first, and then he covered her mouth with his and kissed her thoroughly. He began thrusting his cock between her legs, seeking to climax and hoping to bring her there again. His plunges intensified and all he could think of was being with her forever, that this was only the beginning.

He pulled out of her and pushed in again and then he felt

her surrender to another climax, the convulsions wrapping around him in a fevered pitch. He loved it. He was on the verge of coming, just another couple of thrusts, and then he exploded inside of her. "Love you," he groaned out.

She wrapped her arms around him and hugged him tight. "I love you."

He thought they needed to join the others, but instead, they cuddled and slept.

She finally woke and kissed his chest. "As much as I want to stay here with you forever and ever, let's join the others." Then Lexi smiled at him. "After we take a shower. What did my dad tell you before you got on the helicopter?"

"That he approved of me."

She laughed.

They climbed out of bed and ended up in the bathroom.

She started the water in the shower. "And?" She took Ryder's hand and led him into the shower.

"That you have a mind of your own, which I love about you. But to be sure and have my way too."

Lexi smiled up at him, took the body wash, and began soaping him up. "Did you?"

He leaned down to kiss her smiling lips. "I certainly did."

CHAPTER 23

RYDER KNEW THE GOOD-NATURED TEASING AMONG his friends and the ugly speculations from strangers would begin, and he would have to face all of it by being affable and professional about it. But he couldn't be more thrilled. As his dad would say, "Don't let them get your goat." That reminded him. He needed to tell his parents what had transpired between him and Lexi. He often didn't tell them what was going on with his job when he was on a mission, and they thought he still worked for Aidan and was just on vacation in the redwoods.

Lexi and Ryder showered, dressed, then rejoined the others out back. Mike was scooping a net into the pool to pull out a couple of leaves. Kate was still on her laptop and looked expectantly at Lexi and Ryder. Mike was trying to be less obvious about it. Ryder was sure they'd know that this was a done deal as much as Lexi was smiling, unable to hide how she felt. His own smile couldn't have stretched any further.

They hadn't even discussed whether to wait to tell the world. But Lexi said, "It's done. Drinks are on the house."

"Woo-hoo!" Kate hopped up from her chair. "Can I tell all the other suitors you are unavailable?" She joined them and gave Lexi a hug and then hugged Ryder.

Lexi laughed. "I'll tell them. Or Ryder can."

Mike was smiling as he came over and gave Lexi a hug and shook Ryder's hand, but then pulled him into a hug. "I knew where this was going when you told me you'd met up with a couple of she-wolves in the woods."

"You didn't have a clue." Ryder brought out a chilled bottle of champagne from the outdoor bar.

Mike set up the fluted champagne glasses on the bar. "Yeah I did. You were kind of down in the dumps that I was joining you later. When you told me about the ladies, I knew I wasn't needed. Not right away anyway. I was glad for you."

"Hell, if you had been there, that would have been the end of any chance I had." Ryder poured the champagne into the glasses, the bubbles rising to the top, threatening to spill over, but stopping just at the rim.

They all laughed, knowing that wasn't the case.

With filled glasses of champagne, Lexi said, "To friends for life."

They all said, "Hear, hear," and drank from their glasses.

"To the happy mated couple," Kate said.

They cheered and toasted to that.

"To long life and happiness," Mike said, raising his glass.

"To friends and family, may we always remain healthy, happy, and wise," Ryder said.

They all drank to that.

Kate motioned to her laptop. "More trouble with a competitor."

"What now?" Lexi asked.

They all went over to see what the issue was.

"That Silky Spring is causing trouble again. What *is* her problem?" Kate said.

"What's she up to now?" Lexi sounded irritated as she looked at the monitor.

"People were posting bad comments on the video we did of Ryder and Don. It sounds just like the reviews left on your products pages. Same names used too. They sound like one person wrote all of them," Kate said.

Frowning, Mike watched the video of Lexi applying skincare products to Don's face. "I can't believe Don Morgan agreed to do the video. Hell, all you have to do is tell him about the ugly comments—if he doesn't already know— and he'll be sure to dig up something on her, or make something up, if he learns who she is."

"*We* need to do that." Ryder was irritated the woman was continuing to cause trouble for Lexi, and he felt he needed to do something to stop it. That was the alpha-wolf way. "I mean get something on her that's true, not made up."

"All right. Learn what you can about her, but we're not doing anything until you tell me what you know. We'll decide then," Lexi said.

"Will do." Mike began texting someone.

They might not have a pack that ran a town like in Silver Town, but Rafe had an army of wolf friends who could learn anything about anybody, and no one would be the wiser.

"Okay, one of our guys is looking into her," Mike said.

"I can't believe you all have so many specialists who can do this stuff. I mean, that are wolves." Lexi sounded impressed.

Then Kate smiled. "Oh my, our sales are really hopping."

"Oh? What were the sales from?" Lexi asked.

"It had to be because of our makeup party. We had an influx of orders from Silver Town. I guess they really liked the products after all," Kate said. "I'm glad we had it."

"Yeah, but I didn't mean for them to feel they had to buy the cosmetics. I just wanted them to have fun."

"Well, they had fun and they wanted the cosmetics, or they wouldn't have bought them," Kate said.

"Hey, news flash. One of the men who worked for Rafe said Silky Spring lives about twenty minutes from here," Mike said.

"Okay, so then I think it wouldn't hurt to go speak to her in person," Lexi said.

"Yeah, with real teeth," Kate said, disgruntled.

"I wish," Lexi said. "That would shut her up if the three of you came with me as wolves. Let's go over to her house and see if we can meet up with her."

Kate pointed to her laptop. "She's on Facebook doing a live video, and it looks like it's in her living room. She has pictures posted on her page of her house."

"Okay, good," Lexi said.

"Sounds good to me," Ryder said, having wanted a word with her from the beginning. "We need to discover why she has a grudge against you."

"I agree. Maybe we can settle this. Sometimes people will play games if they feel they're safely anonymous," Mike said. "Once they're confronted in person, it's too real, and they back off. A mention about taking legal action could help too."

Kate agreed.

"Okay, let's go over there." Lexi headed inside the house.

Ryder was glad Lexi wanted to try to resolve this before it escalated. He hoped they could find a peaceful solution. He recalled the way Lexi had run down Don Morgan as a wolf. That scene popped in his mind as they got into her silver Audi hatchback. Except this time, Lexi would still be human, at least.

When they finally reached Silky's small two-story wooden house, they noticed it was on a tiny plot of land very close to each neighbor. Lexi assumed Silky was working on a shoestring budget. She hoped Silky was home and that they could iron out their differences. Issues were bound to come up while managing a business, but Lexi really hoped they could resolve them. She loved her work, but Silky was becoming a thorn in her paw.

A black and white cat was sitting in a window peering out at them. A calico jumped onto the windowsill and joined him. *Pretty cats.*

Ryder stood nearby while Lexi approached the door. Mike and Kate stayed with the car, trying to look less intimidating, but if Silky caused Lexi any trouble, they were all there to help out.

Lexi knocked on the blue door and heard footsteps. It opened, and Lexi stood face-to-face with Silky Spring. The woman's face paled, and Lexi assumed Silky recognized her right away.

"You are Silky Spring?" Lexi asked, even though she recognized the long, red hair and blue eyes from the woman's website photo. She offered her hand in greeting. "I'm Lexi Summerfield."

Silky didn't shake her hand, instead folding her arms across her chest and snapping, "I know who you are. Your dad put mine in jail."

"Joe Tremaine?" Lexi couldn't believe it. Tremaine didn't have any children that she knew of, except the two boys who had died in shootouts. Was Silky an illegitimate daughter?

"Yeah, my dad."

"He killed a district attorney." Lexi figured Silky knew that, but she couldn't help but want to remind her of it. Why would Silky want to acknowledge the bastard was her father?

"He was going to come out and tell the world I'm his daughter. Then your dad had to screw it all up."

"Your dad screwed it up by murdering the district attorney!" Lexi took a deep breath. "Your mother wasn't married to him," Lexi guessed.

"Duh. I'm still his daughter."

True, but Lexi wouldn't have wanted anyone to know that if she'd been her. "He's a crime boss." Lexi was sure Silky wasn't that naive, but why wasn't she put off by it?

"Yeah, so?"

So Silky thought being the daughter of a crime boss would make her somebody? If he hadn't acknowledged she was his daughter all these years, why would he now? She looked to be around twenty-five or so.

"That's why you've been sabotaging my company's product reviews?"

Silky's eyes widened again. She must not have realized she'd be so easy to figure out.

Just then Don Morgan's VW Bug drove up onto the driveway. Lexi smiled at him. He must have read the comments on the video they had made of him and somehow made the connection between Silky Spring and the reviews. "So I see the two of you are becoming fast friends," he said to Silky and Lexi.

Hardly.

Silky stared at Don and then turned her attention to Ryder, finally taking notice of him. "Your two male models are here?" she asked sarcastically.

Don was tenacious when he was after a story, or if someone tried to put him down. He didn't get mad about things. He got even. So it was a good thing he had no idea Lexi and Kate had stolen his camera and equipment while they were wolves. Lexi wasn't surprised when he said, "I know you're the daughter of a heroin-addicted prostitute who was in prison for killing a man, Silky. In truth, your daddy could be any one of a half-dozen different men your mother was seeing around the same time."

Don had pulled off the kid gloves for that one. Lexi felt that was a low blow even for him.

"Joe Tremaine is my dad." Silky wasn't budging.

"Have you had a DNA test to see if you're related?" Don asked.

Silky just glowered at him and didn't say anything. Lexi took that as a no.

"Well, let me inform you, Tremaine's telling a different story. When you left the bad review on my video, I started looking into who had left the comments, and I discovered what else you've been up to. You've been leaving bad reviews on Ms. Lexi Summerfield's products wherever she sells them. On Ryder's video too. I have resources I can access that you wouldn't believe. I learned you and your mother were spreading the word that you are Tremaine's daughter. So I paid Tremaine a visit in prison and learned what he had to say. Why don't you lay off of Ms. Lexi Summerfield's company, and I won't report what you're doing?"

"You can't prove I'm doing anything. I mean, even if I left bad reviews, nobody cares."

"Customers care. Ms. Summerfield cares. Her friends and family care. Okay, how about this. We tell the man you're calling your dad that you're telling the world he and a hooker named Sunflower made *you*. And you want to cash in on some of your dad's wealth. How about that?"

Silky glowered at Don.

"You know he doesn't like it when he's not in control of

a situation. He's bound to put out a hit on *you* next. Why don't you take down all those negative reviews you put up, and we'll call it even?"

"My dad wouldn't kill me."

"You want to bet? He had your mother killed because she was telling other inmates you were his daughter. He doesn't want you for a daughter, whether you're his off-spring or not."

"I don't believe you! She got into a fight with another inmate and got stabbed. My dad had nothing to do with it. Besides, I can't take down the reviews if I had nothing to do with writing them in the first place."

"Didn't you hear the part about me having the resources to learn the truth? The woman who stabbed your mother was just offered a plea bargain if she testifies against who paid her to kill your mother. Tremaine. Not only that, but the reviews are yours. Believe me, I can have this all in print before you know it. Tremaine will hear about it, and he'll end you."

"What about him ending you for putting it in print?"

"All anonymous."

"I'll tell him who did it."

"You'll be dead."

Silky's shoulders slumped and she looked defeated. "What do I get out of this, if I did write the reviews and I can take them down?"

"You get to live and do something with your business. Make it a success with a little work through legitimate efforts," Don said.

"She's got a doctor daddy who helped with her business," Silky said.

"And a mother. Maybe this isn't the business for you.

Maybe it is, but you need to do a lot of work to reach your goals," Lexi said.

"If my dad acknowledged me, he could back my business with the kind of money I need," Silky said.

"And do what? Strong-arm women to buy from you?" Lexi asked.

"Do you want me to take you to the prison to meet Tremaine, and you can see for yourself how he'll react?" Don asked Silky.

"You're just mad because I wrote the truth in a review about you in that stupid video."

"You did it for spite against Lexi, hoping it would hurt her sales. And you're afraid I'm telling you the truth about Tremaine," Don said. "Do we have a deal?"

"I want more of a deal."

Don shrugged. "You write good reviews about Ms. Summerfield's products and Ryder and my videos."

Silky gave Lexi a dirty look and opened her mouth to speak to Don, but he beat her to it. "And I'll write an article about your small startup company."

Silky's jaw dropped, and then she frowned.

"I'm good for my word." Don shoved his hands in his pockets.

Silky gave him an evil smile. "Fine." She turned to Lexi. "If I do this, what will *you* do for me?"

"I won't give your business the trouble you've been giving mine. And that's a promise."

Silky frowned.

Hell, she was lucky Lexi wasn't interested in exposing Silky's underhanded game to the public.

Silky threw her hands up in resignation. "Fine. I'll do it."

"I'll watch you do it, and afterward I'll interview you,"

Don said. "I'll talk to you later," he said to Lexi, then followed Silky into her house.

"Let's go." Lexi was glad that was resolved. She couldn't believe Silky thought she owed her anything for doing what was right, and she was glad Don was offering to handle it.

"I can't believe Don showed up to take her to task." Ryder took over the driver's seat. He figured part of his duties as assigned was being a chauffeur. Besides, he liked to drive.

"I can," Lexi said. "He's like a pit bull when he wants to get something done. And nobody messes with him. Or his wife and two daughters. One time he did a story on a celebrity's extramarital affairs, and the star didn't like it. He hired a man to threaten Don's wife and kids. You don't ever mess with his family. He's just like one of us wolves. And you don't mess with him."

"Well, good. For us, this time," Ryder said.

"I'll say," Kate agreed.

When they arrived at the house, they did the same routine, Ryder and Mike checking the place out and Lexi and Kate waiting outside.

Ryder finally came out and told them it was all clear. "Now what?"

"We can do some guarding and let Mike and Kate have some time in the pool," Lexi said.

"I'm all for it. I'll fix drinks," Ryder said.

"Is there anything you can't do?" Lexi asked as she and Ryder headed out to the pool while Kate and Mike went to change.

"Singing, sewing, and ironing," Ryder said.

She laughed. "Well, I don't do any of those things well either." The doorbell rang, and she headed inside to answer it.

Ryder went with her, and suddenly Mike and Kate were

joining them dressed in swimsuits and carrying guns. Lexi looked through the peephole. "Flower delivery."

Even though she didn't think it was trouble, Ryder still answered the door.

"Delivery for Ms. Summerfield," the man said.

"I'll take it."

"You need to sign here."

Ryder signed *Summerfield*. Not that he was Mr. Summerfield. Which made him wonder, would Lexi even be interested in taking his name? He suspected because of her business, she might not. It was fine either way with him.

Lexi smiled when he signed as Summerfield. Ryder carried the flowers into the house while Mike watched the florist leave. "Does...that mean you're going to be Ryder Summerfield?"

CHAPTER 24

WISHING LEXI HAD ALREADY TOLD HER OTHER SUITORS to take a hike, Ryder set the vase of roses on the bar.

Lexi grabbed the card off the flowers and read, "Hoping to patch things up with you. Dinner tomorrow? Benjamin."

"Do you want to tell him the good news? Or do you want me to?" Ryder asked. At least the guy spent some money on the flowers.

Lexi smiled at Kate and Mike as they applied sunscreen. Kate was wearing a pink-and-black-floral one-piece suit, and Mike was wearing bright-yellow board shorts.

Lexi patted Ryder on the chest. "You tell him, since he doesn't seem to want to listen to me."

"Phone number?"

Lexi handed over her phone. Ryder called up Benjamin.

"Lexi, thank God you called. Did you get the roses? That's probably why you're calling. Does dinner tomorrow night sound good to you?" Benjamin asked.

"Hey, Benjamin, you probably remember me. I'm the guy you told to get lost." Ryder's voice was dark and wolfish.

"Hell, does Lexi know you're using her phone?" Benjamin was irate.

"We're mated. Thanks for the roses. She thought they were lovely. We have them taking center stage on the bar. Sorry you didn't make the cut."

"Let me talk to Lexi."

"Sure." Ryder handed the phone over to her.

Lexi smiled at him. "Hey, Benjamin, yeah, Ryder and I are mated. We just decided on it, or I would have told you about it when I saw you. Thanks for the roses. They're beautiful... No, it has nothing to do with not getting me something from Venice. Good luck with finding the right she-wolf for you. And thanks again for the roses. Bye."

Ryder handed her a margarita. "All done with him?"

"Yeah. Thanks." She took the drink. "Maybe after the pool party, the word will get out and anyone else who still thinks I'm available will get the message."

"I forget you are in the news a lot, so that should work." Ryder set a margarita on one of the lounge tables for Kate and a cold beer for Mike.

Kate and Mike were tossing a beach ball back and forth to each other in the pool. Lexi sat down on one of the barstools and watched them. Ryder grabbed a bottle of beer and sat next to her, getting a kick out of Kate and Mike. He wished something would come between them, but it appeared they were just having fun, nothing serious.

"What do you want to do about our surnames?" Ryder asked Lexi.

She smiled and leaned over to kiss his cheek. "You know, only three percent of men take their wife's name during marriage. I'm more of a traditionalist. Summerfield will continue to be equated with my cosmetics, but Gallagher will be my surname now. I feel more connected to you that way. And unlike with humans, we'll always be together, so I'm eager to make this happen."

Ryder was glad. He would have changed his name if Lexi had wanted him to, but he was glad to carry on his family name.

"Come on, Kate." Lexi sipped on her margarita. "Who's

the guy you're interested in? You've never mentioned anything about him to me before."

Kate laughed and dove underneath the water. When she came up for air, she wiped the water from her eyes. "I am absolutely not saying."

"Ohmigod, Kate, are you kidding? Now you have made me really curious."

Ryder had thought Kate would say when he and Mike weren't around. But something about Kate's tone of voice told him that wasn't happening anytime soon. He knew Lexi was dying to learn the truth. He couldn't help being curious too.

Kate never took off time to be with anyone, so who in the world was the mystery man?

Lexi would have to ask her again later, hoping Kate would finally tell her. "You wouldn't know who it would be, would you?" Lexi whispered to Ryder.

"No. I hadn't met the two of you before."

Lexi let out her breath. She had to know. Ryder was smiling at Lexi, appearing to be amused at her for being so interested. He winked at Lexi.

She shook her head and sighed.

Ryder glanced in the direction of the water, then walked to the edge of the patio and watched a couple of boats bobbing up and down on the ocean.

"See anything?" Mike was treading water in the pool.

"Just a couple motorboats out there. Can anyone reach the house from the ocean?" Ryder asked.

"No, it's too rocky and the waves are too dangerous," Lexi said. "Do you think Tremaine might send men by way of the ocean?"

"Possibly, figuring we wouldn't assume they would for that very reason. Just keeping a lookout from a boat like that, they might be able to tell if you were home or not," Ryder said. "Like now."

"Could they shoot us from that distance?" Lexi had always believed they were safe out here with the ocean at their back.

"Most likely not," Ryder said.

After Mike and Kate finished swimming, they went inside to shower and dress and then fixed dinner—regular fare: roast beef, mashed potatoes, gravy, and carrots.

Lexi was eager to join Ryder in bed after dinner, but he was going to take first guard watch.

Before she went to bed, Lexi said to Kate, "I need to talk to you." She couldn't help it; she wanted to know so badly about Kate's love interest. Didn't Kate need time off to be with him? Now that Lexi had two more bodyguards, she could make time for him.

"Sure."

"Night, Mike, Ryder. I'll see you on shift change," Kate said.

"Night, Mike, Kate," Ryder said. "I'll see you when we switch off." He gave Lexi a kiss and a hug though. "I'll see you soon."

Lexi smiled at him, knowing he'd wake her for some more loving when he came to bed.

"Okay, come on, Kate." Lexi went to the sunroom and Kate joined her.

"If you want to talk about marketing, great. If you want to ask who I'm interested in, I can't say," Kate said as they took seats on the floral cushioned chairs.

"He's not married or engaged or human, is he?" Normally

Lexi wouldn't have considered any of those options, but Kate was being so secretive.

"None of the above, but I'm not saying anything more."

"You're going to have to tell me sooner or later. I will lie awake at night wondering."

Kate chuckled. "Really, it's no big deal."

"Sure it's a big deal. I want you to be able to take off time to go on dates with him. Now that Ryder and Mike are here, I've got protection so you can date."

"And I will, when I meet someone who I can date."

"But you already have someone you're interested in."

Kate just smiled at her. "Are you ready to go to bed?"

"Yeah, sure, but if you ever want to talk, you know I'm available."

"You'll be the first to know. Hey, do you mind if I move my stuff to Ryder's guest room? That will give you two more privacy."

Lexi smiled. "Sure. With your wolf hearing, we wouldn't want to keep you awake at night, or wake you in the middle of the night."

"Yeah, you know me. If I don't get enough sleep, I'm cranky."

"More like quiet and spaced-out," Lexi said. Kate was only cranky when she was starving. "Okay, I'm off to bed."

Lexi went to bed naked and finally fell asleep, but when Mike took over guard duty, Ryder hurried to join her, waking her as soon as he walked into the room.

He stripped out of his clothes, climbed into bed, and didn't hesitate to begin kissing her. "All's well."

"I'll say." Their hearts were both beating out of control before long, and all she could think of was kissing him back, stroking every bit of him, and climaxing with him.

His thumbs brushed over her nipples and she arched her back, wanting him to move his touch lower. She ran her hands over his arms, feeling his muscles tighten. He smiled at her, then moved his hot mouth to her breast and licked the tip of one of her nipples. She let out a pleasurable moan. He feasted on her nipples, taut and expectant. A surge of rife passion raced through her like lightning, igniting a white-hot fire in her veins. He suckled one nipple and then the other, the sensual storm building, their breathing already erratic.

His stiff cock pressed against her, and she wanted him inside her now. Everything about him felt so incredibly good—his mouth, his tongue, his male hardness throbbing against her mound, telling her just how eager he was to have her too.

He moved his mouth from between her breasts, seeking her mouth again. They kissed, his tongue delving deep, then dancing intimately with hers. His leisurely method of seduction was killing her in the most pleasurable of ways.

But then the urgency returned, and he kissed her hard, his hand running over the other breast, cupping and massaging, enjoying the feel of her as much as she was enjoying his touch. She breathed in his musky scent, mixing with her own. He was one hot wolf. She was glad she hadn't let the other male wolves keep her from seeing the good in a male wolf like him. He was perfect for her and all hers. And she was glad she hadn't waited for this either.

He swept his hand downward, his questing fingers finding her sensitive nub. He started slowly, but then his caress intensified, and she arched her pelvis, feeling the heat surging through every bit of her. The ache intensified in her nether region, the sensation building as he kissed her belly with his hot mouth, his breath warming her.

She was so wet for him, and then she dug her heels into the mattress, trying to hold on to the heady sensation building inside of her, trying to let go. "Oh," she moaned, "hurry."

He covered her mouth with his, kissing her deeply again, and then inserted a finger between her legs, swirling and pushing, and then she was coming. Before she knew it, he was pushing into her, and she was relishing every thrust of his hard cock and meeting his thrusts. She loved how powerful and kind and considerate he was. He rocked her world.

Ryder couldn't believe a trip to the redwoods had come to this—a beautiful mate, writhing to his touch and loving him like he loved her. He was thrusting, enjoying her warm, wet heat wrapped around him. He pounded into her, the air filled with their musky scents, encouraging the intimacy to continue between them.

Heat filled every pore, and he couldn't get enough of her. He paused in his thrusts to kiss her again. She was just the person he'd needed to make his life complete.

He resisted coming too soon, but the way she was stroking his ass, he couldn't slow down the rampant need washing over him. He pushed until the end, his blood pumping just as hard, her breath a soft moan as he felt her come again, this time her inner muscles contracting around his cock.

He released, loving how they were in sync, and wanting to do this all over again as soon as they were both ready.

"Hmm, I love you, you hot old wolf." She snuggled against him and he loved the feel of her soft body against his, basking in the afterglow.

"Man, did I luck out when Mike wasn't able to come with me on the hike. I love you, honey."

"Oh, don't tell me you think he would have won me over. You and I were meant for each other." She sighed deeply and kissed his chest. "I never knew it could be this good."

"I feel the same way about you." He combed his fingers through her soft, silky hair. He slid his hand down to her breast and cupped it. "You make my world complete." He just had to make sure he didn't lose focus while trying to keep Lexi safe.

CHAPTER 25

AFTER MAKING LOVE A COUPLE MORE TIMES AND sleeping in late that morning, Ryder slipped out of the room before Lexi finished her shower, and she knew he'd left to help Mike make another special meal for them.

Every meal was a surprise for Lexi and Kate, now that Mike and Ryder had taken over the cooking. Lexi and Kate loved it! But Mike and Ryder had as much fun surprising them.

This morning, they sat down to cinnamon-sugar waffles. Lexi loved cinnamon buns, so these were out of this world. "You guys outdid yourselves. I'm in heaven."

"Kate told us how much you love cinnamon, so we figured we'd give it a shot," Ryder said.

"You both have gone above and beyond. I feel like every meal is a Christmas surprise." Lexi took another bite of her waffle. "I'm so glad we stole you away from Aidan."

Everyone laughed.

"Okay, so next up is the pool party for the new cosmetic line, Summer Breeze. The women are reviewers for magazines, models, actresses, and our very own wolves—Rafe's mate, Jade, and Aidan's mate, Holly. Some of the human females are wealthy and feel entitled. I only invite them because they're important in promoting the new cosmetic line. I try to invite different women each time, but some of the reviewers are the same. Some of the women we've invited in the past were catty and vindictive. Because of my wealth, they're mostly careful not to give me any trouble. But some of them look down their noses on the caterers and Kate. Don't be surprised if one or two of them hit on you guys."

"How do you want us to handle that?" Ryder sounded like he was ready to serve as the bouncer of a club.

Lexi had given this business considerable thought. "I think the best way to go about this is to have Mike greeting them at the front door, and then he remains there, watching for trouble if any of Tremaine's people show up. That will keep Mike out of harm's way, unless Tremaine's thugs show up."

"You have all the fun, Ryder," Mike joked.

"Unless Tremaine's men turn up," Ryder reminded him, smiling. "What do you want me to do, Lexi?"

"You're my mate—to them, my husband—and because of that, I'm hoping they mind their p's and q's with you. If it comes up, we were married in a private ceremony and we'll have the formal wedding where they'll be invited later," Lexi said. "But you know how it is when people start to drink. My goal is to have fun, promote my products, and try to keep the peace. Hopefully, we'll get some good reviews out of it. Because the products are waterproof and have a built-in sunscreen, I've made this one a pool party to prove the products live up to expectations. I doubt everyone will be swimming, but whoever wants to can. Hopefully, they won't smear their makeup when they wipe the pool water from their eyes, or it will ruin the promotional effort we're going for here. Of course, we've tested for that, but you know how things go."

"Agreed," Ryder said.

"What's the attire?" Mike asked.

"Casual. We can figure out something else to wear for later parties—holiday, et cetera, but since you only brought clothes for hiking in the redwoods, just wear whatever you feel comfortable in. Shorts. Jeans. Muscle shirts. T-shirts. The choice is yours." Lexi drank some more of her coffee. "And that brings up another subject. You'll need to move your stuff over here from Aidan's place."

"Aidan said he's having our stuff packed up so we don't have to leave you unprotected," Ryder said. "And a couple of the guys are dropping off our vehicles too."

"Okay, good."

"I need to tell my folks we're mated, and you said you want to have a wedding, right?" Ryder asked.

"Yeah, because of the kind of business I'm in, I'll have to invite everyone I can, hoping I don't snub anyone accidentally." Lexi could just imagine alienating someone important, which could have a ripple effect.

"You're not going to invite that one reviewer who always gives your products mediocre reviews, are you?" Kate asked.

"Yeah, I am. And Silky Spring too."

"All right. Sounds like a good idea," Kate said. "I'll go over the list a few times so we make sure everyone's been invited that we think should be there."

Everyone finished breakfast, and then Kate took charge of setting up the makeup stands under the patio cover out back while Mike and Ryder helped. Lexi hadn't considered what a boon it would be for her to have all this extra help and muscle when she and Kate needed it.

Lexi called her dad in the meantime. "Hey, Dad, are you and Mom working yet?"

"Not yet. We ordered our cars from a dealership, and they should be ready for us at the end of the week. We went on another buying trip. It's amazing what you miss when you can't take everything with you."

"Can you have someone from the pack pick up the things you have where you were staying in the Witness Protection Program?"

"Yeah, Edward said he'd take care of it. We really need to thank Rafe for all of their help," her dad said.

"We will. I'll see his wife and his sister-in-law at a cosmetic party in a little while and mention it too. So you're all settled in?"

"Yeah, we are. We've barely had any time for ourselves, but last night I took your mom to the Silver Town Tavern for a special dinner. The tavern only serves wolves, which was a new experience for us. We can barely do anything, though, without the pack getting involved." Her father's voice was thick with emotion. "You don't know how wonderful it is. Sam and Silva, the owners, brought over champagne and a cake, just to welcome us to the pack. It's like that everywhere. They're thrilled we can help out at the clinic, but it's more than that. They have shared how heroic they think we both are—me for putting a crime boss in prison, and your mother for taking care of the Mexican wolf children and her ordeal after that."

Lexi wiped away tears and sniffled. "I'm so glad, Dad. You both deserve this. And, um, I called to check on you, but I also wanted to tell you Ryder and I are mated."

"Sounds like we need to have another celebration."

"We do. As soon as we can manage it. Oh, and a wedding. I don't know how we're going to do this. Of course I want you and Mom to attend, but it would be too dangerous. I'm thinking we might have two weddings. One there for you and your pack in Silver Town, and one here for friends and associates."

"I'm sure that would work fine for all of us. And I'm glad to hear it. I like Ryder. I think you'll do well with him."

"I will. Okay, Dad, if everything is going well, I'm going

to get back to setting up this party. Tell Mom I'll call her afterward."

"Will do. And congratulations. She's out back putting in a flower garden and left her phone in the living room. I just came in to get us some refreshments, but I'll tell her."

"Thanks, bye, Dad. Love you." Lexi turned to Ryder. "Hey, if you haven't had a chance to tell your parents we're mated, I'll take over from you and you can call them."

"Thanks, I'll do that." Ryder gave her a kiss. "Is everything all right with your family?"

"Yeah. They both love it there." She got a call and looked at the caller ID and smiled. "My mom. Hey, Mom."

Lexi was wiping away tears while talking to her mom when Ryder called his parents. He gave her a hug, but then moved away so she could talk about wedding plans with her mom.

"Hey, Mom, I just got mated," Ryder said to his mother.

His mom tsked. "You know, I figured you'd at least give us some warning."

"Like you did with your parents? We haven't had any time." He explained what had happened, how he and Lexi had met, and all about his new job.

"That sounds like a wild adventure, but I should have known if anyone would have one, it would be you. However, I don't like this business with Tremaine," his mother said.

"Yeah, but you know that comes with the job. I just have to be careful. All of us do. Now, we're going to have a formal wedding, but we'll have two of them."

"Wait, Lexi Summerfield, of Clair de Lune Cosmetics? Ohmigod," his mom said.

Smiling, Ryder had wondered when that would sink in.

"Yeah, so did you want to come to both weddings, or just one of them?"

"Both, of course. We want to meet Lexi's family, and if Lexi's agreeable, since her dad is supposed to be gone, your dad can walk her down the aisle at the other wedding."

Ryder agreed. "I'll ask her." He suspected Lexi would be thrilled, and he was delighted his parents would want to go to both weddings to show their love and support.

"Can I tell my friends?" his mother asked.

"Of course. She'll be announcing it at a party this afternoon, and word will spread like wildfire."

"Hey," Kate said, rushing out to the patio with a handful of sample bags. "The caterers are here."

Ryder said to his mom, "Listen, I've got to go, but we'll talk later about everything."

"Okay, keep her safe, son. And congratulations. I'll tell your dad. Love you."

"Love you, too, Mom."

Mike and Ryder went to check out the new arrivals, even though Ryder was supposed to stay with Lexi. He couldn't help himself. He had to ensure the caterers were who they said they were, and he was checking the list twice. After Rafe had trouble with imposters at a party of his, Ryder knew not to fall for that ploy, and he wasn't taking any chances.

Lexi also joined them to make sure that everything was going okay, while Kate continued to set things up for the makeup session.

The next thing Ryder knew, the guests were arriving. The women were wearing floral dresses or skirts from short to long to in-between, rhinestone sandals, flashy diamond rings, earrings, and necklaces. He was thinking they could really afford to put some meat on their bones. One of the women was a Jamaican actress, starring in a new CBS comedy, and another a Swedish actress he'd seen on the big screen numerous times. He was really impressed Lexi knew these women. He hadn't expected to be so starstruck.

Holly and Jade arrived, both blonds, though Holly had pretty, clear-blue eyes, while Jade's were a beautiful, dark brown. He was glad to see the she-wolves, ready to protect them if any of the women got catty with them.

Kate took everyone else out to the patio to party, while Lexi and Ryder spoke to Holly and Jade alone.

"We're mated," Lexi said. "But we're telling the world we're married and will have the big wedding coming up. I'd love to have both of you as matrons-of-honor, and Kate as a bridesmaid."

The ladies smiled. "We'd be delighted," Jade said.

Holly agreed and hugged Lexi and Ryder. "You're going to Rafe's party tomorrow, right?"

"We wouldn't miss it for the world. Oh, and my parents wanted to thank Rafe for Edward and his men's help with everything."

Jade hugged both of them too. "He was only too happy to offer their services. Okay, we're ready for this party."

"Come on in then," Lexi said.

"Did you warn him about the wild women at this affair?" Jade asked.

Lexi laughed and took Ryder's hand as they walked to the patio. "That's why I'm having Mike stay out front. *I'll* protect Ryder."

Ryder smiled. Lexi went to visit with her guests while Kate started to apply makeup to one of the ladies. Two of the four caterers also started applying makeup to a couple more of the guests.

"Kate and I trained them so they could apply makeup but do the catering, too, when we were done with the makeup sessions." Lexi welcomed everyone to the party and announced, "Some of you might have been wondering. Ryder Gallagher is my husband, but we'll be having a more formal wedding that you will all be invited to, the date to be determined."

"Wow, that was fast." The dark-haired woman eyed Ryder with a small smirk on her face.

"Yeah, we met each other while rescuing bear cubs together, and"—he shrugged—"it was one of those one-of-a-kind life experiences, and we just connected."

"Bear cubs? Oh, really." The woman sounded as though she didn't believe a word of it.

"Yeah, in the redwoods." Ryder ran his hand over Lexi's back and wished he could just take her back to the bedroom now and make love to her.

She smiled up at him, and he kissed her mouth.

Several of the women started taking off their dresses, tops, and skirts, revealing bikinis and tankinis. They were drinking and eating, while some were having their makeup done. The ones who were made up left their chairs to get drinks and something to eat. Then one of those women slipped into the pool, a redhead whose hair was a little too bright to be the real deal.

"This is a little different from working for Aidan and Holly," Ryder told Lexi.

"Yeah, watch that one in the pool though. I think she's already had too much to drink, and we don't want anyone drowning."

"I will." Thankfully, Don hadn't gotten word that Lexi was having a pool party. Ryder could just imagine the guy showing up and giving them grief.

Lexi began applying makeup on another of the ladies, so there were four of them being made up at a time. Two of the women were taking pictures and taking notes.

A couple more women hit the pool, and the redhead climbed out. She grabbed a drink off a caterer's tray, finished it off, and walked over to see Ryder. "Refill it, won't you, sweetie?" She held out her cup.

Ryder didn't recognize the woman, not that he watched TV or movies *all* that often. He noticed Lexi and Kate were watching him. If it hadn't been for not wanting to get bad publicity over this, he would have told the woman she'd had enough to drink.

She was leaning against him, getting him all wet. He took her plastic cup and motioned to one of the caterers to refill her drink.

"I wanted *you* to get it for me," the woman sulkily said.

He didn't figure the woman was a reviewer. She seemed like one of the actresses, though she could be a model.

"That's what I'm doing. Getting you a drink." He asked the caterer to refill the woman's cup.

"You're not really married to Lexi, are you?" the woman asked, her refilled drink in hand.

"Yeah, I am." It seemed strange to say that. He hadn't quite gotten used to the concept yet. He figured word would spread and even Don would hear of it—and probably be miffed Ryder and Lexi had told him they weren't a couple.

The redhead smiled. "Seriously?" She glanced back at Lexi. "Well, she sure has kept the secret well. I'm surprised Don Morgan hasn't published the story even yet, and he's always first to get news like this."

"I'm sure he'll hear about it soon enough."

The redhead shrugged and walked back to the pool.

Ryder smiled at Lexi as she finished up the lady she was making up. "Sorry about that. I never have men here at my parties, and you looked like the perfect target."

"I don't think she believes we're married."

"I thought I was going to have to peel her wet body off yours and throw her in the pool," Lexi said.

Ryder chuckled, envisioning the she-wolf doing just that. "That might not be good for your promo efforts."

"No, but I'd have felt a whole lot better."

Two hours later, the party was winding down, and another one of the ladies joined them, flashing her eyelashes at Ryder. She said to Lexi, "If you ever want to loan him out, I'd be willing to take him off your hands."

Everyone thanked them for the lovely party with promises of great reviews, especially since no one's makeup ran or smeared during the pool play.

The redheaded actress smiled blatantly at Ryder, then left with the others.

"You know she doesn't really believe you'll be faithful to me if she keeps making a play for you," Lexi said.

"Just don't invite her back," Ryder said.

"She's off the guest list," Kate said. "We don't need any trouble from the likes of her, and there are plenty of other celebs waiting to be invited."

Holly and Jade were the last guests to leave the party, wanting to have a private word with Lexi and Ryder.

"I had fun," Holly said. "I can't wait to tell Aidan the news about your mating, but I suspect he realized what was up from the beginning when Lexi called to verify who you were, Ryder."

Lexi smiled. "It's always important to be sure."

Ryder wrapped his arm around Lexi's shoulders. "I'm glad you did."

Jade said, "It was so much fun. Bring your swimsuits to our party, if you'd like. Rafe will have enough bodyguards posted so we can all swim. And congratulations, you two."

Holly and Jade hugged Lexi and Ryder again before they left.

Lexi got a call on her phone and checked the ID. "Don." She answered the phone. "Lexi Summerfield, how may I help you?"

"This is Don Morgan. Why didn't you tell me you and Ryder were getting hitched? I should have had the exclusive story. Doesn't matter. I'd already sent the story in."

"When we told you not to?" Lexi knew he wouldn't have listened to them.

"Aw, come on. I knew you were going to do it, and you did too. So when's the wedding?" Don asked.

"You'll be the first to know."

"Right. Hey, I got Silky to drop the bad reviews she wrote for you products, remember that."

"Ryder saved your life when you were in your burning car, remember that."

"Uh, yeah. You have my wife's seal of approval, by the way. She loved the video of me and your men's skin-care line. It's had over a million views. And I've become a celebrity in my own right."

Not surprised, Lexi smiled.

"My girls said it was silly, but they're only six and eight. What do they know? I've even had a couple model offers."

"Really. Well, let me know how that works out."

"I like what I do."

"Harassing people," Lexi said.

"I'm not just another beautiful face," Don said. "Maybe I'll get into more serious investigative work."

"You'd be good at it."

Don laughed. "I think I'll stick to trying to learn when your big wedding will be."

"I'll be sure to send you and your family an invitation. And you'll be the only journalist who is actually invited."

"Really?"

"Yeah. I've got to go," Lexi said. "Take care of yourself."

"I'll be waiting for the invitation, but I hope you still will give me a heads-up first. Talk later."

"You're inviting Don to the wedding?" Kate asked when Lexi put her phone down.

"Yeah. He'll be there anyway. This way, he'll be there with his wife and daughters and maybe that will help keep him from being a paparazzo at the wedding."

After she ended the call with Don, Lexi got a surprise text. "You won't believe who I just got a text from. Silky Spring."

CHAPTER 26

Lᴇxɪ ᴅɪᴅɴ'ᴛ ᴋɴᴏᴡ ᴡʜᴀᴛ ᴛᴏ ᴛʜɪɴᴋ ᴡʜᴇɴ Sɪʟᴋʏ ᴛᴇxᴛᴇᴅ her.

> It's urgent. I need to talk to you about my dad.

Lexi wasn't sure if she trusted the woman, though Silky had removed all the bad reviews on their product lines and the promo videos. Lexi texted back: What's going on?

> I have something to confess to you. I can't tell anyone else. Please, come see me at my house.

Wary of the situation, Lexi told the others what Silky had shared with her. "What do you all think?"

"Sounds suspicious to me," Kate said, "though she did what she had to do about the reviews. I still don't trust her."

"Sounds questionable to me too," Ryder said.

"There are three of us, if anyone should try to ambush us," Mike said.

"But if she's in with Tremaine on this, she would have told him how many of us would be coming," Lexi said.

"So what do you want us to do?" Ryder asked.

Lexi sighed. "Let's see what she has to say. She sounded really upset, and if I can help her, then I want to. You three can protect me. If you believe it's doable. Unless you think we should meet somewhere else."

"Tell her we'll meet her at her home in two hours, but we'll go now to make sure no one gets there before we do and sets up an ambush. I'll be in the house with you. Kate and Mike can remain hidden outside behind those tall shrubs and let us know if we have any trouble," Ryder said. "Let's go."

Armed for battle, they took off for Silky's house while Lexi texted her that they'd arrive in a couple of hours. She hoped Silky would be there when she and the others arrived at her place. Once they were there, they parked down the street from the house. Silky wouldn't see the vehicle that way.

Lexi rang the doorbell, and then Silky opened the door. "I thought you said you wouldn't be here for about two hours. Come in."

"We decided to come early because we have some other stuff we need to do after this," Lexi said.

"Okay. That's fine. I'd hoped you would come right away. Where are the others? It's just you and your one bodyguard?" Silky escorted them to her living room where the calico cat wound around Lexi's legs, and the black and white cat jumped up on the back of the floral sofa and watched them, his tail waving up and down, looking like he was the king of the beasts.

"They couldn't come." Lexi didn't feel bad about the lie. She had to give them some advantage if Silky had set a trap for them. She glanced around at the eclectic living room—a hodgepodge of decorator items sitting on white shelves, from a jade-green Buddha to a pink metal flamingo, a conch shell, and little framed pictures of a waterfall, a winter scene, and a palm tree.

A wooden rocking chair was covered in pink and

white flamingo cushions; a wrought-iron chair covered in sunflower-on-blue cushions. The sofa was covered in white floral chintz. White box cubes served as a coffee table, and more decorator items filled the boxes. Despite the riot of colors, the decor had a fun vibe and made Lexi feel like she was in a fancy gift shop. She sat on the sunflower chair while Silky took a seat on the sofa. Ryder stood at the window, looking out and listening to their conversation.

"So what is this all about?" Lexi asked Silky.

"I killed the DA," Silky said, her voice soft.

"Why would you even say that? And why would you have done it anyway?" Lexi couldn't believe it. Was Silky thinking she could sway Tremaine into saying she was his daughter if she pleaded guilty to the crime? She had to be nuts. Lexi noticed Ryder had shifted his attention from the window to Silky, probably just as shocked to hear the admission of guilt.

"The DA was after my dad for drug-trafficking and murder. All right? The DA put my mother away when she killed that man in self-defense."

"So you wanted the DA dead because he put both Tremaine and your mother in prison? I don't believe it." Though it could be motivation. "Except for one thing. My father witnessed Tremaine kill the DA." Lexi knew her father wouldn't have fabricated what he'd seen.

"Yeah, sure, that's what your dad saw. My dad did shoot the DA, but he *wasn't* dead. Not then. Not until I shot him."

"That's why they said two different guns were used," Lexi said. "Tremaine saw that my father had been a witness to the shooting, and my father ran before Tremaine could kill him. If Tremaine had run off, my father would have gone to the DA's aid instead." It was possible Silky had shot the

DA after all. Lexi hadn't been at the trial because her father wanted her to stay far away from it. Instead, she and her father had been pretending they hadn't had anything to do with each other for years. They didn't share family photos anywhere, so Tremaine wouldn't have been able to learn it wasn't true.

"If you did kill the DA, why tell me this now? Why not tell the police and get Tremaine off so you could go to prison instead?" Lexi still didn't believe it.

"My dad went into hiding to begin with. I didn't think they'd find him. And they didn't know about me." Silky shrugged. "Why should I go to prison if they think he did it and they can't trace it back to me? He can stay out of jail on his own because he's got so many people working for him that can make it happen. I don't. I thought if he'd admit I was his daughter, I'd have his protection. I didn't expect them to catch him, for your dad to testify—no one ever lives to do that—and that he'd be convicted."

Or she thought if she went to prison, people would look up to her because she was Tremaine's daughter? He already killed her mother in prison. Get a clue, lady!

"But he won't say I'm his daughter, so screw him. It's not like he hasn't killed a ton of other people. Whoever gets in his way is dead. He either orders the hit or does it himself."

Like most everyone, Lexi had figured that, but she couldn't believe Silky had the inside track on any real information that could be used in a court of law to indict Tremaine. "How do you know this for sure?"

"Mom used to be his lover. I mean, she actually lived with him for two years in his multimillion-dollar home, had the diamond rings, bracelets, earrings, necklaces, the Lamborghini, designer clothes, visits to the spas, vacation trips to numerous islands, and gobs of money to throw away. She even had bodyguards like you do. She wasn't a mistress or a one-night stand, or a hooker back then. She shared pictures of the good times with me."

"But she knew how Tremaine made all that money."

"I told you she did," Silky said, her tone snotty. "She saw him kill his own men when they didn't get the job done right. Four different men at different times. Tremaine has a hot temper when things don't go his way. He killed one man just because he smiled at my mother."

"And still, she stayed with him." Lexi figured the money was too good. "How do you know for sure what happened? It's just your word, which can't be proven in court."

"No. She recorded a lot of it, and she gave the recordings to me before she went to prison. She wouldn't turn it over to the police because she still loved Tremaine. Isn't that ironic? Anyway, I have all of it."

"Why didn't you turn it into the police already?" The calico cat jumped onto Lexi's lap, startling her, and she smiled and started to scratch the cat's head between her ears.

"You know what happens when you try to testify against Tremaine." Silky rolled her eyes. "You're dead."

"You've got to do it, Silky. He'll never get out of prison that way," Lexi said. "Really, your mother should have, and not left this for you to deal with."

"I felt sorry for my mom. She didn't get along with her stepdad, and he kicked her out of the house when she was sixteen. She met Tremaine at a local burger place where she was working as a waitress. He gave her a hundred-dollar tip and told her to come home with him, and that was it. Until she got pregnant with me. He wasn't a family man. He saw himself as a hotshot drug lord with all adult fare. Having a crying baby—or even a pregnant lover who was beginning to show—wasn't his style. He kicked her out, and she never got over it. At least she went back to waitressing until I was sixteen and wasn't using until later."

"Okay, so if he did all that, why would you want to acknowledge he's your dad?"

Silky cast her a small smile. "Because he doesn't want me to."

"And that could be dangerous." But there was another possibility. What if Tremaine *wasn't* her dad? What if one of the men in his employ was? The guy who smiled at her mother and consequently was murdered? Or someone else? And Tremaine knew it and murdered him and kicked Silky's mother out of the house. Maybe Tremaine really had felt something for her and couldn't make himself just outright kill her.

Lexi hadn't thought Tremaine would have a soft spot for anyone, but maybe he did.

"You're sure your mother didn't love someone else and *that* man was your father instead?"

Silky's eyes filled with tears.

Lexi thought Silky's reaction was telling. "Does Tremaine know you shot the DA?"

"He knows somebody did, and he wanted him dead. Which means me, but he's clueless about who did it."

"I still don't understand why you told me about it."

Silky didn't say anything.

"Are you sure the DA was even alive when you shot him?" If Silky wasn't making up the whole story.

"Yeah, I think so. I don't know. I never shot anyone before. I just did it really quick."

"Whose gun did you use?"

"I found one in Tremaine's car. I was following the DA, wanting to tell him off for convicting my mom and then getting her killed, but then I saw Tremaine leave his car and I thought he was after the DA. So I checked Tremaine's vehicle—it's always a good idea to lock your doors, even if you're a big-time mobster—and found a gun in his glove compartment and another in his console, but I just took the one."

"So it had his fingerprints on it, unless you weren't wearing gloves. And it would have still been traced back to him. How many times did you shoot the DA?" Lexi figured Ryder could learn how many rounds were fired from the other gun to confirm whether Silky was lying or not.

"Yeah, I was wearing gloves. It was winter. I fired the gun three times. I'm not sure if any but the last bullet hit him. I was really scared, and I was shaking pretty hard. I know how to shoot a gun, but before that, I just shot at cans and not at real people."

"You know what I think? You shot the DA because he put your mother in prison. You might have even planned to shoot Tremaine, but he ran off to kill my father. Tremaine kicked your mother out of the house because he knew the baby she was carrying wasn't his. I think he killed your father, and he was one of the men employed by Tremaine. Maybe even one of the men who guarded her. I think Tremaine loved your mother enough that he forced her out of the house, but that's the only reason he didn't kill her too.

"She told people in prison you were his daughter, and she stuck to her story because she didn't want Tremaine to kill you. But he knew you weren't his child, and he was so eaten up by jealousy over her having an affair with someone he had employed, he finally had her murdered in prison. Then here you are, claiming the same thing. And he knows you're not his kid. I think you're perpetuating the lie because your mom told you to do so or he might terminate you too. Except it's going to get you killed because he's sick of hearing the lie."

Silky was glowering at Lexi, but finally turned her glower to the floor.

"You didn't tell the police you shot the DA because you *wanted* Tremaine to go to jail. He needed to be held accountable for his actions. You said yourself that he'd killed a number of people. But Tremaine killing your mother was the living end for you. She might have been charged with murder, but she would have gotten out of prison eventually. You visited your mother in prison, didn't you?" Lexi had a sneaking suspicion Silky had.

Silky got a tissue and wiped her eyes and nodded.

"You could have had a lot more years visiting her. Cheering her on."

"He took that from me. He took her from me."

"Correct. And Tremaine ordered the hit on your mom only days before he shot the DA. I believe you confessed to me because you were afraid you'd killed the DA, and it's been weighing on your conscious."

Silky sobbed.

"Okay, so you wanted to make sure the DA was dead, and that Tremaine went to prison for it because he'd killed your mother *and* your father, right?"

Silky nodded, tears streaking down her face.

"You're not a cold-blooded killer like Tremaine is. He seems to have no empathy for anyone. Did your mom ever talk to you about anyone she liked while she was living with Tremaine?"

"Murphy Townsend. He went everywhere with her. He was her personal bodyguard."

Very personal, Lexi bet.

Silky let out her breath. "Okay, yeah, he could have been my dad. As much as I hate to admit it."

"Why? Tremaine is no bargain."

"Because he could have taken her away. Okay? If he really loved her, and he wasn't just trying to get even with Tremaine or just proving he could get one over on his boss without getting caught, he would have left with her."

"Unless he was afraid they'd never get away without Tremaine coming after them or sending his men to track them down. When it was Tremaine's idea that she should go, then it was fine. But I doubt your mom and Murphy could have left together without getting themselves killed. If they had been lovers."

Silky begrudgingly agreed.

"Okay, listen, Tremaine's in prison. Quit telling everyone he's your dad and you'll live longer. Don't tell anyone you're Murphy's daughter either. Tremaine could still want you dead for that. But why tell me you shot the DA?"

"I had to tell someone. I…I thought you would understand because your dad was on the side of the law and had witnessed the shooting and then stuck to his guns and testified against Tremaine."

"Okay, Tremaine killed the DA as far as we know." Lexi would have someone verify which bullets from which gun killed the DA. Though both guns were Tremaine's so it still would be on him. She felt sorry for the woman and thought she needed a second chance. "As to your cosmetics business, how are sales?"

"They're okay. I won't make a billion dollars on it like you."

"It takes time, commitment, and passion. I didn't make a mint on my business overnight. I've been planning this for years. But Kate and I can give you some tips on marketing."

Silky's eyes widened. "You would do that for me, even after all that I did?"

"Yeah. I've helped others before with their businesses. It's payback for all the assistance I've had when I was starting out."

Ryder warned, "We've got company!"

Lexi knew he didn't mean the good kind. She glanced back at Silky and thought she looked guilty, her head hanging down. Lexi should have trusted her instincts more, but she'd wanted to see the good in the woman. "It's a setup! You set us up!"

Both cats scattered; one tore off down the hall and the other dove under the sofa.

"No, I didn't. You've got to believe me." Silky's eyes were wide with terror. "Except I posted a video on YouTube saying Tremaine was my dad. I've never said anything about it on social networks before." She pulled out her phone. "Here... Ohmigod, it's had a few thousand views already."

"Get down on the floor now," Lexi ordered her.

Silky hurried to hug the floor.

Gunshots rang out, and Lexi got on her cell phone and called the police. They had to turn the men in to the police if they could. They heard a man cry out, but Ryder stayed inside to protect her and Silky. Lexi prayed Kate and Mike didn't get hit.

"So who is Tremaine after this time? You or me?" Lexi asked Silky, her own gun out.

"Me. I didn't tell anyone you were coming to see me. And I just posted the video about an hour ago."

"Why? If you think your dad could be the man Tremaine had eliminated?" Lexi crouched near the couch, ready to shoot anyone who came through the door, though she hoped she didn't shoot a cop or Kate or Mike by accident.

"I told you. My mother told me to do it. She insisted he was my father. And I did it out of spite since he didn't want to hear me say it. Despite what Don said, I didn't believe Tremaine would really put a hit out on me."

"Well, if they are after you, Don was right."

More gunshots rang out, and then someone barged through the door. The man saw Lexi first and aimed to shoot her, but Ryder came across the floor so fast, the guy didn't know what hit him. Ryder punched him in the side of the head so hard, he knocked him out. The man fell to the floor, out cold, but Lexi could see he was still breathing.

Another man barged in, and Ryder took him down just as quickly. Lexi was impressed. Benjamin would have really had a fight on his hands if Ryder had pummeled him.

"Wow," Silky whispered. "And he didn't even have to shoot anyone."

Kate rushed into the house and saw the two men knocked out on the floor. "I'm glad to see you are both all right."

"How many more were there?" Ryder asked.

"Two. Mike and I nailed them. Nothing fatal. Police sirens are getting closer."

"You won't tell them I shot the DA, will you?" Silky sounded worried she might actually go to prison too.

"I'll check into the ballistics on it," Ryder said. "We have friends everywhere."

"So you set us up?" Kate asked Silky.

"No, I didn't. I didn't tell anyone you were coming. I

thought you weren't coming for another two hours," Silky said, tears brimming in her eyes.

"I think Tremaine put out a hit on Silky. Okay, here's what we're going to do. Men tried to kill you. We were here to protect you. You go into the Witness Protection Program and testify about Tremaine sending these goons to kill you. But I think it would be prudent to get a blood test and verify that you are or are not Tremaine's daughter. And if not, we can try to get some DNA from Murphy Townsend's family and see if you could be Murphy's daughter. And you need to turn over all the evidence your mother gave to you. She didn't destroy it. She probably hoped you'd hand it over to the police eventually," Lexi said. "In the meantime, you'll have to give up what you do, change your name, and just vanish."

"Fine. I'll do it. I'm not really doing great at this business anyway. It's a lot of work and a lot of stress. I think I'd like to do what she does," Silky said to Lexi, motioning to Kate.

"No stress in *my* work," Kate said.

Not unless she was having a shoot-out with gunmen or rescuing bear cubs while their mother watched.

The police arrived while Ryder was texting someone on his phone. While Kate and Mike were giving their statements about shooting the two men outside the house, Ryder said to Silky inside the house, "The ballistics report said the first shots fired from the gun Tremaine had on him were the ones that had killed the DA. One shot from the other gun that was found in an alley nearby—also belonging to Tremaine and with his fingerprints on them—grazed the dead DA's arm. Both guns only had Tremaine's prints on them. So you're in the clear."

Then Ryder made another call. "Hi, I'm Ryder Gallagher,

and I'm at Silky Spring's home where Joe Tremaine's
men tried to murder her. She's looking to go into the
Witness Protection Program for her testimony against Joe
Tremaine."

"Only if I can take my cats with me," Silky said.

Lexi didn't blame her. She'd feel the same way if she had
pets. Which she planned to, once the rehoming pet party
got underway in a couple of days. She wanted them mostly
for companionship, and partly for guard duty, alerting them
if trouble was on its way. She realized she hadn't asked how
Mike or Ryder felt about having dogs in the house. She suspected Ryder would go along with it, just because he'd want
to make her happy. She hoped Mike would be fine with it.

After the U.S. Marshals arrived and took over with the
situation with Silky, Lexi and her party headed out to the
vehicle. When they were on their way, Lexi said, "I'm glad
Silky didn't kill the DA after all. On another topic I wanted
to discuss with you all, Kate and I want to get a couple of
dogs. How do you guys feel about that?"

"Sounds like a great idea," Mike said. "I grew up with a
Lab."

Ryder smiled at Lexi. "I haven't had a pet in years. When
do you want to get one?"

"In a couple of days, I'm sponsoring a rehoming pet
party. I always donate to the Fur Babies Rescue Center's
cause, and I'd love to take a couple of their dogs in." Lexi
thought back to when she had told Kate that taking Ryder
in sounded like rehoming a pet. She smiled.

CHAPTER 27

When they returned to Lexi's home, Kate said, "We're on guard duty, if the two of you want to do some martial arts practice. Then after dinner, Mike and I can get some practice in while Ryder guards you."

Lexi smiled at Ryder. He was all for it. "I'm game, if you are."

"Yeah, sure." But she sounded like she didn't believe she could do well against him.

He had every intention of showing her the ropes and, in time, making her an expert, for her own protection if he couldn't be there for her.

He dressed in a black, skintight compression Lycra shorts and a tank top. She was wearing a bright-pink crop top and black shorts for training. When he saw the way she was dressed, he said, "Hot damn, Lexi."

She laughed. "It's cool and comfortable and made for doing this."

He was thinking he'd rather do some other kind of exercise. Back in bed. Though the workout could be exhilarating, a shower afterward, and yeah, this was just what they needed to finish off the day. The night was another story.

They went downstairs into the basement, the light filtering through several windows that opened out onto the back patio and pool. Part of the floor was covered in gym mats, and two stationary bicycles and a treadmill sat in one corner of the room, a big-screen TV on the wall. Great for getting in shape if the weather was bad. Beach scenes, the ocean, seagulls, and mermaid pictures covered the walls, making him feel as though he was at a tropical resort.

He took Lexi's hand and encouraged her to sit down with him. "First, we meditate for five minutes."

"Oh, this is nice. Usually, Kate and I just stretch and get right to it."

Ryder leaned over and kissed Lexi. "This helps center you." Though he found he couldn't center himself at all, not while he was thinking about what was coming up after the workout. Well, after dinner.

When the five minutes were up, he took her hand and helped her up and pulled her in for a kiss and a hug. He couldn't help it. She was sexy and so appealing. "Hmm, you know after this, we can take a shower, have dinner, and then go straight to bed."

She smiled up at him and hugged him tighter. "Yeah, I like your martial arts plan."

Reluctantly, he pulled away. "Getting back to the martial arts training, to warm up, we can run around the yard, down the road, or jog in place down here for ten minutes, then we'll do sit-ups and push-ups."

"Okay. Let's do it here." Lexi began jogging in place.

Ryder was smiling at her as he jogged in front of her. "You're the perfect martial-arts partner."

She laughed. "You only say that because I won't be able to best you."

He laughed. "I love you."

She smiled at him. "I love you too."

Afterward, they began stretches so they wouldn't injure their muscles during the training.

Then they started with the ready stance, feet together.

He showed her how to find a balance, to move quickly to defend herself. To move from one stance to another. "It's not about muscle strength, but about power and speed."

He showed her how to throw a straight punch, an uppercut, a knife hand, elbow strike, and backfist. And he demonstrated how to block the attacks. Then they alternated between defending and attacking. She was a fast learner. Though she seemed to know many of the skills, she took the training on as though she'd never been taught them, listening to everything he had to say. She was a good student.

"The first two knuckles are the strongest on your hand. If you have to resort to a punch from your hand, use those two knuckles. Line them up with your forearm bones. That will give you the most strength in your punch. Mistakes are made when punching too high, like raising the fist above the forearm or thrusting with the shoulder." He demonstrated the right way again, and then the wrong ways. "Okay, let's practice. You punch, I'll block." After Lexi had a feel for it, he switched off with her and he did the punching, while she did the blocking. "Doing great."

Then they took a breather, and he said, "All right, we're going to practice kicks. But instead of power, we want to do a more fluid motion, just to get used to the moves. Now I know you and Kate have been practicing, but I need to see how far along you are. As you learn the moves, you'll build up power."

She smiled. "I know some of them. But all of this just reinforces what I'm learning."

"Okay, we'll start with the front-start kick. Then the side-start kick." Then he demonstrated the side-thrust kick and the back-thrust kick. "And the last one is the round kick."

After she practiced the kicks, he said, "Okay, we're going to start sparring."

He threw a punch and she quickly blocked it; they did leg kicks, then she punched at him, and he blocked her. He had no idea how she'd react to his teaching her things, but she was eager to learn and quick to grasp the concepts. Near the end, she was tiring, laughing, and not focusing. He was amused and glad she was learning, but also enjoying herself. Then he grabbed her up in his arms and hugged her. "You are beautiful."

"So are you. I love your training techniques. Sorry I started laughing at the end. I was making so many mistakes that I would have been finished off in no time if you were the bad guy."

"I will take care of the bad guys. This is just for your protection in case someone gets past me. Are you ready for that shower?"

"After a workout, always. But with you? Especially always."

He chased her up the stairs and she groaned. "I'm going to be feeling some tired muscles tomorrow."

"I'll give you muscle rubs, chase you around the yard as wolves, swim with you, and do a lot more sparring, and we'll be in perfect shape."

She laughed, grabbed his hand, and hauled him toward her bedroom, but on the way past the kitchen, they saw Mike in there puzzling over something. "I was going to fix salmon for dinner, unless you want to skip it."

"Uh, we're going to get cleaned up, so wait about an hour, and we'll be out," Lexi said.

Ryder smiled at Mike. "I figure we'll run around as wolves after dinner tonight and see the sunset." Before he took Lexi to bed and made love to her.

———

As soon as Ryder and Lexi got to the bathroom, they stripped off their clothes in a rush. She turned on the shower, then they both entered the large stall, shut the glass door, and began kissing each other.

His cock was already swelling with need before she even began soaping him up, their hair wet, their hands covered in soap, stroking and cleaning.

He groaned. "You are a delight." He ran his soapy hands over her breasts, loving the feel of her soft, warm skin, her blushing nipples taut and stretching out under the palms of his hands. Her mouth was on his again, her tongue wickedly teasing his. He kissed her back, her lips warm and soft and supple. He loved the way her hands swept down his sides, his hips, and then slipped around to his back and buttocks, giving them a squeeze, making his cock jump with intrigue. Their mouths were still fused, fueling their passion, their desire.

She reached for her orange-scented shampoo and poured some out in her hand, then slid it through his hair, her fingers caressing his scalp. His breath was ragged, her massage stimulating every erogenous zone in his body.

Their pheromones were swirling around them, encouraging the rapture between them. He kissed her mouth, inserting his tongue, her fingers still doing a miraculous number on his hair. He caressed her tongue with his and slid his hands down her back until he could cup her buttocks. Pulling her tight against his body, he wanted her to feel what she was doing to him. She smiled in a wicked way, but then she rubbed against his arousal and he knew he couldn't last. He slid his hands over her soapy breasts and down her belly until he reached her short curly hairs. She moved her hands over his chest, his nipples aroused and sensitive nubs under her touch.

In earnest, he stroked her feminine nub, and her hands stilled on his chest. Then she wrapped her leg around his, giving him more access to her center. Obliging her, he inserted his finger between her feminine lips and began to thrust as deeply as he could. She wrapped her arms around his neck, the warm shower water sluicing down their skin. Caught up in the thrill of his exploration, she clung to him and arched her back. Her breathing was ragged, her eyes shut as she absorbed his touch, and he loved putting her under his spell.

"Oh…my…God," she rasped out, and he felt her climax rippling around his finger.

Smiling, he pulled his finger out, kissed her mouth, and then lifted her the rest of the way around his hips so he could plunge his cock between her legs. He pushed in slowly, then deepened the thrust. Her ragged breath was whisper-soft against his throat. His mate was pleasure personified.

Lexi would never be able to get enough of being with Ryder like this. She enjoyed how thoughtful he was, always making sure she came before he finished making love to her, completely spoiling her. She was all for spoiling him too. Caught up in the feel of his steel-hard cock thrusting into her, she held on tight and savored the ride. Their hearts were racing, and he kissed her mouth with zeal and love. She was holding on tight to him, feeling the overwhelming urge to come again, his chest muscles glistening with water, his eyes half-lidded, his breath as ragged as hers.

He tightened his hold on her, and barely breathing, he let out a growl and an "I love you."

She was too wrapped up in coming and barely heard him, she was so close to the end. She felt as though the ocean currents had carried her off and deposited her on an island paradise as the climax hit.

He smiled and eased her down so she could rest her feet on the tile floor. Then they were back to soaping each other up, which meant they were caressing and stroking and enjoying each other all over again. "Hmm, Lexi, ready to take this to bed?"

She laughed. "We agreed to eat, and then see the sunset, and then we'll continue this in bed."

He smiled. "I'll take you up on it."

"I knew you were the one for me."

Dinner was great, and then all four of them went out to run outside as wolves—not on the schedule, but they all wanted to do so—listening to the ocean waves hitting the rocks down below, watching the sunset coloring the sky and water in oranges and pinks.

It was beautiful like it usually was, but with a mate and friends, even more so. They chased one another around some more, tackling and play-biting until the sun disappeared and all that was left was the dark-blue night.

Lexi woofed. It was time to go to bed and make love to her mate there.

Kate and Mike followed Lexi and Ryder into the house and shifted. Mike said, "I'll take first guard duty."

"I'm next," Kate said.

Lexi was so glad Mike and Kate were there for them. She woofed at them, thanking them, and took off down the hall. Ryder woofed, too, then he disappeared into the room with her.

She shifted and he did, too, closing the door before he ravished her, like she ravished him.

———∿∿∿———

Early the next morning, Lexi leaned over to kiss Ryder on the cheek, feeling on top of the world, so glad she and Ryder were mated. There was so much more to life than working, promoting, and making money. She and Kate usually greeted the sunrise in the morning, having their coffee out on the patio, sometimes swimming, other times running as wolves. Today, she wanted to run as a wolf. Without telling Ryder what she was up to, and before he could wake enough to pull her into his arms, she moved her covers aside, left the bed, and shifted.

Ryder chuckled, threw the bedcovers aside, jumped from the bed, and shifted. Then he chased after her, but she was already halfway down the hall, and she hit the wolf door before he could reach her. She bolted outside, the thrill of the chase in her blood. She had wanted to do this in the mornings since they arrived home, but they'd been kind of sidetracked.

Now, her mate was chasing her, and she was having a blast. He couldn't catch her though, or at least he wasn't trying too hard. Her tail and his were waving high in the ocean breeze, the sky dark, but lights on a boat out in the ocean caught her eye just as Ryder tackled her to the freshly cut grass.

Ryder paused to watch the lights on a boat bobbing up and down on the water. It was probably a fishing boat at this early morning hour, she suspected. If someone had binoculars, could they see the wolves up on the bluff when the sun rose higher in the sky?

She saw Kate and Mike coming outside dressed in jeans, T-shirts, and flip-flips with cups of coffee in hand, both smiling at them. Ryder released her, and Lexi ran off again with him in hot pursuit. She loved playing with him like this. Not just as wolves in courtship, but as mated wolves.

Then the sky began to lighten, and the bank of clouds on the horizon turned pink and purple, the sky becoming more gold and orange, just beautiful. Panting, she and Ryder lay down on the grass together, their bodies resting against each other, while they watched the sun appearing out of the ocean. She licked his chin, and he nuzzled her face back with affection.

Whitecaps topped the cresting waves, and the ocean breeze ruffled their fur. She took in a deep breath of the salty air, and he smiled at her. This was heaven.

"We're fixing roasted asparagus with pickle-poached eggs and country ham for breakfast," Mike told them, "when everyone's ready."

Lexi woofed to let them know she was ready for it.

Ryder agreed, and Mike and Kate went inside to make breakfast.

Lexi heard a metal clunk against the rocky cliff, and she glanced at Ryder. His ears were perked up, too, and he was looking in the same direction as she was.

They both took off for the cliff to check it out. But as soon as she got near the edge, she couldn't go any closer. Ryder, her beautiful, protective wolf, went to the edge, and that about gave her heart palpitations. She knew the rock was stable, not crumbly like in the redwoods, but it still made her feel as though he'd fall off it at any second.

He was peering down, his ears twitching back and forth, listening, like she was doing. She heard metal clanking against the rocks again, and it sounded like someone was using a grappling hook to climb up the rocks. Only someone with bad intentions would try to reach her property. Another grappling hook hit the rock face, farther away from the other.

Like Ryder, she was glued to where she was standing, wanting to stop whoever they were before they made it to the top. She didn't want to howl to alert the climbers they were on to them either. Nor did she want to run back to the house to alert Mike and Kate and leave Ryder on his own when more than one of them was climbing the rocks.

Still, she thought she might be able to race back to the house and alert Mike and Kate and rush back in time before the men crested the top of the cliffs, but then Mike ran out of the house, shouting, "Tremaine escaped prison. Edward and some of his men are on the—"

Mike stopped talking when he heard the noise down below the cliffs. In an instant, he had his gun out.

At least whoever was trying to climb up the cliff wouldn't be able to get a gun out while trying to reach the top. Lexi couldn't believe Tremaine had broken out of prison. Not that it didn't happen. She was sure he'd had a lot of help to do it. She'd think he'd want to disappear so they couldn't catch up to him. Maybe he had, and whoever was climbing the cliffs were his henchmen. Had to be. She didn't think the paunchy, middle-aged guy would be able to negotiate the cliffs. Even these men seemed to be having a time of it. She suspected this wasn't something they normally did.

Gunfire broke out in front of the house, and Lexi nearly had a heart attack. Kate was alone. Lexi raced off to protect her, running faster than a human could, while Mike and Ryder waited to take care of the men on the cliff.

Her heart pounding, she ran into the house, wondering if she should dress, shift, and shoot. She skidded to a stop when she heard a man in the house, shouting, "Where the hell is she?"

"She's not here." Kate's voice indicated she was sitting on the floor. She had to have been hit or she would have still been shooting, Lexi was certain.

Gunfire and growling sounded in the backyard near the bluff.

"Go help them out," the man said.

Lexi hid behind the sofa, having every intention of taking down the man who was interrogating Kate and then going after the other men, as long as Kate wasn't in bad shape.

One man ran past the couch for the sunroom and back door. More shots were fired outside before the man reached the door. Lexi hated that Mike and Ryder had to face at least three men now, but she had to do something about the one with Kate. She crept around the couch as the man dashed outside and more gunfire was exchanged.

"She left you here? Her personal assistant? I don't buy it. Tell me where she is," the guy said.

"She left with her one bodyguard, Tremaine."

Lexi's heart was already beating double time, but hearing his name made it beat even faster. They had to kill him. They just had to. He was the reason she had to constantly look over her shoulder and couldn't see her parents. He was the reason her father would always fear for his life. And her mother would too.

"They're getting married, and he took her to look at rings. How did you manage to escape from prison?" Kate asked.

"Money can buy anything. What jewelry store were they going to?" Tremaine asked.

Lexi couldn't fathom he would believe Kate's story. Lexi only had one shot at taking him down before he killed Kate. Her body low, Lexi crept behind the long blue sofa in the living room and saw Kate near the foyer, holding her bloodied arm. Then Lexi saw Tremaine, his shaggy, windblown hair a dark-brown streaked with gray, dark stubble covering his blocky jaw. Lexi knew Kate saw her, but she kept her eyes on Tremaine, so she wouldn't alert him that Lexi was standing nearby, just out of his view.

Lexi saw a redheaded man coming through the door, and she didn't have a choice. She had to take the risk and tear into Tremaine. She knew the other guy would shoot to kill her as soon as he saw her, thinking that she was just a large dog with big teeth that could be protective of Kate. Lexi jumped to take Tremaine down before the other man could see her and react. She slammed her large paws against Tremaine's back, knocking him down. Kate scrambled for his gun, aimed, and shot him in the head. Kate wheeled around to shoot the other man before he could respond, but Lexi grabbed hold of his gun hand and bit down hard enough to break the bones in his wrist, forcing him to drop his gun. He pulled a knife out with his left hand and stabbed at her, but she leapt out of the way. She hadn't expected the guy to be ambidextrous.

Kate shot him in the head, and as soon as he collapsed on the tile floor, Lexi and Kate made sure both men were dead. Then they ran for the back door to help Mike and Ryder with the other thugs. Lexi just hoped there wouldn't be any others coming through the front door.

CHAPTER 28

Hell, it was bad enough that two men were coming up the cliff, but then another man shot out of the house. That was bad news since Lexi and Kate were still in there. Ryder was sick with worry that the women were badly injured or dead.

Not liking that they had to shift their attention to the man racing across the patio when the other men could be cresting the bluff at any time, Ryder charged the man, gaining ground on him. When the man turned to shoot at him, Mike shot him. *Bang! Bang! Bang!*

The thug's shots went wild, and he collapsed next to the bar. Still in his wolf coat, Ryder raced back to the cliff to stop the men there. Mike tore off to grab the man's gun and make sure he was dead. Ryder was standing at the edge of the cliff, trying to see where the other men were. After hearing all the shooting, they'd paused in their climb.

When everything outside was quiet, the men began climbing up the cliff again. They must have figured no one knew what they were up to, or they wouldn't risk checking things out.

Then the shooting in the house stopped. Before Ryder could be even more concerned, Kate and Lexi ran outside, Lexi still wearing her wolf coat. Kate's arm was bleeding, and Mike quickly went to assist her as Lexi joined Ryder to defend against the other intruders.

Mike holstered his gun and yanked off his shirt, then wrapped it around Kate's wound to stop the bleeding.

Ryder nuzzled Lexi in greeting, glad she wasn't hurt and praying Kate would be all right. None of them said anything, not wanting to give themselves away to the men climbing the cliff.

Being his protective self, Ryder charged forward as soon as the first man crested the bluff. He heard Lexi's sharp intake of breath as she rushed to keep him from getting hurt. He still didn't bark or growl, but when the guy saw him, Ryder smelled the man's adrenaline-laced fear. Ryder leapt forward, meaning to startle the guy enough that he'd think twice about attacking them and return the way he'd come. Despite his wide-eyed appearance, as if he were in shock to see the wolf so close, the man grabbed Ryder's leg and pulled him toward the cliff's edge.

Lexi rushed forward, growling and snapping viciously at the man, nearly slipping off the edge herself. His heart in his throat, Ryder bit the guy, but the thug still managed to pull him partway over the cliff. Ryder snapped and snarled and bit again, until Lexi made another lunge at the guy, and he lost his grip on Ryder's leg. He plummeted to the rocks below, screaming until he hit the bottom, the other man looking on in horror as he stared at the wolves above, and then at his cohort down below.

Ryder scrambled to safety, but Lexi had been hanging too far forward when she bit at the man, and now she couldn't get enough traction to back up. She looked and smelled as terrified as Ryder was. He moved far enough away from the ledge so that when he shifted, the other man couldn't see him. Then Ryder hurried to reach his mate, leaning out and wrapping his arms around Lexi's waist. He quickly pulled her back to safety. For long moments, he held her in his arms. His wolf. Just as much as he was hers, and he couldn't imagine losing her.

The other man secured himself well enough to the rocks that he could get his gun out and began firing shots at Ryder and Lexi, but he couldn't hit them because of the angle of the rocks, though splinters of rock from where the rounds hit shot upward. But Ryder couldn't get to him either. He didn't want him getting away. Ryder shifted back to his wolf.

Mike hurried to join him. "Kate told me Tremaine is dead. So are the rest of these bastards." He said it loud enough for the man hanging from the cliff to hear him. "If this last guy tries to come up here, *he's* dead."

The guy didn't move. Weighing his options? His boss was dead. The grudge over.

Then they heard him rappelling back down to the bottom of the cliff.

"What the hell happened?" another man asked him from down below.

Ryder hadn't realized there were any more of them down there. A rock overhang was hiding them now, though it didn't impede their wolf hearing.

"Tremaine's dead. Let's go."

"What about Egbert?"

"Leave him. He's dead. Let them deal with it."

"That's it? We don't get paid?"

"Kingston will have taken over. So no. He doesn't care anything about Tremaine's vendetta. Only Tremaine did. He's dead. All right? Let's get the hell out of here before we are too. We could have been far away from here by now if we hadn't done what Tremaine ordered us to do."

"He only helped free us from prison because we agreed to do this. You know he would have come after us if we hadn't done what he'd told us to do." The guy scrambled over the rocks, then fell and cursed. "It's done. Once we get outta here, you go your way and I'll go mine."

Mike was on his phone already. "We had a home invasion—Joe Tremaine and the other escaped convicts are either dead or escaping by boat." He gave the 911 operator the address and everything else he needed to mention about the situation.

Ryder went to see what the blue and white boat looked like, still bobbing in the water. These guys had to have come from that boat, and he wanted to be able to describe it in detail. The name on the boat was *Flossy*, and unless the thugs repainted the boat, at least the authorities had that to go by.

Suddenly, two men in a yellow rubber dinghy came into his view in the rough water. They were trying to motor through the breakers and miss the rocks. A rogue wave headed straight for them, and Ryder sure hoped it would capsize them. Their dinghy hit the rough water wrong and flipped over. He wanted to pump his fist. Instead, he howled. He figured the men would swim back to the rocky beach and the police could apprehend them. Both men went under, the raft carried off by the current. He thought maybe the prison escapees would be under the raft, but then they both bobbed up from the frothy waves, hands flailing, gasping for air, swallowing water.

Neither of the men were swimming for shore, which Ryder would have done. Instead, one grabbed hold of a jagged rock poking out of the foam, only to be ripped away when another wave surged. The other man was still flailing, going under more than he was staying afloat, panicked. Both men disappeared in the rough water, and Ryder didn't see them come up for air again.

Lexi nudged Kate to go back inside the house, and Ryder went with the two ladies so he could shift and dress before the police got there. Mike called Edward after that. "Yeah, we took care of it. The police, and I'm sure the FBI, are on their way because these guys are fugitives. We need medical support for Kate too. You're sending a helicopter. Good. A couple of men tried to make their escape. They're in the water, but the boat that probably was supposed to pick them up left them and took off. It looked like the two men drowned. I know. Karma, right?"

Then Ryder didn't hear any more as he barged into the house and found Lexi dressed in shorts and a T-shirt while she rebandaged Kate's arm with real bandages, Mike's bloodied shirt sitting beside her.

"What happens now?" Lexi asked as Ryder ran past them to the master bedroom to shift and dress.

"The police will probably get the FBI involved, since these guys all broke out of a federal prison. We'll all need to give statements while they're doing a criminal investigation here, and we'll want to try to make up a story about what had happened with the dog that bit several of them." Ryder joined them and looked down at the thug's mangled right hand.

"The guy was ambidextrous and came after me with a knife after I took care of his gun hand," Lexi said.

"Then I had to finish him off." Kate winced.

"The two of you work well together. How are you doing?" Ryder crouched down to feel Kate's pulse.

"Fading."

"A helicopter's coming for you," Ryder said, trying to reassure Kate.

"What about Lexi?" Kate sounded more concerned about her welfare.

"Kate, you're the one who was injured! I'm fine. The bastard who was out to get me is dead. The others who didn't die are already fleeing. Unless they drowned." Lexi held her hand. "Don't you dare die on me. I'll never forgive you."

"Not…going to die. Just want to sleep."

"Don't. You have to stay awake until the EMT tells you that you can sleep," Lexi said.

They heard a helicopter land in the grass out back and sirens out front headed their way.

Doctors Aidan and Holly Denali rushed out of the helicopter, heads down, and dashed for the house. "Edward said you needed us."

"I'm so glad to see you," Lexi said with relief, surprised Edward had called their friends instead of just regular emergency services. She loved them for dropping everything to come to Kate's aid.

"Me too." Kate's voice was pained and tired.

"Kate's the only one wounded?" Holly asked Ryder.

"Yeah," Ryder said. "She might need a blood transfusion. Police are on their way, but she needs to leave now. I don't want them to take Kate to a regular hospital."

"We'll get her out of here," Aidan said.

The police sirens were near the driveway now. "I'll let the police in," Lexi said. "Kate, I'll see you as soon as I can. Oh, and the story is that my dog bit the men but was injured and the Denalis helicoptered him along with Kate."

"Okay. I'll be fine, once I get some blood in me," Kate said.

"You're definitely getting a pay raise," Lexi promised her.

Kate smiled. "Things are looking up already."

Holly and Aidan stabilized Kate.

"Okay, let's get her out of here," Holly said.

Mike and Ryder carried Kate to the helicopter on a stretcher. The doctors climbed into the helicopter with her and took off. By the time Mike and Ryder returned to the house, Lexi was opening the door for the police and a couple of FBI agents.

Then Mike, Lexi, and Ryder gave statements about what had gone down, leaving out the part about them being wolves, of course. That was the problem with being in their wolf coats when they had to fight humans.

"We'll need to speak with your personal assistant, Ms. Summerfield," the agent said to Lexi. He was middle-aged, stern-looking, his hair thinning at the temple, his gray eyes not missing anything. "Why would Tremaine and the other escaped convicts come here? We've been looking for them everywhere, but we wouldn't have expected them to come here."

"He was still trying to discover where my father was so he could kill him for testifying against him and helping to send him to prison."

"Dr. Summerfield. I thought he had died. He must have gone into witness protection." The agent scribbled down some more notes. "What's the kind of dog you own?"

"German shepherd." Lexi offered some tears and hurriedly wiped them away.

The agent paused to observe her.

Ryder said, "She'll come through okay, Lexi."

"And you're Ms. Summerfield's bodyguard too?" the agent asked, directing his question to Ryder.

"Yes. I've only been working for her for a short while. I worked for Doctor Aidan Denali before this. Both Mike and I did."

The agent smiled a little.

"She needed more protection because of the business with Tremaine, as you can see," Ryder said.

The agent flipped through his notes. "I see the reports about the Redwood Cabins and his hired assassins staying at the cabin near hers."

"Correct. That's where I met her."

"I think we've got enough information. Oh, just one other question, why didn't you fire your weapon, Mr. Gallagher?" the agent asked.

"I didn't have it with me first thing this morning. I was enjoying the sunrise with Lexi." Not as a wolf.

"We're getting married," Lexi said. "We were discussing wedding plans. But you know the rest."

The agent closed his book. "All right. You're all free to go. We'll let you know when you can return to the house. Don't leave the state in the meantime."

"We'll be staying with Drs. Aidan and Holly Denali until we can return here," Ryder said.

"That'll work."

Lexi and Ryder went to her room to each pack a bag while Mike went upstairs to get some things. Then Lexi packed a bag for Kate. She hoped the agent didn't notice they had no dog bed, toys, or water and food dishes for the dog. But he didn't seem to notice. Ryder drove them to the Denalis' place a little north of their place in the woods on a lake. "Holly's parents have built a home there, too, so she has her family close by. Both her sister and brother are away at college now and come home on weekends to run in the woods as wolves and play in the swimming pool."

"I've never been to their home, just Rafe's since he always has the big parties," Lexi said. "I'm calling to check on Kate, and I'll put it on speaker so you can hear what's being said." A few minutes later, she said, "Kate, how are you doing?"

"You mentioned a pay raise?"

"The pay raise?" Lexi smiled. "You must be doing all right. We're on our way there now. It'll take us another half hour. And I promise we're *not* going to bring any bad guys with us."

"Good. Aidan said they haven't had any breakfast. And Mike and Ryder will be right on time to make it."

The guys both laughed. But Ryder was thankful the business with Tremaine was over. He never thought he'd be back in the business of cooking meals for the Denalis.

CHAPTER 29

WHILE RYDER AND MIKE FIXED BREAKFAST, LEXI WAS on the phone telling her family Tremaine was dead. She began to cry, and Ryder handed the spatula he was using to flip the omelets to Mike and said, "I'll be right back." Ryder felt bad he hadn't been more sensitive to how Lexi had to be feeling after all the fighting. He joined her and wrapped her in his arms, kissed the top of her head, then kissed her cheek.

"Yeah, Ryder's here with me with his arms wrapped lovingly around me as we speak. It was just upsetting. The whole thing. I haven't had time to process any of it. Kate's going to be fine, but I nearly died when I saw that she'd been shot. And when the thug nearly pulled Ryder off the cliff, I was frantic to save him."

When the thug had nearly pulled his mate off the cliff, Ryder had felt the same way. He still hadn't processed that either. He knew he'd have nightmares about that. She probably would too. He couldn't believe she had managed to get so close to the edge to save him when he knew how terrified she'd been. First chance he got, he was building a wrought-iron fence on that one area, with a gate and a stone path cut into the rocks that would lead to the rocky beach so she could enjoy it. He suspected she'd like to take pictures down there when it was built. His wedding present to her.

"But the good news is we can see each other as a family whenever we want." Lexi smiled and wiped away her tears.

"About the wedding plans. I thought we'd still have two weddings. One for the public here, and one in Silver Town, since you've made it your home and we'll be part of the family there too. Ryder's parents want to come to both. What do you want to do?" Lexi smiled. "Okay, that would be great. Dad can walk me down the aisle twice. I'll be like a bad penny. Dad can't give me away only once." She laughed and Ryder kissed her again.

As long as her father was only giving Lexi away to Ryder, she could have as many weddings as she wanted.

"I have to have the one for the public because I'd promised, and it'll let any male wolf know I'm no longer available. It's all about promotion and goodwill. Otherwise, I'd just have the one in Silver Town. I love you too. We're having breakfast, so I have to go. I'll call you later. Love you."

When she pocketed her phone, she wrapped her arms around Ryder and hugged him tight.

"I'm sorry about everything, honey," Ryder said.

"It's not your fault. We were just having fun as wolves and watching the sunset. Tremaine was the trouble. As usual."

"No more." Ryder took her to the table where Holly, Mike, and Aidan were setting out the food and dishes.

They all sat down to eat their late breakfast and talked about the tea party and dinner at Rafe's house.

"Jade called and said we'd have it later, after Kate's feeling better," Holly said.

"Sounds good to me," Kate said.

"Same here," Lexi said.

"I guess you won't be needing as many bodyguards now." Mike cut into his ham.

"Are you kidding? Just think when we have little ones."

Lexi sipped some of her coffee. "You can have babysitting duty too."

Everyone laughed.

Little ones made Ryder think about the safety of the bluff for wolf cubs and children. And for Lexi's dogs, too, when they picked them out. He definitely thought that putting up a wrought-iron fence around the bluff would be his number one priority.

Then Lexi got a call from Silky Spring and put it on speakerphone. "Yeah, Silky?"

"Okay, I know I'm not supposed to call anyone from my past, even if you aren't all that much in the past, but the U.S. Marshals told me you killed Tremaine and that's the end of me testifying against him. But they have all the stuff my mom had on him, and they might be able to make a case against the others who were on his payroll. So that means I'm out of the Witness Protection Program. Oh, and before I forget, Don called me and said Tremaine wasn't my dad. Murphy was. So you were right."

"You suspected it, didn't you?" Lexi asked.

"Yeah. I was just pissed off at Murphy because he didn't take Mom somewhere safe and protect her if he really loved her."

"I don't blame you."

"So I'm back in the business of selling cosmetics. And Don said my interview will be in a magazine in two weeks. If you want to give me more tips, I'd be grateful," Silky said.

"We sure will. Tremaine shot Kate in the arm, so she's recovering, but once she's feeling one hundred percent, we'll get with you about it."

"Oh, no. He was such a bastard. Tell her to get better. And thanks. I've got to go. Don's still here, and he's going to tell me about the wolves that stole his camera and equipment in the redwoods. Have you ever heard of wolves running around in the park? I think he likes to make up stories. Anyway, thanks for asking Don to learn who my father truly was. Catch up with you later... Oh, and tell Kate I'm sorry. Tremaine deserved what he got in the end."

"He did, thanks, Silky." Lexi took a deep breath and put her phone on the table.

"I don't know about the rest of you, but I'm so tired, I could sleep the rest of the day away," Kate said, and Lexi helped her up from the table.

Lexi took hold of Ryder's hand after that. "If you don't mind having a bunch of houseguests who are all going to bed before it's even noon, Ryder and I are going to slip away for a while."

Ryder was all for it.

"I'll take care of the dishes," Mike said.

After he made love to his beautiful mate, snuggling, and napping, Ryder's phone rang, waking him and Lexi. He glanced at the caller ID. "Don." He answered the call and put it on speakerphone so Lexi could listen in on the conversation. "Yeah, Don?"

"I wanted to tell you I got my camera and equipment back."

"How did that happen?" Ryder feigned surprise.

"Tremaine's men had them in their cabin when the police went to arrest them for possession of illegal handguns and shooting at other people in the campground. Your bodyguards turned the guys in. Anyway, the rangers thought the camera equipment looked the same as what

I'd reported stolen by the wolves. The rangers assumed the thugs found the equipment in the woods when they were after you. Or me. One of my daughters had drawn a bird, and she wanted me to find it in the wild and take a picture, so I had taken it with me. The rangers found that drawing in the camera bag."

"Did you find the bird?"

"No. Not yet. It's a blue jay, but I haven't seen one since my daughter asked me to get a picture of one."

"I took a picture of one on one of our hikes. If you think that would work, I can send it to you," Lexi said.

"Okay, great. Thanks. Anyway, they said the memory cards from my camera were missing. Tremaine's men said that the camera and equipment have been planted on them, and they hadn't found them. Obviously, they found them wherever the wolves had dropped them."

"I'm glad you got your camera and equipment back. Were they in good shape?" Ryder asked, glancing at Lexi, rubbing her arm, smiling a little.

"Yeah, luckily the wolves didn't chew on them."

Ryder asked, "Did the rangers believe you then? About the wolves?"

"No. Not at all. They still say I was making up that part about the stolen camera and bag. They said I probably fell asleep and Tremaine's men stole them. Or maybe I dreamed wolves took the equipment. But it wasn't a dream."

"I believe you," Ryder said.

"No, you don't. Thanks, just got the picture, Lexi. I'll tell my daughter a famous celebrity took it. She will want to thank you in person at the wedding. Got to run. Thanks again!"

———

Lexi snuggled some more with Ryder, glad she had gotten the camera equipment back to Don. She was thinking about making love to Ryder one last time before they rejoined Holly and Aidan when Lexi's phone rang, and she glanced at the caller ID and groaned. "Time to get up. It's the pet rescue center." She figured it was about the rehoming pet party. She answered, putting the call on speakerphone since Ryder would be helping with the event, and said, "Yes, this is Lexi."

"Oh, Lexi, we've got a real problem. I know you're so good at helping us find homes for our pets, but this is an emergency," Mrs. Baluster, owner of the rescue service, said. "Four six-month-old German shepherds were dropped off at a wolf reserve, the owner saying the dogs were part wolf and he can't afford to keep them. The wolf reserve said they aren't part wolf and refused to take them in. Then the dog owner brought them to our facility. We can't take wolf dogs. We're supposed to euthanize them as soon as they're brought in. But with your contacts, I thought you might be able to find them a home when no one else will take them."

"We'll take them," Lexi said without hesitation.

"All of them?" Mrs. Baluster asked, sounding surprised, yet hopeful.

"Yes. Whether they're part wolf or not, we can handle them," Lexi said.

Ryder was smiling at her.

"We'll bring them to your place within the hour."

"We'll be there. Thanks." At least they didn't have the issue with Tremaine and his henchmen any longer. She wouldn't have wanted the dogs to get injured in the fracas.

"Oh, no, thank *you*."

They ended the call, and Lexi and Ryder hurried to get dressed.

"Did you want to leave Kate here while we take the dogs in?" Ryder asked.

"Yeah. Until Holly and Aidan say she can come home. We'll have to put a fence up along the bluff. Something low enough so you can see the view, but high enough to keep the dogs safe."

"Already on it."

She smiled at him.

"It was going to be a surprise, but this is as good a time as any to do it."

"Aww, you're such a sweetheart."

Then they headed out of the bedroom to see everyone and told them what they were doing.

"Wait, what about the crime-scene situation?" Ryder asked Lexi.

"I'll call them to tell them we're taking in some dogs before they're destroyed," Lexi said. "And see what they have to say."

"We're doing it now?" Mike asked. "We're not waiting for the rehoming party?"

"No. We have to take them in now. The shelter will have to euthanize them. Who can better take care of them than a bunch of alpha wolves?" Lexi asked.

Kate joined them, wiping the sleep from her eyes. "I want to see them."

"We'll send you pictures until you're well enough to come home."

"She'll be good in a couple of days," Holly said. "I'd say she could go home with you today, but you're going to have your hands full, and I'm sure she's going to want to help, which she can't do for about a week or two. She needs to give her arm a chance to heal."

Lexi called the detective in charge of the investigation and explained the situation.

"You're going to have to take them somewhere else. We'll need to be there gathering evidence at least through tomorrow night at the latest," the detective said. "I'll let you know."

"All right. Thanks." Lexi let out her breath. "We can't take them to the house until tomorrow night."

"Bring them here then. We have a fenced-in yard. We were planning to go to your pet rehoming party and pick up a pooch," Aidan said.

Lexi gave him a hug. "Thanks." She called Mrs. Baluster and gave her the new address for where to drop the dogs off.

"Okay, I'm sending them now."

Then Lexi gave Holly a hug. "Thanks so much for letting us bring them here until we can take them home."

"You're so welcome. You're going to be here anyway. We'll all have fun with them."

Kate was smiling. "I get to see them, too, then."

"But no using your arm," Holly said, frowning at her.

Kate sighed. "My arm is in a sling. I can't do anything with it."

"As long as you remember that," Aidan said, agreeing with Holly.

Mike and Ryder ran out to purchase toys, beds, dog dishes, and crates for the dogs, while Lexi and the others waited for the puppies to arrive. The guys arrived home with the bounty they had purchased. The German shepherd pups, all of them a bit shy like wolves would be, were dropped off shortly after that. Lexi and the others set out the balls and chew toys, then sat down with the dogs and let them smell them. By their scent, the dogs were definitely part wolf.

"I wonder why the owner had them and didn't want them then." Holly scratched one between his ears.

"We'll give them a good home," Lexi said.

Kate joined them and sat on a chair so the pups wouldn't bump her arm. But she was grinning like the rest of them, talking to the pups as if they were their babies.

Lexi couldn't be happier. "See, I didn't want to take the bear cubs we rescued home, but these little fellows? That's a different story."

Kate chuckled. "And we took two male wolves home with us."

Lexi hugged Ryder. "Yeah, definitely keepers too."

"Finding a mate was the farthest thing from my thoughts when I went to the cabin in the redwoods," Ryder told Lexi.

"Mine too. I never thought I'd find love." Lexi kissed him again, loving him for who he was. If it hadn't been for his protective nature and loving her so thoroughly, she wasn't sure Tremaine would be out of the picture now. If it had been just Kate and her up against all those men? Lexi shuddered to think how that would have gone down. Then one of the pups curled up on her lap to sleep.

Ryder petted her lapdog. "One of these days he'll be too big for your lap."

"But I'm sure he'll always believe he is a lapdog." Lexi noticed Kate had slipped to the floor to pet one of the dogs with her good hand.

When Holly and Aidan glanced her way, Kate quickly said, "Petting animals is good therapy in hospitals."

Everyone laughed. But it was true. Even Lexi was feeling much better about the fight they'd had in her home, now that they had all the puppies to love on. She called the rescue center and said to the owner, "The pups are happy here. If they are part wolf, how did they get that way, and why did the man want to get rid of them?"

"He learned that to be healthy, they'd need some raw meat. It was too expensive, and he was afraid the dogs would be abused if he just gave them to regular homes. He said he'd bred his dog with another German shepherd that he learned after the fact was part wolf."

"Okay, I just needed to know. Thanks." Lexi shared the information about the dogs, and then said, "It's time to celebrate, don't you think?"

"Rescuing wolf dog pups, a new mating, and getting rid of Tremaine? I'll say," Holly said.

Aidan smiled. "I think this afternoon it would be great to have some hand-tossed pizzas."

Ryder and Mike groaned. "Sure, we'll give it our best shot," Ryder said.

Mike agreed.

Lexi loved Ryder for being just as determined to accomplish something as she was.

Yeah, it was time to celebrate, and Lexi couldn't wait to be home with Ryder to do some more celebrating there too.

EPILOGUE

LEXI KNEW THEY HAD A WHIRLWIND OF ACTIVITIES to plan for, once they could return to the house after the scene-crime tape had been removed and cleaners had cleaned everything up. What Lexi hadn't expected was for Mike to take over some of the promotional activities and wedding planning. And they all helped with the pet rehoming party. Ryder contacted a fence company right away to put in the fence and a landscaping company to build the stairs and a gate to the beach. Lexi loved that Ryder had done that for her and for their future kids and all the dogs.

They learned the Coast Guard had caught the boat involved in dropping off the escaped convicts, another of whom had still been in the boat. Kate had shared some marketing tips with Silky, and Don was the first one to receive his wedding invitation. He'd been thrilled.

They'd been wrapped up in all the work that was going on, but Lexi and Ryder still made time for each other, including wolf runs at sunrise and sunset, only now the four pups had to play too.

She realized taking care of the dogs really was like taking care of their own wolf pups when they had some.

Before another day of wild happenings, Lexi and Ryder sat by the pool, watching the sun rise in the morning sky after running as wolves, the pups exhausted from their play earlier and now sleeping on the grass. Mike was preparing wedding invitations, and Kate was on her laptop inside the house, saying if she didn't get back to work, she might get fired. Which wasn't going to happen.

"I love you," Lexi said, moving to Ryder's lap, and he wrapped his arms around her and kissed her. "Sunrises were never this spectacular before."

"I love you back, honey. I can't believe that we're mated, and we have a whole pack of our own. Not *lupus garous* exactly, but…"

She chuckled. "Yeah, I didn't care what breed, mixed or otherwise. Just that they needed a home and would be well loved. So many people who have wolf dogs don't understand how different they are from totally domesticated dogs. And they end up giving them up to wolf reserves because they can't handle them."

"We can. When we go to see your folks—"

"They want us to bring them with us. Everyone in Silver Town has offered to love on them." She sighed. She couldn't believe how much her life had changed—for the good—with Ryder in it. "You know, if you hadn't told me I was holding the map upside down, I might never have met up with my father in time to help my mother out too. You are my life and my love." She kissed him.

Ryder smiled. Here he'd worried Lexi would believe he'd only been there for her money. But she was a wary wolf and had known better. "Did you ever tell your father about the red herring on the map that had thrown you off?"

She laughed. "No, but I'll have to say something when we visit for the wedding. And about burying the message where it ended up underwater."

"God, I'm glad I was there for you. I actually heard you

and Kate earlier, laughing, and I tried to meet up with you just to say hi. You sounded like you were having fun, and it lifted my spirits."

She wrapped his arms tighter around her. "You're not a lone wolf kind of guy. I know because when I invited you to eat with us, you wagged your tail so hard, I figured you needed the company."

He laughed. "I couldn't help it. But I wouldn't have wagged it that hard for anyone else. Thanks for letting me have more than three dates."

"We haven't even begun. Breakfast can wait. Mike can watch the pups. Show me again why I love you so much." Lexi got off Ryder's lap and hurried him into the house. "Pups are yours to watch for a while, Mike."

Mike laughed. "Will do. Dog nanny it is. You know, already Holly and Aidan want one of them. And when they convince you they need him or her, Rafe and Jade will want one."

"We could do that. When we have babies on the way, it will be chaos and all the dogs would get more personal attention that way," Lexi said.

Ryder scooped Lexi up in his arms and smiled at Kate as they passed her by. "We'll be out in a bit."

"No hurry on my account. Lexi will make me get more rest."

Lexi laughed. "Yes!"

"No problem. Lexi is going to do that too." But after Ryder made love to her again. In his wildest dreams, he never thought he'd be mated to Lexi Summerfield, a friend of the Denalis, a high-profile celebrity, and the she-wolf of his dreams.

ACKNOWLEDGMENTS

Thanks so much to Donna Fournier for her hours of brainstorming. After her beta reads, she helps me with ensuring that some of the details that need to be added are not overlooked. And thanks to my beta readers Darla Taylor and Jay Takane who caught stuff I can't ever seem to catch! Thanks to Deb Werksman for always believing in me and to the cover artists who make the wolf world so real that everyone wants to keep them close to their hearts.

Read on for a taste of the story
RT Book Reviews **called**
"Magnificently entertaining."
Where the billionaire wolves began:

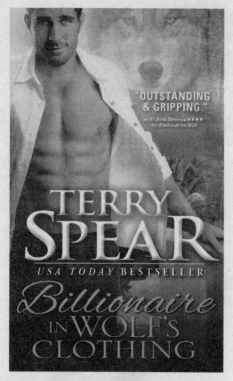

"OUTSTANDING & GRIPPING."

TERRY
SPEAR

USA TODAY BESTSELLER

Billionaire
IN WOLF'S
CLOTHING

Available now from
Sourcebooks Casablanca

CHAPTER 1

JADE ASHTON HAD MADE A LOT OF MISTAKES IN HER LIFE, but returning to her brother's pack topped the list. She should have known the pack members wouldn't accept her son, the product of a love affair with a human, despite pretending they were fine with it. She glanced at her three-year-old son, napping on the daybed in her office in her brother's home where she alternated between sketching new designs for intimate apparel and for a new baby and toddler wear line she had developed when her son was born.

Toby had just fallen asleep, looking angelic with his blond curls resting on his cheek, his dark brown eyes closed as he licked his lips. No way would she ever give him up, despite how everyone in her pack viewed him as a grievous error in judgment.

She felt a little dizzy, probably because she'd been so busy that she hadn't had anything to drink in hours. She got up from her chair and headed out the door, practically running into her twin brother moving silently down the hall like a wolf. She fell back and gasped softly when he grabbed her arm to steady her.

"We need to talk." Kenneth started to guide her to the den, his blond hair much darker than hers, his amber eyes focused on her in a way that said he had serious business to discuss.

Did he know she intended to leave the pack, again? Or did he want to tell her he didn't think her being here was working out? "I need to get some water. And we can't talk long because Toby will be waking in a half hour or so."

"This will just take a minute."

It had better, because she wasn't going to be drawn into any long-winded discussions with her brother. She hadn't told him she was leaving first thing in the morning. She wasn't sure how he'd take it. She had to admit she was afraid he'd try to talk her out of it. But she was determined.

Every time he and the others had looked at her son in judgment, she'd been annoyed. Not only that, but she'd caught Kenneth and the others having secret conversations and then abruptly stopping whenever they saw her approaching. The pack members pretended to tolerate her son, but she saw through the facade. They didn't like her having a human son who couldn't shift. They believed he could be a danger to the pack.

Which was one of the reasons she had left just after her son was born. She had also wanted to save his human father from her brother's wrath. But raising Toby on her own had been tough. When her brother had promised that the pack members wanted her to live with them and have the backup they could provide, she had agreed. She and her son had left southern Texas far behind, so she figured she'd never run into Toby's father again. And Kenneth had sounded sincere in wanting to ensure her protection—just like a pack leader should. She wanted to be part of a family again. She didn't have a lone wolf personality.

She didn't believe Toby would be welcome in any other pack either.

Clearly, the members had changed their minds about having her and her son there. Unless they had never wanted her back and it was all her brother's idea. He was the pack leader, so ultimately, it was his decision—one he was apparently coming to regret. He was just being stubborn, didn't want to admit he'd made a mistake, and didn't want to have to tell her to leave.

Then again, maybe he realized she was planning to leave. Being twins, they sometimes sensed things like that before they really shared with each other. She hadn't packed anything yet. She planned to tell him in the morning, before he left for work at his auto body shop. She thought it would be easier on all of them that way. She'd call him when she got settled and let him know where she was staying. It was for the best—for her son, for her, and for Kenneth and the pack.

Having detoured from the direction of the den to go to the kitchen so she could get something to drink, Kenneth leaned against the granite counter, his focus on her, his expression still ultraserious. "I have a job for you."

She raised her brows, then grabbed a glass from the kitchen cabinet. Between raising Toby and running her own businesses, she didn't have time for a whole lot else. But if this was something quick that she could do this afternoon, she would, to thank Kenneth for taking her in—and then she was through with the pack.

"It's simple. And hell, you might get real lucky."

She snorted, pouring water into the glass and adding crushed ice. "Lucky?" She drank several sips of the water.

The front door shut, and she figured Kenneth's girlfriend, Lizzie, was running out for something. She was a wolf too, which meant they were sleeping together, but he hadn't decided to mate her yet so they hadn't gone all the way. If they did, he'd be stuck with her as his mate for life. Jade didn't know why the she-wolf put up with her brother.

If Jade was in a situation like Lizzie's, she'd tell the wolf that either they mated or she'd look elsewhere. But Jade supposed Lizzie wanted to be a pack leader's mate and was sticking around in case Kenneth decided she was it. Total beta wolf.

"You're living off me so you can put more money into your apparel business that isn't making enough to really sustain you and your son. So, I need you to do this job and—"

"Like hell my business isn't making enough money." She was extremely tight with her money. No fancy food for either of them. No special entertainment. No expensive clothes. Since *lupus garous* lived so long, she had worked other jobs to help pad her bank account before Toby was born. She wasn't wealthy, but she got by just fine. As long as she was frugal. "That's okay. Being here with the pack isn't working out for Toby and me anyway."

Kenneth's eyes widened. "You're not leaving."

"Listen, Kenneth, you know no one wants my son here. And they barely tolerate me. You make Lizzie babysit Toby sometimes when I really need someone to watch him so I can work, but it's not fair to her. The rest of the pack worries about him. I appreciate all you've done for me. I really do." She shrugged. "But…I know this is the right thing for me to do. And for you and the pack too. I'm leaving tomorrow, and we can get together from time to time…later." She really didn't believe that would happen, but she'd make the gesture anyway.

"Like I said, I have a job for you."

What part of she was leaving did her brother not get? He was so stubborn! Or did he feel it was his place as pack leader to decide if she was leaving? He hadn't decided things for her since before she left the pack nearly four years earlier, and she wasn't going to allow him to start now.

Even so, she'd humor him because she *was* leaving tomorrow, with or without his consent. "What's the job?"

"Do you remember when that doctor was taking blood samples from us last week?"

"Yeah, Dr. Aidan Denali. He wanted to take some of Toby's, and I said no. What of it? He's not asking to take blood samples from Toby again, is he?"

"No, but here's the thing. I looked into his background, and his brother is Rafe Denali."

"So?" She'd never heard of the guy. Not that she'd heard of Aidan Denali either before she'd met him at Kenneth's house. Since Toby wasn't a shifter, there was no reason for Aidan to take blood from him. Though she hadn't given the doctor that reason since he hadn't needed to know.

"Rafe Denali's a billionaire. Real estate mogul."

"So?" Her brother was usually much better at getting to the point.

"The good doctor told me he's close to finding a cure for our longevity issues."

"Okay. What has this got to do with me? Or *you*, for that matter?"

"I need you to find out where he's living. Where he does his research."

"What?" She narrowed her eyes. "Why?" She was getting really bad vibes about this.

"His brother is ruthless. Hell, he's the reason our grandparents lost their manufacturing business."

She closed her gaping mouth. She had never known anything about her grandparents. Since her brother had taken over the pack when their parents died, he'd been the one interested in all things family. She'd been rather a wild card growing up. She'd always known she would never run the pack, so she'd done her own thing. After her son was born, she'd thrown herself into her work and raising him. No room for getting into any further trouble. She was faced with enough already.

"Okay, so I don't get the connection between what happened with our grandparents and what you want me to do. Or why you want to know where the doctor lives."

"Rafe is well-known—"

She opened her mouth again to tell Kenneth she had never heard of Rafe, so he couldn't be that well-known.

"—in financial circles. The kind that you don't belong to. I know where he lives. He and his brother are close, but Aidan lives somewhere else. I want you to befriend Rafe and learn where Aidan lives."

"Why would you want to know that? Besides, I don't run in billionaires' circles. You already said so yourself."

"He's a bachelor wolf. He's not dating any she-wolves. I've checked. If he sees you, and you intrigue him, you can cozy up to him and learn where his brother lives."

"I'm not interested. Besides, didn't the doctor give you his business card and tell you to contact him if you have any concerns?"

"It has his phone number. That's it."

"Why do you want to know this anyway?"

"I told you. Rafe is ruthless. When he gets hold of a cure for our condition, he'll sell it to only those who can afford it. What if *lupus garous* begin to age even more rapidly than we are now? What if we don't just end up with a human's life span, but our bodies begin to age rapidly to match all the years we've already lived? Hell, your boy would lose you, and he'd have no one to raise him. Think about it."

She *had* thought about it. But she wasn't one to live with

a fatalist viewpoint on life. She hadn't thought her brother was either. Until now.

"If you really want this information, ask Rafe yourself. Or call his brother. You have his phone number."

"As if either would tell me."

"Send Lizzie." Jade turned to leave, and her brother seized her arm. She rounded on him, yanking her arm away from him, and said, "We're family, Kenneth, but that doesn't give you the right to make me do things that go against what I believe in. If the worst-case scenario ever comes to pass, I'm sure wolves can unite and make the brothers see the right in this."

Kenneth folded his arms. "Lizzie isn't right for the part. She's not as classy as you."

"Oh, wow, give me a break. I hope you didn't tell *her* that." Jade started heading back to her office, but she hadn't taken more than a few steps when her brother cleared his throat.

"I need you to do this. Whatever it takes. After that, you and your son can be on your way. You really don't have a choice."

"Nothing would make lying to the Denalis worthwhile, no matter why you want this information. Toby and I will be leaving tonight." Sooner—once she could get her car packed and Toby ready for the journey. She'd have to plot a course too. Had her brother known about the wolf geneticist *before* he'd asked her to return to the pack? She whipped around. "How long have you known about Aidan? Is this why you asked me to return to the pack? So I could be your spy?"

When Kenneth didn't deny it, she swore under her breath. "I thought you were concerned about me and my son. Or at least me. Thanks for letting me in on the truth." Furious with her brother, she stalked off toward the office and had nearly reached the doorway when Kenneth let his breath out in a huff.

"You will do this for me, and *then* you can have your son back."

His words made her stomach fall and her head spin as she rushed into the room.

Toby and his soft leopard blanket were gone. All that was left on the daybed was his blue rainbow-colored teddy bear.

Lizzie! She must have taken him when Jade heard the front door open. Lizzie was the only one who was close enough to Toby that if she woke him while taking him from his bed, he wouldn't cry out. He'd settle in her arms and go back to sleep. Kenneth had stalled Jade long enough for Lizzie to gather up Toby and leave.

Shocked at what he had done and angrier than she ever thought she could be, Jade hurried out of the room, ready to kill her brother—but only after he told her where her son was. "Where is he, Kenneth? I swear I'll—"

"You'll do this one thing for me, and he's yours. And then you can damn well leave the pack. But if you ever cause any trouble for our kind, I'll kill both of you."

So furious she couldn't think straight, she beat on her brother's chest with her fists, cursing at him until he grabbed her wrists and slammed her against the wall. "I'm serious about this, Jade. Do what I say, and your son won't meet his father's fate."

"What?" Tears filled her eyes, but she tried to get a grip on her emotions so he wouldn't see her as weak. Kenneth had promised he would leave Stewart alone if she left the area before he even knew she was pregnant, and she never had anything more to do with him.

She felt sucker punched. "Why? You said..." It didn't

matter now. All that mattered was Toby's safety. "Damn you, Kenneth."

She kneed her brother in the crotch with one good shove as a final comment on how she felt about him taking her son hostage. Kenneth collapsed to his knees, swearing that he'd make her pay if she didn't do what he said.

Maynard Myer—one of the men who worked in Kenneth's body shop—interrupted them, red-faced. He was a redheaded bulldog of a man who had brazenly shown his contempt for her and Toby when he dropped by the house. She suspected Maynard didn't want to intrude on this scene, but the news had to be serious enough for him to do so.

"What?" Kenneth growled at him, still on his knees on the floor and holding his crotch.

"Grayton wants his money now. You've got two weeks to pay up or..." Maynard glanced in Jade's direction.

She didn't know who Grayton was, although the name sounded like he might be a wolf. If he had loaned Kenneth money, and now her brother was in arrears...

"What are you involved in, Kenneth?" she asked. "Gambling? The horse races? I've got money—"

"Get out of here, Jade. You want to see your son in one piece, leave and do what I told you to do."

No matter how angry she was, she knew she didn't have a choice. She had to get her son back before her brother killed him. She grabbed Toby's rainbow bear and hurried into her room to pack, praying she could pull this off without getting her son killed. If Grayton was threatening her brother, what if he took out Kenneth's debt on his closest relations? Her and her son?

What would the Denalis do if they learned what she was up to?

ABOUT THE AUTHOR

USA Today bestselling author Terry Spear has written over sixty paranormal and medieval Highland romances. In 2008, *Heart of the Wolf* was named a *Publishers Weekly* Best Book of the Year. She has received a PNR Top Pick, a Best Book of the Month nomination by Long and Short Reviews, numerous Night Owl Romance Top Picks, and two Paranormal Excellence Awards for Romantic Literature (Finalist and Honorable Mention). In 2016, *Billionaire in Wolf's Clothing* was an RT Book Reviews top pick. A retired officer of the U.S. Army Reserves, Terry also creates award-winning teddy bears that have found homes all over the world, helps out with her grandbaby, and is raising two Havanese puppies. She lives in Spring, Texas.

YOU HAD ME AT WOLF

First in the Wolff Brothers, an exciting new series
from *USA Today* bestselling author Terry Spear

Private Investigator and gray wolf shifter Josie Grayson is on
an important mission: find evidence to prove the man staying at the Silver Town Resort faked his death for the insurance
payout. When her partner is sent home sick, Josie needs to find
a new fake lover in order to keep her cover intact—and handsome wolf shifter and ski lodge owner Blake Wolff seems interested in the role…very interested.

"Delicious…a thrilling good time."

—Fresh Fiction for *All's Fair in Love and Wolf*

For more info about Sourcebooks's
books and authors, visit:
sourcebooks.com

Also by Terry Spear

Wolff Brothers
You Had Me at Wolf

SEAL Wolf
A SEAL in Wolf's Clothing
A SEAL Wolf Christmas
SEAL Wolf Hunting
SEAL Wolf in Too Deep
SEAL Wolf Undercover
SEAL Wolf Surrender

Heart of the Shifter
You Had Me at Jaguar

Billionaire Wolf
Billionaire in Wolf's Clothing
A Billionaire Wolf
for Christmas

Silver Town Wolf
Destiny of the Wolf
Wolf Fever
Dreaming of the Wolf
Silence of the Wolf
A Silver Wolf Christmas
Alpha Wolf Need Not Apply
Between a Wolf and a
Hard Place
All's Fair in Love and Wolf
Silver Town Wolf: Home for
the Holidays

Heart of the Jaguar
Savage Hunter
Jaguar Fever
Jaguar Hunt
Jaguar Pride
A Very Jaguar Christmas

Highland Wolf
Heart of the Highland Wolf
A Howl for a Highlander
A Highland Werewolf
Wedding
Hero of a Highland Wolf
A Highland Wolf Christmas

White Wolf
Dreaming of a White Wolf
Christmas
Flight of the White Wolf

Heart of the Wolf
Heart of the Wolf
To Tempt the Wolf
Legend of the White Wolf
Seduced by the Wolf